PRAISE FOR S~~ALLY~~

'Sally Franson is a world class en...
this book is a flat out delight m...
turner, and a true 'originell...
cried, and I never, ev...
MEG RYAN

'*Big in Sweden* is full of quick insight and charming detail,
and absolutely packed with one-liners. Sally Franson is a
brilliant comic writer – and one with a deep love for
her characters. It's a dazzling combination'
KATHERINE HEINY

'Swedish pancakes, Viking villages, evangelical relay
races . . . Imagine Ancestry.com meeting the Great British
Bake-Off . . . with ABBA and karaoke. *Big in Sweden*
is a *very* funny novel about the families we inherit and
the ones we ultimately create for ourselves'
JULIE SCHUMACHER

'If you devoured *Pippi Longstocking* as a kid, you will not be
able to turn away from *Big in Sweden*. Reading this hilarious,
heartfelt book was even more fun than watching
reality television. I absolutely loved it!'
JESSICA ANYA BLAU

'A wry, observant take on career success and ambition'
NEW YORK POST

'A gorgeous treat . . . whipsmart, biting and clever. I kept pausing
to re-read parts of it with a huge smile on my face'
JANE GREEN

'Bitingly funny . . . an addictive, escapist novel'
PUBLISHERS WEEKLY

'Wickedly funny'
BUSTLE

'A fast-paced and quick-witted trip . . . with smart, funny
characters and perfectly crafted dialogue'
BOOKLIST

ALSO BY
SALLY FRANSON

A LADY'S GUIDE TO SELLING OUT

BIG IN SWEDEN

SALLY FRANSON

REVIEW

First published in the USA in 2024 by
Mariner Books
An imprint of HarperCollins Publishers

First published in Great Britain in 2024 by
Headline Review
An imprint of HEADLINE PUBLISHING GROUP

1

Cataloguing in Publication Data is available from the British Library

ISBN 978 1 0354 2014 8

Offset in 10.1/13.35pt Garamond Premier Pro by Jouve (UK), Milton Keynes

Printed and bound in Great Britain by Clays Ltd, Elcograf S.p.A.

HEADLINE PUBLISHING GROUP
An Hachette UK Company
Carmelite House
50 Victoria Embankment
London EC4Y 0DZ

www.headline.co.uk
www.hachette.co.uk

For Ben, with Gusto

It occurs to me that I am America.

—ALLEN GINSBERG

*But I would like to spread a general
tolerance for human insanity.*

—ASTRID LINDGREN

CHAPTER ONE

✦

THE CALL

When the phone rang in the middle of an afternoon coaching session, I thought it was the student-loan forgiveness scammers. They'd been hounding me for weeks, four to six calls a day, always from a different number. Sometimes they hustled me, sometimes I ignored them, sometimes I climbed on a high horse and scolded them about greed and my rights as an American citizen. "There's more to life than money, you know!" I'd say. "Like love and friendship and travel and pasta—I mean pasta alone could—" at which point they'd hang up.

This particular number had a +46 at the front, which meant nothing to me except my enemies had grown more sophisticated. In hindsight, I shouldn't have answered, seeing as Tristan's mother was paying a handsome sum to my employer, Premiere Prep, to get her son into colleges a click or three above his ability level. Tristan, high school junior, was parked on the love seat, wrestling with the fact that he didn't want to be a dentist. "But my dad's a dentist, my uncle's a dentist," he fretted. "*And* my cousin's a hygienist."

It was one of those days when I thought I might die if I heard another youth declaim on the subject of their future. Normally I adored Tristan. He had beautiful teeth, as white and straight as the rest of him, and a countenance as genial as a Labrador's. But it was the eighth of January in Minneapolis—gray, subzero, and gloaming at three p.m.—and I was wilting, both from the weather and my New Year's resolutions. (I'd actually started them on the third; one can't simply snap to asceticism like a West Point cadet.) Caffeine-deprived, underfed, my brain as fuzzy as the moldy Parmesan in my fridge, I heard myself murmur, "Oh boy, hmm, that is tricky." Then my phone rang like a bell, and I felt—this is not an exaggeration—saved, even if the source of my deliverance was a cyber-gang out to steal all my money.

"Sorry, but I better take this," I said to Tristan. "Hello?"

"Ah, yes, hello, may I please speak to Pauline Johannson?" A female voice, speaking in posh and accented English. *Yo-hann-sohn*.

"This is she."

"Pauline! *Ja ha*, hello, this is Freja calling from *Sverige och Mig*! How are you doing?"

"Fine." I pointed to the phone, rolled my eyes, and mouthed an apology to Tristan before swiveling around in my office chair. "Why are you calling again? A number of your colleagues have already been in touch, and I've given them at least six pieces of my mind—"

"They have?" The clickety-clack of keys. "I believe I am the only one making these calls. Unless Tocke—Tocke? *Hej?*" A pause. She must have muted me; all I could hear was my lemon-watery breath. Tristan slid his phone out of the pocket of his sweatpants and started scrolling.

"While you're waiting, look up Myers-Briggs," I told him.

Tristan grumped a sigh. "I'm an INTJ."

"StrengthsFinder then."

When Freja returned, she said, "Tocke says you have not spoken."

"Tocke, no, but I have spoken to, let's see—" I counted them off on my fingers. "Jenny, Debbie, Katie, Tom—I'm assuming these are pseudonyms—"

"I do not know a Jenny, Debbie—you are sure they are from *Sverige och Mig*?"

"Mike One, Mike Two," I was saying, not exactly listening as I shooed Tristan off social media. "What'd you call it?"

"*Sverige och Mig.*"

"Sv-air-hee-ya oak mygg?" Nonsense sounds. "It's kind of hard to say—though I guess no harder than Navient—"

"The television program. In Sweden?"

"Wait, what?"

"Your application. We liked it very much. Very, what is the word—"

"My application?"

"Unusual, yes. Pauline—"

"You can call me Paulie—"

"We would like to fly you to New York for the next round of casting."

"Casting?"

While I parroted Freja, Tristan continued to scroll through short videos set to cacophonous pop music. I muted my phone. "Tristan! StrengthsFinder!"

"We would like to meet you in person," Freja said patiently. Her English had a singsong, nursery-rhymeish quality. "Next month. For the tenth anniversary season of *Sverige och Mig*. Are you still interested in participating?"

Finally, at the fourth repetition of the name, a rush of memory returned like the roar of the Baltic Sea. Christmas Eve Eve, my best friend, Jemma, and I had each popped an edible, uncorked a bottle of wine, and eaten an entire pan of homemade gingerbread men before indulging in a relatively new form of relaxation: doomscrolling while watching Christmas movies, in our case *The Shop Around the Corner*.

"Did you see what I posted?" Jemma asked, shoving her phone in my face. A black standard poodle with a voluminous blowout stared balefully from the screen. The caption read *Don't hate me cause I'm bowwowtiful #DOTD*. Over thirty-eight thousand people had hearted the picture, and over a hundred had already commented. *Forty percent of Africanns* [sic] *don't have power u shld be ashamed*, said the first. *Love it and you!!!!!!* said the second. I should explain that Jemma is a celebrity dog groomer. This means she's become quite famous for dog grooming, not that she grooms celebrities' dogs, though I wouldn't put that past her.

I handed the phone back to her. "Some of your best work. Is that Winifred?"

"Prince William. Freddi's the parti." Jemma continued to scroll. "Princie's such a baby. You should've heard him cry while I clipped his nails—wait, oh my God, Paulie, look what my aunt just posted." She shoved her phone back in my face, then snatched it away, laughing. "Some kind of casting call—" Her voice assumed a newscaster's gravitas. "Do you like to *travel*? Do you like *adventure*? Do you have Swedish ancestry and a strong urge to learn about your *heritage*? Apply now, and don't miss this *once-in-a-lifetime opportunity*!"

"What?" I had guffawed. "Your aunt's Jewish!"

"Right?!" Then Jemma explained that Orthodox Aunt Cecille had recently gone hog wild for genealogy. She'd joined a thousand online forums dedicated to ancestral self-discovery, including many with no connection to her own genetic line. "Hold on, I'm texting her." *Tap, tap, tap.* A moment later: "I guess one of Cecille's online friends did this Swedish genealogy TV show a while back and loved it." She reached for the decapitated head of a gingerbread man. We had decapitated all the gingerbread men; we called it dismantling the patriarchy. With her mouth full, Jemma said, "Paulie. You're Swee-ish."

"Yeah." I let out a rather indelicate belch. "So?"

"You could apply."

I felt my eyebrows knit together. "Um, no thank you."

"You know," Jimmy Stewart said from the television, "people seldom go to the trouble of scratching the surface of things to find the inner truth."

"Why not?" Jemma said.

"I don't want to be on TV."

Jemma had laughed at this. "Everyone wants to be on TV."

"That's not true." I raised my voice. "Declan! Do you want to be on TV?"

"No!" came my boyfriend's muffled voice from his home office.

"Everyone but Declan," Jemma amended.

I sat up on the couch. Blood rushed through my ears. "I don't care about being Swedish either."

Jemma snorted.

"I don't!"

"Then why do you always talk about it?"

"I don't!"

Jemma had then rattled off a long list of examples of my supposed allegiance to the motherland, including a holiday party four days prior, where I had declared that if our current president won reelection, I was decamping to Sweden to claim political asylum.

"Oh, phooey, everyone's trying to claim political asylum," I said. "Political asylum is the new black."

"You don't hear me going around telling everyone how glad I am to be Hungarian."

"Lies," I said. "Six months ago you said you were applying for dual citizenship."

"I was." Jemma sighed. "Until I realized their president's even worse than ours." She sipped her wine. "You know, for someone who always leaves the mall feeling depressed about life's spiritual emptiness, you're mighty quick to refuse a once-in-a-lifetime opportunity."

This was true, I had to give it to Jemma. The thing is, unless you get married, buy a house, build an important career, and/or have children, the narrative arc for a thirtysomething woman sort of sputters and stalls. I had recently turned thirty-five, had no career to speak of, and found myself more or less unfit for marriage, property, and procreation, either despite or because of biweekly rummagings through the subconscious in group therapy. I often waxed nostalgic to Jemma about our twenties and the acute sense of purpose that had defined them—the quests for new jobs, new lovers, new dresses and apartments! The delicious suspicion that one's real life was lurking around every corner! I even missed my particleboard bookshelf, which had listed so badly—for years!—it finally collapsed on a guy we called Crotchgrabber while he offered me an unsolicited explanation of cryptocurrency. How he had screamed! It was more emotion than I'd ever seen from him, including the grunt of his orgasm.

He was fine, though: they were mostly paperbacks. Point is, I'd been with Declan since I was thirty-one, had toiled away at Premiere Prep since I was thirty-two, and on an average day the most purposeful thing I did was plan my nightly dessert. Don't get me wrong, I love dessert. I do a lot of baking. But the thrill of chocolate cake is not the same as the thrill of a fresh start, a fresh romance, a fresh pair of shoes one can't afford but buys anyway.

Jemma tapped away on her phone. "We have till midnight to submit a two-minute video."

"And then?"

"Then we see if they like you, which of course they will."

I had poured myself more wine from the bottle. "Give me five good reasons."

"One, you're cute and charming, and any producer would be lucky to have you."

"No, *you're* cute and charming!" I threw a throw pillow at her. "*You* are!"

"Two, you're a photographer, you love the camera."

"*Was* a photographer. Loved being *behind*—"

"Three, you love to travel. Four, you hate your job and would get to escape for who knows how long, and five—five—"

"My family's nuts," I said.

"Five, your family's nuts," Jemma agreed.

"No, that's not a reason."

"Sure it is."

I made a sound in the back of my throat. "It's the opposite of a reason. It's a red flag, or like a steaming hazardous waste—"

Jemma ignored this. "What if your Swedish family's amazing? Just because your parents are . . . your parents . . . doesn't mean you have to slam the door on all things hereditary." She got a funny look on her face. "Damn, I think I'm getting heartburn." She thumped her chest with her fist. "It's like, what if Sweden's where you belong? With your beautiful, blond cousins and their . . . you know . . . social-democratic ideology?"

Oh, Jemma was good. Like all best friends, she knew just how hard she could press on old bruises without my flinching. Still, I was not giving in so easily. "I belong here," I said. "*You're* my family. Declan too. Craziness is genetic—that's a scientific fact."

Jemma took a Tums bottle out of her purse. It rattled like maracas as she fished out a pink tablet. "What if they're members of the royal family?"

Despite myself, I sat up straighter. "Sweden has a royal family?"

How I wish I could blame everything that follows on royal fever, THC, sugar highs, and red wine: in short, temporary insanity. But I would be lying if I said that Jemma's urging wasn't rapping on the door of my heart's secret chamber, the one that longed for the rituals of happy families (Easter-egg hunts, Thanksgiving turkeys, Christmas hams), the one that wanted a clearer conscience than American citizenship could ever offer, the one that wished to scream by Wednesday night from the stress and monotony of working life. It was the chamber, too, that held my shameful desire to be seen, adored, and deemed extraordinary, to achieve fame and fortune from screen to shining screen. And in the end, who or what could stop me? That Christmas Eve Eve, my dad was dead and my mom was in the loony bin, which she checked herself into every year or so, whenever she remembered how sad life was or she just got tired of working. I'd stumbled upon life's sorrows, too, and was sick to death of working, but it turned out I was also a gal who'd endure plenty of horrors for the chance to have a bit of fun.

"Oh, what the hell," I'd said to Jemma. "Not like anything will come of it."

"Pauline? Are you there?" Freja was saying on the line while Tristan laughed at a video that involved someone screaming in agony.

"Sorry, sorry." I whumped back to the present, and my eyes landed on the framed photograph of Jemma and me in front of the Centre Pompidou, the summer after my mom's third hospitalization. Both of us were flushed with rosé, joie de vivre, and the giddy thrill of plopping oneself in a foreign country with no attachments save a phone charger. "Yes," I heard myself say through a weird bubble in my throat. "I'm definitely still interested."

Beside the photo of Paris was a formal portrait of my Swedish grandmother, or *farmor*, as I was soon to learn, that had been taken at about my age. She was the person who'd taught me everything I knew about baking, about *krumkaker* and *lefse*, *chokladbollar* and *semlor*, *kanelbullar* and *kardemummabullar*, and—until she died when I was ten—everything, and I mean everything, I knew about the good parts of family and about maternal love.

I cleared the throat bubble with a cough. "What was that about flying me to New York?"

"Dude, I love New York," Tristan said without looking up from his phone.

"Tristan!" I barked. "Go find your strengths!"

THE ADRENALINE THRILL from this news was unfortunately short-lived, and not only because of Tristan's attention deficit disorder. Though most of Premiere Prep's clients had applied early to the Ivies and Ivy-adjacents, January 15 was a big deadline for a number of respectable academies, and my boss, Garance, had foisted a pile of procrastinators upon me after returning from holiday break. I spent the rest of the afternoon and early evening breaking my resolutions not once but thrice (potato chips, gummy worms, Keurig K-cup), talking clinically anxious teens off the proverbial cliff, and sending out emails pleading for at least partial drafts of personal statements. It didn't take long for the replies to start rolling in:

hey Paulie sorry but i need more time. I'm at my dads house in Florida and the frogs and toads are super loud, none of us got any sleep last night.

I know I'm supposed to write about the trip I took to Guatemala but honestly it was pretty boring, could I do my ACL instead? The recovery took way longer than they thought

paulie i dont know if you heard but the prince of S— died yesterday. im not from S— but my friend is and im really upset. ill try to work on my essay but i can't make any promises

It was hard not to feel demoralized about the future of my job, not to mention my species, as teen after teen bowed out of responsibility due to acute crisis, either real or imagined. Did these rich youths—if not the one percent, then the two-to-five—not comprehend their position on the world stage? Or did comprehension lead to chronic despair and lethargy? How it vexed me to witness them squander their time and good fortune, as if time and good fortune came in bulk from Costco and supply chains never ran dry. But while I would never admit it aloud, not even to Jemma, a tinge of envy commingled with my vexation—if not for their good fortune, for their belief in eternal life.

Just as I was about to throw up my hands and give up for the day, two more emails arrived: one from Freja, with a round-trip e-ticket to New York attached; and one from Sophie, an apple-cheeked dancer desperate to get into Case Western. *Paulie don't be mad I know this is last minute but could you edit this tonight??? My mom and I are going to Joffrey in Chicago tmrw for a training and I want to try to finish my app on the train. Thank you!!!! You're the best!!!!!!!!*

Sighing, I emailed back, *No problem, kiddo!* and stuck my work laptop into my bag, though I was tempted to throw it out the window. By the time I got to my car, the temperature on the dashboard read negative eighteen—enough to freeze my nostrils together and kill me within the hour. It's strange to live somewhere so hazardous, or so my college roommate liked to hazard. (She was from San Mateo.) "I could *never* do it," she'd say before I'd haul off for winter break. "You're so *brave*." But I did not feel brave when she said this. I felt like I did when I was fourteen and strangers, with a mix of horror and pity, tried to console me about my acne.

When I opened the back door of our duplex, I saw Declan standing in the kitchen holding a platter of Sloppy Joes. He wore his new Christmas apron, which read May the Forks Be with You alongside a picture of a pronged Lightsaber. I was caught off guard, as I often was after a period of absence, by how handsome he was. Declan's hair, I liked to say, deserved its own social media, to which Declan would reply that he hated social media and I should too—privacy matters and so forth. (Software engineers love to talk about privacy.) But his locks were so dark and thick and wavy, should the world not bear witness? The same could be said for his eyelashes.

The other thing about Declan that I should say straight-out is that he's a Good Person. Definitely a better person than I am. It's hard to say exactly what makes him a Good Person: the goodness is just there, the way some people have knobby knees. A surprising problem about falling in love with a Good Person is that unless you, too, are a Good Person, you end up looking Bad in comparison. Or at least Worse. The one in the pair who cuts off old people in the airport security line and says horrendous things about the host on the way home from a party.

"Voilà!" Declan said, and wafted the smell from the platter toward me. "I cooked again."

"I can see that." I took off my mittens, unwound the scarf from around my head, removed my hat, and struggled out of my neck warmer, all while kicking off my heavy boots and shrugging off my sleeping-bag coat. Thus untrussed, I kissed him on the cheek. "Thank you, duckie."

We sat down at the table, as we always did in the evenings, to tell each other about our days. Normally I cooked and Declan did the dishes, but his New Year's resolution was to learn the fine art of cuisine. His approach was more methodical than ambitious, and so for the past week we'd been eating like a daycare: macaroni and cheese, grilled cheese and tomato soup, rice and beans, BLTs, and Cream of Wheat.

"You'll never guess who called today," I said after half a Joe.

"Your sister?"

"Nah, she's still deep in the Movement."

My older sister, Else, was a polyamorist, conspiracy theorist, and serial joiner of wellness cults. Every other January she'd call, euphoric, to extol the Secrets of a Happy Life before hitting me up for a bulk order of essential oils. Else and I could have a civilized conversation for about fifteen minutes before our incompatible worldviews began to chafe like inner thighs:

"Well, you guys do live near a cell tower," Else had said with a sigh the last time we talked, after I'd told her our next-door neighbor had been diagnosed with breast cancer. "The research shows—"

"Oh no," I'd said, standing up at the kitchen table. "I'm gonna stop you right there."

"There're hot spots wherever there's 5G," she'd continued, as if I'd said nothing. "Just because nobody's talking about it doesn't mean it isn't real."

"Actually, it does mean that."

"I'm not saying it's her fault—"

"That's exactly what you're saying!"

"I'm saying it's AT&T's fault! God, Paulie! If the electromagnetic radiation doesn't kill you, your judgmentalness—"

"You mean your *lack* of judgment!" Then she'd hung up on me.

The Movement, Else's latest book of revelations, had my sister staring at the sun for five minutes every morning, dancing ecstatically for three hours a night, and trading in skin-cancer pseudoscience, e.g., its invention by Coppertone at the behest of a sinister little man named Dave. We'd texted on Christmas but otherwise gave each other a wide berth, like gorillas in rival bands.

"Your mom?" Declan said, and plucked a chunk of Sloppy Joe from my plate.

She hadn't called since Christmas, I told him with my mouth full. Even then we hadn't talked for long. She'd grown close to a horse named Chester in equine therapy, and he was struggling with abandonment issues.

"Then who?"

"Remember the night Jemma and I made you watch the end of *The Shop Around the Corner* four times so you'd finally realize how perfect it is?"

Declan took a sip of water. "I remember watching it once and then you and Jemma shouting about red carnations—"

"Well, after you went to bed, Jemma and I kind of—" How did one go about explaining insensible deeds sensibly? Declan's face bloomed with concern. "Drank more wine and filmed me doing, like, a one-woman show in the kitchen and"—I cleared my throat—"submitted the video to a Swedish reality-show casting call?"

I tended to end sentences with questions when I knew Declan would find the content questionable. His concern furrowed into confusion, the same look he got debugging code.

"Anyway," I concluded, "they're flying me out to New York in a few weeks, isn't that fun?" I popped the last of my Sloppy Joe into my mouth and answered my own question. "Super fun."

Declan said nothing, just let his gaze drift toward the right. Over the years I'd learned his silence was neither a form of withholding nor poor listening. Declan needed time to think. I wanted to give him this time, but I also wanted him to be my mirror. A free trip to New York! A free trip to Sweden—maybe!

"Is it like those shows you watch while you put on your potions and creams?" he said finally, referring to my nightly skincare regimen, during which shows about feuding rich women kept me company. Declan hated these shows. They were mean and stressful, he said, and life was mean and stressful enough. I'd explained to him that I'd been tuning in for so long that the feuding rich women felt like family. "Be nice to my moms," I'd cajole when he'd roll his eyes at the screen—a joke, though Declan never found it funny.

"No, not at all." I drank some water. My armpits were getting sweaty.

"What kind of show is it, then?"

"It's a family show," I said, though I had no idea what kind of show it was, because I hadn't bothered to look it up.

Declan pulled out his phone. "What's it called?"

I told him, reluctantly. He was spoiling the fun. After a moment he held up a clip of a blond woman weeping.

I pointed at the screen. "She's crying because she's *happy*."

"I'm just so glad," the blond hiccupped over a soaring orchestral soundtrack, "I got to come here, and see this place—"

"Manufactured epiphany," Declan said, and for a split second I wanted to go back in time and blow up the liberal arts college where he'd majored in media and cultural studies.

Before I could retort, he tapped on the next suggested video. A group of people in matching T-shirts were racing around a maypole, screaming.

"You saw this?" he said. "And you still applied?"

"I applied," I said carefully, "but did not see that."

I could tell Declan was trying very hard not to sound exasperated. "Tell me you googled the show before saying yes to New York."

"Um," I said.

Karen Hamburger, my group therapist, often said that I protected myself through humor and willful ignorance. Not to mention defensiveness, hence the following: "Anyway, thanks for being happy for me."

Once again, Declan said nothing. The silence comes from his German side. He's half German, one-quarter Irish, and one-quarter English: in other words, three-quarters colonizer. The first time I met his mother, she'd shown off her gold-plated china and claimed descent from two passengers on the *Mayflower*.

"That was sarcasm, in case you didn't notice."

"A ficus would have noticed."

"Why aren't you more excited for me?"

"I am excited for you," Declan said in a voice less animated than a chatbot.

I puffed air from my mouth and stood to grab two beers from the fridge.

"I thought you weren't—"

"This is hardly the time for New Year's resolutions!" I trumpeted. I opened the bottles with the can opener and thumped back down at the table. "I know what you're going to say, so you don't have to bother saying it. You're going to say reality TV is bad."

"That's not what I was going to say."

"You're going to say it's destroying America, blah blah blah, politics have become entertainment, nobody wants to actually do stuff anymore, they just want to be famous, and once you're famous you go crazy." I pointed at his phone screen, at the group of people frozen mid-flight around a maypole. "But this is a *Swedish* show. It won't even air here. And Swedish TV is a lot better because"—here I had to drink some beer, to buy time to come up with a reason—"because their society actually cares about people. The planet. *Women*." Now the engine was revving. "They get free health care and education, and, like, a *lot* of parental leave—"

"I was going to say there's no such thing as a free trip. You end up paying one way or another—'member Puerto Vallarta?"

He was referring to the "Free Boat Ride!" I had signed us up for during our one and only tropical vacation, which ended up being the prelude to a three-hour time-share sales pitch.

"That was different," I said. "How was I to know Derek was a flim-flammer?"

"Look, if you want to go to New York, it's not like I'd ever stop you—"

I clacked my beer down on the table. "But not stopping me is not the same as wanting me to go!"

We were dangerously close to having the same fight we had every few months. I'm too impulsive, Declan's too circumspect; I say yes too much, he always says no. The fight never resolves itself, exactly—we just pop it like a pimple, knowing full well we'll break out again.

But this time, Declan stopped us before the argument could really begin. He said, "I love how excited you get. You know that. I just don't want anyone taking advantage of you."

"Taking advantage!" I said. "I'm the one taking advantage! It's a free trip! I don't even know if I'd do the show—*if* they picked me. But they seem really nice, and I get a per diem and everything—"

Declan frowned. "See, that's how they get you."

I think it's much easier to be wise if you're a person like Declan. Declan's favorite pastime is sitting in a chair and staring into space. When he's not coding he's thinking about concepts, which run the gamut from the Shaker movement to the Chinese Communist Party. One night, when I got home from work, all the lights were off, and Declan was sitting in his office with fifteen browser tabs open to various waste treatment facilities and the Paris sewer system. "I was wondering how toilets worked," he'd explained, and then admitted he'd forgotten to go grocery shopping.

Back when I was in charge of cooking, instead of calling him to the table when dinner was ready, I'd holler: "Time to reenter the physical plane!"

But me, I'm struck dumb by most everything in the physical plane. Ripe strawberries, perfume samples, a cute guy from the hardware store giving a perfunctory hello. *Obsessed* is my most frequent text to Jemma, last used in reference to homemade marshmallows. I suppose Else and I have that in common, a certain willingness to be bowled over by life.

"I'm excited for you, too, you know," Declan said. He put an arm around me, and I smelled his Declan smell: sweat and skin and soap and deodorant. Desire zinged through my lower belly.

"Yeah?"

"Yeah."

We kissed—the love kind, not the lust kind. I missed making out with Declan. We mostly neglected matters of foreplay these days, though we still had plenty of sex. Why was that? I put my hand on his thigh, an invitation for more. He cleared his throat.

"I've got some work I need to finish up," he said, and kissed me on the cheek. He stood up with a half-guilty, half-apologetic expression. Declan worked a lot. He was still wearing the Forks Be with You apron, which he'd probably forgotten about, and probably wouldn't remember until I said something.

"Okay."

"That okay?"

"Of course it's okay." I smiled a titch too broadly. "I have an essay to read anyway."

"Maybe tomorrow?"

"Okay." I drank my beer. "Sure."

"You don't mind cleaning up?"

"Not at all."

He kissed the top of my head, and I said, "Thanks again for dinner."

As I did the dishes, looking out the window over our frozen street, I caught sight of the storefront that had been vacant for over a year, ever since the bespoke candy shop had gone out of business. For several months, Declan and I had talked about setting up shop there ourselves. It would be a graceful exit strategy from Premiere Prep—follow your dreams, kids!—that would sidestep the fact I found the clientele increasingly deranged. One day, in a burst of hopefulness, I'd even called the landlord, a charming old Minneapolitan, to ask about the rent, which was surprisingly affordable given the neighborhood. "You sound like a great tenant," he'd said. "What are your plans for the space?"

"Well," I'd said. "I'm, um, working on a few concepts," and then in a panic hung up. I had so many ideas, ideas coming out of my ears. One day I'd be gung ho about opening a gallery, the next a coworking space. I read an article about animal cruelty and for a week became hell-bent on a doggy daycare. Last autumn, when Declan and I walked past it, we'd batted around the idea of a web-design business wherein Declan would build the sites, I'd create the images, and everyone who walked in would get a free hot dog. But then I decided the only fun part of the plan was the hot dogs, which was around the time Declan decided he needed a break from my ideating.

I rinsed soapy water off the big frying pan and placed it on the rack while wiping my eyes on my sweater. It was dumb to get teary over an empty storefront, dumb to cry at the loss of an imaginary, better me who went sprinting toward challenges like a pole vaulter instead of persevering on the starting line. Hot water scalded my hands as I scrubbed away at a stained wooden spoon—at last, a challenge I could meet! Else once sent me a self-help book I'd never read (actually, she'd sent me many I'd never read) called *Manifest* after I'd complained to her about Premiere Prep. *Your job isn't the problem Paulie*, she'd written on the front flap. *YOU are the problem. Love your big sister xo Else. p.s. The book cost $20 so you can mail me cash!!!*

I checked my phone after drying my hands and saw that six more students had emailed over the dinner hour, all with brutal, almost corporate urgency. They needed me *now*, they needed feedback *now*, they were *freaking out* and so were their parents, and if I didn't help *ASAP* everything would be *ruined*. I sighed, and, in lieu of addressing these concerns, went down the hall to draw a bath. Baths are like breaths during Minnesota winters: you have to take them or you'll die. I'd been trying to convince Declan to build us a sauna, but he's not a fan of extreme temperatures—extreme anything, really. As I passed his darkened office, I saw him tapping away on a glowing black screen, far above the physical plane.

I lit candles and threw in a bath bomb before wiggling out of my clothes and sinking into the warm water, or sinking as much as a woman of six feet can. (I am not rich enough to have a tub that fits me, and if I ever am, perhaps it will be a sign that I'm *too* rich.) I held my phone at arm's length from the tub, and for the first time in my life googled "Sweden." I scrolled past facts about geography, history, and culture until I arrived at a site entitled Notable, Noble, Nobel Swedes. Interesting. There were more than I thought. Ingmar Bergman, Greta Garbo, Greta Thunberg, Alfred Nobel and ABBA and Alexander Skarsgård—

I stopped scrolling when I got to Alexander's picture. My, he was handsome. Different from Declan, who was rather hirsute. He looked—well, he looked kind of like me. Blond hair, blue eyes, fair, tall, slender. I put his name into the search engine, clicked over to videos, chose one: "Alexander Skarsgård Speaking Swedish." There he was, in a plaid shirt, burbling away in an unintelligible tongue.

Before I knew it, the fingers on my free hand were creeping under the water toward my inner thighs. *"Fleur mann shekta beelteeya ha,"* Alex said confidingly to the camera. His eyes were as blue as moonlight, dark and piercing—

Oh! Oh! I would go to Sweden and everything would be different. I'd be surrounded by tens of hundreds of Alexander Skarsgårds. They'd put flower crowns in my hair and go down on me constantly, a symbol of their egalitarian society, where excellent public universities rendered Premiere Prep irrelevant. These men would carry IKEA furniture instead of guns, hunt moose instead of people, willingly give up fifty percent of their earnings to maintain a functional government, elect women instead of lunatics, go to museums instead of football games, wear interesting shoes, cook, do all the dishes, find me endlessly fascinating, and make it a breeze to turn an abandoned storefront into a fetching business, even if one had no experience nor plans nor, I daresay, discreet desires to start manifesting—

I was so caught up in my fantasy that right before I was going to climax, I dropped my phone in the bathwater. "Criminy!" I crabbed my hands through the bubbles and tossed the phone on the bathmat. "Declan?" I shouted, dabbing the phone with a towel. "Can you help me?"

After a moment, Declan's head popped through the bathroom door. "Jesus, it's hot in here."

"I dropped my phone in the tub."

"Again? How'd that happen?"

"Um," I said.

"Keep drying it off," he said. His head disappeared. After a moment he returned with a mixing bowl filled with dry rice.

"Thank you, duckie," I said, nestling the phone in the rice like a hen in straw.

"No problem," he said, without any criticism, my personal knee-jerk reaction to human error. See what I mean about him being a Good Person?

As Declan went back to his office, my phone rang, miraculously. I fished it out of the rice. It was Jemma. "Hello?" I said, putting it on speaker as I stepped out of the tub. "Hello? Hello?"

"Why are you talking so loud?" Jemma said.

"I dropped my phone in the bath. I have a bunch of work to do but I just couldn't—"

"Again?"

"It doesn't happen that often!" (It did.) I grabbed a towel. "You can hear me?"

"Yeah, fine. I saw your text!"

We cackled over the absurdity of it all. Jemma told me she was going to be in New York at the same time I was, filming a segment on doggie deep conditioners for one of the morning shows. Thanks to her wildly popular social channels, she flies out to New York or Los Angeles every month to film one of these guest segments. My favorite video of hers is a slo-mo montage, set to "Every Breath You Take," of a recently blow-dried Pomeranian.

"We'll meet for lunch in Midtown," Jemma declared. "My treat."

"I mean, I guess if I get to see you . . ." I said.

"You guess? This is a coup!"

"Can we go somewhere fancy?" I pumped lotion into my hands and slathered it up and down my arms. "Somewhere with three courses and starched tablecloths?"

"Of course." Jemma paused. "What's up? Did Declan say something?"

"Just the usual stuff. 'Paulie, slow down. Paulie, stop and think. Paulie, why do you always say yes before you know what the question is?'"

"You can't say he's inconsistent."

"Maybe a little too consistent."

"Frankly, I wouldn't mind a little consistency."

Jemma is bisexual, though at this point she mostly dates women; Lucy, her on-again, off-again, was flakier than lead paint. "Anyway," she said, chewing on what I guessed was the olive oil cake I'd dropped off at her condo that morning. "I've got a good feeling about this. Aunt Cecille said her friend who did the show is really close to her Swedish family now. She visits them twice a year, speaks Swedish and everything. Says it was the best experience of her life."

"Really? You have a good feeling?" I trusted Jemma's intuition, which had never let us down, except the time we got food poisoning from roadside empanadas in the Yucatán.

"Really," Jemma said. Her voice turned thoughtful. "Who knows, maybe it'll be healing."

"Ha ha!" I said. "Reality TV! Healing!"

We laughed and laughed.

CHAPTER TWO

✵

THE CASTING

Whoever invented the six-a.m. flight was either a sadist or a masochist. Or both! A few weeks later, I almost missed mine to Newark because I'd stayed up too late trying on clothes for my audition. Jemma'd been helping via FaceTime from New York, and by eleven thirty half my closet was on the bed. Declan had kindly decamped to the couch, where he'd dozed off with my grandmother's copy of *The Joy of Cooking* on his chest.

"What says 'pick me' but also 'I don't care'?" I'd asked Jemma.

"A bustier and sweatpants?" she'd said.

Eventually we'd settled on a fun yet respectable plaid miniskirt suit, dressed down with tights and Doc Martens. I was feeling great about my prospects until I slept through two alarms and had to run through the airport with my dirty hair streaming behind me and my backpack flapping like an open mouth. I boarded the plane right as they were closing the gate and slept through both the flight and the bus to Manhattan. When I finally skipped down the shuttle steps near Grand Central and caught sight of Jemma, the exhaust-filled Midtown air seemed to me the sweetest nectar. Jemma screamed when she saw me, and I screamed right back. There's something thrilling about seeing your best friend in an unfamiliar location, like having sex in the kitchen when you're used to the bed.

"You look beautiful!" I said as we embraced. Jemma's dark, curly hair and makeup had been heavily zhuzhed by network professionals. She wore high-waisted trousers and a powerfully purple cashmere sweater that I was certain popped in HDTV. I took my vintage Polaroid 600 out of my backpack—a black, squat loaf with a rainbow stripe and pop-up flash—and snapped a picture fast enough that she didn't have time to pose. Jemma is excellent at posing—one million followers will do that to a person—but I preferred her pose-free.

"Good girl!" She pointed to the camera. "I haven't seen that in for-ever."

"Grabbed it on my way out the door. Why not?" I turned the lens toward us both and smiled cheesily. Click and whir went the Polaroid. I threw its box chain strap over one shoulder and adjusted my backpack on the other.

Jemma leaned forward and took a big whiff of me. "You smell good. Perfume and—what is that, cookies?"

I confessed I'd eaten a dozen Biscoffs on the plane as we linked arms and headed for the Italian restaurant where Jemma had booked a reser-vation. Heads turned, as they always did when we were together: Jemma was only an inch shorter than me, which meant we towered over almost everyone on the street. At the restaurant's best table by the window— a perk of Jemma's influencer status—we attacked the bread basket and olive oil before ordering two glasses of French champagne, cacio e pepe, gnocchi, and a pear-Gorgonzola-walnut salad to share.

"*Grazie mille!*" I said when the server put the cacio e pepe in front of us. I snapped a Polaroid of the plate and stuck it under my butt to develop.

"I'm so happy you're taking pictures again," Jemma said through a mouthful of gnocchi.

I pointed my fork at her. "Don't."

"Don't what?"

"Don't use that Make-A-Wish voice on me."

"I think of it more like 'encouraging aunt.'"

"I don' nee' encoura'ement," I said through a mouthful of pasta. "I haf' an MFA."

Inspired by the greats—Diane Arbus, Dorothea Lange, Nan Goldin, Gillian Wearing—I'd taken up portraiture in my late teens, only to be trampled in university art departments for what (male) faculty and (male) peers decided was boring, domestic, sentimental drivel with "unlikeable subjects" and a lack of "gravitas" and "positionality."

"I'm just saying, it's been, what, five years since you quit?" Jemma said during dessert, after I'd taken a picture of our tiny espressos and tiramisu. "The world's lucky to have you taking pictures again."

"Your butt's lucky to have me taking pictures again," I said, and leaned under the table to snap a Polaroid of our long legs tangled up together.

Jemma sighed and held out her hand. "Will you at least let me post some of these?"

I shrugged and passed her the stack of film. "It's a free country."

"One of these days," Jemma said, flipping through, "you're just going to have to get used to the fact that some people are never going to like what you do, no matter how well you do it." She waved the Polaroids. "But then you'll figure out it doesn't matter and do it anyway."

I scraped the bottom of my ramekin with my tiny spoon. "That's always been true. The difference now is that every Tom, Dick, and Harry can pillory you virtually."

Jemma signaled for the check. "If I had a dollar for every time I was pilloried virtually, I'd be even richer than I already am." She was referring to the various crazy people, antisemites, homophobes, and misogynists who slid into her DMs and demanded she feel like crap.

"How do you do it?" I picked up my espresso cup. "I mean it—how do you do it?"

Jemma rummaged through her purse and took out her Tums and her credit card. "I close my eyes and imagine their terrible childhoods, their broken relationships, all the love they long to have and all the love they're lacking." She handed the card to the server with a radiant smile, then turned back to me. "And if that doesn't work, I picture myself fifty feet tall and crushing their houses with my bare feet."

She signed the bill and we began walking toward the hotel where my interview would be held. Strolling, I thought for the millionth time about how remarkably well-adjusted Jemma was for a celebrity dog groomer. She was one of those emotional ninjas with an intact-enough selfhood that the world's slings and arrows bounced off her harmlessly, like Nerf foam. Yet her selfhood wasn't so hard or inflated that she couldn't weep at soldier-dog reunion videos or get all revved up about my minor successes, like when I learned to make flaky croissants or started taking Polaroids again.

But for me, the world's slings and arrows pierced hard and fast, like a steak knife to taut plastic wrap. Take my time in the art world. Because I'd been so impressionable, I'd been unable to sift through my colleagues' valid critiques (my technique *was* sloppy) from the absurd ones (photographing women's lives in a naturalistic fashion was either boring, stupid, or exploitative). The nadir came when I took a series of photographs of my great-aunt—my Swedish grandmother's sister—for my MFA thesis show that paid homage to Sally Mann. My aunt was autistic, and I'd spent months visiting her at the nursing home before taking a single picture, hoping to capture her particular form of beauty, by which I meant her lack of artifice. What I loved about photography, specifically portraiture, was how it could draw a viewer's attention away from the manufactured images of advertising and social media and toward something more startling. The best picture from my show emerged after I had spent ten minutes rubbing my great-aunt's shoulders after she complained of back pain. "How does this feel?" I had asked her gently, but with Lady Bountiful undertones.

She'd cocked her head. "I don't like it."

I'd been put off at first, ruffled by her lack of gratitude, until offense gave way to delight. How often in this world did a person say exactly what they meant? I'd started laughing, and I took a picture of my aunt as I did. She'd looked right at me, pleased, as if I'd finally grokked something she'd understood for a long time. In short, it was a joyful project, and by the end of it I had a small yet unmistakable sense that I was onto something. And then:

"If I have to look at one more pathetic fucking portrait of someone's grandma," I'd overheard my professor mutter to a colleague at the opening, "I'm going to shoot turpentine in my veins."

I'd blanched at this remark, then wilted. Then I'd decided to throw out everything I was interested in—intimate pictures of people I loved—in order to throw myself into formalism, the coin of the realm during my school days. My portraits became stiff, stilted, intricate shoots with other white women that took weeks to arrange and days to develop. Think Cindy Sherman, but with less of a wink. There was Jemma on a rocking horse. There was Else in a cemetery. There was Martha, the owner of the coffee shop where I baristaed, surrounded by creepy Victorian dolls. These portraits were sad and solemn and lifeless, and what's worse, I *knew* they were sad and solemn and lifeless, but I also knew my truer impulses had thus far led to humiliation and failure. After finishing my program, I spent two years submitting this work to residencies and galleries and juries and got precisely nowhere. And then I just kind of . . . gave up.

Well, I didn't give up entirely. I got the job at Premiere Prep, started dating Declan, enjoyed lolling about on weekends instead of staging hopeless shoots for hopeless fellowships. Once in a while I'd take pictures at a party the way a lapsed musician might pick up a guitar. It was better that way, I said to myself and anyone who asked. Less pressure. My Pentax and lenses were in a closet somewhere; I used a Diana or Polaroid when I picked up anything besides my phone, which was rare. But for some reason I'd grabbed the camera that morning, even grabbed an extra box of film from the fridge.

"Everyone should have a friend like you," I said to Jemma when we got to the hotel. "If they did, we'd have world peace."

She enveloped me in a hug and lifted me off my feet. I grunted from the pressure to my rib cage. "If they don't fall in love with you in thirty seconds, call me and I'll make them. Actually, call me anyway." She set me down gently, like a mother with her child.

"I will." I pulled out my phone and checked the time. "Oh no!"

"Don't forget to call me!" Jemma said as I took off at a dead sprint toward the entrance.

"My battery's almost dead!" I shouted.

"Borrow their phone!" she hollered.

"I can't borrow their phone!"

"Why not?!" We were both bellowing now. Luckily we were in New York, where no one blinks unless you've got a gunshot wound to the abdomen.

"It's rude!"

"Be rude!" Jemma shouted. "Be shameless! This is reality TV!"

"Okay!" I huffed as I flung open the lobby doors. "Okay! Okay!"

I WAS GREETED at the door of a sixteenth-story suite by two enormous Swedes.

"You are very tall," the black-haired man said. He looked exactly, I'm afraid to say, like a Viking. This is not a stereotype. His biceps were the size of rump roasts.

"*You're* very tall!" I said, and threw my arms open in greeting.

"You *are* tall," the blond woman said, and opened the door a little wider.

"As are *you*!" I said.

"And you are late," said the woman with a smile.

"Just a couple minutes—"

"Swedes are very punctual," said the Viking, also smiling.

"Oh—" I faltered.

"Don't make it a habit!" said the woman.

Because they were smiling, I couldn't tell if I was in trouble. "I'm . . . sorry?"

"It's all right, Pauline. Come in." The woman opened the door wider. I could tell by her lilt that this was Freja. She introduced the Viking as Tocke, the executive producer of *Sverige och Mig*. "Would you mind taking your shoes off?"

In fact I did mind, for I had a large hole in the toe of my tights. I thought of what Jemma had said. *Be shameless.*

"Actually, I can't," I said.

Freja turned to Tocke with a puzzled glance. "You can't?"

"I can't," I said, and shrugged helplessly, as if an invisible overlord had handed down the decision. "It's not possible."

A brief pause, during which Tocke appeared to assess the politics of the situation, as well as my feet.

"All right, then," he said, and gestured toward a squat armchair. "Please, sit."

"All right, then!" I said. "Here we go!" I felt a little drunk as I eased into the chair, less from the lunchtime champagne than from the euphoria of refusal. Without asking for permission, I took my camera out of my backpack. *Snap*—the giant harness boots and chunky sneakers on the floor. *Snap*—the cords crisscrossing the patterned carpet. *Snap*—Tocke and Freja settling themselves onto a comically small love seat. Though we were technically in a suite—a sitting room opened out from the foyer, the bedroom was to my left—the word overstates the size and quality of the place, if not the price.

"I thought we were the one taking pictures, ha ha ha," said Tocke, gesturing to a tripod and camera set up in one corner. There were no windows in the sitting room, just two lamps, one of them neon, like a down-market bar and grill.

"You are a photographer? I do not remember this from your application, only the baking," Freja said. She wore an oversized black jumpsuit and thick black glasses, which made her fair hair and skin seem even fairer. Stockholm women, I knew from fashion blogs, had a certain je ne sais quoi, though different from the French, of chic minimalism and casual disregard of the gender binary.

"No, it's just for fun." I held up the still-hazy pictures. "I'll give them to you, if you'd like."

Tocke waved his hand in a no-thank-you manner, and I noticed the red light on the camera was blinking. I hadn't even checked my teeth for parsley!

"Tell us why you want to be a part of *Sverige och Mig*," Tocke said. "This means '*Sweden and Me*' in English, you know this, yes?"

"Oh! Right. Of course, definitely," I said. "But first, um, why don't you tell me a little about your journey?" I interlaced my fingers over my knees. "I mean, why'd you create *Sweden and Me*, and what makes you keep at it after a whole decade?"

This put Tocke back on his heels for a second. I had learned this approach to interviewing from a quick Google search in the elevator.

"Actually, it all started with our sister show in Norway," Tocke said after a beat, and went on to explain that the Norwegians had years before schemed up a competitive reality show called *Sjokkere Meg!* (*Shock me!*), in which Americans with Norwegian heritage flew to their homeland to compete in a heartless boot camp with challenges like gutting fish, binge-eating lutefisk, and skiing cross-country with no prior experience. "The winner met their Norwegian family and got ten thousand dollars," Tocke said, snapping a rubber band on his wrist, "but they learned nothing about their ancestors and their family stories. It was obvious that viewers were interested in that. We saw the DNA tests and the popularity of your genealogy shows here in the States—as you know, Sweden lost twenty percent of its population to immigration in the nineteenth century . . ." He trailed off, looking fondly into the distance. "So we thought, why don't we relax the show, bring in a historian, keep the competition but not have it be so . . . what is the word . . . ?"

"Harsh," Freja supplied. "The Norwegians are very harsh."

"Yes, not so harsh, and also change the focus of the show from the culture shock to the family, to meeting the family."

"They are also very rich, Norwegians," Freja said. She shook her head. "From the oil. It is almost disgusting."

Inflatable dollar signs were dancing above in my head. "And the ten thousand dollars?"

"Never." Tocke looked horrified. "That is not what our show is about."

"Oh," I said. The dollar signs sputtered across the room, deflated. "Right."

Tocke cleared his throat. "They are beautiful stories, the family stories. Every one. You have watched online, yes?"

"Um, just a little," I said, recalling Declan's screaming maypole.

"This is smart." Tocke nodded. "It is better when you are surprised."

"It is the most popular show in Sweden," Freja said. "Last year we won an Emmy."

"Did you?" I said. "I don't remember seeing you on TV."

"Well, it was an international Emmy," Freja conceded.

"I keep it in our offices," Tocke said, and to my great surprise I saw his eyes mist over. I had never seen a Viking cry before. The incongruity was touching, like watching a bear use a fork and knife.

"Congratulations," I offered. "I mean, wow, that's amazing."

Tocke smiled. His eyes were still wet. "Why do Americans always say 'amazing'? Everything is either amazing or awesome. What if something is not amazing? What if it is just fine?"

"My six-a.m. flight was just fine," I said.

Tocke laughed at this. Or I hoped it was a laugh—a brief, guttural bark. "You are funny," he said with a granite expression.

"Beautiful too," Freja said to him, as if I weren't there. She whipped her phone off the coffee table and started taking close-ups of my face. "Look at that," she muttered to Tocke as she showed him the screen.

I patted my left cheek, then my right. I had never taken pictures of myself during all my years of portraiture. Jemma said I was too Midwestern for self-documentation; Karen Hamburger, my group therapist, said it was my fear of being seen. I told them both it was a protest against a culture of rampant narcissism, and somehow neither of them believed me.

"But tell me now"—Tocke leaned forward on the love seat—"why do you want to be a part of *Sverige och Mig*?"

"Um," I said.

His question posed the same problem as all job interview questions: Did you answer candidly, or did you say what the interviewer slow-pitched you to say?

Because I want a new job, I could have said.

Because I want a new family, I could have said.

Because I want to be on TV! I could have said.

"Because I've, um, longed for years to understand who I am and where I come from," I said. I put my chin in my hands and tried to gaze in a ponderous manner toward the neon lamp. "My whole life has maybe, um, led to this moment?"

"And why is that?" Tocke said, nodding along and scribbling something on a notepad.

"Um," I said. I thought again of what Jemma said. *Be shameless.*

I took the Altoids tin out of my backpack and popped four in my mouth. "Because my family's a teaspoon of yeast short of a cinnamon bun, if you know what I mean," I said as my mouth burst into flames. I'd started mega-dosing cinnamon Altoids in art school while my classmates puffed on Parliaments. It satisfied my oral fixation, and the panic brought on by overwhelming flavor functioned as a natural upper.

"I do not know what you mean," Tocke said, at the same time Freja said, "What is a teaspoon?"

So I gave them the whole rigamarole. When I was eleven, my minister father came out of the closet, just ten months after his mother, my Swedish *farmor*, died of cancer. Shortly thereafter, Dad decamped to Santa Fe with his parishioner-lover, Len, who was fifteen years Dad's junior and Jemma's and my piano teacher. This, of course, scandalized everyone in town, no one more than my mother, a champion of abstinence-only sexual education with stricter morals than the Vatican. But bully for Dad and all that, everyone should live their truth, though Jemma and I agreed it would have been much easier to wave the pride flag on his behalf if Dad had not regularly called Len a "fruitcake" when he picked us up from our lessons.

Anyway, Dad forgot about Else, Mom, and me for a while. He never paid child support and didn't invite Else and me out to visit him until Else had graduated high school. In the end, I'm not sure which was more painful: his five-year abandonment or the dream catcher he wore around his neck when he picked us up in Albuquerque. His graduation gift to Else was a visit to a sweat lodge, during which she threw up twice and flipped the switch on her commitment to woo-woo spirituality. I didn't go, nor was I invited. I spent the week sulking by the apartment-complex pool, refusing to eat Len's chicken enchiladas, and attempting to elicit an apology from my father that was as likely to arrive as a UFO in Roswell.

Which was too bad, since Dad dropped dead of a heart attack—they called it a widow-maker—six weeks after the visit. I didn't have much time to grieve, seeing as I was busy taking care of Mom, who took the news just as hard if not harder than his initial skedaddling.

"He was a wonderful man," she would weep at night.

"Mom," I said. "He lied to you. He left you. He owed you money."

"You should have seen us when we first met," she would continue, her eyes glassy with tears. "He couldn't take his eyes off me."

Her glass of Crystal Light at dinner became a glass of Chardonnay, then two, then an entire bottle, then vodka. When I tried to talk to her about her drinking, she'd put her head on my shoulder and interlace my fingers with hers. "You were the sweetest of my babies," she would say. "Always wanted to be held. You'd cry and cry when I'd put you down."

If that didn't work, she'd get angry: "You've got a mean streak, Paulie, you always have."

Then she'd move on to denial, then bargaining, then all sorts of impressive logical fallacies (Mom was a lawyer by trade) before ending with an aria of despair. "Oh, I tried to be a good mother. But there's been too much calamity in our family. Too much!"

Still, I probably could have survived the rest of high school in this fashion had I not come home from track practice one sunny spring afternoon to find Mom unconscious on her bedroom floor. No one used the term "suicide" in front of me, neither the paramedics nor the doctors nor the family friends—as if the word would hurt me, not the action. They said my mom was "very sick" and she was going to Baltimore to "get better." When I said goodbye to her at the airport, her eyes were as flat as paper.

The only person who was straight with me this whole time was Jemma.

"This is all so fucked," she'd said at the gas station we stopped at on the way home from the airport, sloshing Mountain Dew slushy into a forty-eight-ounce cup.

"So," I said to Freja and Tocke as I popped three more Altoids in my mouth. "I moved in with Jemma's family that night and have been something of a free agent ever since."

The Swedes looked like children sitting before a birthday cake.

"Can you look over to the camera and say all that again?" Tocke said. So I did, and my mouth was burning.

"You are very brave." Freja tapped her pen against her notepad.

I balked. "It's not brave when you don't have a choice."

"In Sweden people do not talk so openly about these things. Though the world as you know is changing."

I cocked my head. "In America we're open about some things, but not others. Like you can say you have anxiety, but you can't say it's because, for example, someone roofied you at a party. Isn't that strange?"

"I believe it is good to be open," Tocke said solemnly.

I swallowed. "Are you open, Tocke?"

There was a pause. "No."

Swedes, I would learn, are so reserved that my forthrightness was the conversational equivalent of a mushroom cloud. In the fallout I thought of Jemma, whom I could almost see cheering me on through the fog. *Be shameless.*

"Well, I promise to be open on the show," I said. "There's no point in doing it otherwise, is there? Even the embarrassing stuff."

Tocke raised his eyebrows. "What stuff?"

"Oh, gosh," I said, blowing air out through my mouth. "Well, this one time, Jemma and I were in London, and I got diarrhea in Westminster Abbey and I couldn't find a bathroom 'cause it turns out the abbey's really big? And I was at Target last week and I had this big pack of paper towels in the bottom of the cart that I forgot to pay for at checkout? And then I didn't go back and pay for it because I was afraid they would arrest me? I still feel guilty about that." I fished around for more Altoids. "And years ago, I used to close this shoe store I worked at early so my boyfriend and I could smoke pot and hook up in the men's wides. Ha! We were pretty stupid." Chomp, chomp. Swallow. "I don't mind talking about my bad behavior. It's secrets I don't like. Hate them, actually. My grandma always said the truth will set you free. Which is funny 'cause her son—my dad—could never do that with her—or me, for that matter—"

And like the abrupt onset of a raincloud, tears filled my eyes. I blinked and blinked. The hotel room's neon light swirled and swam in front of me.

"This is your Swedish grandmother, yes?" Freja said, scribbling something on her pad. "Your *farmor*? Father's mother?"

"Yes." I dabbed at my cheeks with the pads of my fingers, trying to keep my mascara from running. "Sorry. I don't know what came over—"

"You miss her," Freja suggested.

"I do." From a distance, I heard my voice, which did not sound like my voice. "She's the one who read me *Pippi Longstocking*. It's weird, I haven't thought about her for a long—"

I closed my eyes and saw my grandmother lift me onto her kitchen chair, saw her level the cup of flour I held in my hand, saw her face as I regaled her with one of my own, made-up Pippi Longstocking stories, saw the tenderness behind her eyes.

There was a pause.

"It's hard to lose someone," I finally said, "who understands you."

"Excellent," Tocke said. He lifted his phone. "Smile, please?"

I smiled through my tears. Like I had nothing left to lose. And maybe I didn't.

On our way to the door, Freja opened her palm and revealed a plastic circle. She opened it and showed me a small pile of white sacs, like those preservative pouches you see in vitamin bottles. "Do you know *snus*?"

I did not. "It is very big in Sweden. Better for you than smoking. Or this." Freja motioned to my Altoids tin. "You take one of these little pouches? Of nicotine?" She demonstrated. "And stick it above your teeth to your gum. It feels quite nice. Would you like to try?"

I didn't see why not. I took one, shoved it above my right incisor, and after a moment felt a pleasant buzz.

"We will be in touch," Tocke said. He clapped a flipper-sized hand onto my shoulder. "Good job today."

"When will I know if I'm on the show?" I said, high upon a floaty cloud of stimulants.

"Within the month," Freja said in a much more formal manner as she basically pushed me out the door. "Goodbye, now. *Hej då*."

"Byeeeee," I echoed to the closed door. "Oh, wait!"

I pounded on the door until Tocke opened it with a puzzled expression. "My phone's dead," I said apologetically. "I promised to call Jemma—my best friend. Would you mind if I borrowed yours for a sec?"

"I—all right." Tocke fished his phone out of his back pocket. I thanked him while dialing Jemma's number—one of the few I knew by heart, along with Declan's, Karen Hamburger's, and the number I used to call as a kid to get local weather updates.

"How'd it go?" Jemma said as soon as she picked up.

"How'd you know it was me?"

"Who else is gonna call from a Swedish number?"

"Right, right." I stole a glance at Tocke, who was pretending not to listen. "I did everything you told me."

"Were you shameless?"

"Yes."

"Were you rude?"

"I think so."

Jemma whooped. "Call me later, okay?"

"Thank you again," I said to Tocke when I handed the phone back over. "I swear, I'm usually much more civilized than this."

"I hope not," Tocke said. And then he winked at me. A Swedish wink!

"SO THEN WHAT happened?" Group therapist Karen Hamburger asked the following Tuesday at noon. All five of us—Me, Kira, Ayisha, Sheila, Todd—were sitting in Karen's softly lit beige office with Panera sandwiches nestled in our laps.

"Then I went to catch the bus back to the airport," I said, taking a bite of my Mediterranean Veggie. "And threw up in a trash can on Forty-Second Street."

"I see," Karen said in a neutral voice. "And what do you think that's about?"

"Why does everything always happen to Paulie?" Kira complained. "Nothing ever happens to me."

"Nothing ever happens to *me*!" I said. "That's why I went to New York in the first place!"

Our group, hand-selected by Karen Hamburger, had met every other week for four years. We all came from broken families of one kind or another, and most of us had developed weird relationships with food to cope with the stress—hence the mandatory sandwiches. Kira just poked at her chicken salad every time, which drove me nuts, except when I remembered she'd lost her own mom to suicide two years before and was still hanging on by a thread.

"Sometimes I get nauseous when I tell my story too," Todd said. He reached out and squeezed my hand. Todd's mom was schizophrenic, and they'd been homeless for a while in Los Angeles. Somehow he'd managed to get himself to art school and now he worked as a full-time cartoonist.

"I dunno, maybe it was the *snus*," I said.

Sheila sucked in a breath through her teeth and shook her head as if to say, yeah, right. Sheila was the group's elder and resident malarkey detector, perhaps because when she told her parents about Uncle Bud's bad touch they patted her on the shoulder and said she was imagining things.

"But I guess I want to ask the group," I said. "Do you think I should do it if they ask me?"

I took my group's advice as seriously as I took my own life. Though I did not know their last names or their employers, and though they frequently maddened me with their self-saboteurship, they were, I suppose, family, or a version of it. "The thing is"—I halted—"what if spending all this time thinking about family just causes me more—"

"Don't do it," Kira said quickly. I narrowed my eyes at her.

"It's a big risk," Ayisha said. Ayisha was an actuary and notoriously risk-averse. Her dad was bipolar, alcoholic, and a bunch of other things too—eventually she'd had to block his number. But the truth is, all of us were as risk-averse as Ayisha, at least when it came to things that mattered. Sometimes this saddened me about group, how shaped we all were by things that had happened a long time ago, by people who weren't really thinking about us.

"What does your intuition say?" Todd asked, still holding my hand.

"My intuition—" I said, and then paused. The excitement of New York was wearing off, and I could feel my heart curling back into its shell. In the past few years, my life had become rather small, it was true. But maybe it was better to live a small, manageable life than a big, un-manageable one. Maybe big lives were for sturdy people who had taken fewer lumps, people who didn't quit after initial failure, people who didn't panic after sending emails and reread them not once but thrice—

I looked toward Karen Hamburger for guidance, but of course she didn't offer any, that professional sphinx. Sheila spoke up after swallowing the last of her Bacon Turkey Bravo. "Out of all the reality shows you could have tried out for, do you not think it *peculiar* that you chose one about family?"

"I don't think it's peculiar at all." I put down my sandwich. "It's incidental, really."

Sheila made a noise with her lips.

"I just wanted an adventure," I insisted. I picked up my sandwich again. "I was bored. But I got my fix, and I think I'll stop here."

"Paulie, everything happens for a reason," Todd intoned, a vestige of his twelve-step days.

"I'm tired of talking about Paulie," Kira complained. "We talk about Paulie more than anyone else. Paulie's commitment issues, Paulie's indecisiveness. It's the same thing every week. 'Declan's not a marriage person. Paulie doesn't know if she's a marriage person. Should she try talking to him about marriage—oh wait, you missed a session? No worries, we'll talk about it next time, seeing as Paulie never follows through on anything.'"

"Actually, Kira, we talk about *you* more than we talk about anyone else," I shot back.

"Let Paulie have some space," Sheila said, holding up a warning finger to Kira. "We all have the right to take up space, remember?"

"We actually talk about you not wanting to talk about Paulie more than anything else," Ayisha clarified to Kira with her great and noble exactitude.

"Fine, Kira, what do you want to talk about?" I asked.

"I want to talk about cleaning," Kira said. "I think I like it too much. Sometimes I can't sleep until I bleach all the countertops."

I swear I saw Karen Hamburger's eyes flicker ever so slightly toward the back of her head.

LATER THAT AFTERNOON I got a text from Freja: *Hej Paulie! We have talked to the network and they have a few more questions for casting. Can we Skype tonight 8 Minneapolis time and with high lighting? Tack så mycket, puss puss!*

"More questions?" I said to Declan when I got home from work. "I feel like I told them everything already."

"I'll say." Declan spooned a pile of rice into my bowl and motioned for me to help myself from the wok on the stovetop, where a pile of stir-fried tofu and vegetables waited. Declan had recently learned to stir-fry and had subsequently stir-fried everything but the kitchen sink. I never thought I would long to crunch through a meal as much as I did after three weeks of pan-softened cuisine.

There was a hint of tone in his reply, but I ignored it. We had argued plenty about the show in the past week, beginning when he picked me up from the airport. "Why are you doing this to yourself?" he'd said from behind the wheel of his reliable Japanese import. This was after I told him about the puking. "It's too crazy!"

"No, but it felt good!" I'd unrolled my window and flung my arm out into the bitterly cold night. "Like pulling out a tapeworm! Karen Hamburger says the more we tell our stories, the less power they have over us!"

"It's freezing." Declan had pressed the button on his side to roll up my window. I'd pulled my arm back in, affronted. "But they want you to tell it for their reasons, not yours. What's painful for you is ratings gold for them."

"You don't know that," I'd huffed. "You've never even met them. They seem really nice."

"Everyone's nice when they want something from you," he'd said, and turned up the radio just as Prince started praying that we get through this thing called life.

"Why are you being so cynical?"

He gripped the steering wheel. "Why's it so easy for you to think the best of strangers and the worst of me?"

"Why's it so easy for *you* to think the worst of *me*?"

"I don't. I think the worst of *them*. Genealogy's a scam, anyway. Have you talked to Karen Hamburger about the show?"

This set my heart aflame, and not in a good way. "Don't do that."

"Do what?"

"Use Karen Hamburger against me."

He'd laughed. Meanwhile, Prince was wondering if the reason we got so excited was because we knew we were going to die. "You use her against me all the time."

"Declan, come on. I'm serious. I'm trying to be brave here."

"You're already brave," he'd said, putting on his blinker. "You're brave all the time. You don't need a reality show to prove anything to anybody."

"But the point of life is to live!" I'd unrolled my window again and flung my arm into the sky. "To try things! To suck the marrow out of every opportunity!"

Declan knew how much I hated that adulthood was basically just one long march into conformity and repression. He hated it too. That was one of the reasons we fell in love, two strange people delighting in the strangeness of the other. You should have seen us when we first met. We never slept. We read poetry aloud in bed. We had sex in a theater bathroom, then cleaned ourselves up and watched avant-garde dance. Yet somehow, over four years, the pressures of long-term monogamy had encased our strangeness into tidy sausage links. On Sunday mornings, those golden hours when we used to ravish each other—what did we do now? Fried bacon and meal-planned. Declan seemed to enjoy these routines, took comfort in their steadiness, whereas I found them constraining, like playing the triangle on a four-four beat while an entire drum kit beckoned.

"I'm not satisfied—" I had continued, and to my surprise my voice broke. "I won't be satisfied with a life that looks like everyone else's."

Declan flicked off the radio. "And I won't be satisfied if I can't ask questions about you throwing yourself into this show without you turning it into a referendum on your identity."

Oh, how I had fumed at this! That night, we'd gone to bed angry with each other, which almost never happened. I knew Declan was hoping I wouldn't be cast, and I tried not to resent him for this. Though obviously I did.

Over stir-fry that evening, I kept up a cheerful patter of conversation about current events and teenage drama (Tristan, high school junior, had just bombed a chemistry test) before pushing my chair back from the table. "I should probably get ready for this call," I said, taking one last swig of water. "I'll be glad when it's over. You'll be happy to know that in group today I decided I'm not gonna do it."

"You did?" Declan looked up from gathering our plates, unable to keep the eagerness out of his voice.

"Don't worry about those," I said. "I'll do them after, okay?"

"I've got it," he said as I headed for our bedroom, which was either a gesture of truce or a stab at martyrdom—it was hard to say. Amazing how you can live with someone, love them, look upon them first thing every morning and still not have a clue about what goes on in their head.

A half hour later, after turning on all the lights in the bedroom and reapplying mascara, I accepted Freja's Skype call. Swedes were fiercely loyal to Skype, even as the rest of the world abandoned it. "Hello?" she was saying. "Hello? Hello?"

"I can hear you, but your screen is black!" I said. Shadows flitted across my laptop.

"Hello, Paulie, yes, that is on purpose! I am in L.A. and just received a vampire facial ha ha and I am afraid it is better if you do not look my way!"

"A what?"

"Anyway, Paulie, I am so happy to see you again after our nice time in New York! You look beautiful as usual!"

"I do?" I touched my cheek. It was a little spongy from all the dairy I'd eaten that day. "Thank you? Anyway, you said you had more questions for me?"

"Yes, Paulie, we will get to that." There was a dramatic pause from the shadows. "But first, Paulie, I want to tell you that you are going to Sweden!"

A brief, pregnant pause, into which the whole history of the universe seemed to yawn. Then:

"Ahhhhhhhh!" I screamed.

"Ahhhhhhhh!" the shadow-blob that was Freja screamed. "*Välkommen till Sverige!* Sorry to trick you, but we needed the surprise factor! We are recording this call for the first episode so keep in mind you are already on TV!"

"What's going on?" Declan hollered from somewhere in the house. "Are you okay?"

"I'm more than okay!" I screamed. "I'm going to Sweden!" The decision that I had been rationalizing and worrying over, in the end, wasn't a decision at all. The endorphins in my body were all surging the word *"yes"* symphonically, like a flock of birds drunk on juniper berries.

Meanwhile, if silences could talk, Declan's would have been swearing a blue streak.

"Paulie!" Freja said. "Could you please explain how you are feeling right now?"

"I am excited!" I said. My cheeks felt hot; I was regretting my red wool sweater. I fanned myself with my hands.

"And what else?"

"I am shaking!" My hands were trembling like an Oscar winner's.

"Anything else?"

"I am so happy!" And I burst into tears.

"Good," Freja said in a more normal voice. "Good, good." She must have stopped recording, for she said brusquely: "Great job, darling. Inga, our contestant manager, will be in touch in a few weeks."

"Contestant?"

"It's a competition, remember? Only the winner will meet their family. *Puss puss*, darling!"

She hung up. I stood and flung open the door, where Declan was standing with a blank expression on his face.

"I'm going!" I was still teary. "I'm going to Sweden to meet my family!"

Declan's expression turned to gobsmacked. "You just told me you weren't going to do it."

I reached out and put my palm on his chest. He flinched ever so slightly. "I had to say yes. It felt right, you know? Finally, I'll have a family!"

He didn't say anything, but I felt his heart beating through my fingertips. "I thought I was your family," he said at last.

"No, you are," I insisted, and put my arms around his neck. "You are."

It seemed like a long time before he hugged me back.

"You're leaving," he said over my shoulder. "Just like that."

"Not till May."

"Why didn't you talk to me first?"

I pulled away, stiffening. "It all happened so—anyway, why do we have to talk again? We've already talked. And talked and talked—"

"What about Micah and June's wedding?"

"Oh, right," I said. "Guess I'll have to miss it."

The muscles in Declan's face rippled unhappily.

"I forgot," I said. I put a hand on his arm. "Sorry about that. But you'll have fun without me—"

"I would never say yes without talking to you first."

My cheeks flushed again. "Here we go."

"I don't even say yes to a happy hour without checking in."

I stepped fully out of his embrace and crossed my arms over my chest. "I don't ask you to do that. I'm not your ball and chain. You can do whatever you please."

"Right, right." He took a step back from me, then another. "Of course I can."

I followed him into the kitchen, where he started putting away dishes from the dishwasher. "*What?*"

"You don't think about me when you make decisions," he said, clattering plates in a stack. "You don't think about us. You think about you and that's it."

"I give you the same amount of freedom as I want for myself," I said, grabbing a measuring cup. "Not every decision needs to be an endless negotiation."

"I'll get that," he said, reaching for the roasting platter I had my hand on.

"No, I've got it," I said.

We both grabbed it, then both let go. It dropped to the floor and cracked in two.

"Great," Declan said.

"I said I've got it," I said.

We went to bed without saying another word.

CHAPTER THREE

✣

DEPARTURES AND ARRIVALS

Three months, two suitcases, one twenty-page contract, and a flurry of emails and phone calls later, I was on an overnight flight to Copenhagen with knots in my stomach and my grandmother's copy of *Pippi Long-stocking* in my lap. Denmark was a strange place to start filming a Swedish reality show, but Freja said all would be explained when I met up with Inga, the contestant manager, and seven other Americans at the airport. *Soon you will form little Swedish family!* Freja wrote in the email with my itinerary. *You will love you're* [sic] *fellow Americans!*

I wasn't so sure. Jemma and I had alarmed ourselves one night by watching half an episode of *Sverige och Mig* from the previous season. The contestants had been quite a different vintage from what you find on American shows. To wit: a guy named Boomer, covered with Norse rune tattoos; a woman named Lucia who wore only white in honor of her namesake saint; an old man, Hud, who wore a giant Swedish flag like a cape. They all cried prodigious amounts and panicked before minor challenges like building houses out of playing cards and memorizing

the Swedish alphabet. The whole enterprise looked as dignified as a
three-a.m. trip to Wendy's.

"So at what point does Swedish pride become—" Jemma had said,
lowering her voice as Boomer stripped to his skivvies and ran the Swedish
flag up a pole somewhere in the Arctic Circle.

"*Skoooooollllllllll!*" Boomer roared as he beat his tattooed chest with
his fist.

"You know, like"—she dropped to a whisper—"white supremacy?"

"Hmmm," I'd said, thinking of the scholarly article Declan had emailed
the week prior, explaining the link between genealogy, eugenics, and
fascist movements. He'd been surprisingly generous in spirit in the
intervening months, in that passive way of keeping his mouth shut.
Yet he also couldn't help himself—he'd been researching the show
and fine-combing every document I received from production. (You
may have guessed this already, but I'm not a fine-print kind of gal. The
only document I've read closely in my life is the Blizzard menu at Dairy
Queen.)

I wouldn't say Declan and I were in a great place when I left Minneapolis, especially when he'd figured out from my contract that they'd be
taking away my phone as soon as we started filming. I'd be able to call
him from hotels on our free days, twice a week at best. His refrain about
the show, when he was not remaining silent, was "This is insane." Our
goodbye at the airport had the warmth and intimacy of a paper cut.

"I love you," I'd said, and kissed him on the cheek, the lips, the other
cheek, then sniffed his neck. There was nothing my animal self loved
more than that smell. "You're my family."

"When something makes you uncomfortable, say so," he'd said. "You
don't have to please anyone. Okay?"

"Okay, fine, jeez," I said, and turned my face away.

It was hard enough leaving behind a partner who disapproved, but
Declan wasn't the only one making my transition to television difficult.
Garance, my boss and Premiere Prep's founder, had clicked her tongue
and narrowed her eyes when I'd asked her if I could take a month off with
earned vacation hours.

"That's a big ask," she'd said, tapping her Harvard pen on her glass-top desk. (An intra-office joke: Q: How do you know if your boss went to Harvard? A: Oh, they'll tell you.)

"I know," I'd said. "But it's a big opportunity—"

"I have a drawerful of applicants who would jump at the opportunity to work here," she'd interrupted.

"I know, I know," I'd said. "And in this economy"—I stumbled—"not that it's just about the economy—"

"It's a very good job," she'd said, almost to herself. "Very good."

"I know," I'd said again. "And I'm so grateful—"

"I'm a very good boss," she continued as she adjusted her four-hundred-dollar blouse.

"That's what I tell everyone—"

She raised her voice. "And a *very* good person!"

Eventually Garance had agreed not to fire me on one condition: that I mention Premiere Prep on camera at least once per episode. "But naturally," she'd coached. "Like you love it so much you can't help but talk about it all the time."

"Of course," I'd agreed while scuttling backward out of her office. "It'd be my honor."

The plane landed in Copenhagen with nary a bump. I'd been too excited to sleep on the flight, yet I wasn't tired. I'd reread *Pippi Longstocking* instead of watching movies, a book with pages as thin and as soft as my grandmother's kerchiefs. Reading it returned me to the feeling of sitting on her lap, her sun-spotted and pillowy arms holding me like a seat belt as she slowly turned the pages. Pippi'd had an alchemical effect on us both, as memorable characters will. Once, Grandma actually let me strap sponges to my feet and skate across her kitchen floor to "clean" it. When my grandfather complained of the mess, she'd snapped at him, something she never did. "Leave her alone," Grandma had said, and in her voice, I swear, was the voice of a small girl, essentially orphaned, who could lift a horse.

That Pippi-feeling—that sense of possibility, that eschewal of convention, that buoyancy—carried me off the plane, through customs, and to the baggage claim, where it was quickly punctured by a phone call from my mother, which came through five seconds after I turned on my phone.

"Mom?" I ran for my first suitcase, which had whumped onto the conveyor belt.

"Hi, honey!" From her voice, it sounded like a good day.

"What time is it there? Are you still in the—I mean, are you at Healing Waters?"

"Oh, yes!" she said gaily. "I've moved in, actually. Gail's hired me—well, technically I'm not getting paid—to be her full-time assistant."

"That's great?" I had no idea who Gail was.

"Because I'm so good with Chester," she explained. "We have a special bond. I swear, he's the son I never had."

"Chester the horse?"

"Say that again, honey?" I heard a rustling. Her voice sounded distant. *Whump* went my second suitcase onto the belt. "Your reception's awful. Chester can feel me getting agitated."

"I'm in Denmark right now. I'm doing a TV show," I said, heaving the second suitcase. I heard another rustling, then a cooing. "Mom? You still there?"

"Here I am," she said breathlessly. "Just checking in with Chester—the wind's a big trigger for him."

Strong gales stiffened in my chest. "They're taking my phone soon, Mom, so I guess we won't be able to talk for a while."

"Oh dear, I'm not hearing any of this." She sighed. "Bad connection." She hung up.

My two suitcases blurred into four and wobbled in front of me.

"Pauline?" said a voice from behind. I turned around to see a handsome woman in her twenties with a thick mane of dark-blond hair. She wore an oversized button-down, bike shorts, and a cell-phone chain strapped around her torso.

I took a step back. "How'd you know?"

"We have a file on each of you with pictures," she said, in a manner that was neither friendly nor unfriendly. "You're the first to arrive." She looked me up and down. "You are very tall. Taller than your picture."

"So are you!" I stuck out my hand. "Not that I've seen your picture. Call me Paulie."

Inga did not laugh, but rather surveyed me coolly as a nanny would her charge. I trailed after her to the meet-and-greet area outside the airport to look for the others. Inga had their photographs, which she wouldn't share with me, but over the course of ninety minutes of first impressions, I eventually found myself with:

TOM HOLM: A taciturn, handlebar-mustached Milwaukeean in his fifties whose hobbies, when I asked him, were "beer." Inga said that years ago Tom had won fifteen thousand dollars on *Wheel of Fortune*, but it was hard to imagine him spinning the wheel while jesting with Vanna and Pat. He worked at a meat-packing plant on the South Side and dabbled as an electrician, though his wife wanted him to quit now that he'd been electrocuted. Twice.

MATTHEW "JUNIOR" MATTSON: An out-and-proud ex-Mormon, reality-television devotee, amateur genealogy nut, corporate director, and local cabaret star in Omaha. I knew Junior and I would be fast friends when he quoted *Oliver!* to sum up his flight to Inga. ("Shut up and drink your gin.")

BROCK HANSON: A tall, fair, and fashionable mountain biker and Liberty University graduate. His parents had been Jerry Falwell devotees, and he had the pain in his eyes of all former evangelicals, along with the tattoos and stories of epic drug use. Brock lived in Colorado, played in a band, and worked as a project manager for some IT company when he wasn't cycling and jamming.

BECKI LINDBERG: As soon as Becki came along I knew she'd be a tough nut. Her T-shirt read Don't Mess with Texas; she didn't crack a smile with anybody, save whomever she was texting on her glittery phone. When Inga told me Becki was an amateur MMA fighter, I bounded over and told her I'd taken kickboxing a few times and found it cathartic. She looked down her sunglasses at me—it was raining, mind you—and said, "What I do isn't kickboxing." I slunk away like—well, like I'd been TKO'd.

HONOR BERG: Honor, in her forties, lived up to her name: her first act upon arrival was to present the rest of us with U.S. Capitol magnets. (None of the rest of us had thought to bring gifts.) She'd gone to the Kennedy School, worked for the Department of Housing and Urban Development, and had the kind of student council president energy you might expect from someone living and working inside the Beltway, though not in a bad way.

DEBORAH MESSING (THE OTHER ONE): Oh, Deborah! I'm a sucker for lesbians in their sixties; they have great taste in food and books and never look around at parties to see if there's someone better to talk to. Deborah was the writer of the group. She'd recently published a memoir, *Fruits of the Spirit*, about running a vineyard in Sonoma County, and the previous month had been arrested at a climate protest. "I got to ride in the paddy wagon with Jane Fonda," she confided, her eyes crinkling at the corners. "I would've asked for her autograph, but our hands were zip-tied."

KEVIN AXELSSON: The first thing Kevin asked me was not my name but whether I'd ever heard of his podcast, *The Forty-Hour Body*. Kevin, aged thirty-three, was a self-appointed personal trainer, wellness expert, dating guru, and solar-panel salesman from Panama City Beach, Florida. Before I could escape his monologue, he tried to sell me on the Wim Hof breathing technique, HIIT workouts, twice-daily saunas, and the law of attraction. A book by a famous cultural conservative poked out of his backpack.

Not to put too fine a point on it, but we were all white. The white of Wonder bread, soft serve, mashed potatoes, picket fences, musical theatre, Teva sandals, one-drop rules, and Daughters of the American Revolution. As fair as a county fair, as pale as unfair comparisons. Inga led us to a black Mercedes Sprinter van in the parking lot, and we waddled behind her with our luggage like white ducklings. Our first stop was the town of Helsingør, alleged home of Hamlet's castle, located forty-five minutes north of Copenhagen. As rain pattered on the roof of the van and the windshield wipers *whump-whumped*, I tried to remember everything my fellow Americans said so I could repeat it to Jemma later, though with everyone talking over each other I caught only snatches:

". . . to see the land my ancestors worked will be profoundly healing," Deborah confided to Honor. "For decades I didn't even know I was Swedish; mine was a closed adoption—"

". . . it's like, being Swedish was something I could hold on to when everything else turned out to be a lie," Brock was saying.

". . . I might even move to Sweden after this," Kevin boasted to Tom. "Depending on how far I get in the competition. It's an underdeveloped solar-panel market, like Australia—anyway, I have a podcast, you should listen to it sometime—"

". . . it was working with Native American communities at HUD that made me start to wonder: What made *my* ancestors come to America?" Honor mused. "And was it worth the cost, not only on them but on the indigenous—"

"Wife signed me up," Tom said. "Said she wanted me out of the house."

". . . Lord, I'm just here to apologize," Junior said. "For the religious colonization."

". . . it was my dad's last wish," Becki said flatly.

As Inga pulled up to a modest motel on Helsingør's outskirts, I pulled out my phone. Nothing from Declan or Jemma yet; they were probably still sleeping. "So," Inga said, turning around after she'd lurched into park. "We start early tomorrow. I'll knock on your door later with the call time—probably between seven and eight." Her English was as bright and crisp as a green apple. She handed us each a hotel key in its sleeve. "Try to get some rest, because these next days are going to be pretty tiring." She emphasized these last two words: *pre-tty tie-err-ing*.

"What are we doing that's so tiring?" I asked.

"They don't tell us," Junior said from behind me. I turned to look at him. *I'll explain later*, he mouthed.

"Correct, everything is a secret," Inga said, opening the driver's-side door. "Do not worry. You will do better if you think of yourself like a kid, and we are your parents. We take care of the details so the surprises are really a surprise." She came around and opened the van's sliding door.

I clambered out, marveling at Inga's ability to be both cordial and withholding. "Have you done this show before?" I asked as I helped lug suitcases out of the back.

"No, not this one," she huffed as she hurled a bag onto the pavement. "Just *Big Brother* and *LEGO Masters*." She shook her head as if trying to get water out of her ear. "That almost killed me—eleven million pieces." And louder: "Everyone have everything? We have a production meeting in ten, but I'll be in Room 185 if you need anything."

"Thank you," we all echoed, even taciturn Tom. "Thank you, thank you."

"Before I go, a few rules," Inga added. She interlaced her hands behind her back. "Number one, please stay in your rooms tonight. This is important, because you all need your rest. Number two, this is your last night with your phones. I'll take them in the morning and keep them until you leave the show. If we find out you have a secret phone, which happened in another season, you will immediately be eliminated. Please call your loved ones tonight and let them know you will be out of touch for a few days—they already have my number in case there is an emergency."

"What if we actually need our phones, though?" Becki said.

Inga blinked. "You signed the contract. You can make calls and check email at the hotel in Stockholm on your days off."

"What if I need to transfer money?" Becki insisted.

Inga ignored this. "Number three, I will only be giving you the information you need to know, not the information you want to know. For example, if you ask me, 'What time are we leaving tomorrow?' I will be able to tell you at some point, but maybe not right away. If you ask me, 'What should I wear tomorrow?' I might say, 'Dress to be outside for the day.' But if you ask me, 'Where are we going?' or 'What are we doing?' or 'When is the next competition?' or 'When is the next day off?' I will not tell you. Do you understand?"

"Really, that much secrecy?" Deborah said. "Would knowing when we get a day off actually ruin the surprises?"

"Yes," Inga said. She smiled, but in this smile was the glint of metal. "This is how reality works. I'll come around to your rooms at sixish with dinner. Till then, just relax. It's been a long day."

"Okay!" I said. Because as much as I hate being told what to do, I actually, secretly, love it.

"Lobby. Twenty minutes," Junior, the ex-Mormon, hissed into my ear before rolling his giant bag toward his hotel room's exterior door.

"But—" I glanced over at Inga, who was stalking toward the other end of the building. Then I looked at Junior, then back at Inga, then back at Junior. When two confident strangers equally assert their authority, whose authority does one choose?

"I'll buy you a beer," Junior said, and waggled his eyebrows, thus breaking the tie.

I pointed a finger gun at him. "Salut."

"CHEERS TO THE religious trauma unit of the cast!" Junior said an hour later in the hotel lobby bar. He raised his giant glass of Carlsberg, and Brock and I clinked it. It was only four p.m., but anytime is a great time to drink Carlsberg in Denmark. We were on our second round, and the jet lag and high ABV had already given me a buzz. *Snap, snap, snap*. Polaroids of Junior laughing, Brock sticking his tongue out and giving the rock-'n'-roll salute, the two of them kissing on the cheeks. Brock was married with a kid, but he had that former evangelical "down to party" energy that transcended heteronormativity. A sign above the bar quoted Hans Christian Andersen, a Dane himself: *To travel is to live*.

"Another round?" Clara, the rosy-cheeked desk clerk, asked from behind the bar.

I put a hand up to refuse just as Junior said, "*Absolut*," and gestured to our three glasses. Both Junior and Brock had been studying Swedish for months in preparation for filming. When they'd asked me what I myself had done to prepare, and I told them I'd bought fetching new sneakers, Junior had patted me on the back and sighed, "Paulie, Paulie, Paulie," the same way Jemma did when I forgot to look where I was walking and crashed straight into a telephone pole.

"Tell me, Clara," Junior said, with an easy familiarity. "Have you heard of *Sverige och Mig*?"

Clara shook her head. Junior continued, "You get Swedish TV here, though, yes?" Clara nodded. "So you might have come across it? Americans with Swedish heritage finding their roots?"

"Oh, you mean *Crying Americans*!" Clara put a fresh pilsner glass in front of me. Foam sloshed a little down the side. "I love that show."

"No, no, it's called *Sverige och Mig*," I said. "Means *Sweden and Me*. You must be thinking of something else."

Clara wrinkled her nose. "No, I do not think so. I know the show you are talking about. They are always crying, ha ha, like babies, it is crazy. No one calls it by the real name. Wait—" She looked at us. Beer from the tap sloshed into the rubber mat. "You are not from *Crying Americans*?"

"Surprise!" Brock spread out his very long arms.

It took us a minute to convince Clara we weren't pulling her leg. "But why would you do this?" she said once Junior had pulled up the contract on his phone. "Me, I would never want to do reality. Yes, it is a nice show, but still, it is so . . ." She trailed off.

"Vulnerable?" I supplied.

"What is this word?"

"It means you have to open your—"

"Oh!" Clara brightened. "Humiliating. This is the word I am searching for."

"Oh!" I said. "Well. That's maybe a little too—"

"How many people in America auditioned for this show?" Clara asked.

Brock cocked his head. "There are eight of us. So maybe nine?"

"It's gotta be more than—" I said.

"Americans don't mind humiliation, so long as people are paying attention," Junior explained to Clara.

I said, "I wouldn't say that exactly sums up my—"

"You are interested in ancestry, yes?" Clara said. "Me, I do not find this so interesting. My family has lived in the same village for hundreds of years. So what is big deal?"

"See, I think that's rad," Brock said. "I've been a tumbleweed my whole life." He mimed a rolling tumbleweed when Clara looked confused. "When I got my test results and it said ninety-six percent Swedish, dude, I'm telling you, I lost my mind. I was so happy."

"You are the same?" Clara looked at Junior and me.

"It's a Mormon thing, genealogy," Junior said, swallowing. "Pretty messed up, actually, BroJo was all"—he pulled out air quotes—"'go forth and multiply' but also 'let's baptize dead people starting with Napoleon.' Ancestry dot com, that's a Mormon company, did you know? Believe me, their interest in your family's not altruistic." He drank his beer thoughtfully. "I might have quit the church, but I still love researching my family, maybe 'cause I'm gay and don't want kids." He corrected himself. "But it's not just that. This fourth cousin of mine, she lives in Hawaii but she found me on Ancestry—it turns out we have the exact same sense of humor—"

"And you?" Clara's eyes were fixed on me. I felt color rising up my neck.

"I'm like the opposite of an ancestry person." I took a very long slug of Carlsberg. "My closest family's my best friend, Jemma, but technically we're not related. Actually, most of the time I try to think about my blood relatives as little as possible . . ."

I trailed off. No one said anything. There's something about Scandinavian silence, different from in America, where it's accompanied by a great rush to fill airtime. In Junior's eyes I saw compassion. Something stirred beneath the murky surface of my consciousness, something—what was it? Grief? Longing? My grandmother reading *Pippi Longstocking*?—I tried my best in daily life to shove aside.

I swallowed the stone in the back of my throat and said lightly: "But I mean, it's a once-in-a-lifetime opportunity. How could I say no?"

Halfway through round three, as we became increasingly sloshed, Junior interrupted our lively debate over the best subgenres of ASMR to distribute a bit of intel he'd accumulated about the show. "So here's what's gonna happen next," he said, wiping foam off his beard. "Each episode takes three days to film. After every one or two episodes, we'll get days off for the crew to rest. This first week is big because they want to knock us off our axes. Want us vulnerable, want us to bond. Then, boom, the first elimination: high stakes, great drama. Loser gets sent on the next flight home."

"How do you know all this?" I bellowed. Beer makes me bellicose.

"I interviewed a bunch of past contestants. Who, by the way, were dying to talk. Fifteen minutes of fame goes by too fast for most people—"

"Dude." Brock tapped his index finger to his forehead. "Smart."

"Some sour grapes." Junior took another sip. "Not as bad as the drama on *The Bachelor*, though."

I made a mental note to ask him about that drama later, insatiable as I am for the hardships of people more beautiful and famous than me.

Junior continued, "It's like, really? This is the hill you're gonna die on? Your episode-four elimination six years ago?"

"I don't want to compete," I heard myself say. "And I do *not* want to get eliminated." I was surprised to hear these words coming out of my mouth. I'd told Jemma and Declan and Karen Hamburger I didn't care about winning the show; I only wanted an adventure. But it turned out I did care about winning insofar as I did not want to lose.

"You won't," Brock said confidently. He stretched his arms out again. "The three of us, we're staying till the end."

Normally I resented peacocking male confidence, but because Brock included me in his, I threw myself into his feathery plumes. "I love you guys," I bellowed. Beer also makes me sentimental.

"What are you doing?" a voice said from behind us. "I told you to stay in your rooms!"

We turned. Inga was standing in the hotel's entryway, an umbrella in one hand and her phone in the other. "This is serious," she said. She looked furious. I felt a lurch of guilt. "We need you to be rested."

"You mean you need us not to bond off-camera," Junior said, and winked at her.

"Sorry!" I held a palm up. "So sorry." With my other hand I chugged the rest of my beer and slid off the bar stool. "We'll leave right now."

"You have to follow the rules," Inga insisted.

"Mom, don't be mad at us," Brock said, and went over and put his drunken arms around her.

"It's Tocke, he'll kill me," she said into his chest. "He'll kill you too. They're spending a fortune this season."

Junior gestured loosely to the tap. "How would he know if we don't tell him? You want one?"

"I'm leaving, I promise. I love you guys." I started weaving toward the door. "It feels like we've known each other forever, doesn't it?" *Snap.* A Polaroid of Inga nestled in Brock's arms. I threw my arms around them both. Junior threw his arms around me.

"Look!" I slurred. "A Swedish sandwich!"

"You mean *smörgås*," Brock said as he tucked Inga into his armpit.

"*Smörgås!*" I threw my head back and laughed. "*Smörgås!* You sound like a Muppet!"

"I love Sweden." Brock laughed. "I love it so hard and I've never even been there."

"No, *I* love it," Junior said into my hair. "I want to marry it." He raised his fist. "To Sweden!"

There was only one way to answer him. Brock knew it too. We raised our fists alongside Junior's and hollered, "To Sweden!"

"You Americans, you are crazy," Inga said. But her tough facade cracked just a little, for her fist was in the air too.

MY HOTEL ROOM was about what you'd expect, save the mystery of the bed. It appeared to be two twin beds pushed together, with separate fitted sheets and duvets.

"Doesn't that defeat the entire purpose of a king-sized bed?" I asked Jemma from the bed's right side when I called to say a proper goodbye.

"That'sh the mosh Proteshtan shing I ever heard," she replied, chewing on the rhubarb cake I'd baked her as a going-away present.

I shoved a pillow under my back. "And here I thought this was a social-welfare state, emphasis on *well*—"

"Speaking of faring well, you better win," Jemma said. I could almost see her, lying on her own bed despite the time difference (Jemma was an avid indoorswoman), her nightstand crowded with mugs of half-finished beverages (though not a housekeeper), flexing her right wrist in her brace (from phone-induced carpal tunnel). "Think of it, the two of us. You, big in Sweden, me, big on the internet, our generation's Oprah and Gayle—"

"I'm not going to win—yeow!" I shifted my legs and got my left ankle stuck between the mattresses. On the telly, which I'd turned on for companionship, *The Manchurian Candidate* was playing with Danish dubbing.

Jemma sighed. "Don't do that."

"Do what?" I pulled the covers up to my neck. "I bet Kevin'll win. Or the MMA girl. Someone who likes the smell of blood."

"That thing where you don't try because you're afraid of succeeding."

"*Hurbya flurba shopperya klarena*," Angela Lansbury said onscreen in a sinister fashion.

"When have I ever done that?!" I said. "I'm afraid of failing. That's different."

"No, you're afraid of things changing," Jemma said. She laughed. "Though it's a little late for that."

After the normal effusions, and after promising a hundred times to call as soon and as often as I could, we hung up. Then I called Declan. It was early afternoon in Minneapolis, which meant Declan was reading *The New York Review of Books* on our front porch, engaging with thorny matters of politics, religion, and science while neighbors gardened and drank light brewskis.

"I miss you!" I said as soon as he picked up.

"I miss you too," he said mildly. "How was the flight?"

I gave him the rundown on my fellow Americans, including my illicit rendezvous with Brock and Junior. Then Declan told me some truly awful news coming out of the Middle East and described a photograph of a newly discovered black hole. While he detailed its doughnut shape— mmm, doughnuts—I made a Maginot Line of pillows down the entire length of the bed crack and muted the masterminding happening on the telly.

"Oh! Don't forget to water the plants on Sundays," I said once he was finished.

"I know. I have it written down."

"And check my email every few days to make sure I'm not missing anything—"

"It's insane they don't let you have your phone," Declan said for the millionth time.

"I know," I said. "You've made that perfectly clear."

"And they're not even paying you."

"Yes, they are," I said, more defensive than I needed to be, seeing as the network was paying me eighty dollars per day. "It's called a *per diem*."

We'd run these lines so many times I knew exactly what Declan had cued up next: "I made more in college doing work-study."

"Also," I said, cutting off the next act of this particular argument, in which we debated pay disparities across lines of race, gender, and industries, "you'll probably need to buy more toothpaste since I took the extra tube—"

"Anything else, m'lady?" Declan said. "A shoeshine, perhaps?"

"Ha ha," I said without laughing.

"Shall I schedule a dental checkup upon your return?"

"You know," I said, "I bet Penelope didn't get this crabby when Odysseus left on *his* big trip—"

"Penelope's not a person, she's an archetype—"

"And he was gone for *twenty years*. And she was loyal the *entire time*."

Unfortunately my knowledge of *The Odyssey* stopped there, seeing as I'd "read" it when I was fifteen, and then only to impress a senior boy who'd gotten into Stanford. Which is why I didn't know how to reply when Declan said, "Odysseus wasn't, though."

"He wasn't?"

"You don't remember?"

I did not remember, but neither did I want to say so. In the silence, my thoughts lurched toward, of all people, my parents. Even before Dad came out and left my mom, their relationship had always felt funny to me, like a pantomime put on by amateur actors.

"Do you and Dad love each other?" I'd asked Mom once after she'd picked me up from piano.

She'd sucked in her breath like I'd slapped her. "Why would you ever ask me that?"

Mom hated when I asked prying questions. "She's always watching, it's unnerving," I heard her complain to her sister on the phone. (I was spying on another extension.) In the car she'd told me I was too young to understand marriage, and for that matter, too young to understand love. But even then I knew that being a kid gave me an upper hand in matters of love, for I had not yet bricked a wall around my heart like the ones on which grown-ups were constantly working.

On the telly, a sniper took up residence in Madison Square Garden.

"Just because they couldn't do it doesn't mean we can't do it," I said to Declan, though I wasn't sure if I was referring to my parents or Odysseus and Penelope.

"You think?"

I heard uncertainty in Declan's voice, a rare note. He was the sturdy one of us, as reliable as a Honda; it had not yet occurred to me that he might sometimes need help with the engine.

"I *know*." Because when you love someone, part of your job is to offer certainty, though none exists under heaven.

"I was going to keep this a surprise," Declan said after a pause. "But I'm learning to roll sushi."

I clapped my hand against my bare thigh. Sushi was my favorite food. Not the real kind though, the Americanized version, rolls slathered with sauces and stuffed with cream cheese.

"I thought I'd make it for you when you get back."

"You," I said, affection surging through my chest, "are one hell of a guy."

"And you one hell of a girl. Sorry—woman."

I fell asleep just a few minutes after we hung up, curled up on the left side of my Maginot Line, a smile curling the corners of my lips. Life, that night, seemed utterly wonderful. A warmhearted adventure with unexpected delights—not unlike the adventures of Pippi Longstocking. Anyone who said otherwise, I remember thinking before dropping off, was either a pedant or a miser, and no friend of mine.

"I HATE THIS," I said not ten hours later. "I'm not doing it. If they try to make me do it, I'll quit."

I was standing next to Junior and Honor in the Helsingør Harbor, staring down a leaky, rickety rowboat—the *Hoptoad*, Pippi's father's ship, this was not—with four benches and eight oars, swaying in the lapping waves. There was something rotten in the state of Denmark, all right. Five minutes earlier, a chipper, visibly pregnant producer named Anna

had greeted Inga and all eight of us Americans with the unpleasant news
that we would be kicking off season ten of *Sverige och Mig* by rowing
across the Øresund Strait to Helsingborg, Sweden, a distance of approxi-
mately four kilometers, while a three-person crew filmed what I was sure
would be our capsizing, hypothermia, and untimely demise.

"The way your ancestors rowed themselves to the ships that took
them to America!" Anna had told us in a falsely cheery tone, the tone
managers use when tasking employees with drudgery that managers
themselves would never deign to perform.

"I got up at six to wash my hair," I told Junior, who was wearing a
baseball cap with a rainbow stitched across the front. "I put on blush!
I never wear blush!"

"I wouldn't waste your time on that." Honor sniffed. Her hair was
pulled back in a practical braid. "You have to try and sleep as much as
you can before competition days."

"I knew it would be bad, but I didn't think it'd be this bad," Junior
said. He pulled at his beard. "Then again, last season they flew a helicopter to Gothenburg and it almost crashed."

"Yeah, well, there's dignity in tragedy," I grumped.

"Paulie, have you even seen the show?" Honor asked in that student-
council-president way.

"*Yes*," I said. "Some." Pause. "A little." Another pause. "I mean, enough.
Probably."

"'Member what I said last night?" Junior bumped his shoulder against
mine. "Their job isn't to make us happy, it's to make us react. Happy, sad,
angry—it's all the same to them."

It was a depressing thought, made more depressing by a drizzly, dreary
morning, cool enough that I wore both a wool sweater and a flannel-
lined coat. We could see Sweden across the strait, its centuries-old architecture with its muted reds, blues, and yellows, both close and impossibly
far away. Sailboats and fishing boats filled the harbor; above and behind
us, the Hamlet castle loomed through light fog. On the promenade,
older Danes with shiny canes sat and chatted on benches despite the crap
weather, and blond mothers pushed strollers with older blond children
in tow. Everyone looked rich—or, if not rich, comfortable—and neither

a panhandler nor piece of litter was in sight. Meanwhile, Inga and two other crew members—I recognized them by their official raincoats—were huddled around Anna, receiving instructions. We Americans shivered under umbrellas, clumped in already-forming affinity groups: the jocks (Becki, Brock, Kevin); the olds (Deborah, Tom); the try-hards (Honor, Junior); and me, the self-identified misfit.

"Five minutes!" Anna called to us as one of the raincoat-wearing guys hefted a giant, expensive-looking camera onto his shoulder.

"No," I said. "No, no, no. There's got to be a way out of this." I turned toward the others. "If we all refuse, there's no way they can make us. Right? Like a general strike. Like a union!"

"You can't form unions in an autocracy, Paulie," Honor said, rolling her eyes, and then started prattling on to Junior about the decline of liberalism in the West.

"And you signed the contract," Becki said, in the same tone Inga had used with her the previous day. Becki had told Junior over breakfast that she ran her own landscaping business. I could easily see her as a business owner with numerous underlings—someone who not only craved self-determination but other-determination. She wore a Gulf Shores sweatshirt, jeans with rhinestones on the butt, and a somewhat incongruous pearl necklace. "Suck it up already."

"I think it's awesome," Kevin said, laughing for no clear reason.

"Me too," Brock was quick to add, in that tone men use when they want you to know they lift weights.

"Yeah, man." Kevin gave Brock a fist bump. His T-shirt was so tight I feared the seams would split. "It's like, I train in all weather, so—"

Tom didn't say anything, just chomped on his chewing tobacco. Inga marched over and pointed at his mouth. "Get rid of that before we start." She was still holding the plastic tub into which we'd deposited our phones after arriving at the harbor. Becki's beady blue eyes latched onto it.

Tom spit tobacco on the ground. "Yes . . . ma'am."

Horrified, Honor pulled a tissue from her coat, ran and picked up the tobacco, and then ran over to one of the trash cans on the promenade.

"I am going to need my phone in a couple days. To transfer money," Becki said to Inga.

"I thought you said to suck it up already," I said under my breath.

Becki gave me a sharp glance. "What was that?"

I saluted her. "I said this rower's at the ready!"

Becki glowered at me. Her high blond ponytail pulled at the skin on her temples, giving her face a pinched look. Meanwhile, Deborah looked as displeased as I felt. "This is ridiculous," she said, crossing her arms over her chest. "I thought the point was to welcome us to Sweden. I thought this was a family show." To Inga: "Is Tocke around? Some of us want to talk to him—"

Kevin whispered something in Becki's ear. They both laughed.

"You won't see him till you're in Sweden," Inga explained. "He's waiting for you with the rest of the crew."

"What about hair and makeup?" I said.

Inga's face twitched. "No. No, this you will always do for yourself."

My face must have fallen. Becki burst out laughing. "What do you think this is, *The Young and the Restless*?"

From the dock, Anna interrupted us by clapping her hands: "Walking shots! Time for walking shots!"

"It's not fair," I complained to Deborah as Inga hustled us toward the boat. "They shouldn't be making us do this."

Junior laughed. "Oh, honey, you thought this was going to be fair?"

Anna lined us up, shortest to tallest. I said, "I thought it was going to be fun. Or at least not so . . . punishing."

"I thought the same thing about prison," Deborah said, patting my back. She was referring to her climate-protest arrest, when she'd been stuck in the slammer for six hours with Jane Fonda.

Nearby, Kevin was complaining that he was actually taller than Becki, it's just that her shoes had a small heel. Inga shooed him to the front of the line. Deborah continued, "But you think people with this much power over us are gonna try to make our lives *easier*?" She let out a rueful laugh. "Where on earth did you learn that?"

CHAPTER FOUR

✤

VÄLKOMMEN!

What is it about America, anyway, that cultivates mean-spiritedness
like an invasive species—kudzu in the South and French broom in California, deer ticks in New England and ranch dip in the Middle West?
I pondered this question as the cameras turned on and my castmates
began battling for first place on the proverbial call sheet. Brock tried to
dominate by walking faster than the rest of us; Honor launched into a
prepared speech about immigration, homelessness, and displacement;
Becki began shouting about what awaited us on the other side of
the water ("Cobblestones! Meatballs!"), loud enough that no one else
could get a word in. Kevin kept stepping in front of Deborah so that the
camera could catch his "good side," and Tom, irritated with the others,
started talking over Anna by saying he had to "take a piss." The latter
offended Deborah, and doubly so when Tom walked over to the edge of
the dock and started to unzip his pants. Junior, who didn't like fighting
any more than I did, ran over to Tom and told him about the café with a
bathroom right across the square, and I ran over to Deborah for a tête-
à-tête about the turpitude of straight white men. "No respect, except

for each other," she complained. "You think if Anna was a man Tom'd interrupt her like that?"

Meanwhile, ten feet in front of us, producer Anna not only looked quite pregnant but quite devoid of her chipper demeanor. "These walking shots should take five minutes!" she called through gritted teeth. When Tom got back from the café bathroom, we tried the walking shots again, but first we walked too fast, then too slow. Then there was too much shoving, then we looked angry, then our smiles were fake, then we were smiling too much. By the time we were all arranged in the boat, including Anna and the sound and camera guys, we were exhausted, hungry, and about ready to throw each other overboard. And yet:

"What an incredible opportunity!" Becki boomed into the boom mic as we pushed off from the dock. "To reverse the path of our ancestors!"

Yet it soon proved difficult, even for the athletes (Becki, Kevin, and Brock), to row and chew scenery simultaneously. We listed to the left, then the right. Then Deborah's arms grew tired. Then my arms grew tired. Then Honor's arms grew tired, we were only a quarter of the way across the strait, and Becki said she was tired of us bellyaching. "Get over yourselves and move!" she roared.

She looked at me as she said this, probably because I was using my oar as a chin rest. The camera panned to her face. She said, "Our relatives gave up everything to come to America. They were starving. Some of them died on these boats and some of them died when they got to our country. But you know what? They never gave up and they never stopped grinding."

"I'm sorry, I just need a minute," I said. "I haven't been to the gym in a long—"

"That's the problem with our country," Kevin chimed in from the back of the boat. "Some people want to sit around while the rest of us do all the work."

It was true that Kevin was working hard, in that he was rowing furiously. But it's also true he wasn't working with the rest of us, which meant that, in a rowboat, his effort was mostly wasted. Perhaps we could have sorted ourselves out, gotten into a rhythm eventually, but over time— how much time I could not say; time grew slippery like the sweat on my temples—the light fog of the morning turned to a thick creamy soup, until we could see nothing but six inches in front of us. Disoriented, I took the Altoids tin out of my coat pocket and popped a half dozen into my mouth, letting the curiously strong cinnamon soothe/torment me as the others wrestled over leadership. Brock was counting oar strokes, Kevin was counting breaths, Honor told us we needed to make a plan, Tom told us he needed a beer and did anyone else, 'cause he had some in his backpack, and Becki told the camera guy to get a close-up on her glittery nails. The rest of us obeyed, or pretended to obey, or flat-out ignored these orders, because who died and made these clowns emperor? When it became clear we were just rowing in circles, Anna told the crew to take a break and stop filming, it was too foggy for the footage to be useful anyway.

"We'll just have to wait till this clears," she said. "I'll text Tocke." I heard the crew thunk down their equipment.

"Coulda made it before the fog if we went faster," I heard Kevin grumble. I couldn't see Kevin, but I could *see* him, if you get my drift, spreading his legs out so wide they bumped up against Deborah's.

"Anna, why don't we take a minute to chart our next steps," Honor insisted. "Happy to take the lead on this."

Anna ignored this, as did I. I closed my eyes and sucked my Altoids as the discourse devolved into rancor and recrimination. Kevin called out Deborah, Honor, and me for not working out more prior to the show, Junior blamed Kevin for what he called "toxic masculinity," Becki blamed Junior for what she called "PC bullshit," Honor blamed Becki for what she called "internalized misogyny," Brock blamed jet lag, which really "messes up the vibe," Deborah blamed Tom for what she called "numbing," and Tom silently blamed all of us for not, I think, being more like the guys he hung out with in Milwaukee. I suppose I blamed them all, too, by gobbling Altoids and refusing to blame myself, but this did not feel like blame in my heart, but good judgment. At some point I must have wandered into that twilight before sleep, for I became a child again, sitting on my grandmother's lap, reading the thin, soft pages of *Pippi Longstocking*, and the grown-ups in her little town were scolding her, always scolding her, for living by herself and doing exactly as she liked.

"I can't believe you just said that," Honor said to Becki.

I opened my eyes. Above us, a blue iris: the fog was slowly clearing. I could see the others now, looking cold and pale and furious. I could see Sweden, too, its muted colors and gabled architecture. We must have drifted in the fog, for we were surprisingly close to shore, so close I could see scores of people in matching raincoats swarming the harbor.

"Nature doesn't care about equality," Becki proclaimed. "Nature wants the strongest to survive."

"Finally." Anna sighed. She stood up and waved. I craned my head and could just make out Tocke's thick frame and long, dark hair standing on the dock: part Viking, part Jesus of Nazareth. He waved to Anna. We all waved back.

"Hurry up!" he shouted through a bullhorn.

And for whatever reason, our desire to please him trumped our desire to best each other. We took up our oars and rowed in perfect rhythm, like Harvard men. Anna counted our strokes with one hand, her other hand resting on her swollen belly. The cameraman stood and swooped his equipment over our arms and legs. Our oars sliced through the gray water, the breeze blew back our hair. It was almost majestic, or would have been, were we not so riled up by each other's company.

And speaking of riled up: as soon as Kevin and Brock threw the rope to the dockworkers, as the boat rocked and pitched, the others jumped up, threw down their oars, climbed over the wooden seats, clambered onto the dock, and raced for shore, shoving each other out of the way like Black Friday doorbusters. I saw Becki stick her foot out, saw Honor go flying, saw Tom trip over his own shoelaces, saw Kevin throw himself upon the sidewalk headfirst and split his chin open. I wish I could say that I stopped to help the others, but what I did instead was breeze past, flinging off my coat and shoes as I went. "My native soil!" I heard myself holler as I went flying into a flower bed.

"And how does this make you feel?" Anna said from behind me.

"I feel like I'm finally where I belong!" I cried. Where on earth were these words coming from? Was that true? Was I mad? Why was I in a flower bed? Before I could answer these questions, Becki thumped down in the dirt beside me, rumpling the nonnative begonias as cameramen stuck their lenses in our faces. In the middle distance I saw a banged-up Honor touching a tree, a bloody-faced Kevin gazing across the water, and a teary Brock with his palms on a statue.

Oh dear, I thought. We were entering a house of mirrors, and some part of me knew that if I wanted to maintain a shred of perspective, I'd be better off flying straight home to Declan. But the reality wheels were turning, turning, had been turning as soon as Jemma had read that casting call aloud, so all I could do was open my mouth and recite the line that was waiting right there for me, despite this being an unscripted series:

"My grandma would be so happy!"

THIS MELEE WENT on for a while, and when it was over, it wasn't even over: we were whisked off for individual interviews, which producers called "syncs," in which we had to explain our inexplicable behavior using "feeling" words with dozens of people watching. Not only the crew, made up of sound guys (they were all guys), cameramen (all men), producers, and PAs. Maybe a hundred others, both locals and tourists, had gathered in Helsingborg Harbor, and were filming us on their phones. A woman with three towheaded children came up to me and said, in perfect English: "I will be cheering for you!"

During a production break that included catered meals of meatballs, lingonberries, and mashed potatoes, I asked Anna about the bathroom situation. She waved me toward one of the upscale hotels that lined the harbor. Feeling like an interloper, I hugged the perimeter of the first lobby I entered, keeping my distance from the front desk, and ducked into the first sign of a toilet area. Unfortunately, it happened to be the men's room. A good-looking guy in his early forties wearing a cream fisherman sweater looked up from a line of urinals in surprise.

"Oh!" I said, backing up. "I'm so sorry." I could not help but notice that even in muted lighting, the man's jaw was so chiseled you could slice a lemon on it.

"Do not be sorry," he said in accented English. *Zip* went his pants. "You are just the person I'm looking for."

I gave him a double take. He smiled at me, a slow, easy grin, one side higher than the other. Was this the start of a porno? A horror movie? I panicked, turned, and fled straight down the hallway into the women's bathroom, where I ran into the last stall, climbed up onto the toilet, and plunked myself on top of the tank. My pulse was racing, my hands sweating, my knees jiggling. I stilled the latter with my palms. Who was he? Who was *I*? What was I doing? What was *he* doing? What were *we* doing, we Americans, and what had we been doing all morning? I needed to hit the reset button; I needed my dignity. Yes, that was it: dignity! I clenched my knees with my fists. What would Pippi Longstocking do? She'd climb off this toilet, for one thing. Walk out the door with head held high, lift that strange man straight up over her head and deposit him onto a tree branch, jeté out the hotel doors with balletic elegance, and return to set, as immune to mean-spiritedness as she was to all pernicious human traditions, inner poise rising above the fray—

And yet just as I started collecting my wits, which were scattered all over the stall, I was interrupted by the same male voice I had heard in the men's room: "Pauline? Are you in there?"

"No!" I heard myself say. I cleared my throat. "I mean—she's not here!"

"Pauline, I am Lars. I am one of the segment producers of *Sverige och Mig.* I am sorry I scared you."

I found that presumptuous. "You didn't scare me. I left of my own accord!"

"Do you have a moment to talk?"

Obviously I did, since I was trapped in a bathroom stall. But how did he know I wasn't suffering from explosive food poisoning and/or diarrhea? "Not really!"

I heard what I thought was a laugh. Then footsteps, which increased in volume. Then the tops of a pair of brown leather boots were peeking through the bottom of the stall door. The voice sighed. "This was not the introduction I was hoping for."

I crossed my arms. "What were you hoping for, then?"

"A handshake. A cup of coffee."

"I don't like coffee." This was a lie.

"You don't like coffee?!"

There was playfulness in his voice, and I must admit there was some in mine: "Liking coffee is so boring. It's like saying you like vacation. Who doesn't like vacation?!"

"A handshake and some tea, then."

"Have you ever had a fun conversation with someone who loves tea? Besides the British, I mean."

"My ex-wife loves tea."

I felt my lips twist into a smile. "Is that why you divorced her?"

"That, and she said she could no longer look me in the eyes."

"That must have hurt."

"Not as much as her sleeping with her coworker."

"You're kidding."

"We Swedes are not known for our humor."

I reached out and unlocked the stall. The door swung open. Lars stood there with a half-smile on his face. He ran one hand through his hair and then turned, almost bashfully, to the side. I had an urge to reach out and run my thumb over the crisp line of his jaw.

"Well, I can barely look at you either," I said instead, motioning around the toilet stall. "Given the circumstances."

He rubbed his jaw with one hand. "What if I closed my eyes?"

So he shut his eyes, and at the same time reached out his hand as if to shake. The second we touched, desire slammed into me like one of those superconducting magnets, the kind that lifts frogs right off the ground. I stared at him, watching the smile tug at his lips and the muscles in his forehead relax. His palms were large, warm, and slightly damp. Our wrists bobbed up and down. His eyes still closed, he said, "It is nice to meet you, Pauline."

"Call me Paulie," I said, in a voice that didn't quite sound like my own.

Without letting go of my hand, Lars opened his eyes and helped me off the toilet as if assisting grown women off toilets was something he'd done a thousand times before. His palm grazed the small of my back. We went to the sinks and washed our hands in silence, occasionally looking at each other and smiling. I felt drunk. As self-contained as an open screen door, the one out of which my dignity had fled.

"I don't wish to scare you again, but I must tell you that you are not going back to the others," he said as we dried our hands on the hotel's rolled white terry towels.

"You didn't scare me." I tossed my towel in a wicker basket.

Lars raised his brows at this as we headed toward the exit. "If you say so, Pauline. You are the talent, yes?"

I laughed at the word "talent." Besides Jemma, no one had called me talented since high school. "Paulie. And that's right. Cross me again and I'll lock myself in my trailer."

As we stepped outside, Lars waved to Tocke, who was in the hotel garden with the rest of the crew. Tocke waved back. We kept walking, heading for a busy avenue. "Where are we going?" I said, jogging to keep up with his long legs. He must have been at least six-four.

"You know I cannot tell you that. You are very tall, you know this?"

"I've been made aware. And rules are made to be broken."

He cocked that half-smile of his again as we crossed the street. "Only Americans say this. How tall are you?"

I hurried to step in line with his gait. "Six feet—I don't know what that is in metric." I fished my Altoids out of my coat pocket and stuck two on my tongue. After half a block, I added, "I'm not like those other Americans."

"Which Americans?"

"You know . . ." I said, gesturing with one hand. "The kind you see on TV."

Lars laughed. "But you are here for TV."

"It's different. This isn't real TV. It's more about . . . going on a journey."

He side-eyed me, amused. "'Journey.' Another word only Americans use."

I puffed cinnamony air out of my mouth. "That's so not true."

He laughed again. "You love to argue, don't you?"

For some reason, this made me blush way more than any innuendo could. Stupefied by pheromones, I walked in silence beside him down the street, feeling the energy of his body reverberate off mine. I hadn't been so charged up by a man since—well, since I met Declan, really.

Declan. Declan. I shook my head like it was an Etch A Sketch. Declan, goddammit. Declan!

No, Paulie, my brain said as Lars took my elbow with his hand and guided me around a corner. *No, no, no, no, no.*

Yes! my body sang.

When we arrived at a parking lot, two more tall, handsome Swedes were waiting beside a shiny, black station wagon. Lars opened a backseat door and motioned for me to slide inside. "Wear this," he said once I was seated, and tugged at the seat belt hanging beside my shoulder. His fingers brushed the fabric of my sweater, and the skin beneath it burst into flame.

"Guess it's going to be a wild ride," I said, and then promptly died of humiliation. Who was this ridiculous person talking, and where did she come from? What a baffling day this was turning out to be. I wonder if Odysseus ever felt the same.

WE DROVE FOR four hours after that. It was me, Lars, a funny, bearded sound guy named Magnus, and a serious, gray-haired cameraman named Jonas, both of whom I cottoned to on sight. Mostly the trio spoke Swedish to one another while I stared out the window, marveling at the tall pines and spindly birches and lakes with complicated names. Once in a while, Magnus and Jonas spoke to me solicitously in English. How was I liking Sweden so far? How did I find my fellow Americans? What was my life like back home? What kinds of TV shows did I like to see? Addled by the various shocks of the day, I answered in basic phrases: I liked Sweden very much, the other Americans were very nice, my life in America was pleasant enough, and I'd watch anything, really. I came up with marvelous answers in my head well after the fact as I gazed out the window, but one of the small tragedies of life—or is it a gift?—is that you cannot edit a conversation.

At six o'clock, we arrived at a city called Midköping. Just a month out from the solstice, the sun was still sky-high. "Mid-coping," I read aloud from the blue-and-white sign as we entered the city limits.

"Mied-shope-ing," Lars corrected from the passenger seat.

Magnus, who was driving, pulled up in front of a stately hotel beside a wide, blue river. Flags fluttered at full mast: Sweden, Norway, Denmark, and the European Union. As Jonas pulled bags from the back—my suitcases, their overnight bags and equipment—Lars headed for the front desk. I followed him like a beagle, sniffing the faint remnants of his cologne. "Here," Lars said, handing me a key in a paper sleeve. Room 225. I snuck a look at his sleeve. Room 222. "Would you like to come to dinner with us in one hour—"

"Yes!" I shouted. "Yes!"

The hotel desk clerk blinked twice and pulled his neck in like a tortoise.

I showered when I got to my room, changed my clothes and put on makeup, then halted, put my hands on my hips, marched back into the bathroom and scrubbed off all the makeup I'd just applied. This was not a *date*. I was not trying to *impress* anybody. Lars was probably contractually required to ask me to dinner and, if not, did so out of pity. I flopped onto the twin-sized bed (what was with Scandinavian beds?!) and watched a half hour of a reality show called *Mormor Lagar Mat!* (Grandma Is Cooking!) while replaying happy memories with Declan in my head: country drives, dancing in the kitchen, nights reading by the fire, doing dishes companionably.

Before I went downstairs, I looked at myself square in the bathroom mirror after reapplying mascara and said, "Now, Pauline Johannson, you are not to drink too much or toss your hair, and, most important, you are not to laugh at a single joke that isn't funny."

"HA HA HA!" I found myself saying two and a half hours later, glass of aquavit in hand. "Ha ha ha!"

I had broken all my rules by then and a few more to boot, the way I knew I would when I made them. Magnus, Jonas, Lars, and I were sitting at an outdoor table at a restaurant in the pedestrian center of Midköping, right across from a huge, old brick pile that had once been the Swedish king's hunting castle. The air was cool, the sun high, the sky clear, the breeze glorious, and the atmosphere euphoric, as palpable as humidity:

late May, in the far north, the long-awaited reward for the rest of the year's meteorological misery.

The euphoria was infectious; it coursed through my body. These Swedes were as dreamy as I'd first fantasized after googling their country: good listeners, egalitarian, their horror over American violence balanced out by their love of American TV. There was not an interruption in sight, nary a monologue to forebear; the four of us had been telling stories all evening, mostly about the bad jobs we'd survived. I regaled them with tales of Premiere Prep's helicopter parents; Jonas and Magnus countered with war stories from shows like *Ninety-Day Divorce* and *Farmer Needs Fiancée*. Lars spoke less than the others, but he was communicating a great deal every time our eyes met. He poured me more water without asking and gave me his unused fork when I, a notable hand-talker, knocked mine to the ground five minutes in. My body, despite my best efforts to subdue it, practically groaned with the pleasure of being near him.

"Dessert?" the server said in English when she came for our empty plates, which had been filled with toast, mayonnaise, lettuce, and tiny shrimps.

We looked at one another. I held up my glass. "*Mycket* aquavit?" That meant "more," the only Swedish word I thus far knew, and maybe the only one I needed.

"You really don't know what's happening tomorrow?" Jonas said to me when the server had left. I shook my head.

"You do not watch show before you come?" Magnus said. "Ha ha, that is so stupid!"

I took a sip of water. The water glasses were tiny, barely bigger than a shot glass. "I tried, but one episode was all I could get through." I remembered the guy running around the Arctic Circle in his skivvies, remembered my own tootling about in the flower bed that very morning. Oh dear. "Give me a hint?"

The Swedes looked at one another as the server returned with the aquavit. "We call it your special day," Lars said, taking one of the glasses.

We clinked, the four of us, and sipped our shots. Aquavit has a bracing taste, as bracing as Sweden's climate. I said, "Special like 'surprise party' or special like 'we're making you eat tarantulas'?"

Lars exchanged a glance with Jonas and Magnus. "Always you try to know more, and always we cannot tell you."

"Listen, it takes me twenty minutes to get in a swimming pool. I need time to prepare for these things." I noticed I was drumming my fingers on the table in a not-very-self-contained way, bordering on frenetic.

"Paulie." Lars leaned forward. He was sitting right across from me, and I could feel the warmth from his breath. "Paulie, are you nervous?"

I bristled. "*No*. Why would I be nervous?"

Jonas said something to Lars in Swedish. Lars nodded, glanced at me, and said something back. The three of them laughed. I bristled again. "*What?*" I said. "What?"

Jonas raised his eyebrows a couple times and mimed zipping his lips. Lars pulled the plastic off a toothpick and stuck it in the side of his mouth. "We will tell you tomorrow, after everything."

The nerve of him! The withholding! I hated it. Loved it. Hated it. Loved it. One of the two, at least.

WE WALKED THE long way back toward the hotel after our nightcap. Magnus had lived briefly in Midköping, a town of thirty thousand; he knew all the cobblestoned streets and tiny alleys. Pots of cheery red geraniums sat outside the cafés, electric vehicles sat in parking spots; in a small park, two accordion-playing alte kackers wheezed old-timey ditties. Here is what I didn't see: cigarette butts, bumper stickers, bus stop ads for personal injury attorneys, Arby's wrappers, graffiti, 1-800-GOT-JUNK signs, In This House We Believe placards, meth-heads, street preachers, homelessness, pickup trucks, payday-loan outfits, chain pharmacies, or billboards reading Heartbeat at Six Weeks. It was ten thirty and still relatively bright out; my heart was light and my bloodstream full of aquavit. I drunkenly longed to take Lars's hand. Instead I nudged him toward a small bar, where, according to a chalkboard on the sidewalk, a DJ was spinning.

"It's late," Lars said. As segment producer, he was the boss of procedural matters. "We have to be going tomorrow by seven thirty."

"Just for a song or two." I looked at him. Thunk went the frog to the magnet. "Please?"

"Please?" Magnus mimicked.

Lars smiled, rolled his eyes, and shook his head. "You are trouble, aren't you?"

"Me, trouble?" I said as we all went inside. "Please. I'm a house cat."

"I knew it the minute I saw you!" he shouted over the music. "When your picture showed up in my email."

The thrill! Lars had been thinking about me while he read his email? Before I could think of a clever reply, the DJ double-clicked a new track on her laptop and the speakers emitted a huge slide across piano keys. Immediately, the crowd started cheering, stood up from their chairs as the synth and guitar fired up, and the disco drum started kicking. That kick drum! I started dancing, started jiving, started having the time of—

What is it about "Dancing Queen" that makes it Pavlov and the world its dog? I felt my mouth grow wet, blinked. When I opened my eyes, everyone in the bar was dancing, and Jonas was dancing, and Magnus was dancing, and Lars was dancing, and I could tell they loved to dance; there was not an ounce of self-consciousness in their hips and arms and feet. Magnus handed me a Carlsberg and I brought the green bottle to my lips. It was eleven at night and outside the bar, the sky was pink like cotton candy. Next to us, two women were kissing. I closed my eyes and threw my arms out—

"ABBA, they are Swedish, you know this?" Lars shouted over the music.

Instead of answering him I grabbed his hand, made him twirl me around, then made Jonas twirl me around, then Magnus, and all that twirling made time swirl away in an eddy.

It was well after one by the time we got back to the hotel, or I think it was. The ancient elevator was tiny, creaky, and made for one at most. Magnus and Jonas squeezed in and motioned me to join them. "No worries, I'll walk," I said, waving at the hotel's circular staircase.

"I will walk with you," Lars said.

We ascended the red-carpeted stairwell in silence save for our breath, still heavy from dancing. Lars's hair was damp, his forehead shiny; he had rolled up the sleeves of his button-down, revealing taut forearms. I'd sweated off some of the alcohol, but I was still pickled from a day of aquavit, adrenaline, euphoria, intense physical exertion, and the narcotic effects of the camera's all-seeing eye. "You're the one who's trouble," I said as we got to the landing, poking my index finger into his arm, knocking him slightly off balance. Part of me regretted saying it, but only part.

"You have no idea," he said, and stopped walking. We were in front of his room, which happened to be right across from my room.

"Well," I said. I turned to face him. "Good night."

"Good night."

A beat—two—three—four—of utter aliveness. Possibility pulsing like galaxy stars. I stared at him, throbbing. To want is to live. To want is to live. To want is to—

"Good night," I said again, though it was the opposite of what I wanted.

He half-smiled. "Good night, Paulie."

We fumbled for our key cards at the same time, opened the doors and closed them in unison. I leaned back against the door, breathless. Thunk went the frog to the magnet.

No, my brain said. *No, no, no, no, no.*

Yes! my body sang.

THAT NIGHT I dreamed of a farmhouse. I was standing in a field of grain, staring at a white clapboard A-frame, beside which sat a squat, brown shed. House and shed were surrounded by fields and three small fruit trees, and in the back was a vegetable garden. As I walked closer to the house, I saw two sun-weathered women standing by the tomato trellises, wearing aprons and homemade poplin dresses and holding shovels. These women looked strong, sturdy, wrinkled from hard labor, fearsome from privation. When I saw them, I sucked in my breath. They appeared to hear me, for they started heading toward the field.

I ducked down and hid. For some reason I didn't want to meet them yet—I wasn't ready.

When I awoke, I was damp and hot and guilty and hungover. I washed off the sweat in the room's tiny shower, braided my hair, swiped on lipstick, and lugged my suitcases down to the lobby, where Magnus, Lars, and Jonas were waiting. Lars had a coffee and croissant in his hand. He handed them to me. I sipped the coffee gratefully.

"I thought you did not like coffee," he said, and smiled wryly.

My brain knocked wetly against my skull. How embarrassing had I been last night? "No, I do." Heavenly Father, why did I order *mycket* aquavit, why, why—

"It is a nice dress," Magnus said. "Like old farm woman, ha ha! And too bad for you, no one to help with hair and makeup, ha ha ha ha ha!"

"It's a *prairie* dress, and thanks a *lot*," I said. To Lars: "Thank you. For the coffee, I mean."

"What is 'prairie'? Is this like 'prayer'?" Magnus mused.

Lars showed me the time on his phone. "You are late."

Seven thirty-two. "Two minutes! Jesus."

"You will need to pray, Paulie, to get through your special day without any sleep, ha ha ha ha ha!" Magnus was cracking himself up.

"In Sweden on time means early."

What happened to our crackling energy from the night before? Lars seemed as cold as pickled herring. "Okay, fine, I'm sorry."

"Don't listen to him," Magnus said. "He is so excited he is waiting here since seven. Ha ha, like a creep!"

"Not a creep," Lars said, though I noticed he didn't correct him about the excitement.

We piled into the station wagon and drove. It was a gorgeous late-spring morning, all blue skies and long shadows. We passed a hockey rink, a vegetable canning factory, little wooden farmstands, newly planted fields. Wildflowers lined the narrow roads that led us out into the country. After twenty minutes we stopped the car so that Jonas could fly a drone over some rye fields. B-roll, this was called. Houses flew Swedish flags and all bore the same color, a warm and rusty red. We drove until we arrived at a park by the river. The same river, Lars said, that ran through Midköping.

"Come back!" Jonas called when I'd slid out of the van and started down a dewy walking trail. I turned and saw him hefting his camera onto his shoulder. "You go nowhere till we're rolling!"

Blasted walking shots! I walked twenty steps in forty-five minutes. Lars directed me to look thoughtful but not morose, emotional but not weepy. I got stung by a bee and developed a pained expression, which Jonas said worked nicely. Lars remained all business, sporting aviators and a baseball cap. I was just picking up steam down the trail when he pointed to a moldering tree stump. "Stop!" Time for a sync.

"Sync what?" I complained. "We haven't done anything!"

He ignored this. I parked myself on the tree stump as Magnus fiddled with my mic and Jonas instructed me to fiddle with my hair. Lars took off his sunglasses, crossed his arms over his chest, and stood behind Jonas and the camera. They exchanged a few words in Swedish as Jonas adjusted the shot. Lars nodded approvingly. "Very nice, with the dress and sunlight," Jonas said to me, and my feathers puffed with pleasure.

Lars interlaced his fingers at his lower back and straddled his legs to make his gaze level with mine. "Look at me when you are talking, not the camera," he ordered, and began rattling off a series of network-approved questions. How was I feeling? Was I nervous? What did I think was happening? What did I hope to discover? Did I think my whole life would change from today's discoveries, and how did I think it would change? I was to answer these questions in complete sentences, the better for the editing bay. I was also to follow the question's lead. For example: "I do think my whole life will change from today's discoveries because that is the premise of this television series."

"No, no, no. Go deeper," Lars said when I answered his question about my "growing fears" with a concern that, due to a lack of public toilets, I'd have to pee in the woods all day.

"Can't we just"—I made a gesture—"get on with it already?"

The answer was no. The answer was, as Jonas informed me, ninety percent of the footage from today would be thrown out by editors, but Lars still needed to hand it over so the executive producers felt they had the ultimate say. Therefore, I needed to answer a billion more questions, which swiftly ratcheted up in intimacy. To wit:

- Do you think your grandmother would be glad you are here today?
- Tell us about her dying and how it ruined your childhood forever.
- Also how being Swedish provided you some relief and identity.
- What about your father, who is also dead but who abandoned you some time before dying?
- And how he was closeted, yes? And a priest? And ran away with a much-younger man?
- Tell us how terrible that was. Use the word "traumatic."
- And speaking of trauma: your mother, who we have heard is crazy? And suicide, wow, eek.
- And your sister, who stares at the sun all day?
- Don't you feel sad, being all alone here, with no family? Explain.
- Don't you wish your family were here to love and support you? Explain.
- How would your ancestors feel about the sad state of your relations? Explain.
- What do you believe your ancestors wish to show you today?

Have you ever been listened to, and I mean *really* listened to, by a near-stranger whilst spilling painful details of your private life? It breeds affection, like that time years ago, after an individual sesh with Karen Hamburger, I hugged a pillow, wrapped myself in a blanket, and called her mommy. "I care about you too," she'd said, as calm as a millpond, as if it were standard for thirtysomething women to goo-goo-ga-ga at three on a Tuesday. "You did a great job today."

Yes, radical disclosure makes a person pliant, a sapling in the breeze. In this case, the breeze was a series of industrial fans constructed by the network, but the effect was the same. Lars handed me a packet of tissues to dry my eyes, but then he told me not to use too many, for I would need them to pee in the woods all day. (I knew it!) I nodded and wobbled to my feet while Lars and Jonas looked over the footage. When they concluded they'd gotten what they needed, Lars came over to hug me. "I am sorry to make you cry," he said into my hair. "I must ask these for my job. Forgive me."

But I realized, nestled there in his arms, dizzied from spilling so many beans, that I was not mad at Lars: I was falling, infatuated, at his feet, just as I'd fallen at Karen Hamburger's that long-ago Tuesday. I buried myself in his shoulder, let his arms wrap around me more tightly. *Incredible!* I thought, googly-eyed from tears and acceptance. *He's perfect, he's just perfect—*

"Okay, Paulie, we have to keep going," Lars said, extricating himself from my straitjacketing embrace. I barely heard him through the scrim of adoration, which filters out everything except goodness and gentility.

I followed him, of course, enchanted as I was, as Gretel follows Hansel, the children of Hamelin follow the Pied Piper, Pippi follows Papa to the South Seas. We walked farther into the woods, where the trees were tall enough to block out all the morning sunlight. The river made a soft, gushing sound somewhere in the near distance; the air was a cool compress on my forehead. Jonas walked backward in front of me, filming my every look and gesture. Magnus kept the boom mic above my head. Lars charted the path, notifying us of potential tripping hazards. After a time we rounded a bend in the trail, and the trees gave way to a clearing. What I saw there nearly made my heart stop. This is not an exaggeration: I clutched my chest and started gasping.

Because what I saw, just ahead of us, was the farmhouse from my dream. Not exactly, of course: some of the details, like the vegetable garden, were missing. But the white clapboard, the brown shed, the fruit trees, the surrounding fields of rye and wheat. I heard crickets buzzing, birds singing. I doubled over and put my head between my legs. I might have started screaming. I do not consider myself a spiritual person, despite my pious upbringing. The closest I've come to God is sausage ravioli.

"Stand up, Paulie!" Jonas was saying, as if through a tunnel. "We need to see your face!"

I straightened. Magnus rushed in to adjust my microphone. "Where are we?" Lars asked in a quiet voice. Despite the bright sun in the clearing he kept his sunglasses tucked into his pale-blue button-down, kept his hat in his hands.

"My grandma's house," I heard myself say, though I did not know why I said this or how I knew. My hands crabbed through the air, looking for something to hold on to.

"Your great-great-great-great-grandmother's house, yes. And your great-great-great-grandmother's. Your great-great-grandmother's and your great-grandmother's, too, before she left for America."

I'm sure I fell to my knees at this point. What else could I do? You go through life explaining the world to yourself, building it out in your head with tidy, LEGO-sized pieces, and then something beyond your puny brain barrels in and sends the heuristics sailing. I remembered filling out a basic family tree on the *Sverige och Mig* application, listing my grandparents' full names and dates of birth and death, but I had no idea that supplying such basic details could lead to something like this.

"This is for you," Lars said, and handed me a piece of paper scrolled up with red ribbon. He sat down on the ground next to me; Jonas and Magnus did, too, adjusting their equipment. They were as silent as monks, reverential even. I untied the ribbon and began to read.

"Out loud, please," Lars said.

"Oh. Right." I cleared my throat.

Dear Pauline,

The story of your family can be traced well back into the eleventh century. From state church records we find generations of scholars and clerics. In the seventeenth century, your seventh-great-grandfather became the vicar of Varnhem. This is an honored post, admired by kings and nobles, and a sign of your family's influence. Indeed, centuries went by with your family situated comfortably in Sweden's priest class. If your ancestors grew weary of religious life, its traditions and hypocrisies, the weariness was passed over for the sake of education, noble patronage, and plenty of food on the table.

Yet this tradition starts to change in the eighteenth century. We take up the tale with your fifth-great-grandfather, Mattias Andersson. When Mattias, the son of a priest, finishes his religious studies, he is granted a post at a country church in Harjevad, just one kilometer from this place. Mattias and his wife and children travel by boat down the River Lidan, the same river you see today, and move into the vicarage (this unfortunately burned down). Mattias is known

*as a doting father. He and his wife, Kristina, have four children,
including your fourth-great-grandmother, Svea. Some parishioners
whisper that Mattias spoils his children, and they grow wild. His sons
forgo an education and the priesthood and set off for Göteborg, losing
precious social standing. Your grandmother Svea learns to read and
runs around the village barefoot. This scandalizes parishioners, but
Mattias will not abide criticism. "Do not worry about Svea," he writes
in a letter to his sister. "In some ways Svea's life will never be easy
because it will be different. But it will be easy in other ways because
the differences she does not mind."*

*Yet Mattias and Svea are both put to the test when, at the age of
seventeen, Svea announces she is pregnant. The father of the child is a
local farmhand, Jonas—*

"It's a common name," Jonas clarified.
"Shhh," Lars said.

*—of a much lower social standing. What's more, at that time,
sex before marriage was not only a sin but a violation of civil law.
Svea is taken to court for her crime. Court records show that the
judge is willing to grant leniency to Svea on the condition that she
marry Jonas. Svea refuses the marriage, which scandalizes the town
further. Will she be cast to the street? Sent to jail? Forced to work in
a city factory?*

*Fortunately for Svea, none of these fates befall her. Though Mattias
is a man of the cloth, and some of his more vicious parishioners have
accused him of moral degradation, he uses his influence to convince
the judge to let Svea and her new son, Per, live with him. This shocks
everyone, except Svea, who knows her father's golden heart. Now a
widower, Mattias dotes on Per as he did his own children and takes
on all the housekeeping. Svea continues to live as she likes, ignoring
the conventions of the day. She meets a new man, Per Anders, at the
market, and the two spend a glorious summer sailing across Lake
Vänern. Mattias cares for Per alone during this time and teaches him
to read. When they return in autumn, Svea and Per Anders marry,*

*and soon two more children arrive. Together they build the farm you
see before you. Mattias retires from the church and comes to live with
them. For several years the farm is full of life.*

*Tragically, however, these two children die of fever at four and
six years of age. It is a painful time. Svea and Per Anders find
solace in each other despite their grief. Mattias takes to the garden,
now grown-over. The shadow of sorrow remains over the farm for
years, yet the wheel of fortune is always turning. Per Anders has a
head for business, and though the family has lost its status, the farm
starts to succeed. Joy returns to the farm when Per, now eighteen,
meets a milkmaid named Maja. Per and Maja marry, and Per
starts building a farm nearby. Maja bears two children. Svea is a
grandmother for the first time!*

*Indeed, it seems the family has at last put their sorrows behind
them when tragedy strikes for a second time. Disease sweeps through
the village, killing Per Anders. Two weeks later, Per dies. Maja is
alone with two young children, one of whom also dies from fever. Svea
is a widow, and Mattias is long buried. The situation seems hopeless.*

*Some of the old townspeople are almost pleased by this bad news.
Finally, Svea has received her due punishment. Yet Svea, since childhood,
has confounded their expectations, and she manages to do so again. In a
remarkable turn of events, she convinces Maja and her remaining son,
Johan, to move here to the farm, and the two women learn to run it on
their own. Within a few years it is even more successful than it was
under Per Anders. This is not to say it was easy for your grandmother.
But Svea is, as her father understood, someone whose circumstances can
drastically change without changing her spirit entirely.*

*After one particularly successful harvest, Svea buys an apple tree
and plants it, which you see before you. Go on now, stand up, pick an
apple from the tree. It is a gift from your fourth-great-grandmother to
you. Your life is a continuation of her story.*

The letter went on from there, but I had to stop reading. I stood up
and walked over to the old apple tree. It was thick and tall and gnarled,
like something from a fairy tale. I reached out and tugged a tiny green

apple from a branch. Jonas, Magnus, and Lars were hovering behind me, but I barely noticed.

"What is going through your head right now?" Lars said, as if through water.

"I—" I said, putting my palms on the trunk of the tree. "I—"

But some moments are beyond words, even moments that are choreographed to elicit certain words for an unscripted reality series. And I was not made of words in that moment, only flashes of memories: the unhappiness my father exuded every Sunday afternoon, the rage in my chest when my mother called me "untidy," the pride with which my grandma displayed her college diploma, my great-grandmother in the nursing home, her arthritic hands and weather-beaten face. I could not make sense of these memories, just heard them rustling through the rye fields, willing themselves into place.

"I—"

More images kept appearing: My sister, Else, pouring water on her head at a fancy restaurant after my mother told her to behave. My father, standing alone at parties. My grandma, changing the subject every time someone mentioned my uncle, who had died in a car wreck at seventeen. I felt like if I just had time, just a little space away from the camera, a little peace and quiet, I might be able to put all these images together into some kind of—but then again, maybe not. Maybe their significance was as temporary as all things, as temporary as the sun passing in the sky.

By this point, it was only one p.m. We filmed till eight thirty. Whatever profundity I'd stumbled into would have to wait, if it stuck around at all. I had to finish the letter, which told the story of my family's emigration from Sweden, but I was too overwhelmed to take it in, despite the fact that Lars made me reread it ten more times while Jonas mucked about with the camera. Jonas also reshot my arrival at the farm with the drone and then from across the field. Later, I went inside the farmhouse, wandered through the fields, hugged all the fruit trees, and lay on the grass, staring up at the sky, each of which demanded several of Jonas's permutations. Hours wandered by in this fashion. We ate lunch at some point, cold-cut sandwiches and a thermos of coffee. I took maybe three bites and put the sandwich down. It was not a corporeal kind of day.

Sometime in the late afternoon or early evening, Lars plunked me down on the farmhouse's front steps for another sync. I answered his questions in a daze. Yes, I blathered to the camera, I saw myself in Svea. Yes, I saw Else in Svea. Yes, I saw my grandmother in Svea. Yes, I saw my father in Svea. Yes, I saw Pippi Longstocking in Svea. Yes, my life was part of a much larger story, a consequence of hundreds if not thousands of small decisions and fates. Over and over I repeated these answers, with camera shifts and verbal variations, but it was too soon for words. I cried a lot. Lars, Magnus, and Jonas cried too. Have you ever seen three hand-some, grown men cry simultaneously? Declan never cried, but rather sublimated his intense feelings with house projects like gutter cleaning. The air felt thick and sweet with the milk of human kindness.

"In ancient Greece," Lars said, standing up to put one arm around my shoulder, "you were not considered a true soldier until you could cry."

"There is one more thing—" I said to him, then started crying again. He nodded at me to go ahead and stepped back behind the camera. So I told them about my dream.

"That is really something," Lars said when I was finished.

"Told you," Jonas said to Lars in English. He turned off the camera.

"Told him what?" I said. I grabbed the Polaroid from my backpack, which was sitting on the steps.

"Last night," Jonas said. "At dinner. When you asked me what I said. I said, 'This girl does not want change, but I think she will change more than anybody.'"

Lars said, "And I told him, 'This is why she is perfect for *Sverige och Mig*.'"

I wiped my eyes. "You don't even know me."

Which made them laugh, which made me laugh, for it seemed both equally true and untrue. And then I was crying, and laughing, and crying and laughing, and they were laughing too. It was a lovely sound, an aria rising above the singing birds and waving wheat and buzzing insects and rustling forest and the faint *woosh* of passing cars in the distance. A human sound. A humane sound. I took a Polaroid of the three of them standing on the farmhouse steps. Then I went over and threw my arms around Magnus. "Thank you." Threw my arms around Jonas.

"Thank you." Paused in front of Lars. We stood there, six inches apart, staring at each other.

Finally he reached for me. "I love you," I heard myself say over his right shoulder. *What?!* I pulled away. "No—sorry—I meant to say *thank* you. Sorry—God—it's been such a long day—"

"It's okay." He pulled me back into him. He smelled so good, like fresh air and soap and the adrenal heat of sexual restraint. I felt his lungs swell against me, his heart thud into my chest. Standing there, on the same spot my grandmothers had stood, I knew I was losing my mind, the way I lost my mind at ripe peaches, the way Svea lost her mind with farmhand Jonas. Life was bursting through me; tectonic plates were shifting. I felt the ground open beneath my feet. What could I do but meet the moment? I jumped in all the way.

CHAPTER FIVE

VIKINGAR!

We drove north that night after we finished filming, to meet up with the others. Lars sat next to me in the backseat. I fell asleep for a while, and when I woke up my head was resting on his shoulder. The more darkness fell, the more I felt cocooned by mankind's benevolence, Lars's in particular. Perhaps Declan, and to a lesser extent Junior and Deborah, had been wrong about Tocke and the show: they were not here to *exploit* us; they were here to *expand* us! Expand our sense of who we were and where we came from, expand our sense of history both large-scale and small. When we got out of the car to buy gas and sandwiches for the road, I found myself staring at Lars, Magnus, and Jonas like a newly adopted dog, slobbery with gratitude. Were they my family now? They certainly felt like family; the affection among us was sure as my sandwich. But that was demented, wasn't it? Or did it only *seem* demented because I'd bought so fully into the nuclear-family industrial complex? Or was "demented" just another word for *magical*, or perhaps *meant to be*?

Though I had no definite answers to these questions, I think it's fair to say that my own personal dementedness was by midnight well established.

By the time we pulled into a campground outside of Karlstad, a medium-sized city in the Värmland province, I could barely remember my last name, let alone any other details of my life back home. Minneapolis, where's that? Declan who? Why had I been so upset about losing that storefront? About quitting photography? Who cared, when all that mattered was love?

I fell out of the car, feeling as if I'd been given the keys to the universe, only to be set upon by my fellow Americans, drunk and reeking of campfire.

"Dude, where'd you go? We filmed all day without you!" Brock crowed, looping a long arm around my shoulder.

Before I could answer, Becki pushed him out of the way, hugging me so tight I thought my eyes would pop out of my head. She touched my cheek with her sparkly fingernails. "And then we went swimming and I was super hungover," she said, her breath sour with wine. "And we went shopping for food and we barbecued, and Honor got mad because she thought Tocke was fat-shaming her on the beach—"

They were all hot to the touch, their faces as juicy and red as rare steak. "It was your special day, wasn't it?" Junior said, pulling Becki away from me. To the others: "I told you it was her special day!" To me: "Did you have fun? Was it amazing? Let me guess—you went to your ancestors' house? What'd you learn? Did you cry? What am I saying, everyone cries, they don't stop filming until you—"

"Um—yes," I said, letting him shepherd me toward the fire as Brock handed me a bottle of tequila and Becki a plastic cup of wine filled to the brim. I heard the station wagon behind me. My suitcases were sitting on the gravel; in the passenger seat, Lars put a hand up in farewell. Blushing, I turned back to Junior and stuttered, "It was amazing. Or—I don't know, more than that. It's hard to describe—"

"Junior says tomorrow's the first competition," Becki babbled. "No way in hell I'm going home. We just got here—"

"Yaaassss, so glad you had a good time!" Junior said. "I wanna hear all about it later, but right now we should focus. Based on my research I think tomorrow's gonna be something mental, probably a puzzle—"

Oh, but I did not want to think about competitions and puzzles.

I wanted to focus on this life force bursting inside me, to flop on a bed and stare at the ceiling and play back every second of this extraordinary day. "Actually, I'm pretty tired," I said, handing the tequila bottle to Junior. "I should probably go to bed—"

Meanwhile, Brock had sat down by the fire and picked up his traveling guitar, crooning, "*How many toads must a man walk on before they can call—?*"

"I think it's roads," I said.

He shook his head while still picking the strings. "Lotta people think that."

Junior handed the tequila back to me.

As I swigged, he explained that while Deborah and Honor had scored their own tiny wooden cabin, a traditional accommodation in Swedish campgrounds, the rest of us would be "sleeping" in a fluorescent one-room rec hall with all the privacy of a prison shower. No point in tucking in for the night, then. We decided to make the best of our imprisonment with a "when in Rome" attitude, sipping lukewarm tequila and taking Polaroids of the following:

- a drunk Brock malapropping Dylan's entire canon ("*Once upon a time you dressed so fine, never used a dime since they weren't primes . . . DIDN'T YOU?*")
- a plastered Becki trying to sell me on FLUFFY, her lash-extension side hustle
- Tom getting drunker and silenter and drunker and silenter until he fell asleep sitting upright on a log
- Kevin, doing shirtless push-ups in the firelight

It had been a long time since I'd tried to capture a night with my camera, but the muscle memory was still there: tugging at the box chain strapped across my chest, flicking the plastic flash up and down, feeling my back pocket for another film cartridge. For years my camera had been like another appendage, and even now, my hands on the old black box betrayed none of the paralyzing self-consciousness I'd developed in art school. *Snap*. Junior poring over charts of previous competitions. *Snap*.

Becki doing the splits. My hands didn't seem to notice that I no longer trusted my eye. Or perhaps, with the help of tequila, they didn't care.

Which was fun, way more fun than taking pictures had been for ages. Junior and I were still giggling when we finally turned in for the night. Yet the gaiety didn't last long, for Tom discovered he hadn't packed his sleep-apnea machine, and Junior lost his Ambien somewhere in his sleeping bag. Between Tom's snoring and Junior's tossing and turning, I barely slept, and at around five a.m., the rose-colored glasses from my special day turned to polarized black antipathy.

Yet there was no time to nurse this antipathy, any more than there'd been time to nurse the previous day's exaltations. The show must go on! We woke, dressed, drank coffee, ate cereal, brushed our teeth, repacked our bags, and met Inga at the campground's entrance at eight. She and the crew had slept at a hotel, Junior told me as we rolled our bags over. Honor and Deborah were already with Inga, looking as fresh as Sweden's drinking water. "It's all about preparation," Honor was saying to Inga, her oxford shirt neatly tucked in. "People can decide how chaotic they want their lives to be, don't you think?"

I greeted Honor with an unfriendly wave. Inga was ignoring her; she had a serious look on her face. "Hey, pay attention," she said to Kevin, who was chatting with two scantily clad teens. "This isn't a game."

Technically it was, but this was no time to split hairs. "No, it's not," Becki said. I turned around and saw that she had donned a camouflage sweatshirt and smeared black grease across her cheekbones. "It's a competition. Someone's going home today."

"Gimme some of that," Brock said, and plucked the grease compact out of Becki's hand.

"I know it's a competition, but let's be kind," Deborah said. She folded her hands in front of her chest, as if in blessing. "I hope you all do great today. We don't need to be every person for themselves."

Becki gaped at Deborah. "That's literally what a competition is."

Honor huffed, "Well, that's not the right way to use 'literally'!"

AN HOUR LATER we arrived at an open field about fifty yards from a weedy sand beach. I saw lawn games set up in the field, charcoal grills, a plastic kiddie pool, a forty-person crew, and a camera on a giant crane. The air smelled like the Fourth of July; the sky rumbled with distant thunder; gray clouds rolled above us in a menacing fashion.

"But where's the puzzle?" Junior bayed as he climbed out of the Sprinter. Lars was standing by what looked to be a ringtoss, and I raced toward him. We exchanged pleasantries, but they seemed different now, charged with intimacy. I touched him on the arm when I laughed; he picked a bit of fluff off my shirt. Tocke lumbered over to us, wearing a gray T-shirt, leather vest, and dark sunglasses despite the ominous weather. "Thank you," I said to Tocke. "Thank you for yesterday. Thank you—what a gift."

Tocke smiled, seeming pleased by my genuflections. "You are welcome." He motioned to Lars. "You are very close now, yes?"

"Oh, yes," I babbled. "Yes, yes. He's like my—um"—crush? lover? therapist? soulmate?—"a brother to me now—"

"We had a nice day," Lars said. He shifted his weight, and his T-shirt brushed my bare arm. I looked at him, and he smiled at me.

"Bonded for life," Tocke said gravely. He looked between us. "It is like war. When you experience something like this together, it is a bond you do not forget."

I tried to look impressed. "Wow, I didn't know you were in the military."

Tocke looked at me funny. "I wasn't. Sweden barely has military." Then he gave Lars a pointed look and walked away just as Magnus wandered up.

"Not a small-talker," said Magnus, thumbing toward Tocke. "Actually, not big talker either. A yeller, ha ha!"

"What was that look about?" I said to Lars, who looked embarrassed.

Magnus put up a finger. "Is funny you ask, Paulie." He explained that *Sverige och Mig* had a storied history of intercourse between cast and crew members. "Is no surprise, maybe. We spend so much time together, having fun and getting cozy. It is like kids at the summer camp but with the sex and the drinking. And the crying, hello, Paulie, remember? Ha ha! Plus Swedes, we are free with our bodies. Very open about sex, no biggie. And four couples, they have gotten married from this show! That is even more than *Swedish Bachelor*!" Magnus lowered his voice. "But some not so fun Americans say to Tocke, hey, this is bias, what if I do not win because crew is telling show secrets to cast member after hanky-panky? This is why we do not stay in same hotel as Americans anymore. But to be honest, Paulie? It is like your laws in America with the . . . what do you call? LBGT?—"

"Um," I said.

Magnus continued, "Anyway, point is, rules do not stop the people from doing what they want to do but make the other people feel better or something."

"Tocke was just reminding me to sign the code of conduct," Lars hurried to say. "Everyone has to sign it. You probably already did."

"Oh, right," I said. I had a flash of stumbling back to my hotel room in Denmark and scribbling my signature on a document with a bunch of buzzwords: "sexual harassment," "alcohol impairment," "bullying," "verbal abuse."

"Stop that, you idiot!" Tocke screamed at Kevin, who had taken off his shirt and was taking selfies in the kiddie pool with a thumb-sized digital camera.

"*Hej, allihopa!* Walking shots!" Chipper pregnant producer Anna was clapping her hands behind me. "Time for walking shots! Pick up your matching polos on the picnic tables, please!"

"Good luck today," Lars said to me, just as I said, "Matching polos?" He lifted his hand as if to touch my shoulder, dropped it, and then gestured to a pile of royal-blue polyester.

GENERALLY WHEN I think about competitions, I imagine something tough. Alpha-male-like. *Braveheart* mixed with Ironman mixed with Olympics mixed with *Survivor*. I definitely don't imagine a festive Swedish barbecue circuit that on this day included the following activities: ringtoss *kubb* (similar to a ringtoss, but with wooden blocks) ball-in-the-bucket toss apple-bobbing in the kiddie pool and grilling a supersized Halloumi burger to sixty degrees before balancing it on a life-sized Jenga tower. Junior hung his head in disappointment when Tocke announced the puzzle-less plan. And if there is a moral to be drawn from his error, which is unlikely, it might be that reality television, like life, turns out so rarely like we imagined.

That this circuit, which we would complete one by one, was gentler than a Silver Sneakers class at the YMCA had no bearing on our collective adrenals. We started pacing, stretching, babbling positive self-talk. We cracked necks, knuckles, and flimsy attempts at jokes during our precompetition syncs. Tocke decided that Tom would go first, and while the two men marched toward the starting line, Inga locked the rest of us in the public bathroom. "So you do not get advantage," she explained, and then shut the door in our face.

I was the last to run the race. After ninety minutes of anxious confinement in yet another toilet stall, it was my turn, and I galloped through the party games like a spooked racehorse. I knocked over the Jenga tower due to a tremble in my hands; I broke a permanent retainer on a Red Delicious. When it was over, I flopped down on the weedy beach with a still-pounding heart, smelling of charred Halloumi and certain I would be sent home shortly. Others coped with the stress somewhat differently:

Brock: "Dude, I smashed that."

Honor: "Like Junior, I was hoping it was a puzzle. I'm very good at puzzles."

Junior: "Should've seen this coming! Season six, episode two—"

Kevin: "Horseshit, is what that was."

Deborah: "The ableism! What if someone had false teeth? Can't very well bob for apples with a flipper like my Sherri has."

Becki: "Grind it out. That's what I tell my guys on hundred-degree days. Just grind it out."

Tom: "WHAT? Can't hear anything with water in my goddamn ears."

When it was all over, Tocke called us back to set, and we lined up next to the kiddie pools like victims of a firing squad. The host of the show, Erik Lundgren, an affable Scandinavian TV star whom we saw only on competition days, solemnly informed us, after an unendurable pause, that Honor had lost by four minutes and would be the first person sent back to America. Honor, whose stringent ethics and formidable intelligence had been repaid with a veritable spanking from the rest of us, due to severe astigmatism.

"Ableism!" Debbie exhaled as the rest of us turned to Honor, who was crying silently behind her glasses. As if in sympathy, the clouds started weeping a light rain.

"This is the last time you will see her!" Tocke shouted from behind Camera One. "When camera cuts, she is cut! So make these goodbyes count!"

"Honor! I'm gonna miss you so much!" Becki said, shooting toward Honor like a rocket. "We were just starting to get to know each other! I'll come visit you next time I'm in North Carolina!"

"I live in D.C.," Honor said, stiff within Becki's vise grip. "You called me a snowflake."

"Ha ha! You're so funny! Funny joke!" Becki let her go. With her hands on her hips, she said in her radio-announcer voice: "It's hard to say goodbye to these people we're getting so close to so fast!"

"I'm sorry, Honor," I said, patting her arm. And I was. But I also wasn't, because I'd rather it was her than me. But then again I was, because I'd rather Kevin or Becki went home instead of Honor so as to prove, once and for all, that human beings needn't be ruthless to thrive in American society.

"'There is always light,'" Deborah intoned, putting both hands on Honor's shoulders, "'if we're only brave enough to see it.'"

Honor nodded, sniffling, before she let out a big boo-hoo. "But what will my coworkers think?!"

Kevin, who had won the circuit, according to Erik Lundgren, appeared unmoved by Honor's suffering. He was strutting around, holding his biceps unnecessarily far from his torso, offering unsolicited high fives to the crew. Tocke had to scream at Kevin to say farewell, which Kevin did with the perfunctoriness of a frat boy waking up beside a stranger on Saturday morning: "Hey, nice to meet you, I'll see you around."

Honor nodded through her tears and even managed to compliment him on his victory, at which point Tocke called the goodbye segment complete.

"That's a wrap on episode one!" he announced, just as the light rain accelerated into a downpour. "Episode two starts tomorrow! Rest up!"

Chipper pregnant producer Anna ushered Honor away from the rest of us. A moment later, we heard a car door shut and an engine start. And that was the last we saw of Honor, pun most certainly intended.

"Are you going to talk to Tocke about the ableism?" I asked Deborah as we ran toward Inga's van, holding our matching polyester polos over our heads like makeshift umbrellas.

Deborah said, huffing as we jogged, "He walked away as soon as I started talking." She frowned. "You know, I think it's worse 'cause they pretended before I signed the contract that we'd become a happy little Swedish family. Did they tell you that too?" She glanced around. Tocke was screaming at the crew to protect the equipment from the rain, Inga was tapping on her phone, Brock and Kevin were doing push-ups in the wet grass, Becki was calling them pussies, Tom was stuffing six packets of *snus* into his upper lip, and Junior, bless him, was jogging up beside us, having tied his regulation polo into a crop top.

"They did." I snapped a Polaroid of Junior giving me a hang-ten sign. "I still kind of believe them. Is that naïve?"

"Yes." Deborah laughed, but in a sad way. "I try not to be cynical, but Tocke's not making it easy."

"Oh, forget him, hon," Junior said, affectionately pushing Deborah's damp hair out of her eyes. "His job's to make good TV, not run a charity. We want to feel like family around here, we have to do that ourselves."

"You sound like Declan," I said to Junior, pulling open the van door. "He says I'm too gullible."

"Who's Declan?" Junior said as we clambered inside.

"My boyfriend," I said. The van smelled like feet. "He hates reality TV. I'm sure I've mentioned him."

Junior cocked his head and fished a bottled water out of a plastic bag. "I don't think you have."

"I definitely have," I insisted. Just then, my wet bra started driving me crazy. I scratched my sternum and reached for the Altoids in my backpack. "I talk about him all the time."

"Maybe to other people," Junior said. "But I'd remember the name 'cause it's the name of my ex-boyfriend's cat."

"You're crazy," I said. I scratched madly with one hand and popped open the tin with the other. "It's this bubble we're in. We don't have any sense of people's lives outside it."

"Funny," Deborah mused. "I thought you were single this whole time."

LATER THAT AFTERNOON, Inga drove us five or so hours to Sweden's eastern coast and dropped us off at a modest lodge called the Harbor Hotel to get a decent night's sleep. When she arrived the next morning, she took us straight to an actual harbor, where a cruise ship–sized ferry, emblazoned with the words *Destination Gotland*, hulked above the other boats. Tocke, chipper pregnant producer Anna, Lars, Magnus, and numerous other crew members stood in the weak sunshine amidst a long line of cars waiting to board. Inga honked her horn and waved at them out of the driver's-side window.

I had never heard of Gotland, but Deborah had cannily packed a guidebook in her rucksack. On the cushy, four-hour ship ride, over sandwiches filled with tiny shrimps and paprika-flavored potato chips, we learned it was the largest island in the Baltic, boasting a long history, sparse population, and a walled medieval city called Visby. The pictures made it look like something out of a Bergman film—rocky beaches, tall grasses, windswept cottages—because, it turned out, it *was* something from a Bergman film. Bergman had lived on the adjoining island, Fårö, and made movies there all the time.

"There's a lot to process," Deborah said, adjusting the scarf around her neck after I'd filled her in on what I'd learned about Svea and the rest of my ancestral line. "For all of us, but for an adoptee? I knew nothing about my birth family until a few months ago, and let's just say my family and I don't always see eye to eye."

I asked her what she meant and Deborah said that recently, while cleaning out her deceased aunt's house, she came across an elaborate family tree from which she herself had been omitted. Her breath caught as she said: "I'll never know. Is it because I'm gay? Or because I'm not blood-related?"

"Jesus." I puffed air out of my mouth. "I'm so sorry."

Deborah shook her head. "Between you, me, and the lamppost, my aunt was a real . . ." She trailed off. "Sherri and I've been together thirty years, and right up till she died she'd say to me, 'Now, how's that roommate of yours? What's her name, Terry?'"

I made a sympathetic sound. "Do you think being over here will give you any sense of—"

"Of course not." Deborah laughed. "But I trust the mess. Anyone who's got an easy answer about anything but wine pairings can stay the hell away from me."

Right before it was time to disembark the ferry, I ran into Lars in the ship's café. I was looking for napkins; Tom had gotten seasick and thrown up chewing tobacco all over his seat's upholstery. Without my asking, Lars helped me find them and bought Tom a bottle of sparkling water. My whole body vibrated as we walked silently toward the back of the ship, the fabric of our clothes occasionally brushing.

"Did you have a nice sleep?" he said finally.

I nodded. "You?"

He nodded. "You did very well yesterday."

"Oh"—I blushed—"I don't know about that."

I had, of course, been acutely aware of Lars's presence the entire time I'd been careening around the obstacle course. Like proprioception, but for another person. The idea of him observing me closely as I made a fool of myself was both horrifying and arousing.

"You are a natural, I think. The camera wants to follow you."

"It does?" My mind flashed to when I face-planted on the grass after getting a little too ambitious with the ringtoss, and then flashed again to Declan. I needed to tell Lars about Declan, to tell everyone about Declan. I needed to proceed with caution and grace and the kind of strict ethics that Honor had demonstrated. Instead I heard myself say, "Well, you make it easy."

Paulie! Must get brain and mouth in proper working order. Before my mouth betrayed me any further, I peeled off toward where my castmates were sitting. I didn't see Lars again until we were on land and well inside Visby's stone walls, being directed by chipper pregnant producer Anna toward a crumbling stone cathedral. It turned out we'd arrived in Gotland just in time for *Vikingaveckan!* (Viking Week!), a six-day celebration of the island's history of sacking and being sacked.

"Now, please enter the ruins and find your costume," Anna trilled after we'd finished the walking shots. "It will have your name on it!"

My castmates and I rushed into the once-grand cathedral, whose caved-in ceiling now revealed an expansive blue sky. On the stone wall, I found my name pinned to a hanger on which hung a scarlet velvet gown. I put it on and turned to see Deborah in an ornate embroidered emerald dress and cape and Becki in a shapeless burlap sack. I laughed at Becki, and she scowled at me. The only person who looked as displeased as her was Kevin, who was dressed as a court jester. "I was born for this," Junior told me breathlessly, with his velvet cloak and scepter, and then started singing a song from *Camelot.* A woman with ornate braids and a dress so corseted I feared her breasts would pop right out the top came into the ruins and introduced herself as Ilsa. As the cameras rolled, Ilsa explained in English that she would be leading us to Viking Village, an area outside of Visby's walls where visitors during Vikingaveckan "lived like true Vikings." (Ilsa pronounced it *wikings.*) Together with the crew we followed Ilsa outside of town, scrambling up grassy hills and across wildflower-filled dales, until we came upon a hand-painted wooden sign, the printing thick and black:

VÄLKOMMEN TILL VIKINGABYN
INGEN EL
INGEN GAS
INGA ARMSBANDSUR
INGEN VVS

Snap. I took a picture of the sign. Behind it was a large encampment. Flags with crests fluttered atop medieval tents; fires burned; somebody, somewhere, was playing the fife. "What's VVS?" I asked Ilsa as Kevin and Tom undid the bands of their wristwatches and handed them to chipper producer Anna. Apparently the crew had gotten special dispensation to film inside the village, though they were not allowed to sleep there.

"Plumbing!" Ilsa replied cheerfully, adjusting her breasts in her corset.

"If you need a shower, you must ask for jug of water, and if you need the toilet you must dig a hole."

I hadn't used a hole for a bathroom since Jemma's and my road trip through the Yucatán. A smelly campsite with no plumbing or electricity was hardly my ideal accommodation, but if Pippi Longstocking could be a good sport with the cannibals on Kurrekurredutt Island, I could do the same here. "Oh! Okay. Well, hmm—very period-appropriate!"

Before I could finish applying my brave face, a pair of enormous identical twin Vikings, clad in matching leather pants, tunic shirts, and belts that carried enormous swords, crashed into the campsite. Ilsa introduced them as Björn and Häger and informed us that they oversaw the grounds but unfortunately didn't speak English. Silently, the twins, with their interchangeable, André the Giant–like aspects, led us through a maze of smoky, odorous campsites to a trio of tents, in the center of which roared a large cooking fire. A tween boy turned a pig on a spit, two women in similar getups to Ilsa's sliced black bread, and a group of male Vikings sat at a thoroughly modern picnic table, drinking beer out of pewter steins as a Russian wolfhound dozed at their feet. The Vikings waved at us as Björn—or was it Häger?—pulled back the flap on one of the tents, revealing seven straw beds, each covered with a coarse white sheet and raw wool blanket. Björn/Häger grunted in welcome and/or indigestion.

I saw Kevin's jaw clench. He stalked over to Lars, and I strained to hear him say, "I think, with my back and all, I'll be in better shape for tomorrow if I could sleep where the crew's crashing tonight?"

That a man obsessed with his physique might also be a prima donna was not surprising, but it was satisfying. I went over and nudged Lars. "Sorry Kevin, was sleeping on hay not part of your training regimen?"

He opened his mouth to retort, but Ilsa interrupted him. "Before we sleep," she said to the cameras while rubbing her hands together. "We feast!"

At the picnic table, over a surprisingly delicious meal of suckling pig, black bread, and homemade beer, we learned that this particular band of Vikings, who'd attended university together, had been coming to Gotland for a decade. "We look forward to it all year," said Viking Anders as he tore boar meat off the bone with his teeth. Anders worked in IT but moonlighted as a barbaric warrior. His wife, Annika, who was too busy tidying the hearth to sit with us, spent her days at camp hand-sewing costumes, foraging mushrooms, and welding amulets to sell in the village.

"Can women be Vikings?" I asked Anders, glancing at Annika, whose boobs were quivering like Jell-O in her corset.

"One or two," he said. "We try our best to be true to history." Then he told me about the remains of an elite Viking warrior that had been found on a Swedish island, which were for over a century misidentified as male.

"But what about the Valkyries?" I pressed. My grandma had given me an illustrated book about Norse gods and giants, and I'd spent countless hours thumbing through it as a kid.

Anders shook his head. "But they are not real. Not like the real Vikings." He motioned to the campgrounds. Nearby, two large men were blowing into curved horns. *Wah-waaaaaaahhh*. "This is not, how do you say, make-believe."

I frowned.

"Dude, Paulie, let the guy eat," Brock said, laughing in that pointed way that meant: *Cut it out.*

"I was just wondering," I bristled. Of course Brock had no interest in cosplay gender equity; he already had a bear fur draped over his shoulders, a hand-forged knife tucked into his belt, and a lute he'd borrowed from God-knows-where. Meanwhile, Becki had solved the problem of male dominance in her own way: by stealing Häger's sword and swashbuckling around with one of the teenage boys. Elsewhere, Deborah and Junior were listening, rapt, as Annika told tales of Old Norse mythology to the children.

I wanted to be a good sport like the others, but there was the matter of the hay beds, not to mention the sexism I sniffed in the air. Did Ilsa *want* her bosoms popping from her corset like tennis balls from a serve machine? Did Annika *want* to be making amulets all week instead of fake-killing IT guys from Gothenburg? Straight answers seemed impossible to gather, especially under the influence of Anders's potent home-brewed ale.

"But you've had a female prime minister," I said to no one in particular. "Right?"

Everyone ignored me, caught up in singing Norse drinking songs, which involved guttural shouts and lots of pounding on the table. If I had been a Good Person, as Declan was, perhaps I would have gone over and sat with Kevin, who was staring moodily at the fire. But that would mean I had found common cause with Kevin, who I'd already determined was a boor. So I ignored him, waved good night to the others, and crawled into my hay bed while thinking about how easily Pippi had befriended the Kurrekurredutts and their strange customs on their South Pacific island, and how impossible such diplomacy thus far was for me.

THE NEXT MORNING, I awoke to rain pouring down the sides of our tent. The air reeked of body odor and wet straw, my back ached, and I'd spent half the night sneezing from the hay. I groaned, reached out, and opened the tent flap. Lars was crouched there, holding a golf umbrella and drinking espresso. He smiled. "How did you sleep?"

"Ugh," I said, and dropped the flap of the tent on him. Emerging from their straw nests, everyone looked as terrible as I felt. Tom's face was puffy from drink, Becki had bug bites on one cheek, Junior was coughing, Deborah had half-moons under her eyes, and Brock was green from what he described as a four-a.m. "crisis" from suckling pig. Kevin, too, was a little storm cloud of displeasure. He fished a pill bottle out from under his pillow, pulled on his jester outfit, and stomped out of the tent. "I can't eat that," I heard him say to a Viking. "Do you have any eggs?"

But there were no eggs. No coffee either. We ate the same pig and black bread for breakfast that we had for dinner, and received a cup of water we could use for either drinking or bathing. This seemed preposterous, given that the crew was drinking lattes and eating thick croissants right in front of us, but producer Anna said that authenticity was a big part of *Sverige och Mig*'s appeal. "Technically none of this is authentic?" I said, gesturing to my pewter mug while eyeing Anna's croissant. "This says 'Made in China'?"

"You love asking questions, don't you Paulie!" Anna tucked the last of the croissant into her cheek. "Walking shots!" she called while walking away and clapping her hands. "Time for walking shots!"

While a small camera crew whisked Tom away to the far side of the island for his own "special day," the rest of us walked. We walked and walked and walked. We walked to the entrance of *Vikingaveckan* and took tickets from visitors. We walked to the crafts area and learned how to weld. We walked to the food tents and ate turkey legs; we walked around Visby and picked up trash; we walked to a rocky beach to watch grown men race toy ships. Due to our rustic lodgings and, as Magnus loved to remind me, lack of hair and makeup teams, I had turkey meat in my molars and pimples on my chin and felt like a greasy hamburger in my velvet dress. My mood did not improve when Tocke, who came to supervise filming in the afternoon, kept critiquing our performances. "LOOK EXCITED! YOU BETTER NOT BE HUNGOVER!" he kept shouting. "THIS IS A TRIP OF A LIFETIME FOR FUCK'S SAKE!"

The climax of the day, and indeed of Viking Week itself, was a staged reenactment of a historic battle, the real name of which I never caught, at a pageant organizers were calling Valhalla. Our job as American volunteers, according to a bespectacled Viking Week organizer, would be to wave flags and hand out extra swords to the (all-male) actor-participants on the battlefield as a thousand spectators cheered them on. The only problem was that the show couldn't start until dusk, and in late May in Gotland, there wasn't much dusk to be found. It was after eleven by the time the Vikings lit the torches, and by then, after something like fifteen hours of walking, all of us—save Tom, who was still filming on the other side of the island—were barely upright, clinging for dear life to the metal fence separating the arena from the battlefield. If the hay beds from the night before represented our psychological straws, we were down to our last ones.

"Watch it," Deborah snapped at Brock as he reached over her to grab a flag.

"That's my foot!" Becki barked at Kevin, shoving him away after he dropped a sword on her toes.

Junior and I exchanged a meaningful glance. After filming for several days, we were beginning to adapt to the cameras' omnipresence, even cooperating with each other at times, but low on sleep, fuel, hygiene, and personal space, we reverted to baser impulses. Becki wouldn't stop talking over everyone, Deborah wouldn't stop crafting a narrative, Brock wouldn't stop calling everyone "Dude," and Kevin wouldn't stop boasting about how much more fit he was than these Viking goons, who were slowed, he said, by beer and other carbohydrates. Only Junior retained his stiff and cheery upper lip, for I—well, I'm afraid my contrarian nature emerged under duress. "If you're that jacked, why don't you go out there and join them?" I shouted to Kevin over the roar of the crowd, as on the field, one half of the Vikings smashed on the other. "Or are you one of those guys who lifts weights but can barely run a hundred feet?"

If Kevin heard my sarcasm, he certainly didn't respond to it. "I love cardio, actually!"

"Imagine!" I shouted, my sarcasm simmering into contempt. "If the time and energy you put into perfecting your body went into something useful, like . . . you know . . ." Hmmm. "Dismantling the patriarchy?!"

One of the Vikings in the arena fell off his horse. People gasped. He clambered back on with a wave to a mix of cheers and jeers. Kevin didn't bother turning from the melee to shout, "What, Paulie, do you, like, hate men?!"

I startled. "No!"

"Seems like you do!"

I shouted, "Just you, actually!" Another roar from the crowd as faraway bugles blared.

Kevin hollered, "Lemme guess—everything bad that's happened to you is some guy's fault!"

"Wrong!" I roared.

"'Cause you love being the victim!" he roared.

"I've never called myself a victim!" I screamed, smashing the tip of the wooden sword I was holding into the ground. "You can't call people victims just 'cause they show you problems that you don't want to—"

"Stop telling me how to talk!" Kevin roared back. "You don't know anything about me!"

"You don't know anything about me!" I screamed.

At this point we both had our wooden swords clutched in our hands, which we were supposed to be passing out to the (all-male) actor-performers. For a split-second it seemed we might start dueling, for I was overcome with an urge to bonk Kevin on the head. But before I could give physical violence the old college try, Björn or Häger, I still don't know which, ran over to us, screaming a word in Swedish that sounded a lot like *sword*. Kevin and I thrust our swords high in the air, trying to get him to choose ours instead of the other's, and through a rapid sequence of movements I'll never be able to grasp, let alone adequately narrate, Björn/Häger ran straight into both of them, forehead first, and fell backward to the ground with a *clomp*.

A clean line, like a tree felled in a forest. Everyone around us gasped. After a few seconds, Björn/Häger sat up, dazed, his expression mushy as oatmeal. Though the larger battle continued to rage on the field, unfazed by the fracas, from somewhere behind us I heard Tocke scream, "CUT! GODDAMMIT! CUT!"

"What is going on?!" he shouted as he stormed up, face purple inside his black hoodie. On the other side of the fence, a medic was crouching beside Björn/Häger, holding up three fingers to his face.

I pointed my finger at Kevin, and at the same time he pointed his at me. Deborah, Becki, and Brock pointed their fingers at both of us. Junior shrugged in confusion. "It was an accident," Kevin explained just as I burst out: "You should have heard what he said!"

"No." Tocke shook his head. "No. I fly you halfway across the world and—"

"We didn't do it on purpose!" I complained as Kevin added, "She started it!"

Tocke exploded. "You are children! You think you are so special? You think you are the first Americans on this show who do not get along?" He started pacing in front of us, taking his time to formulate what he would say next. I crossed my arms over my chest. Kevin scuffed his shoes into the dirt. In the distance, a group of Vikings roared in triumph. Tocke continued: "You have your American basketball, yes? Your so-called Dream Team? Does the coach pick only the best point guards for his team? Only the best defenders? No! Do you understand what I am saying?" It was clear from his tone of voice this was not a question we were meant to answer. "I do not care if you do not 'like each other,'" Tocke taunted. "I do not care if you never speak again, though you should know this has never happened in ten seasons. What I care about is that you show up on time, with energy, you don't party too hard, you learn to respect each other, play as a team, and stop"— his voice rose to a shout—"GETTING IN THE WAY OF MY PRO-DUCTION!"

"Okay, Dad," Kevin said under his breath, and for once I agreed with his sentiment.

"Then that's a wrap on Viking Week," Tocke said before turning off his walkie-talkie and handing it to Anna. Just before he stalked off, he said: "You all better show up differently in the morning."

WE LEFT THE arena in a sullen silence. Dad was mad; he said we'd been bad; we sulked about it like the children he'd said we'd become. Inga drove us to the northern tip of Gotland, where we took a car ferry to the island of Fårö, Bergman's island, one of the most remote islands in the Baltic. The water was still, the air cool and fresh, the sky the color of blue silk. To be at sea in the midnight sun was a balm to my jangled nerves.

It was after two a.m. when we were back on land. We wound through dusky roads to a bed-and-breakfast hugging the sea, where Inga told us our call wasn't until the afternoon. I slept until eleven and, upon waking, took my breakfast: strong black coffee, bread with butter and jam, and a hard-boiled egg, all served on a big wooden tray with chipped yet sturdy crockery. I ate to the sound of birds hopping on my windowsill, to the rush of wind and sea.

How wonderful it was to be alone, to be silent, to be cloistered from the world and all its insane inhabitants! I wondered if Pippi felt that way at Villa Villekulla, the relief of no longer having to participate in a society where people yelled at you for walking backward and hiding toys in trees. Perhaps, I thought, biting into my toast, I could do a Buddhist retreat when I got home, take a vow of silence with the guarantee that everyone else would be silent too. Once I'd told Karen Hamburger, after a scuf-fle with colleagues at work, "Generally I like people, but the problem is all these other people!" This had made her laugh so hard she spilled her chamomile tea. "That wasn't a joke," I'd said, my voice becoming uncertain. "Oh, I know!" she'd said gaily. "I wasn't laughing because it was funny!"

Brock knocked at my door, then, interrupting my quietude. He said the B&B had bicycles, and did I want to go for a ride? I did. We spent the following hour pedaling up and down Fårö's rolling hills. The landscape was dotted with small farmhouses, the fields full of poppies and sunflowers, the roadside covered in tall grasses, the sky dotted with sheep's-wool clouds. We passed the Bergman Center, which was crawling with tourists, just as Brock told me that I should take it easy on Kevin. "He's young for his age, he's listening to these dumb podcasts . . ." Brock paused to stand up and pedal. "You know this is his first time out of the country? He's only been on a plane twice. Give him some grace."

"*Pfffft.*" I stood up to pedal myself. "Don't try that Christian bullhonky on me. You think Kevin's ever turned a cheek in his life? Why am I the one who always has to turn a cheek?"

Brock's face turned serious. "Take it from me, Paulie, I've been married ten years." He sat back on his seat as we started coasting down a hill. "It's not worth it, keeping score."

"Because the score is, you always win," I said, the breeze ruffling my ponytail. It was a beautiful day for an argument. "Because you didn't grow up learning to concede and be nice and want nothing. Tocke, talking about teamwork—I'm sick of it!" I started talking faster. "*I* bend. They *never* bend. Guys like Kevin—my dad was like this—I bend till I break. That's why I loved hearing about Svea. *She* didn't bend. The thing about our ancestors is—"

"They're dead," Brock interrupted.

A laugh erupted from my lips, more surprise than anything. "No," I amended. "What I was going to say is—"

Then I burst out laughing again. Brock did too. We laughed a long time as we pedaled down that glorious country road, maybe more than Ingmar Bergman ever laughed in his life. I can't explain why. Whenever one of us would pause, the other would get us going again, until we were doubled over, nearly losing our balance. My sides were aching once we got back to the inn. It felt wonderful. Oh, to be cleansed by laughter! An inside-out bath is always better than an outside-in one, no matter how smelly you get.

THAT BEING SAID, I did shower when I got to my room. As soon as I put my hair under the spigot, the bathroom filled with the smell of campfire and hay, a disgusting combination when mixed with vanilla bodywash. When I climbed into the van at call time, Kevin was already inside; to honor Brock's pleas for tolerance, I ignored him. Tom was in the front seat with Inga, saying more words than I'd ever heard come out of his mouth: "My goddamn *farfar*'s *farfar* drowned at sea . . . and my *farfar*'s *far*. No wonder he didn't let Pop join the navy—put him in the mines instead. But that was just the same shit, different pile . . ."

He kept up his patter on the shortish drive up to Fårö's lighthouse at the eastern tip of the island, either oblivious to or disinterested in the tension brewing between Kevin and me, and to our collective nerves as we headed into the second elimination. We knew it was coming, for as Junior had explained in Denmark, each episode took three days to film: two focused on Swedish culture and activities, and one on the competition. At the rocky beach, ancient, fossil-filled rocks jutted into the air like alien figures. Affable host Erik Lundgren was waiting for us, standing next to an enormous chessboard with giant plastic pieces and what appeared to be black-and-white inflatables.

We donned our polos and mics, the cameras started rolling, and Erik Lundgren explained that this contest riffed on the famous chess scene from Bergman's *The Seventh Seal*, wherein Max von Sydow's medieval Knight plays a long match against Death personified. Brock, Deborah, and I would be playing the white pieces (the Knight); Kevin, Tom, Junior, and Becki the black (Death). As a team, we would be in charge of both moving the pieces and wearing them, hence the inflatable chess suits. (That the sides were uneven didn't matter, since this was a group challenge based on strategy.) Whichever team won the chess match got immunity; the losers would take up bows and arrows for a sudden-death archery contest, and the person whose arrow missed the bull's-eye by the widest margin would be sent home.

"Uh, so either of you know how to play chess?" Brock said to Deborah and me as Anna zipped him into a giant inflatable white knight.

"No!" came Deborah's muffled reply from her inflatable rook.

I shook my head from inside an inflatable white queen. With a sense of foreboding, we waddled over to the chessboard, where Tom (inflatable black knight), Becki (inflatable black queen), Junior (inflatable black bishop), and Kevin (inflatable black rook) were waiting. Cameras and mics were adjusted accordingly. "*Ett*," Erik Lundberg said from the center of the board, "*två, tre*—" He brought his arm down like a checkered flag. "White goes first—*Går*!"

Kevin checkmated us in two moves. The clips are still circulating online: inflatable-queen Becki triumphantly hopping over to square H4, past our pawns on F3 and G4, as Brock, Deborah, and I look on in horror from inside our suits in the back row. "Know what this is called?" you can hear Kevin shout to us from the other end of the board. "The Fool's Mate!"

I found out later that Kevin had been playing chess since he was a kid. "You're the fool!" I shouted at him. In the clips you can see me start to run in his direction—to do what, I have no idea—but then I trip on my shoelaces. The air from my inflatable queen suit lets out a hissing fart as I face-plant between the rows of pawns.

"Cut!" Tocke shouted after I'd scrambled to my feet and Kevin and Becki had tried to enroll Tom and Junior in an inflatable-chessman victory dance. We were given a meal break while the crew set up for the archery competition. Brock, Deborah, and I huddled together eating meatballs and fretting while Kevin, Becki, Junior, and Tom fist-bumped, sore-winnered, and otherwise celebrated with the crew.

"I don't want to do this," I said to Deborah after Tocke called us back to set. Anna zipped me back up in my inflatable queen suit. "I think I'm gonna puke."

"You know I love you two," inflatable-knight Brock said in a patronizing tone. "And I'm a gentleman. But this is sudden death, and I'm not gonna go easy on you."

Deborah snorted from inside her inflatable rook. "What the hell makes you think I'm gonna go easy on *you*?" Deborah, who had faced so much hardship in her life—alienation, rejection, government persecution—and yet, at sixty-eight, remained puckishly undaunted.

Brock turned to me, put a hand on my shoulder, and said in a low voice: "Paulie, can I ask you something?" He didn't pause before continuing. "Since you're doing the show just for fun, how would you feel about giving this contest to Deborah? Since she still doesn't know anything about her birth family, you know? It hardly seems fair for her to go home right away."

I took a step back, heat rising in my cheeks. "No offense," Brock added.

It was hard to say what offended me most: being given instructions by a (male) peer who had taken it upon himself to serve as my superior, being called out publicly for the self-interest I thought I'd so skillfully hidden, or having to confront privately that I was not as altruistic as I liked to think. "Um, well, if you care so much, Brock, maybe *you* should let Deborah win!"

Brock gestured to the landscape with his inflatable arms. "But this is really important to me."

I made a sound in the back of my throat and tried to thump my chest with my inflatable hand. "It's really important to me!"

"But I want to meet my family."

"*I* want to meet my family!" More than that, I needed it. *Do you know what it's like,* I wished to say, had wished to tell him ever since we'd been drinking in Denmark, *to be lonely your whole life among the people to whom you ostensibly belong? Do you know how much that wears on a person? How stooped you get from lugging that around?*

Brock looked at me pityingly. "But I'm going to win."

I'd had it with him. "No, *I'm* going to win!" I clapped my inflatable hand over my mouth as I said this. It was the first time I'd said it to anyone, including myself. For it was one thing for a gal to be ambitious, but, at least where I came from, one had to disguise it, including from oneself, with a gradient of self-effacement to -loathing. I felt naked there in the crisp wind, despite my inflatable queen suit, and my hunger to best Brock was quickly replaced by shame.

"Oh for heaven's sakes, neither one of you is winning, or letting me win," Deborah said, stalking off with as much dignity as she could muster while tucked into an inflatable rook. "Because I'm going to beat the pants off both of you."

Unfortunately for those interested in justice, Deborah's prophecy did not come to pass. Yet this should not undercut the authority with which she rushed to her bow and arrow, calling "Ayiyiyiyiyiyiyiyi!" like Xena, Warrior Princess, only to tump over in her inflatable suit and miss the bull's-eye by about ten feet. She was the oldest contestant ever to appear on *Sverige och Mig*, and despite this final tumble, she had done herself proud, which is more than the rest of us could say, including Tocke, whose competitions were not only ableist but ageist.

"Goddammit, Deborah, I'm so sorry," I said over her shoulder as we hugged goodbye, after Erik Lundgren had declared that she was heading back to America. "I should've let you win."

"No, you shouldn't have!" She held me at arm's length and looked me dead in the eye. "You give 'em hell, Paulie, you hear? You hold yourself back on no one's account. 'Specially your own."

Before I could apologize again, or ask her what she meant, Becki came crashing through our embrace with one of her death-grip hugs. "Debbie, I have to try your wine! Does it by chance come in a box?"

We had to rush out of there after Tocke yelled "Cut!" to make the ferry from Fårö to Gotland, and from there, the last ferry back to the mainland. Before I could take my seat on the ship, Brock nudged me, said we needed to talk, and led me out to one of the observation decks. I clenched my fists and prepared to continue our fight from earlier, but there, in the desolate gray middle of the Baltic Sea, as the wind whipped our hair and sucked our windbreakers against our bodies, he took me by surprise by offering a simple yet eloquent apology. "I had no right to ask you to do something I had no intention of doing myself," he said. "No right to question your motives either." He stuck out his hand. "Friends?"

Amidst the intensity of the past week, I had plum forgotten the power of a small kindness. "Friends," I said, and hugged him in lieu of a hand-shake.

And with that, not unlike young children, we wiped the blackboard clean. With an air of lightness, we went inside to buy beer and sand-wiches and potato chips at the ship's restaurant, and then Brock peeled off to take a nap. My seat was next to Becki's, not that you'd have known it from the way she pretended I didn't exist. I decided to pretend the same thing, but after about ninety minutes I busted through my vow of silence by confessing, "I miss Deborah. Don't you?"

Becki was leafing through a Gotland tourist magazine. "It's only been, like, four hours."

"But I feel bad."

"It's a competition," she said, turning the page. "Someone's gotta go. We all knew that going in. Deborah too."

"They should get rid of the competition part of the show—it'd be better that way." Tocke was six seats away. I leaned toward Becki and lowered my voice. "It's supposed to be about genealogy, not these stupid games, you know?"

"If you feel as bad about Deborah as you say you do"—Becki licked her index finger and turned another page—"then why didn't you offer to go home like Brock said?"

I leaned back. "Because—"

"See? You don't want to," she said. "You want to win. Just like me and Brock and Kevin. So stop pretending you're better than us and shut up already."

I crossed my arms. "I don't think I'm better than you."

Becki snorted at this. After a pause she added, apropos of nothing: "My dad always said nature's gonna have her way. The strongest of the species—that's who survives."

I'd had a couple beers, which is why I said: "But didn't your dad die of cancer?"

"Yeah. So?" She turned the page again. "Didn't your dad die of a heart attack?"

"Yeah." A pause, then an impulse: "My dad wasn't strong, though."

She looked at me. For the first time, I saw no hostility in her gaze. "Yeah, well, neither was mine."

Another pause. In the silence, I heard the strike of a match, a flicker of understanding. "Not that I'm a social Darwinist," I added, for clarification's sake. "I don't think the heart attack was his fault. I just mean he was emotionally, like, a coward, probably because he was afraid of his own—"

"Social what?" Becki frowned. "Stop using big words, Paulie."

I made a face. "Darwinism's not a big word. Darwin? Charles Darwin?"

"Ugh, you're so annoying," she said, and as she said this, she angled her body away from mine in the plush ferry seat and stuck her magazine in her face. Which goes to show that as suddenly as a person might reveal their secret heart to you, and you to them, more often than not, the both of you might just as suddenly yank them away.

CHAPTER SIX

✣

NORDEN MINNS

Three days' leave in Stockholm is what Tocke granted us. Three un-
encumbered, glorious days. It was evening by the time we got off the
ferry, and by ten p.m., Inga was pulling up to a marquee-lit, four-star
hotel called the Rival in Södermalm, one of Stockholm's main islands.
"Rooms are in your name," she said with utter exhaustion before speeding
off in the Sprinter.

There on the street, with dusk only beginning to fall thanks to the
impending solstice, I felt darkness fill my belly at the thought of Deborah
spending the night alone in a random motel or watching B movies in
coach on her way back to California. This darkness only expanded when
I saw a soused Tom stop a chic couple walking down the sidewalk with
their small dog. (He'd been pounding beers on the ferry.) He whistled.
"Hear that?" he said. Despite the Swedes' nonplussed expressions, he
slapped them on the backs and whistled some more. John Philip Sousa,
"The Stars and Stripes Forever." Tom hacked a smoker's laugh. "That's the
sound of America!"

"Hello?" I said into my room phone once I'd checked into my room, showered, and flopped down on yet another king bed split straight down the middle (!!!). Other than that, the shore-leave accommodations were excellent: tasteful lighting, cozy chairs, and enough pillows to build a medium-sized fort. According to the hotel binder, Benny Andersson from ABBA was an owner, which explained the large, built-in CD rack filled with pop albums. Clad in a plush hotel robe, I'd dialed Declan's number, but there'd been a long pause before it started ringing. "Hello? Hello?"

There was a click. Then: "Hello?"

"Duckie?!"

"Paulie?!"

The sound of Declan's voice after a whole week—I felt myself get whooshed back to our bedroom, could smell the deodorant under his arms, see him take off his undershirt and toss it at the laundry basket, looking pleased when it went in. Things I didn't know I noticed till they were missing, things I didn't know I loved. Tears pricked my eyes. "I miss you!"

"Are we gonna get charged for this? Should I call you back?"

I wasn't sure. "No, no. Stay on."

"I'm gonna call you back."

He hung up. Twenty minutes later, the phone rang. "Sorry, no one at the front desk knew how to work the landline."

"Boy, that's sad." I flopped back on the bed and put my feet against the headboard, twisting the phone cord around my fingers. I loved talking on the phone, had spent years of my youth in this very position, gossiping with Jemma after school. "How are you? What've I missed? Tell me everything and don't stop till you've got dry mouth."

Declan laughed at this. I loved making him laugh; I knew, unlike me, he'd never fake it. Sometimes at parties I wished he'd fake it at least a little—swim, as I always did, with the evening's current, abiding the stories and posturing, like a shark just *keeping things moving*—but it was not in Declan's nature to be mutable, any more than it was in my nature to be static. Declan was the same wherever he went, which is why I loved him, and also why he drove me nuts.

He filled me in on work, his latest attempts to make pie crust, our wilting pot of basil, and the new lightbulbs he ordered for the bathroom. It was wonderfully ordinary stuff, the stuff of life, yet after a week of extraordinary stuff it also sounded bizarre, like he was speaking pig Latin. "Someone named Inga texted and said you'd been filming all week," he said. "So? What's it been like?"

I tapped my heels against the wall. "Totally incredible—I went to my family's farm and learned about this ancestor named Svea—way, *way* ahead of her time—we've done two episodes so far—a welcome episode and a Viking episode—and I almost lost today—Brock tried to make me throw it, don't worry, he apologized—but it was actually sad because *Deborah* lost and got sent home, which was awful—Honor, too, a few days ago—I was hoping it was gonna be Becki or Kevin 'cause they're, I'm not joking, the *complete worst—*"

"You've been in Stockholm this whole time?"

You know after friends would study abroad in college, they'd come back with feather earrings or tattoos or words like "pardon," but you could never quite figure out what had happened over there because every time you asked they'd get a faraway look and talk about night trains and flea markets without the details ever cohering? I was running into the same problem. "We've been traveling—we were somewhere in the middle, and then we went to Gotland—we sleep in hotels but one night I stayed at a campground and another night on a hay bed with a bunch of Vikings? And another night we went to this club and did you know they listen to ABBA and it's not, like, ironically—"

The words sprayed fast from my mouth, like water from a suddenly unkinked hose. Interestingly, however, the word "Lars" refused to pop out. Declan said, "Did you say Vikings?"

"Yeah!" I wiggled my toes. "We did a whole episode at this big famous Viking reenactment. I thought I was gonna hate it"—I considered—"actually I did hate it, except for the giant turkey leg . . . did you know there were lady Vikings? But most women at the festival weren't Vikings, they dressed like—I don't even know what to call them—they had very tight leather brassieres—"

"So you went to a Ren Fest?" Declan said. "What does that have to do with meeting your family?"

"Well, I mean, that part didn't as much," I rushed to say. "But this Svea? The ancestor I was telling you about? Total Pippi Longstocking—single mom, went sailing with her boyfriend for an entire summer, not her kid's dad by the way, she'd dumped him a while back—and the farm she built was so beautiful, I have to take you sometime—"

"How many generations back is she?" Declan said. I heard him clicking his computer mouse. "Because it turns out, after five there's no actual genetic link between you two—"

"I can't remember—it's hard to explain, but hearing about her life, I swear, it was like I made so much more sense to myself—"

"No more than any other person off the street—"

"You know I've always felt like such an alien in my family—but everything I saw and heard looked so familiar, like it had somehow imprinted on me?—"

"And anyway, ninety-nine-point-nine percent of human DNA is the same," he concluded. "And most of that we share with mice."

I paused, stopped wiggling my toes. "You're not listening."

"Yes, I am," he said mildly. "You learned about Svea's life and it made you feel better about yours."

I thought of Lars, crying along with me as I sat on the steps of Svea's farmhouse. I sat up on the bed. "But you're not *hearing* me. Or understanding. It wasn't about feeling better. About the past, I mean. It was like being there touched something deep inside—"

"I'm glad." Click, click went the mouse. "I didn't mean to minimize. I've been doing research, is all, and the study of genealogy tends to"—click, click—"historically at least, oversimplify and overdetermine—"

"Lars says this show changes people's lives. That's the reason he's done all ten seasons. He says you can actually see people transforming, right before your eyes—"

"Who's Lars?"

I froze. "Oh," I faltered. "Just this producer on the show."

Declan let out a *ha*. "Of course he's going to say that."

I ripped open a bag of roasted peanuts from the basket on the nightstand, poured a handful into my cupped palm, and shoved them in my mouth. Chewing, I said, "But there's this whole other, like, spiritual dimension to ancestry that you can't just *read* about. Like, I had this dream the night before my special day about a farm. And then when I actually saw my family's farm, it looked *exactly* like my dream, I got this overwhelming sense of déjà vu and—"

"Well, that makes sense." Click, click. "Déjà vu's caused by stress."

I shoved the rest of the peanuts into my mouth. "I' noh' streh."

"You sound stressed."

"Well, now I am," I huffed. "Thanks to you!"

I heard him sigh. "It's getting late," I said. "I should go to bed."

"Really?" he said. "Right now?"

An argument in a long-term relationship is like a game of chicken. Who dares to concede? Declan and I were both stubborn, but as a Good Person he usually veered away from impact first. "I don't want to end like this," he said. "Not after a whole week."

"Fine." I twisted my fingers around the telephone cord. "Let's talk about something else."

"Fine."

We switched to safe subjects, stuff we easily agreed upon: the insanity of our upstairs neighbors, who screamed at the television during every sporting event; the superiority of some prestige television shows over others; the dreadfulness of people like Kevin and Becki. Thus returned to a safe, us-versus-world orientation, we exchanged I-love-yous without subtext or resentment and hung up.

Speaking of subtext and resentment, without quite knowing why, I then found myself dialing my sister Else's number, which I still knew by heart.

"Hello?"

"Else, it's me."

"Mandy?"

"No, Paulie. Your sister?"

"Oh, hi." I could hear traffic in the background. "You sounded like Mandy. What number is this?"

"I'm in Sweden." Mandy was Else's partner Sean's other partner. "Are you driving?"

"Sweden? Why are you in Sweden? Yeah, I'm picking up groceries for Mandy."

"I texted you. The genealogy show? I'm researching our family?" Researching was perhaps too strong a word, but then again, Else had once called a weekend sound bath training "graduate school" and included her Reiki certificate in her email signature.

"One sec, Paul, Mandy's calling." Else put me on hold. When she came back a couple minutes later: "Sorry, what was that?"

"I said I'm researching our family. The genealogy show in Sweden? I wanted to tell you—they took me out to our family's farm, and Else, it was so beautiful. Our ancestor, Svea, who built it? She had a child out of wedlock—which was illegal by the way—and went sailing with her boyfriend—a bohemian just like you—"

Else interrupted. "Dave says we shouldn't fetishize biological relatedness. He says it reinforces vertical patriarchal structures that prioritize toxic group identities."

Dave was the long-haired, long-winded leader of the Movement, the organization I called a cult and Else called a family. I'd watched videos of Dave online after Else had taken up with him: he spoke like he'd drunk a blender full of quaaludes, Deepak Chopra, Slavoj Žižek, and Neil deGrasse Tyson. "Now, is this the Dave that has four girlfriends and hasn't cleaned a toilet in a decade?"

"Very funny," Else said without laughing. "I don't know why you're so into family all of a sudden. Dave says the only thing Mom and Dad passed down to us is shame and secrecy."

"Yeah, but also, like, our actual lives, which it turns out are tied to all these other lives—"

"Dave says that to save the planet we should get rid of nuclear families and form like-minded interspecies kin groups, isn't that great?" She took a breath. "Anyway, Paulie, I have to go. We're doing a naming ceremony today for Mandy's new baby. I'm one of the godmothers. All of us are going in together on a bunch of land outside Santa Cruz—Dave's gonna build a yurt—"

"Oh." I felt tension grow behind my eyes, which evolved into pinpricks.

How could my own sister also be a stranger? Families didn't make any sense. "Well, um, have fun, I guess. Are naming ceremonies supposed to be fun? What's her name anyhow?"

Else sounded exasperated. "God, Paulie, we don't name the baby—she names herself!"

After Else hung up, I dialed Jemma. She answered right away. "Paulie?! Is that you?!"

I thought my heart would burst. "It's me!"

"I want to talk to you so bad but I am up to my elbows in Prince William's anal glands." I could hear the poodle whining in the background. "Can I call you back in an hour?"

"I have to go to bed. Can I call you tomorrow?"

"Of course. I love you so much! I miss you so much!"

"I miss you so much! I love you so much!"

As I fell asleep, I thought, As nice as it was to visit Svea's house, the thing that makes life most consistently worth living is a friend who understands.

STOCKHOLM'S NICKNAME IS the Venice of the North. Also the Paris of the North, the Jewel of the North, the Capital of Scandinavia, the Beauty on the Water. A city comprised of fourteen islands separated by canals and joined by bridges, it opens up eastward to the Baltic Sea and over twenty thousand islands in its eponymous archipelago. Guards on horseback flank the Royal Palace, fashionable citizens fill sidewalk cafés, leafy parks spill into stately neighborhoods, and sculptural fountains bubble in the center of tree-lined public squares. In these fountains you might see small children playing, accompanied by parents and/or big, scrumptious dogs with heads the size of bears. On benches surrounding the fountains you might see elderly women, their hands resting on top of canes, staring up at the sky anytime the sun peeks through. You might also see teenagers licking ice-cream cones, singletons eating lunch, a fastidiously dressed businessman reading a physical paper. And you might not see any of them using their phones, because these squares have long been places for people to pass the time, and, it turns out, they still do the job splendidly.

But while I loved these public squares, it was Stockholm's waterways I became most enchanted with during my three days' leave—cold, blue, and fresh, carving nature through civilization's Old World achievements. Junior and I walked miles together, winding our way from island to island, neighborhood to neighborhood, Södermalm to Gamla Stan to Östermalm to Skeppsholmen, hugging the canals' edges and marveling at the dreamy, late-spring light. In Gamla Stan, Stockholm's old city, we poked our way through skinny cobblestone streets, where antique stores carrying vintage copper and ornate *rosemåling* snuggled in next to minimalist design shops. In hipster Södermalm, Brock joined us, and we took turns trying on clothes in secondhand stores carrying famous Scandinavian labels. At one such establishment, I bought a pair of used wooden clogs just like Pippi's with per diem cash, and Brock, Junior, and I clomped our way up to Monteliusvägen, a famous Söder lookout spot. Here, twentysomethings, families, and tourists gathered to drink beer and gaze out upon a panoramic vista of Stockholm's central city. It was our last afternoon of freedom, and I was determined to soak it in. Snap, snap went my Polaroid. Two teens necking against the metal railing, a Japanese family eating kebab pizza on a bench. The city was so breath-taking, the temperature so temperate, I'd almost forgotten that just four days prior I'd been trying to murder Kevin from inside an inflatable chess suit.

"Isn't it crazy?" I said as Brock passed us beers from his backpack, nodding toward the view. "That our ancestors left *this*?"

"Not this-this." Junior cracked open the tab with a fizz. "Mine were poor as hell."

"Well, mine too," I conceded. I had learned from my genealogy letter that after a disastrous three-year drought, my great-great-grandparents had had to sell their land and take work as servants at a nearby estate. We clinked cans and drank, looking out at the three golden crowns flanking the top of City Hall. "But Sweden's so rich now, and America's so . . ."

But I couldn't think of the right word for what we were. Brock pointed his can at me. "Dude, there're just as many chances to climb the ladder as there's always been. But you've gotta put yourself out there."

He went on to explain the superiority of American entrepreneurship in the tech space over companies in the EU, and how his project management skills were so in demand he was making a mint from his side consulting business. He spoke at length, at times seeming to mistake the privileges that accompanied lifelong good looks as proof of his own virtuosity.

"You're very . . . confident," I said when he paused to finish his beer, without bothering to hide my irritation.

"If you want to call it that." Brock sipped his beer. "I do a lot of visualizations. Have you guys tried? You should. That's how I know I'm going to win the whole thing."

I groaned. "Not this again."

Junior rolled his eyes, though he seemed more amused than irritated. In his other life as a corporate director, he encountered guys like Brock all the time. He'd even had to put a few on improvement plans, or so he had explained during one of our long car rides, when their beliefs about their abilities and their actual abilities failed to synchronize.

"It's nothing personal," Brock clarified, a phrase used when a matter is most certainly personal. "I'm gonna help you guys as much as I can till the end, okay?"

Brock was such a funny mix of a person, I thought as we walked back to the hotel. Both emotionally intelligent and emotionally stupid, equal parts self-aware and oblivious. I supposed this was true of many people of certain looks, sexual orientation, and pallor, who were groomed to stride up to the world's buffet table and gobble up as much as they could. Though Brock's entitlement had been complicated, even softened, by his turning away from evangelical Christianity, he still, however unconsciously, had trouble taking Junior and me seriously, and had no problem maneuvering ahead of us to the front of the line.

"You got quiet," Brock said from beside me. "What's on your mind?"

"Oh, well—" I faltered. My irritation, however righteous, always sounded petulant when vocalized. I said, "I'm just hungry, I guess."

When we arrived in the Rival lobby, which also functioned as a bar and lounge, Becki, Tom, and Kevin were plopped on the couches, eating sandwiches and drinking beer while surrounded by shopping bags from fast-fashion outlets. At the bar, Junior, Brock, and I ordered burgers and fries. "We saw two H&Ms on one corner!" Becki told Brock by way of greeting. "Hey, have you guys seen all the male nannies walking around?"

"I think they're the kids' dads," I said.

Becki scrunched up her face like a raisin. "No, I don't think so," she said as Kevin fished what looked to be a child's T-shirt out of his bag. It had a picture of a grizzly bear and read California Golden State. "Dude," Kevin said to Brock, "what do you think?"

Brock laughed. "Why'd you get an extra small?"

"You don't like it?" If I hadn't been convinced Kevin was a psychopath, I would have sworn his feelings were hurt. He put the shirt back in the bag and pulled out a boy band jacket. "This is cool, though." His voice was almost pleading. "Right?"

"It's great," Brock said in a big-brothery way. Junior asked Tom what he'd done that day, and he said he'd gone to Fotografiska, the photography museum on the water.

"You like photography?" I said in surprise.

Tom narrowed his eyes. "Something wrong with that?"

"No, not at all, I just didn't know there was anyone else here who . . ." I trailed off as Tom turned away from me and told Junior about some exhibit called *Migrations*. It was then I noticed the DSLR camera around his neck, which I guess I'd never clocked.

"I can't wait for my special day," Becki said, apropos of nothing. "I'm gonna scatter my dad's ashes. I've got about a cup in this cute little—"

"I'm pretty sure that's illegal," I said. Actually I had no idea whether it was legal or not, but what a beautiful sound, the *pffft* of punctured certainty!

"No, it's not," Becki said, but she looked uneasy. It was then I saw she was sitting on one of her plastic bags; every time she shifted her weight she crinkled like a bag of Fritos.

Tom stuffed a new packet of *snus* into his upper lip. "Maybe your people're sailors like mine. Seamen through and through." He cleared his throat wetly.

Brock grinned. "Sorry, what was that?"

Tom missed Brock's expression. "Whaddya got, corn in your ears?" he said, depositing the old *snus* into a round container. "I said seamen through and through." *Snap* went my Polaroid.

"Seamen," Brock repeated. "Seamen through and through."

"Don't be an idiot," Becki was saying, but it was too late, the rest of us were giggling like sixth graders on the back of the bus. She rolled her eyes. "I'm going to bed."

"You don't want to hear more about Tom's big, strong seamen?!" Brock called to her retreating back. Becki shook her head in what I'm sure was disgust and, in farewell, raised her middle finger.

I WAS IN the hotel lobby at the ungodly hour of five the next morning. Tom, Becki, and Brock helped Inga load the van while I sipped my strong black coffee. "This will be a long day," Inga said as we settled into our seats. She corrected herself: "A very long day."

"How long can it be?" Kevin said. "Sweden's not that big a country."

I saw a hint of a smile pass across Inga's face in the rearview mirror. "If you need *fika* there's a bag at Becki's feet."

"This isn't *fika*, it's candy," Becki said, rummaging around in the bag. "My dad said *fika* meant coffee break."

Inga explained that *fika* was not only Sweden's national pastime but a catch-all term meaning snacks in general, a pause at work, an invitation to one's house for coffee, a cozy afternoon with a friend at a café. Did we have any words like this in English? We all thought about this, stumped, as Inga put the Sprinter in drive. "Party?" Brock offered after what seemed like twenty minutes.

Inga looked incredulous. "Party?"

We all agreed that "party" was about as flexible a word as we had in English, for it could cover everything from a one-year-old's smash cake to Burning Man to three teenagers getting wasted in the basement with a box of Franzia. I felt almost proud of my mother tongue, for what it lacked in grace it made up for in flexibility. We continued to brainstorm additional uses for "party" (hosting a dinner, smoking weed with more than one person, snorting cocaine off a public toilet with a stranger) as Inga drove and drove and drove. According to Deborah's atlas, which she had kindly left for us in the van, we were traveling north up a highway that hugged Sweden's eastern coast: every so often we'd get a peek of sea through the trees. At lunchtime we stopped at a roadside Max for burgers and milkshakes. Kevin made his keto by eating his patty plain, holding it with waxed paper like a cookie. While we took turns using the bathroom before hitting the road again, Becki asked Inga, "Are we almost there?" We'd been driving six hours.

"No," Inga said.

So we kept driving. The groves of pines and birches thickened in density along the highway, but their trunks remained as spindly as teen models. We passed Sundsvall, Umeå, Piteå, Luleå. The van grew stuffy with body heat. I'd barely spoken a word to Kevin since our chess match and didn't plan to, considering his unkind use of the Fool's Mate. But I was stuck with him sitting right behind me, driving me crazy with his self-help jargon and sales tips. "There's gold behind that fear," he was saying to Tom. "You know who the greatest salesman in history is? Jesus Christ."

Actually, by late afternoon, all of my fellow Americans save Junior were driving me crazy. Tom, dumping toxic fumes in the air about the gangs coming up to Milwaukee from Chicago and allegedly ruining his city; Brock, singing songs from his band's newest album while using Inga's seat back for drums; and Becki, trying to befriend Inga via a graphic recounting of her sexual history: "I love ass play, don't you? . . . my ex-boyfriend, I met him at a strip club . . . no, I wasn't stripping but I would . . . not much I'll say no to 'cept girls, no way."

Despite the fracas, I managed to hold on to a little sanity, thanks in no small part to the occasional wink Junior would give me when the others weren't looking. I slept, I snacked, I stared out the window. I took Polaroids of the others in unbecoming positions when it was their turn to doze. I also spent a fair amount of time fantasizing about Lars. You would think this was difficult, seeing as I didn't know his last name, let alone anything else about him, save he smelled nice and made me tingle when he stood nearby. But in fact I preferred my fantasies without facts! In this particular one, Lars and I became a husband-and-wife documentary team, traveling and shedding light on dreadful issues like, hmm, the dearth of bees, and in our spare time shagging each other like some type of endangered monkey we would also (nobly) document. And at the awards shows we would be photographed together, but then our handler would pull me aside in my whimsical Rodarte pantsuit and say, Ms. Johannson (for I would keep my maiden name), the pool would now like you to step and repeat solo—

"I don't vote," Brock was proclaiming proudly beside me. It was late afternoon by then. "But when I do, it's third party."

"Same," Kevin said, reaching up from the back-back to give Brock a high five.

Becki turned away from Inga and looked at them. "What's wrong with you?" she said. "You don't like—?"

She proceeded to name the foulest politician I could think of, a man even more oily than his toupee. "Amen," Tom said hoarsely from the back-back.

Next to me, Junior frowned. I must have gasped, for Becki's head snapped in my direction. "Oooh, Paulie's offended," she taunted. "What's the matter? Is he a big, bad man, Paulie?" She switched to a fake baby voice. "Is he out to destwoy ouw democwacy?" It was then I noticed her T-shirt read, in swooping Austenian cursive, I Get Slotty in Las Vegas.

She was laughing as I ransacked my brain's chest of drawers, trying to find a clever yet devastating retort: "Well, as a matter of fact . . . um . . . he is . . . and . . . I don't even need to explain why . . . because . . . um . . . history is going to speak for itself . . ."

"History?!" Tom said.

"He is awful," Inga said from the driver's seat as Tom started ranting about how the party opposing the oily politician had for decades driven Wisconsin into the ground, what with all the rich politicians, professors, and lobbyists in Madison who "didn't give a rat's ass" about working people.

"Agreed," Junior said to Inga. "Not to mention an idiot."

"Right?" Inga said. "In Sweden we look at America and think, 'How can they take him seriously?'"

Becki looked genuinely hurt. "It's the media," she insisted to Inga.

"You know how many guys've lost their jobs?" Tom continued. "GM plant—gone. Cheese plant—gone. Paper mill—gone. Meatpacking plant—still there, but we're a skeleton crew. China company plant—goddamn thing never even opened—"

"Guys, let's chill about politics," Brock said as he rustled through his backpack. "Here, everyone have a gummy."

"How long have you had these?" I said, accepting one. "I thought weed was super ill—"

"Narc!" Becki screeched.

"You guys, I don't care," Inga said into the rearview mirror.

I raised my head high, used my hand like a visor to shield my peripheral vision from Becki's face, and asked, "Inga? How much longer till we get there?"

"Four hours," she said without turning around.

"Four hours!" we all groaned, not simultaneously but close enough. And something about having a common enemy—time in this case—calmed us all down about politics, Tom and Becki especially, though I suppose it could have also been the gummies.

WE ARRIVED IN Kiruna at around nine that evening. Not that I'd have known it without looking at the van's clock—the sun was still well above the horizon like a plump egg yolk. Kiruna was the most northern city in Sweden, over two hundred kilometers north of the Arctic Circle in Lapland, according to Deborah's atlas. It was also a company town, founded in 1900 after a mining firm discovered an enormous iron ore deposit; many of the twenty thousand inhabitants were either employed by or otherwise affiliated with the mine. Sadly, the atlas said one could only see Kiruna's famous northern lights in winter. But then again, not so sadly, because filming during a Kiruna winter would have meant weeks of total darkness.

Climbing out of the van in front of the hotel, I was shocked firstly by how light it was, and secondly by the emptiness of the streets. No one was walking or biking or driving; shops on both sides were either boarded up or plastered with posters announcing fifty to ninety percent off inventory. It reminded me of ghost towns in the American West, skeletons of boom-and-bust economies. Unease traveled like signal lights down the length of my body as we dragged our bags into the hotel, whose English-pub theme and traditional wood paneling seemed dropped from another movie set entirely. "Why's it so empty out there?" I asked the young male clerk when he gave me my room keys. He either didn't hear me or chose not to answer.

"Creeeeeeeeeepy," Junior sang as we headed for the elevator.

My modest room came with both blackout shades and curtains to keep out the intense sunlight, yet I still slept poorly after collapsing on the bed, my body restless from sixteen hours in the van and jittery from the city's ghostly atmosphere. Then there was the matter of the mysterious crashes—BOOM! BOOM! BOOM!—that startled me from a doze sometime around one thirty. I climbed out of bed, went to the window, and pulled back the curtains to unearth the source of this clatter, but all I saw was a big brown bear lumbering through the deserted street, the summer fat on his body swaying with his gait. I watched him for a long time as he headed down the hill. He was beautiful, or by beautiful I mean he had a kind of surety.

I was late to breakfast in the morning, and whatever hopes I had that a bright new day would calm my nerves were quickly dashed. For the breakfast room was not, in fact, a room, but the atrium of an abandoned shopping mall to which the English pub–themed hotel was attached. I went through the buffet, gathering smoked salmon and yogurt sauce, scrambled eggs, yogurt, and muesli, while staring at a vacant hair salon and darkened shoe store holding a single box. When I turned around, I was relieved to see the familiar faces of Lars and Magnus, who were sitting beside a haggard-looking Tocke. Inga had said last night that the crew was staying at the same hotel because, thanks to tourism's high season, there weren't rooms elsewhere.

"Did you guys hear that sound in the middle of the night?" I said as I sat down at their table. "It sounded like some kind of explosion."

"Paulie, it is explosion!" Magnus said. "Kaboom! In the mine!"

"You have ten minutes," Tocke growled. "Hurry up."

I managed to wolf everything down before scrambling to meet the others outside. The temperature was surprisingly warm for the Arctic Circle, in the mid-60s Fahrenheit. A coach bus wheezed up in front of the hotel and chauffeured us to the outskirts of town, where, following a series of strict security protocols, we entered the iron mine's world headquarters, a massive campus that included a restaurant, numerous office buildings, and a sauna for underground workers coming off shifts. A weathered, bird-faced woman in her sixties wearing reflective gear hopped on the bus at a stop sign and announced into a headset microphone that she, Karin, would be our tour guide for the day. "Today we will take this coach five hundred forty meters underground," she proclaimed in a hard, flat English, "into the largest iron ore mine in the world."

"Bullshit," Tom said. He stood right up and went to the back of the bus, where Tocke was sitting, and I watched as Tocke brushed him off and told him to sit down. As Karin explained how they regulated temperature and air quality underground, an enormous door opened on the side of a mountain and the bus shuddered inside.

"You see," Karin said as the bus curved downhill in the darkness, hugging the edge of a one-lane paved road, "the city of Kiruna and the mine have a special relationship. Some say the mine is the city's mother, for without the mine, there is no city. It is the greatest mother in the world, with the purest iron ore, which is sent all over the European Union."

The bus paused to let a transport vehicle squeeze past, headed the opposite direction. It barely fit. Meanwhile, my ears were starting to pop. I heard Tom say from somewhere behind me, "I told you, you're either gonna have to stop the bus or send me back up after you drop 'em off. I ain't doing this."

"Yes, you are," I heard Tocke say. "Everyone is here to get out of their comfort zone, and now it is your turn."

"I told you, this was the one thing I—" Tom said, but that was all I heard before the bus squealed to a stop and Karin instructed us to head into the visitor entrance hall and grab a hard hat. "You are very tall," she said from behind me.

I turned around. "Yes?"

"It is your American food, so much of it," she said brusquely. "Look at you, you are all giants."

"Um," I said, plunking my hard hat on my head. "Thank you?"

We scuffed our feet on the massive cement floor as Karin launched into a well-rehearsed speech, which covered the region's geology; new, environmentally friendly mining technology; and the exciting new deposits of rare earth elements the company had discovered, which could be used to power electric vehicle batteries and wind turbines. The state-owned company gave much of its profits back to the Swedish government and, from Karin's perspective, would solve much of Europe's energy problems. Alas, science was never my subject; instead of listening, I flopped around, rapped on people's hard hats, tried to escape to the bathroom but got yelled at by Karin for breaking "safety protocols." In fact, I didn't tune back in to the lecture until I heard Karin say, "The city is not falling into the mine. The mine is leading the city toward its future! This is an exciting opportunity for Kiruna!"

Wait, what? I straightened and stopped flicking Brock's head. Karin continued, "The mine is paying for everything. The new city center is state-of-the-art, not to mention much more beautiful. Three kilometers is not very far, but it is far enough for a new beginning."

I figured I was mishearing her, or misunderstanding, but then Becki let out a low whistle. "Damn, I thought sinkholes were just in movies."

I raised my hand, thinking of our anachronistic English-pub hotel. "But what's going to happen to the old buildings?"

"The historic buildings, we are paying to move to the new city center," Karin said pleasantly. "The largest and most ambitious move ever attempted."

"So you're leaving everyone else behind," Tom said loudly. "That it? Out with the old, in with the new. That it?"

Karin's smile took on a forced quality. "The company buys the non-historic properties from the owners at market rate, plus twenty-five percent. When the mine can extract more iron, not to mention these rare earth elements, from deeper in the earth, it benefits not only the whole city but the whole country, all of Europe. We have invested billions of dollars into Kiruna already, and we have committed to staying here for . . ." She paused, checking her notes. "Another fifty years."

"Then you're outta here," Tom said. "That it? Leave 'em to starve up here?"

I said without raising my hand, "But does that mean that in twenty, thirty years you might have to move the town *again*?"

Karin's forced smile became more of a showing of teeth. "We cannot say, but if we do, we will work together with the city to find the best outcome for all."

As she led us into an underground cafeteria and tried to stuff down our questions with fresh coffee and an enormous cookie buffet, I couldn't help but think of the old Rondo neighborhood back in St. Paul, a thriving, middle-class Black community that had been destroyed in the 1960s when the federal government decided to run their new interstate straight through it. The residents of Rondo, too, had been told it was the best outcome for all, and then they'd lost hundreds of millions of dollars in community wealth. And while I drank the mine's coffee and ate several pounds of digestive biscuits, the taste in my mouth was primarily disappointment at the fact that Sweden was not quite as immune to putting profits over people as I had previously thought.

After *fika*, Karin granted us leave from her chaperoneship to explore a whole cavernous corridor of enormous, discontinued mining equipment. From my perch in the cab of a giant digger, I spied Tom and Tocke going at it in front of a train car full of iron pellets. Tom's face was red, and the veins in his forehead were pulsing, as if the hostility he had mostly swallowed and silenced over the course of our time together was about to blow off the top of his head. "You wanna push me?" Tom said. "How 'bout this: I quit." He ripped the mic pack off his belt and threw it on the ground.

Tocke threw his hands in the air and said something I couldn't hear. Brock jogged over, picked up the mic pack, and said something to Tocke. Tocke said something to Tom, and whatever it was must have really set him off, for the next thing I knew he was shoving Tocke, and Tocke was shoving back. Brock got between them, put Tom in a bear hug, and started leading him away so he could collect himself. By then I was standing up, and I had one foot placed on the step of the digger. What on earth was going on?

Yet my intense curiosity, coupled with my slightly less intense desire to help, was stilled when Tom broke free of Brock and went charging back to Tocke, getting in his face and pushing him in the chest. "You're a liar, and you're a piece of shit, and if you think for one goddamn minute you're gonna tell me what to do you can bet your ass that—" At which point both Brock and Kevin grabbed him by the arms and started dragging him away. I lifted my foot and prepared to take another step down the digger but found that I could not. My heart was beating rapidly, recalling my father's tantrums, which, like Tom's, were explosive in nature, in large part because he sublimated his rage ninety-nine percent of the time, along with the rest of him. I don't know which was more frightening, really, Dad's rage or its incongruity with the generous and genial man he presented to the public. Once, when I'd called him a liar after he'd disappeared for thirty-six hours without explanation, he'd cornered me against the kitchen cupboards, slammed his hands on the maple wood, and hissed something not that much different from what Tom had just said to Tocke. I was ten at the time. Which is why, instead of running over to Brock and asking what was going on, I gripped the door of the giant digger for dear life until the old terrors subsided.

When I climbed down, shakily, I was met with Jonas's camera in my face.

"What did you think of the tour?" Lars said from behind Jonas.

"They're moving the whole town three kilometers!" I said. "For a sinkhole they made!" And then I burst into tears. It was sad, but it wasn't that sad; I guess something about the truth just got to me. The truth does that, don't you think?

THE NEXT MORNING, a crew whisked Kevin away for his own "special day"—apparently his family came from somewhere in the region. Brock looked like hell when he came down to breakfast; he'd been up half the night talking Tom off the ledge. Apparently Tom's father had been killed in a lead-zinc mining accident in Wisconsin when a tunnel sixty feet underground collapsed. As a result, Tom had never been underground, not even in a basement. (Brock didn't call it a phobia, but that's what it sounded like.) Anyway, Tom had told Tocke this during his audition and felt that subsequently sending him down into the mine had been a betrayal of his trust. Which it was. In fact, it was ghastly, about as far from the "Swedish family" narrative as you could get. Tocke had always made me nervous—giant, powerful men generally had this effect—but that morning I found it hard to even look at him. Whatever his justifications for doing that to Tom—pushing him out of his comfort zone, making good television—I could not get around a general sense of *wrongness*. Meanwhile, Tocke was frowning and stalking around the breakfast room complaining in Swedish into his phone, as if he were in fact the injured party.

While Brock ate peanut butter and bacon on knäckebröd, he told me that around midnight, Tom had made a list of "demands" in order to ensure his continued participation in the show. Alas, not only had Tocke ignored the list, he'd threatened to sue Tom in an American court for breach of contract *and* give him a bad edit in post. Tom had conceded, albeit unhappily, at around three in the morning, and had yet to show his face.

"Why'd you stay up with him?" I asked Brock as we cleared our dishes. I knew he liked Tom slightly more than I did, but that wasn't saying much.

"I love ministering," he said, putting his tray on a rack. "Reminds me of my old men's group at Liberty. If Tom had more support, chances are he wouldn't blow up like that."

"No one should blow up like that, period," I said as we walked outside. "There's no excuse."

"Jesus, Paulie." Brock shook his head. "You're so hard on people. Kevin, Tom—"

"Because they suck!"

He laughed. "Don't we all suck sometimes? 'Member when you knocked that Viking unconscious?"

"I'll admit I'm not perfect," I said, pulling my hair back in a ponytail and scowling at him. "But you have to admit that compared to Kevin and Tom, I suck a lot *less*."

Before we could properly establish a hierarchy of who sucked most to least in our cohort, Tom was storming toward us, Magnus was sticking a mic pack into my jeans pocket, and we were setting off on another filming day. This time we were on foot, traipsing through the neighborhood around the hotel. Some of these streets were already taped off by mine workers. Some buildings had already been razed. Tocke led us to an intact block of tidy houses with geraniums and had Becki ring a door-bell. Jonas's camera hovered just behind Becki's right shoulder. After a moment, a woman who looked to be in her seventies opened the door. She had short gray hair and slate-blue eyes and wore a soft, hand-knit wool sweater. "*Hej, hej,*" she said, stepping aside to let us through. "*Väl-kommen.*"

This was Gullvi Persson, as I would soon learn. Gullvi was a lifelong resident of Kiruna and had lived in her home for forty years. She was one of six thousand people being relocated because of the sinkhole; the mining company had already bought her house, and our job for the day was to help her pack up her belongings for her forthcoming move to the opposite side of town. As Jonas filmed, Gullvi showed us photographs of her children and grandchildren in her living room as we drank coffee and ate thumbprint cookies. "We do every holiday here together," she said, pointing to her grandchildren. "Sometimes I wonder if—" Her eyes were growing shiny. "They act like it is a good thing, the company, especially since my husband is dead. 'This is your reward for his thirty years of hard work,' they say. They give me money. Not a lot, but they say it is generous. They say I will get a nice flat but my daughter says I cannot afford the new ones. So I rent instead. Nothing will be mine. Soon this whole area will be . . ." She trailed off. "Sometimes I wonder, what will be left of my life? What will happen to Kiruna? Will I have even existed?"

She drifted away then. We waited in silence, all of us, for her to return. I could hear the click-click of the kitchen clock and the hum of some appliance. Eventually Gullvi cleared her throat. Her voice was different, synthetically cheerful. "But the children have been very helpful. And you too. Shall we begin?"

Production had brought in a pile of cardboard boxes of varying sizes, waiting to be assembled. Tocke assigned Becki and me to the living room and Brock, Junior, and Tom to the guest bedroom. Gullvi pottered back and forth between us, pouring more coffee in our cups and refilling our plates of cookies. Lars, Magnus, and Jonas alternated getting B-roll and filming us doing stupid things we did to amuse ourselves. Becki put a lampshade on her head; I attempted to shuffle a deck of Dala Horse playing cards, Vegas-style, and instead sent them flying across the room.

"No, no, no," Tocke said, coming into the living room as I was crawling around, picking up the cards. "I want it more like this." He sat on the couch, motioned Jonas over, and modeled paging through Gullvi's photo albums. To Becki and me: "See?"

Becki and I exchanged a glance, the same look Else and I would exchange when our mom frantically vacuumed before company came over. "Uh, fine," Becki said. "Whatever you say."

So we sat down on the couch, opened the albums, raised the pitch of our voices by half an octave, and gave the requisite oohs and aahs over cheerful family pictures of Jul and Påsk and Midsommar while Jonas filmed dutifully.

"Now," Tocke said after a few minutes of watching this, "talk about how looking at these photographs makes you think about starting your own families."

I looked up with alarm, and from my peripheral vision I saw Becki do the same. A surprising yet inevitable twist, familiar to any woman over thirty. If I had a dollar for every time someone casually probed my uterus, I'd be able to buy a baby on the black market and have money left over for a pair of python heels.

"How you are getting older," Tocke continued encouragingly, "and time is running out, and you are realizing how important family is because of the show."

"I'm not doing that," Becki said flatly. She took the photo album off her lap.

Tocke crossed his arms over his broad chest. "Why not?"

I hadn't heard Becki take this tone with Tocke before. "Because I don't want kids."

"You say that now . . ." Tocke said suggestively, or as a kind of warning.

"No, I say that forever." Becki stood up. I stood up too. She crossed her arms over her chest. I did too. She continued, "I always have. I always will."

"Fine," Tocke said, motioning to me. "Paulie, you do it."

"No," I said, surprising myself.

"Why? Because you also do not—"

"No, because—" There was so much I wanted to say, but it was all gobbed up like a hair ball in the back of my throat. Because I didn't know. Because I didn't like the pressure. Because I didn't want my life reduced to a single, albeit important, decision. Because I was tired of being scolded for living exactly how I liked.

I tried to explain my position: "Crrrbbbpph."

"Because you're violating the code of conduct!" Becki burst out. "No bullying!"

I could have hugged her, even though the thought of hugging Becki was like hugging a porcupine. "Yeah!" I said, my voice returning, albeit tremulously. "No bullying!"

"It's not bullying, it's reality," Tocke said, but his voice sounded uncertain.

"Yeah? You sure?" Becki said. "You want to tell that to the network? You think they'll go out on a limb for"—she gestured to the white, male bulk of him—"*this*?"

I saw Tocke startle. It was small but marked, a psychic sneeze. The energy in the room recalibrated, gathered on our side of the coffee table. "You want us to talk about kids?" Becki said. She nodded toward the guest bedroom, where Brock, Junior, and Tom were folding blankets. "Make them talk about kids. Hell, make Brock talk about *childcare*. Then we'll *think* about it."

"Yeah, then we'll *think* about it," I repeated. I felt big as I said it, as big as the whole room or even bigger: undiminished. I pushed my shoulders back and held my head high as Tocke stalked out of the room, presumably to lick his wounds and/or suck up to the network.

"That was amazing," I told Becki as soon as he was out of earshot. "How'd you do that?"

Becki shrugged, but I could tell she was pleased. "You think he's bad, you should hear the MMA guys. My staff too." She uncrossed her arms and flexed her impressive biceps. "I don't take crap from any of 'em."

It wasn't that I hadn't heard anyone say that before, or that the words were particularly profound. I suppose it was the conviction behind them, their matter-of-factness, as frank as frankfurters. My eyes welled up. I stumbled over what I said next: "Wow, that's beautiful, honestly you're an inspir—"

"No." She started waving a hand in front of my face. "Don't start. I'm not a feminist."

"Okay," I said, wiping my eyes with my sleeve. "Okay, okay." But she was smiling as she said this, she wasn't barking at me, and I wasn't barking at her. And then she swatted my arm, and I swatted back, and something was different in the air after that. What that something was I couldn't say, but if I had to put a word to it, I guess the closest approximation is love.

THE REST OF the day sped by, the way filming days often did. We spent a couple more hours with Gullvi, then went over to the towering wooden church with the striking windows, which was once voted Sweden's most beautiful building, and would soon be dismantled and rebuilt in the new city. We ate reindeer pizza with a Kiruna city planner and marveled over his 3-D architectural models. Though Tocke had thwarted Tom's threats to quit the show, Tom was retaliating by becoming the most disagreeable version of himself. "Bullshit," he slurred loudly after drinking a whole bottle of wine by himself on top of several cocktails at the restaurant.

"Pardon me?" said the city planner, a thin-haired, mild-mannered Swede.

"You don't give a rat's ass about the city. You just love that money. That big, dirty mining money—you know as soon as they've taken what they wanted they're gonna leave, and you're gonna done fuck yourself right in the—"

I shook my head and tried to give the planner an apologetic glance. "He's had a tough couple days," Junior said in a low voice. "He's not usually like this."

"Okay, buddy," Brock said, removing Tom's wineglass from arm's length. "How 'bout you and I go get some air—"

"I don't need air," Tom interrupted. His voice rose in volume and pitch. "What I need is you all to stop being such fuckin' liars!"

Brock stood, then, hoisted Tom up, and took off with him, stumbling, to the front of the restaurant. Thank God Tocke had taken the night off, or who knows what might have happened. After the city planner excused himself and went home, looking significantly more down in the mouth than when he'd met us, Junior and I went over to Lars, who'd been put in charge of filming the dinner, and was packing up with the rest of the crew. "I'm so sorry you guys," I said. Junior whistled, and I added, "Tell us the Americans are always this bad so we'll feel better."

Lars stood, wiping his hands on his jeans. "What do you have to be sorry for?"

"Well—" I had no good answer. Social apologies were as much a reflex as kicking my leg at the doctor's office. Once I'd even apologized to the woman who'd plowed right into me with her cart at Target. "You're welcome," she'd said, an even stranger reflex.

"I mean—" I finally said. "I'm guess I'm sorry—"

"On behalf of our people," Junior finished.

"Exactly."

"We think he is crazy man," Magnus said, straightening. "Paulie, you agree?"

"Before this, you were the most normal cast we have had," Jonas said. He laughed. "If you can believe this."

"You handled it well, though," Lars said to us, stepping away from the others. "You changed the topic, moved the discussion back to the planner, you did not let Tom take all the attention as hard as he tried . . ."

"Yeah?" I said, suddenly hopeful. "You think?"

He smiled. We stood there, not saying anything, letting the energy hum between us. How I loved that Lars took *Sverige och Mig* so seriously— took me so seriously. He made it feel like we were accomplishing something important, life-changing—or, no, not just that, he actually believed we were. His attention, not to mention lack of irony, felt like seventy-five-degree sunlight: warm, caressing, just the right intensity.

"Well, I should let you sleep," he said, stepping aside. "Since tomorrow is a competition day."

"Right," I said. "Of course."

"I will hold my thumbs for you, Paulie." He held up his hands, his two thumbs pressing together. And, as if an afterthought: "And you, Junior."

"What does that mean?"

"It means good luck," Junior explained. "Like crossing our fingers."

"Like this?" I held out my thumbs.

"No, like this." Lars took my hands in his. Whoosh went the frog to the magnet.

I WOKE UP the next morning with a pit in my stomach. My fellow Americans, especially Brock, looked equally ill at breakfast—he'd stayed up late with Tom again. The rest of us hadn't slept well, all dreaming about the show, or should I say nightmaring. Junior said he dreamed that Tocke had hired a private investigator to dig up dirt on him; Brock dreamed he accidentally knocked a whole building down while filming and was terrified the show didn't have enough insurance; Becki dreamed her sister had been hit by a car and Tocke wouldn't let her call home.

"What about you, Kev?" Brock said, biting into a hard roll.

Kevin, ashen-faced, shook his head. "He's freaked out 'cause yesterday they told him he's part Sámi," Becki said, glugging some orange juice. She punched him. "Didn't know you were Indian, did you?"

I put my napkin down. "He's not Indian, he's indigeno—"

"Whatever, Paulie," Becki said, cutting me off. "Close enough."

"Dude, that's rad," Brock said to Kevin. "My kids love *Frozen*."

Kevin was rubbing his temples. His eyes were on his plate. "So what's the big deal?" I said.

"He wasn't expecting it," Becki explained. Apparently she'd become Kevin's interpreter overnight. "Some kind of family secret. The church burned all his great-great-grandmother's drums. She converted to Christianity after that. Never told anyone in America about being Indian."

"Who's Indian?" Tom said, thunking his tray down at the table. I looked at him warily.

Becki explained again. "Yeah, well, I gotta bit of Chippewa blood myself," Tom said, slathering a bun with butter.

"Are you an enrolled member, Tom?" I said, with perhaps more tone than was warranted. I'd heard Honor talking about tribal enrollments in the van one day. Complicated stuff!

Tom ignored me. "Most people prob'ly won't look at you any differently."

Kevin lifted his eyes from the table. They were red-rimmed. "You think people are gonna look at me differently?"

I found myself at an impasse, standing before my enemy with a sword on his neck. Which was nobler, victory or mercy? I remembered when Pippi Longstocking came across a group of older boys beating up a little kid named Willie. She'd lifted them up, one by one, and hung them on the limbs of a birch tree as the biggest one insulted her hair and her dress. And while, technically, Kevin was not beating me up at this *second*, had in fact been brought as low as the bottom of one of his infamous push-ups, he sure as hell had done plenty to warrant—

"Why, yes," I heard myself say, slicing the proverbial blade across his aorta. "Starting with me. And of course you'll have to look at yourself differently. Probably you'll need a brand-new personality to replace the whole 'inflammatory podcast disciple' thing."

"Shut up, Paulie," Kevin said.

"Was that really necessary?" Brock said to me.

No. And yet the superfluity felt delicious. Junior sighed and clucked his tongue. "Paullllliiieeeee, bad girl."

I doubled down. "And here I was thinking there is no God!"

Kevin pushed his chair back from the table and stood up. Without saying a word, he stalked out of the breakfast room. Becki shook her head. "You're such an asshole."

"Oh, so *he* can have *his* feelings but *I'm* not allowed to have *my* feelings?" I said.

"You have too many feelings," she informed me matter-of-factly.

I sputtered something about internalized misogyny, Cartesian dualism, and the origins of the word "hysteria," but before I could reach the apex of my argument, which in truth I hadn't come up with in advance, Inga came over and herded us into the van. We had to sit in the parking lot for ten minutes while Tocke coaxed Kevin out of his hotel room; when he thumped into his seat I could smell the artificiality of his cologne, the musk of his anger, and something else: the heaviness of his heartache.

But wait, that didn't make sense: Kevin didn't have a heart. Did he? No. I'd already decided he didn't.

WE ARRIVED ABOUT twenty minutes later to a small Sámi museum and cultural center in the village of Jukkasjärvi. I snuck a look at Kevin as we pulled into the parking lot to see his reaction, but his face was drawn, his gaze downward as he fished a prescription bottle out of his back pocket. We donned our competition polos and followed a narrow path from the parking lot to the open-air museum, where we were greeted by a twenty-something man in a black sweatshirt and ponytail who introduced himself as Tomas.

Tomas was Sámi, and his family had been herding reindeer for generations—his father and grandfather were currently up in the mountains with the herd, as they were every summer. Tomas, too, was a herder, but also an activist. He explained that the competition, which he himself had designed, was a symbol of the Sámi struggle against Swedish colonialism:

"You see, before there was Sweden, there was Sápmi," Tomas said as we ducked into a traditional Sámi dwelling, complete with a fire pit in the center and thick reindeer pelts. "Our people's area covered the northern parts of Norway, Sweden, Finland, and parts of Russia. We did not recognize borders; we moved with the reindeer. But when Sweden realized that the land up here had many natural resources and was not just the wasteland they had imagined, they did everything in their power to destroy us because we stood in the way of those resources."

We ducked back out of the dwelling, and he led us to an exhibit on traditional Sámi religion. Kevin ran his fingers over a traditional drum as Tomas continued: "They killed us if we did not convert to Christianity. They sent our children off to terrible schools. They built churches and mines on land we had honored for thousands of years. When we became alarmed about the climate because our reindeer were starving, they ignored us. When we said the mine is destroying biodiversity, they laughed at us. When they had the chance to ratify the Indigenous and Tribal People's Convention, they refused." He led us over to a wooden canoe and sled. A sign said they had been used by Sámi herders for centuries, though snowmobiles were now the norm. "Now the government and the mine are celebrating the discovery of rare earth elements beneath Sámi herding lands. They announce to the European Union that mining these elements is part of their 'green revolution.' But I do not see extraction of resources for the purpose of consumption, to the point of environmental failure, to be very green, do you? After decades of ignoring the climate crisis for their own enrichment? And their exploitation leaves my family's reindeer with almost nowhere to go."

This was sounding dreadfully familiar. Minnesota's Native population had been shunted onto reservations generations ago, and a battle currently raged in the state's northern regions between conservationists, many of whom were Native, and mining conglomerates hell-bent on sucking up all the precious minerals that they could. I might have noticed the parallel earlier, for Declan had sent me an article about the Sámi some months back, but of course I'd never read it. It'd been my naïve assumption, based on a high school world history class and a steady diet of Scandi noir, that Sweden had never been a colonial power. Certainly not one that whaled on its indigenous population as hard as we did.

But dismay often followed naïveté, at least in my experience, and it was with a sense of defeat—hardly the first of this trip—that I followed Tomas to a wooded area that was prepped with cameras and cranes and crew for the day's competition. Between two trees, a double neon slackline was dangling; the top line had fabric rings hanging from it like a jungle gym.

Tomas explained, "This slackline represents the bottleneck my reindeer must go through because of the unsustainable development in Kiruna. Whereas once we went directly through the town, now we are cut off by the mine, the airstrip, the railroad, and the sewage plant, which prevents the creek from freezing. Each year, over a hundred reindeer die making this passage. You, too, will 'die' if you fall—you will leave the competition. So I suggest you move carefully."

Affable host Erik Lundgren came over, then, and announced that I was going first. On the ground beneath the slackline were wrestling mats with signs reading Mine, Infrastructure, Railroad, Airport, Mild Winter,

No Food, Bigotry, and Poachers. Chipper producer Anna led the others away so they couldn't copy my strategy, which was maybe unnecessary, since I had none. My mind was still spinning from what Tomas had told us, seeing as it was the complete opposite of what tour guide Karin had told us, yet they both had spoken with such conviction that it seemed impossible that one of them wasn't telling the truth. The world was so confusing; was everyone as confused as me? It seemed probable, and yet the internet blazed with certainty.

"Paulie!" Tocke barked as I lapsed into befuddlement. "You have thirty seconds!"

So I threw myself at the slackline without a whisper of a plan. It took me about six tries just to get up on the stupid thing, and then about five minutes to let go of the tree and grab the first fabric loop above my head. I think I took at least a half hour to get across; about three-quarters of the way through, I saw members of the crew start to yawn and check their phones. But I did not fall except after I had finished, at which point I lost my balance and star-fished onto a wrestling mat.

"Ha ha! Wow, Paulie, very bad to watch!" Magnus said as he helped me to my feet. Becki and Kevin went next in quick succession. Unsurprisingly, they were quick and agile, zipping across the slackline like kids on a playground. Junior followed, and while he wasn't nearly as coordinated or in shape, he had the laser focus of someone who studied reality-TV competitions, so mind won out over matter.

Junior came and stood next to me as Tom approached the slackline. "Do you think he's gonna throw it?"

"He's got to. Right?" I whispered. "It's not like he wants to be here."

But as we watched, Tom clung to the ropes like a boxer, bruised but refusing to be beaten. He nearly toppled several times, but he righted himself after each near-fall. "He doesn't want to lose," Junior whispered. "He's too stubborn. He'd rather break a leg than give Tocke what he wants."

Whether from spite or stubbornness or ego, Tom made it across in one piece. Which meant only Brock was left, which meant I breathed a sigh of relief. Brock's love of mountain biking and skiing meant his balance had to be superb. But for some reason—the need to prove something to us, the need to prove something to himself—Brock decided to forgo using the top slackline's rings as aid, and instead, started across using only his two feet for balance. Junior sucked in his breath. "Don't be an idiot!"

Idiot or not, the fatigue from Brock's late nights with Tom or the pressure to perform a task he'd already dismissed as a snap must have gotten to him. Halfway across, as Junior and I watched in horror, Brock put his right foot down just a little bit sideways and bounced right off the line onto the mat labeled Poachers.

"Kevin, you are the winner," Erik Lundgren announced. "Brock, I'm afraid it is your time to go home."

One would think that watching an overconfident man fall from grace would inspire schadenfreude, or at least satisfaction. Yet the feeling that hit me like a basketball was awful, awful: I braced myself but could not avoid the bitter punch to my diaphragm. Even if Brock was a braggart, he was *my* braggart. I ran over to him—he was crying—but before I could throw my arms around him, Becki swooped in and wrapped him in one of her barnacle hugs. "No, please," Brock was saying through his tears. "Let me do it again—I do this all the time in Colorado—thirty feet above—"

"Just like that *Amazing Race* challenge." Junior panted as he jogged up beside me. "It took a pair of Olympic gold hockey players fifty-six shots to hit the five-hole. It's almost worse if you're good at something, 'cause everyone's expecting you to knock it out of the park—"

He knelt down to console Brock, who was still on the ground. My eyes locked on Tom, who was right behind him. The horrible feeling in my chest bounced straight out and into him, morphing from anguish to anger. "This is all your fault, Tom! You hated it here? You wanted to quit? You should have thrown it and gone home!"

Tom tucked his chin back and winced, as if a fly had flown onto his nose. "Say your goodbyes!" Tocke barked.

"You only think about yourself!" I said to Tom, and though I was talking to him, I was back at home, ten years old, talking to my father, and my mother too. "It's all about you! I can't take it anymore!"

Tocke barked, "Paulie, shut up! You have thirty seconds before Brock leaves forever!"

I threw my arms around Brock. I meant to say, *I love you.* I meant to say, *I'll miss you.* I meant to say, *You're a true-blue friend.* But what I said instead was, muttering into his ear: "I'm gonna kill Tom. I'm gonna kill him. This is all his fault and I promise I'll get my revenge."

WE DROVE BACK to Kiruna in the late afternoon. I wish I could say for propriety's sake that my fury had subsided, but in fact it was more like the door to my inner steam room had burst open, hissing hot rage onto every surface. Life was unfair. Life was terribly unfair! I hated Tom and I hated Tocke and I hated the show and I hated what Sweden had done to the Sámi and I hated what the mine had done to Kiruna and I hated feeling like a puppet on a string, getting jerked around every which way by cold-blooded production decisions. What had I been thinking that spring, when I'd gone around proclaiming to everyone who'd listen that Sweden was Shangri-La? That *Sverige och Mig* was a family show? That everything over here would be better because they hadn't turned their country into a privately owned fortress/dump? That my fellow Americans would become my best friends, when the only thing we for sure had in common was that we'd auditioned for a *TV show*?

Perhaps, for someone else, these questions might have led to introspection, but for me, they simply dumped coals on my rage. I hated Sweden and I hated America and I just wanted to go home but—oh, wait, I hated that too. And I hated my father and, sure, why not, hated my sister and mother and I hated my job, and while I was at it, hated the profiteers and politicians and power-seekers and, hmm, everyone I went to college with who was more successful than me. Meanwhile, throughout this hating, I should tell you, I was alone in my hotel room with my pants off, shouting into a pillow and blaring the television to muffle the sound. It was tuned to the kids' channel of Swedish public television, and every so often interrupted my screams with a sound of an animated pig's giggle and a chorus of voices singing *Bink! Bonk! Bork!*

Eventually I tried to calm myself by pulling out my grandmother's copy of *Pippi Longstocking*, but it only made me despair further. Pippi was so goddamn self-sufficient. There was no problem she couldn't solve with superhuman strength, a pile of gold coins, and, as Brock would have called it, a positive mental attitude. "Riddle me this, Pip," I said to the grinning redhead on the book's cover. "How's a normal, not-rich, not-superstrong person supposed to maintain a positive mental attitude when everything's such a mess?"

I went downstairs to the hotel's English pub sometime around seven that evening, not because I'd calmed down but because I hadn't. There's a lot of energy to anger, have you noticed that? Sometimes I think if I weren't so busy repressing it I could do crazy stuff, lift a car even. So there I was, trampling toward the bartender like a rabies-laden elephant when I saw Lars, Jonas, and Magnus sitting at a big brown leatherette booth. *Please, God, no.* I skidded and put my hands out on the bar.

"*Alkohol,*" I said to the bartender, angling my body away from them. "*En stor alkohol.*"

He looked at me like I was insane, which I probably was. Lars appeared beside me. "*Två* 'gin and tonics,'" he said. He looked at me. "Is this okay?"

I was trapped. I nodded. The bartender gave me the drink. It tasted more than okay. I went and plopped down with Lars and Jonas and Magnus.

"You are all right now?" Magnus asked me. "You come in here so mad, I think, 'Is Paulie going to burn down hotel?'"

"We lost a friend today," I said. "I am not all right."

Magnus said, "Ha ha! He is not dead, Paulie!"

"But basically!" As I said this, I somehow felt a little more all right.

"To Brock," Lars said, raising his glass. "*Skål.*" We locked eyes, clinked glasses, and swapped memories of our fallen comrade: his music, his confidence, his potent gummies.

"I hate Tom," I said after a while.

"You don't hate Tom," Jonas said. "You miss Brock."

"Same thing." With a mighty swig, I finished my gin and tonic.

"You Americans, you would rather be angry than be sad," Magnus said. "Swedes, we are a little bit depressed all the time, we don't mind it. Ha ha!"

I leaned back in my chair. "Just what I need, more men explaining things to me." But I did not begrudge him his insight, not really, I just didn't want to have to be grateful for it.

They explained some more things to me over a few rounds of drinks.

About the Institute for Racial Biology at the university in Uppsala that, in the 1930s, deemed the Sámi an "inferior breed." About the government's refusal to grant the Sámi property rights. I explained some things to them, too, like what an "emotional vampire" was and how Tom likely qualified, and how in America, women were often shamed for expressing anger. Then we stopped explaining things to each other and started having fun, not that learning isn't fun. I made them play Never Have I Ever, which was new to them, which eventually got us to this impasse:

"Never have I ever," Lars said, licking his lips before taking a swig of Guinness, "swam in a pool."

Jonas, Magnus, and I exclaimed in disbelief. Lars was shaking his head. "It is true. My mother didn't like the chlorine, and I would rather swim in the sea." Lars was from Varberg, a coastal town south of Gothenburg.

"We must find you one," Jonas said, whipping out his phone for a quick google. There was another hotel, a seven-minute walk away, with an outdoor pool and sauna. Giggling like teens, we paid our respective bills and drunkenly swayed down the hill, passing abandoned apartment buildings with broken glass and shuttered family businesses. It was around nine o'clock, but the sunlight and long shadows looked like midafternoon. Profoundly disoriented, whether from the midnight sun or the crumbling city or booze or grief or being pushed to the breaking point for two weeks, I tripped on a cobblestone and fell, scraping my knees and hands. Lars rushed over and helped me up. "Are you all right?" he said, putting one arm around me. He smelled clean. Strong. Sane. Much saner than me.

"I am now," I heard myself say.

When we arrived at the hotel, we ducked down a corridor to avoid the front desk. I smelled the pool before I saw it: humid, chlorinated. The door was propped open, and we ran through it, laughing, yanking off our sweaters once we realized no one was around. The air was cool but warmed by the eerie sunlight. I stripped down to my bra and underwear and, instead of taking my usual twenty minutes to inch into the water, jumped in feetfirst, screaming as the cold touched my body. Jonas and Magnus, down to boxer briefs, followed. Lars stood at the edge, looking skeptical. "It smells awful," he said.

"Just do it!" we shouted at him. "Do it!"

So he did, eventually, coming up for air sputtering and shaking his wet hair like a dog. Magnus swam to the edge of the pool and pulled a flask of *snaps* from his pants pocket, which warmed us. Who knows how long we stayed in there, paddling around, joking, laughing, doing stupid tricks. Eventually Jonas said he wanted a sauna, and Magnus said he'd go too. "Not me," I said. I was floating on my back, staring up at tufts of pink and purple clouds. "How could you give up this view?"

Lars stayed at the pool with me, and we were quiet for a while. I forgot where I was until cold struck my body. Shivering, I looked down at my fingers, which were wrinkled and turning blue. Lars was already out of the pool, a hotel towel snaked around his trim waist. He was holding a pile of towels. "Come here," he said, and looked at me.

I climbed the steps out of the pool slowly. Without saying a word, Lars opened a towel and wrapped me inside it, rubbing my arms through the terry cloth. I closed my eyes and said nothing, my head spinning from *snaps* and the exquisite pressure of his fingers.

"Are we going to talk about this?" he finally said.

I opened my eyes. "About what?"

"Do not do that," he said, shaking his head, and I felt heat burst through my body. "You know what."

"I—" I coughed and tightened the towel around my body. "I have a boyfriend."

He took a step back. Silence. Terrible silence. Then: "Why did you not say something?"

"I—I dunno—" I faltered as he went over to a pile of clothes and pulled out his jeans. I stared at his lightly tanned body, at the lines of his hip bones, as he tugged on the denim. "It never seemed like a good time—"

Lars pulled on one sock, then the other. "How about before now? Or when I say to you my wife has left?"

He was angry, fair enough; I would have been angry too. "I guess I didn't want to—" I turned my face away, as if looking at him burned my retinas. "I like talking to you, I didn't want anything to change—"

Lars's shoes were on now; he pulled on his shirt. "Now they have changed," he said. "They always had to change."

"But they don't have to—" I went over to him, resisted the impulse to touch him. "We can still be friends—"

"Paulie, this is not friends." He motioned to the space between us.

I felt the hint of a whine enter my voice. "I'm sorry, I just really like being around you—"

He walked toward the exit without saying anything, then turned back around. "You don't get to have everything you want." I heard something hard and metallic in his voice. "When are you people ever going to learn?"

Before I could ask him to what people he was referring, he left. I put my clothes back on, waited five minutes, counting the seconds in my head, and then silently, shakily, made my way to the parking lot. I started running the way I thought we'd come, weaving my way through street after deserted, broken-down, shattered-glass street, but the hotel was nowhere in sight. I kept running, heart pounding in my ears, until I was passing the same buildings: the abandoned jewelry store that had opened, according to the sign, in 1920; the boarded-up community center; the city's original firehouse. Or was my vision just blurring? My body smelled of sweat and chlorine, was both hot and cold, when at last, at a distance, I saw the bright, incongruous outline of an English pub in the middle of this ghost town. My hotel key was in my pocket, and I ran straight upstairs to my room, where the Swedish kids' channel was still blaring, while in my head I kept repeating, *I'm sorry, I'm sorry.* Though we'd been instructed not to use the hotel phones, I had to talk to Declan. Declan, who really knew me. Declan, whom I'd betrayed.

I dialed his number. "Paulie?" he said as soon as he picked up.

I got a lump in my throat at the sound of his voice. "It's me."

"I'm on a work call, things are really crazy, there's like fifteen—can I call you back when I'm done?"

"I don't know the number," I said, and started, silently, to cry.

"Well, call me back, then," he said. "All right?"

I nodded, not that he could see that, and hung up. Then for some ill-advised reason, I called my mother.

"Who's this?" she said breathlessly. "Jean-George, is that you?"

"Mom, it's me. I'm—"

"Oh, hi, Paulie," she said, sounding disappointed. "I was hoping to hear back from Jean-George. He's the best equine therapist in the country. Where are you? This is a funny number."

"Mom—" I paused. Tears were still streaming down my face. "I'm in Sweden, remember?"

"Oh, right." Rustling sounds. "I'll send you an article about Jean-George. It's wonderful what he's doing. He told me I have quite a knack for someone my age. He said—"

"Mom, I'm upset. I think I—"

"Oh, honey, you're always upset. My goodness, you're just like your father—"

My heart thudded irregularly. "No I'm not, I'm *not*, I'm nothing like—"

"Between him and your adolescence, I swear, took years off my life—"

"Your life!" I stood up from the bed. I wasn't crying anymore. "Your life! The life I—holding your hair back and turning—I was supposed to be doing my math homework!"

"Paulie, you're telling yourself stories now, that's not the way it—"

But I couldn't listen, not again, to the alternative facts of her personal history. I took the phone away from my ear and let her go on. I couldn't bear to listen, nor to cut the connection. After about five minutes, when she still hadn't taken a breath, I put the phone down on the pillow, got my jacket out of the wardrobe, grabbed my room key, and headed back out. It was eerily bright, the air cool as a mausoleum. I stuck my hands in my pockets and started walking down the abandoned avenue. Inside a broken window, a white teddy bear clutched a soft red heart.

Then I saw him. The brown bear. Lumbering down the lane. Not a care in the world, it seemed, or not a care that I could see. He swayed right past me, unimpressed by my turmoil. It struck me, in a brief bolt of clarity, that I was the wild creature, I was the savage, made feral by my inability to accept—well, anything. I felt the thud of his great paws on the pavement and sensed, as a wave, insight swelling up inside when—

BOOM! went the mine. BOOM! BOOM!

CHAPTER SEVEN

✦

HJÄRTAT ÄR EN
ENSAM JÄGARE

In real life, when I've lost my mind, I make tracks for Karen Hamburger. Over the course of forty-seven to fifty-two minutes, we diagram my foolishness like a compound sentence until each cause and consequence is laid out in neat diagonal lines. "So let me get this straight," I could almost hear her say. "In order to cope with the distress caused by your friend leaving *Sverige och Mig*, the distress of isolation from friends and family, and the distress of creating reality television, you caused yourself more distress by getting drunk and crossing boundaries with your producer?"

"I know, Karen Hamburger, it's bad," I said, though I meant to just think it. It was seven thirty in the morning, I hadn't slept a wink, and I was sitting on top of one of my suitcases in a fake English pub, waiting for Inga to pick us up.

"Who are you talking to?" Junior said, rolling his suitcases to a stop next to mine.

"Oh," I said, fishing Altoids out of my pocket. "Um, no one. Just my morning meditation."

He gave me a funny look. "Crappy weather. Someone said it frosted last night."

I inhaled cinnamon and looked out the automatic glass doors and saw that it was pouring just as Inga pulled up. We got soaking wet loading our bags into the back of the Sprinter, which was much easier now that only five of us remained. After Becki, Kevin, and Tom straggled out, Inga set her GPS and launched us on a drive headed southeast, according to Deborah's atlas. We crossed out of Lapland, back into Norrland, and set a path toward what can only be described as the middle of nowhere. Towns were few, tiny, and far apart, made visible only by their red and yellow siding far back from the road. I'm not sure I would have known they even were towns, were it not for the blue-and-white signs announcing their names.

After lunch at a rest-stop buffet, we turned off the main road and arrived after twenty minutes at a lone, red-and-white cottage tucked deep in the woods off a gravel driveway. I'd slept for most of the drive but still felt loony from fatigue; my faculties didn't exactly improve when the first person I saw once I clambered out of the van was Lars, holding five pairs of waterproof boots. I couldn't look at him. I doubt he could look at me either. "These are for you," he said shortly, dropped the boots on the ground, and stalked off.

"What's with him?" Tom said.

"That's rich, coming from you," I shot back.

"Paulie . . ." Junior said in a warning tone. Tom just ignored me. Kevin was also ignoring me, and I was ignoring him. Junior wasn't ignoring anyone, though he was quieter than usual, but Becki was ignoring all of us, because she'd already put on her waterproof boots and was squelching about in the mud. It was misting, still, and freezing cold, so while we waited for the rest of production to arrive, Inga passed out navy-blue down vests that read *Sverige Och Mig* in small letters on the breast pocket. I took a Polaroid of Kevin looking like a wet rat. He scowled at me. "Are we going to be outside all day?" I complained, shaking the film. "Because I'm really cold and really tired." Everyone ignored me, including Inga. "And really wet."

"Shut up, Paulie," Kevin said as a small, blond pistol of a woman shot

out from the cottage's gabled entrance. She wore clompy boots, camouflage pants and jacket, and a camouflage trucker hat. Behind her trailed
two hunting dogs and a doting middle-aged man. "*Hej!*" she shouted to
us in a thick northern Swedish accent with a cigarette rasp, waving with
gusto. "You want to kill today?"

And just like that, I fainted. I'd never fainted before. Magnus said later
I'd looked like a tree—"The sound ha ha! Like big log falling!" The first
thing I saw when I opened my eyes was the blond pistol woman slapping
my face. Tears pricked my eyes; my cheek stung with needles. "*Hej! Hej!*"
she said. "You like this?" Whack, whack went her palm on my face. "You
want some more?"

"Ow—stop that—" I swatted her palm away. "Ow!" I struggled to
sit up on my elbows while Inga passed me a water bottle and Magnus
passed me an energy bar. Everyone was gathered around, staring, including the unblinking eye of Jonas's camera. Everyone except Lars.
"I'm great," I said with a mouthful of energy bar, getting on my knees
and holding a hand out to block Jonas's lens. "Really I'm fine. Nothing
to see here."

Still, Tocke exiled me to a plastic patio chair while the others filmed
the introduction to the episode. Turned out this tiny pistol woman,
Carolina, was the most famous female hunter in Sweden; the butler-
man, Hans, was her husband, fellow hunter, and biggest fan. Carolina
and Hans had had their own reality show on Swedish public television,
which had focused on a twenty-person hunting group they'd founded
that shared, in a socialist fashion, the spoils of their expeditions. It soon
became clear that Carolina was "out there," as my grandma would say.
As she spoke she lurched across the grass like she'd just gotten off a horse;
she'd frequently stomp her foot or thrust her fist into the air for emphasis.

"Here in Sweden we have something called *Allemansrätten* in our
constitution," she proclaimed while I drank orange juice from a child's
straw. "That means we can hunt, forage, walk, camp on all lands, but we
must not destroy or—" She searched for the word.

"Disturb," doting husband-butler Hans supplied.

"Yes, disturb. But not disturb-disturb—" Carolina circled her finger
around her ear. "More like, you must respect the people. Do not camp

too close to someone's *stuga*. Do not take all the morels and lingonberries like forest troll. It is the right for *all* people to use *all* the land in Sweden, not just you."

Becki said to Carolina: "Where I live in America—Texas—if someone trespasses on your property, you can force them off. You can't kill them but"—she paused, considering—"you can do pretty much anything else."

Carolina laughed at this. "Crazy, crazy," she said, shaking her head between guffaws. Then she said to Becki, without an ounce of hostility, "You and me, we have different ideas about property."

Now it was my turn to laugh. Carolina seemed to embody something I'd once heard about aikido: using an opponent's own energy to maneuver them gently to the ground. Becki opened her mouth, closed it, opened it again, closed it. Carolina smiled at her. "Guess we do," Becki said finally. "So what are we hunting today?"

We were hunting birds, it turned out. Becki and I would hunt with Carolina, and Tom, Junior, and Kevin would hunt with Hans. Because I'd never hunted before, let alone held a gun beyond the Nerf variety, I was placed in charge of the birdcall whistle while Becki peremptorily thunked Carolina's twelve-gauge shotgun over her shoulder. Tocke paired Lars, Magnus, and Jonas with the men, and we were paired with a crew I'd barely met, thank God.

"Got six of these at home," Becki explained to Carolina, gesturing to the gun as we tromped out into the woods behind Carolina's cottage. "Shooting range near my house has a great deal on date night. Me and my boyfriend go. Nineteen bucks a couple and his and hers lanes."

"Hmmm," Carolina said. I blew into my whistle. *TWEEEETTHH-HHBT! TWEEEEEEETTTHHHHHHBT!*

"Paulie, not like this." Carolina took the whistle away from me and blew into it gently. "Like this." *TWEE TWEEEBT.*

"Like this?" I blew again. *THEEEEBT! THEEEEBT!*

"No, like this." *TWEE TWEEEEBT.*

We went back and forth a few times until Becki stuck her fingers in her ears. *THEEEBT!* Soon I was tootling away like a fifer in brigade. And after an hour of rustling around in the woods, I blew into the whistle and a bird called back. I screamed. To talk to a bird! It felt like I had made an important discovery, something about the oneness of all things. I whistled again. The bird whistled back. My heart soared! My hangover abated! We're not so different, all living things!

"Even if we are trying to—you know," I said apologetically to the birch trees.

"Paulie!" Becki groaned. We had to change locations, needing the element of stealth and so forth. Then we changed again when I screamed again, slow learner that I am.

Finally, much later, after the rain had stopped, we settled on a mossy log somewhere deep in the forest, with the camera crew crouched on a boulder behind us. I worked the whistle, Carolina the binoculars, Becki the shotgun. We must have sat there for two hours while we called to the birds, who came close but not quite close enough to shoot. Besides the assassination element, it was a peaceful afternoon. We snacked on lingonberries and wild blueberries and whispered like schoolgirls about nature and deadly weapons. I told them that my great-grandmother Esther had become a hunter after immigrating to Minnesota because her husband went off logging for months at a time. My grandma said she had killer aim and knew every way to skin and cook a deer.

"And you've never shot a gun?" Becki whispered. I shook my head. "Do you want to try?"

"Oh," I whispered. "That's all right. I'll leave it to the experts. Thanks, though."

"Can we teach her?" Becki whispered to Carolina.

"She is too clumsy, no?" Carolina whispered back.

"It's really fine," I whispered, waving my hand. "I'm good."

"How can you say you hate guns when you've never even used one?" Becki whispered.

"I say the same thing about Danes!" Carolina whispered to us.

"I never said I hate guns!" I whispered. I hated guns.

"You didn't have to!" Becki whispered.

"But Danes, they throw good party!" Carolina whispered. "Come to Copenhagen, I show you! Crazy dancing! I drink many drinks, take many drugs. Bye-bye, Carolina!"

"Wait, what?" Becki whispered. "At a club? Which one?"

"My friend." Carolina made an obscene gesture. "In bathroom with big Dane."

"Fine!" I whispered. "Jesus! I'll shoot the stupid gun!"

So that's how I ended up on that mossy log, choked up on a twelve-gauge for the first time in my life, Carolina on my left side and Becki on my right. "That safety, that's your best friend," Becki murmured. "And here, I want your shoulders to go up and over—no, both feet planted—yup, even when you're sitting—eyes at the sight—the sight does it all for you—exhale when you pull—"

I closed my eyes. "For God's sake, open your eyes, Paulie," Becki said. I opened them and breathed and felt myself, briefly, at one with the gun. Then I pulled the trigger and felt it shudder into me along with a huge burst of adrenaline.

"Holy cannoli!" I stood up. The bullet appeared to have lodged into a tree, more or less where I was aiming.

"No, Paulie—be careful with the—"

Whoops, I'd put the muzzle of the gun straight into the dirt when I stood. Carolina grabbed it from my hands. Giddy with adrenaline, I gave Becki a double high five and hopped up and down. "That was incredible! You're such a good teacher!"

"Oh, it's nothing," Becki said, but I could tell she was pleased. "I think all females should know how to work this equipment—for safety reasons."

I wasn't sure I agreed, but I also wasn't sure that I cared. "I'm so glad you made me do it," I was babbling to Becki. "It was scary, and I didn't want to do it, but I did it." Carolina motioned to the crew to turn around. As we started walking I said, "Now I want to try something else I've never tried. Skydiving? Bungee jumping? Should I get a tattoo? And Becki, now it's your turn, I'm gonna make you do improv or something—"

"Ugh," Becki was saying. "Never, ever," as I crowed, "Yes and!"

THAT AFTERNOON, I basked in the healing powers of nature while also coming to the limits of what nature can do. For while I'd been enchanted by the birds and the brush with Carolina and Becki, enriched by the wild berries at my feet, and emboldened by firearms, I still had no idea how to solve the intractable clashes I had with my fellow cast members, let alone recover from that disastrous encounter with Lars, let alone fess up or even make peace with Declan about said encounter, dear impossible Declan, who was tending the proverbial hearth some thousands of miles away.

But that night, returning from the forest to Carolina's cottage, I decided that nature could at least help me fake it till I made it. As soon as we walked in the door and felt the warmth of the woodstove in the kitchen, I let the giddiness and bonhomie of our time in the forest carry me through the evening. We were all staying in the cottage that night along with Carolina and Hans, and I tried strenuously with my cast members to err on the side of solicitude: forgoing the small hot tub so they could enjoy it, showering last and in cold water, taking the smallest and mustiest bed. I imagined spending my remaining time in Sweden in the forest, marveling over ferns and moths, far above the human fray. And whenever anyone annoyed me or appalled me, Tom and Kevin especially, I would take to the trees and think about the nature of time and the miracle of existence. Yes, that was it!

I felt sure I'd cracked the code on being a person well into the next day. Under Carolina's supervision, we went foraging for chanterelles in the morning, then spent the afternoon learning to cook them in butter over an open fire. We also went about preparing a number of other typical Norrland foods: moose stew (with meat frozen from the previous fall's hunt), savory cheesecake, beef meatballs, gravy, potatoes, and lingonberry sauce. Becki and I were getting along splendidly after bonding over the shotgun, and Junior and I were thick as thieves, so when I heard Kevin give Hans advice about losing his "spare tire," or a drunk Tom tell Carolina about an off-the-grid militia he knew of in northern Wisconsin, I simply veered away like a cautious bumper-car driver. Lars seemed to have adopted a similar methodology, for I barely saw him all day. When I did he appeared to be birding, staring out at the woods with binoculars as Jonas gathered up B-roll.

Indeed, it seemed that the power of nature, coupled with Tocke deciding to use his immense power over us for good, had softened our jagged edges. We joked, clinked beers, felt our cheeks grow pink from cooking. With its outdoorsy sights and domestic smells, Carolina's land was by far the most pleasant location we'd had for filming. So pleasant, in fact, that by early evening, despite my strenuous attempts at its suppression, paranoia was brewing in my abdomen. *They have something up their sleeve*, my paranoia belched as I clattered pans in the cozy cottage kitchen, making the savory cheesecake. *But what?*

I found out soon enough. We sat down to our Norrland feast in the dining room with Carolina and Hans. The small room was packed: Lars's crew, the second crew, and Tocke were smooshed into the corners as the rest of us squeezed around the dinner table. After we *skål*ed with Norrland beer and exclaimed over the deliciousness of moose stew, I saw Tocke make eye contact with Carolina and give a small nod.

"So!" Carolina said in a falsely casual manner after swallowing a massive bite of moose stew. "As you learn these days, here in Sweden we have very, ah, strict laws about hunting. When to hunt, how to hunt, how to get weapon. But you know what we are not so strict about?" She looked at Hans, who mouthed a word to her. She nodded. "Abortion!

"I wish to tell you story. Hans and I, we have three beautiful children. But when I am pregnant first time, we find out baby has big genetic problem with brain. There no way he can survive in world. Yes, yes, this is very sad. I say, 'Doctor, what do we do?' She says we must end pregnancy. Hans and me, we cry and cry and say okay, fine, this is what we must do. We go next day to hospital. Everyone is so nice, and we pay no money. Someone even brings us cake! This is sad story, but it has happy ending, for I am pregnant with my daughter three months later.

"I want to tell you story because Tocke says that in America you do things opposite way. It very easy to get gun and very, ah, tricky to get abortion. He says that in some states, you cannot get any abortion but you walk into store and walk out with big weapon! Same day! On credit card so you are not even paying real money! For Hans and me, we do not understand this. Will you explain?"

The room suddenly got extremely hot, or so it seemed to me. I took off my sweater and scratched the skin beneath my wool socks. My heart was pounding. Why was I scared? I had no reason to be scared. *Above the fray,*

Paulie, above the fray. Kindness and reason, ferns and moths, what would
Pippi Longstocking—

"I mean, the Second Amendment is basically our *Allemansrätten*,"
Junior started. He was using his corporate-director voice: lower, crisper,
and less campy than usual. "Constitutional right to bear arms, never mind
its historical context. Personally I'd rather have an amendment about
public land use, 'specially after growing up in Utah, but that's America
for—"

"Personal responsibility," Tom chimed in. "You get a gun, you gotta
learn how to handle a gun. You get pregnant, you gotta learn how—"

Kevin shifted in his chair. "I grew up hunting. Been going since I was
a little kid. Dad bought me my first gun when I was twelve." Though this
was not remotely an answer to Carolina's question, it was also not a direct
endorsement of Tom's position.

"I've had an abortion." Becki shrugged. "Don't see what the big deal is."

I tucked my chin back. "In *Texas*?"

She shrugged again. "It was a little easier back then. Didn't have to
drive far."

Tom looked at Becki. "That surprises me."

Her voice sounded irritated. "Why?"

"More potatoes?" Hans asked me politely. I took the whole bowl.

"You strike me as a woman with a good head on her shoulders."

"I do have a good head on my shoulders." Becki's voice was icy. "Which
is why I got the abortion."

I felt compelled to jump in and defend her. "I'm surprised you care so
much, Tom. What's it to you whether she did or didn't?"

Tom, who I must remind you was, as always, drunk, started explaining
in a rambling fashion that while his dad had been Swedish, his mom, still
living, was Polish and a devoted Catholic, and while maybe he didn't go
to church every Sunday he still believed in everything it taught, for its
teachings had been around a lot longer than any government. Which of
course rankled me to no end, the way selective morality always will. "So
the whole, 'thou shalt not kill' thing," I interrupted. "You feel good about
applying that to Becki, but there's some wiggle room for folks going out
and buying assault rifles?"

Tom snorted. "I don't talk about guns with people who don't know anything about 'em."

Junior countered, "Couldn't Becki say the same thing to you about abortion?"

"I definitely think it should be harder to get a gun," Becki agreed, and I nearly dropped the potato I'd speared with my fork. She amended, "But I don't think there's anything wrong with guns. They're pieces of equipment. Would you ban chain saws if people were dying from chain saws? Do we ban plastic bags when kids put them over their heads?"

"And what about you?" Carolina said, turning to me, but I found my brain empty. Everyone I knew hated guns and supported a woman's right to choose, but because we were in total agreement, we rarely talked about such matters. Which is why all I said was: "They're both, um, public health issues? And, you know, like everything else in America, they're arbitrated by a bunch of rich old guys who—"

Tom snorted again. "Don't ask Paulie, she doesn't know anything. Doesn't even read the news."

"Um, yes I do!" I did not.

Kevin, glancing at the cameras, said, "I definitely think we should have more gun education. And even if I'm personally against abortion, I would be open to discussing it—"

"Open to discussing!" I burst out just as Tom shoved a whole meatball into his mouth and cried, "You wan' education? Go learn hishory—you remember why 'he Founding Fathers did wha' they did? 'Caush they were living under tyranny!" He wasn't bothering to chew. "A governmen' more consherned wi' isshelf than ish people! Like all thosh politishians! You think they give a rat's ass about you and me? Tryna tell us how to live, thinkin' they're better'n us, wouldn't last a day on the Soutsh Shide, I can tell you that." He was talking fast now, careening toward the decline of the American dream and Milwaukee in particular. It was the cri de coeur of a man aggrieved by and at odds with the world he found himself in. "And if the gangs in theshe inner shities wan' to all kill each other, and raise ten kidsh in poverty wif' shix different mothersh, well, I say, ish abou' pershona' reshponshibil—"

But then he stopped talking. His eyes bugged out, looking furious.

Insane. In the silence Kevin said to Carolina, "It's still the greatest country in the world. You should see the beaches where I live—sunshine, white sand, even the hurricanes can't—"

He was cut off when Becki jumped up from her chair, rushed around the table to Tom, stood him up, and started administering the Heimlich. At the moment I registered that Tom was choking, Becki punched him smack in the sternum with her fists. Half a meatball sailed out of his mouth, whacked me on the cheek, and rolled across the floor, stopping at Tocke's feet.

"Cut! Cut!" Tocke said as I wiped the saliva off my cheek.

"Jesus," Becki panted. "That was close."

Tom croaked, "Could've died, Tocke. You'd like that, wouldn't you?"

"Jesus!" Junior said. "Tom! Stop!"

"You think so, right? It's the greatest country in the world?" Kevin said, looking at Carolina. And then, after he saw her face: "You *don't*?"

I'M NOT SURE that was the conversation Tocke was hoping for when he staged that confrontation, but it was the conversation he got. Our discussion of guns and reproductive rights ended strangely, with Kevin spiraling into an existential crisis as it dawned on him that America, in Carolina's eyes, was a backward shithole; Becki ignoring Tom's feeble attempts at gratitude as she finished her moose; and my horror at Tom's awfulness, coupled with the horror of my own ignorance, getting sublimated via a thorough scouring of the kitchen, which Junior, thankfully, joined. Carolina and Hans went to bed as soon as they could, looking more tired than if they'd killed and gutted a sixteen-pointer. Tocke sent the crew packing. He gestured to Tom, who was supine on the kitchen bench. "Go to bed for chrissakes." I heard him swearing in Swedish on his way out the door.

"I'm going swimming," Becki said after they'd left. "Anyone wanna come?"

I raised my hand, made shy by Becki's quick thinking in a crisis and her brave admission of her abortion. I, too, had a strong urge to get out of the house and away from Tom's emotional geysering. He had not left the bench, at Tocke's instruction, but was double-fisting beers like some kind of Scandinavian Jabba the Hutt, his handlebar mustache drooping along with the air in the room. "Lemme just get my suit—"

"Oh, for God's sake, Paulie, who's gonna see us?" Becki said, halfway out the door. "The moose?"

Though the water was initially shallow in the lake at the edge of Carolina's property, it was still freezing. I yelped as I ran in to shoulder depth, covering my breasts with my hands. Becki was already swimming around like a dolphin, more at home than I'd ever seen her on land. "The Heimlich," I panted from the cold. "Where'd you learn that?"

Becki explained she was first-aid certified, as were all her employees. "Just in case something happens on the job," she explained matter-of-factly before she kicked off and swam away.

You never knew what talents people had, what might happen when their mettle got tested. I treaded water and contemplated the unknowability of other people, also the unknowability of myself. How could it be that I kept doing and saying things that did not make sense to the mind attached to the doings and sayings? Over time, the cool water relaxed my tense muscles and quieted these heady thoughts until all I could hear was the lapping of the water against my skin, the hum of insects, and the splashing of Becki in the water. The latter was distant at first but became less so. Until—

"Thanks for backing me up in there," she said from right behind me. I turned around.

"Anytime," I said, making figure eights with my hands. "Sorry Tom came at you like that."

"I should've let him choke." She laughed an uneasy laugh. "He's really on one right now, isn't he?"

"The mine set him off. I don't know why he's still here."

"Tom's head is so far up his ass—" Becki made figure eights with her hands too. "I didn't realize it at first, 'cause he was so quiet. But all he thinks about is himself—even more than the rest of us, and that's saying something. Like, I feel bad that Tocke made him go to the mine, but I'm also pissed. You know?"

"I do know." I started mirroring her in the water, making my figure eights like hers. Becki looked off in the distance.

"My dad was like that," she finally said.

A pause. "So was mine." I pictured him, my dad, sucking up admiration from people like a giant curly straw but always seeming empty. Pictured him sitting on my twin bed with the Pippi Longstocking comforter, explaining to me why I hadn't seen what I'd seen when I walked in on him and Len in his church office, continuing to talk and talk, shrinking me down and down, until his words weren't words, just a wall of sound, and I was tiny in size, a speck on a brightly colored bedspread, until he thought I couldn't see the cruelty and anguish lurking just beneath the surface of him, though I always did.

"I can't deal with that again," she said frankly. I knew better, somehow, than to ask exactly what she meant. Becki was like those cats who only snuggle you when they think you aren't paying attention. She stuck out her hand. "So. Let's make a deal. If either of us sees the other getting railroaded by Tom, we get them the hell outta there. And if helping the other in the competition means Tom'll go home sooner, we help each other too. Deal?"

"Deal."

We shook hands solemnly, naked in lake water, but as officious as if we were under oath. "You're all right, Paulie," she said, and I swear, something about the way she said it—it was one of the nicest things anyone's ever said to me.

I smiled. "You too."

"I hated you at first," she said amiably, rubbing her face like she was just waking up.

I laughed. "I hated you too."

"I still hate you," Becki conceded. "About fifty percent of the time."

"I still hate you too!"

She smiled at this. The loon cooed to us, the water caressed our sides, the leaves on the trees rustled their approval. Much seemed to pass between us in this brief silence, much seemed to be understood. Then Becki hugged her chest tightly. "I'm so cold!"

Come to think of it, so was I. My fingertips were turning blue. "I'm so cold too!"

"Oh my God," Becki said, heading for shore. "Stop copying me!"

I ran past her in the water. "Stop copying *me*!"

Together we ran screaming from the water, naked as can be, giggling like teens out after curfew. We huddled under too-small towels as we bolted back to the cabin, exposed but for the wet shoes on our feet. Becki held the door after she beat me to it and even let me shower first, and I guess that's when our friendship really began.

THE DAY DAWNED—OR really, it didn't dawn, since the sun was no longer setting—on our fourth competition day. Carolina and Hans made us all a giant breakfast of fried eggs, sausages, bacon, Swedish pancakes, and homemade toast with Carolina's cloudberry jam. Oh, and coffee of course, made the Norrland way, over an open fire and with cheese instead of milk. It was so hot and so strong it felt like one step away from just chewing on the beans, but I drank it gratefully. While Inga waited in the driveway, we thanked Carolina and Hans for their hospitality.

"Now it will be strange day for Hans and me," Carolina said as we zipped up our vests and suitcases. "American tornado came, American tornado leaving." She gave us each a small jar of cloudberry jam. "Now, bend over," she instructed, and obediently we complied. She snapped our rears one by one with a dog towel she kept by the front door. "For the competition. It means 'good luck' in Norrland."

"It does?" I asked, straightening and rubbing my gluteus minimus.

"No," Hans supplied politely from behind Carolina's shoulder.

After we loaded the van, Inga drove us to an open field about a half hour away from the cottage. There were glass beer bottles lined up on a fence, and a white circle spray-painted on the grass, but that's all I saw before Magnus pulled me aside and started fitting my microphone. Jonas sat me on a folding stool, and Lars began asking me the usual pre-competition questions for a sync. It was the first time we had locked eyes since the pool in Kiruna; at once my face and neck burst into flames. Lars, too, was beet red: unfortunately this made him even more good-looking, virile, even, like the flush of—*God, Paulie, stop!*

Instead of looking at me, Lars appeared to address his questions to the pine tree six feet to my right. "Are you nervous for the competition?"

"Yes, I am nervous for the competition," I said to the twelve inches of air above his head. I was trying very hard not to notice the tingling in my pelvis.

He coughed into his fist. "Do you hope to win today?"

"Yes, I hope to win today."

"Will you be sad to go home?"

"Yes, I will be sad to go home."

"Wow," Magnus said. "This is terrible."

"Really bad," Jonas agreed from behind the camera.

"That is good," Lars said to the pine tree. "You are done now."

"Done?" Magnus said. "This is worst interview I have seen!"

I tore off toward the other Americans, who were being greeted by affable host Erik Lundgren. "A marksmanship challenge," he was saying. "But you must only hit the bottles labeled with animals we can legally hunt in Sweden."

I squinted across the field toward the bottles, which were, in fact, labeled with impossible-looking Swedish words. "You will have one minute to memorize the list of animal names. It is hidden in a box out in the woods," Erik Lundgren said. "Then you will run back here, pick up your gun, and shoot the targets. The contest will be judged on speed and accuracy."

Terror rose up into my throat from my guts. I sat down on the grass. Visible relief passed across Becki's and Kevin's faces. I was toast. We all knew it. Bye-bye, Paulie. Bye-bye, Swedish family. Bye-bye, sticking it to Tom and/or Kevin. Bye-bye, finally belonging—

But true to her word, Becki dropped her naked ambition just as soon as it came over her. She plopped down next to me, told me to pay attention, and then, as she physically maneuvered my arms and shoulders to the correct position, went through the same checklist of shooting instructions she'd given me in the woods two days before. "You have a chance," she said. "Tom's memory's bad. Just don't give up too soon, all right?"

I nodded. I must have looked a fright, for she gazed at me pityingly and said the exact words my gym teacher used to say to me the day of the Presidential Fitness Test: "Oh, Paulie, just do your best."

I'M AFRAID I can't tell you what happened out there in the woods that day. You're going to have to look it up. What I remember exists only in flashes, like what a fox might recall after escaping an English hunt: crashing through the bushes; panicking when I couldn't find the hidden box with Swedish animal names; shouting, on repeat and with incorrect pronunciation, Swedish animals; running back to the field whilst still shouting; crying as I loaded the BB gun; forgetting how to load the BB gun; offering myself a pep talk while I flopped belly-down on the earth inside the spray-painted circle and took aim at the glass bottles. "You've got this," I said to myself. "I'm not afraid of you," I said to the gun. "This one's for you, Grandma Esther!" I said to the sky. "You and Pippi!"

By some miracle—perhaps the miracle of my friendship with Becki—I didn't miss a single shot out on the course. I limped off once I'd hit the last bottle and burst into a fresh round of tears. Kevin, who had completed the course already, was sitting on the sidelines, popping one of his pills into his mouth and shoving the orange bottle in his back pocket. He said, "And here I was thinking there is no God!"

I knew he was throwing back the exact words I'd said to him at his own nadir, but I was too overcome with humiliation to argue. I scowled at him, limped toward the far end of the field, and spent the next hour with my heart in my neck as Becki, Junior, and Tom went through the course. We waited around while the crew took an ill-timed but legally required break and then changed the cameras for the results shot. During this pause I ate a dozen cookies from a plastic bag I found on the ground and mentally composed my farewell speech. I also made plans for what I would drink on the plane (everything), eat on the plane (ditto), and the number of baths I would take upon my return.

Finally, at what seemed like the end of my Swedish adventure, affable host Erik Lundgren strolled out on the field wearing a crisp polo and windbreaker. "Congratulations, Becki, you are the winner of this competition," he said.

Becki's mouth opened in surprise. Kevin looked like he wanted to turn Erik Lundgren to stone. "You did it!" I threw my arms around Becki. "My hero!"

"Which means the sad news is next," Erik Lundgren continued. A pregnant pause, during which I considered whether to take potshots at Kevin during my farewell address. Yes. No. Yes. No. Yes—

"Tom, I am afraid you are going back to America."

"*What?*" Kevin said.

"*What?!*" I said.

"*What?*" Junior, who was only slightly more familiar with guns than me, said.

"*What?!*" Becki said joyfully.

"It's 'cause I threw it!" Tom burst out. "Listen, everybody, I threw it! I threw it! I threw it because I don't want to be here anymore! So actually I didn't lose." He was lurching toward Erik Lundgren, then lurching toward the crew, then lurching back to us in a Frankenstein fashion. "I choose to go home, you little fuckers. Okay? I'm the winner here!" he shouted to Tocke. "I'm the winner! Sick of your bullshit mind games. You better believe, the first thing I'm doing when I get home is calling up a reporter—no, a goddamned lawyer—and we're gonna—"

Tom's tantrum devolved into a tapestry of obscenities, delivered with such physical passion it became almost slam poetry. It took four crew members to corral him into a corner of the field. The rest of us busied ourselves with post-competition syncs, and I avoided looking Tom's way until we climbed back into the van. What I saw surprised me: he was taking a group photo of the entire crew with his DSLR camera, and then handed it off to chipper producer Anna, so he could go stand in the middle with all of them and say cheese. He beamed and gave two thumbs-up. I nudged Becki, made her look. "What the hell?"

She rolled her eyes. "He's the center of attention. Of course he's happy."

We hit the road, and Inga turned on the music. Swedish rap, which I understood about as much as I understood anyone or anything, which is to say not at all. We drove in silence for a while. Then Junior said, "Call me crazy, but I kind of miss Tom."

"I was just thinking that," Becki said.

"*What?*" I said. "After all that?"

"He took a great picture of me and Kevin," she mused, turning back to look out the window. It was raining, which made the world look blurry and unfocused, like an Impressionist painting. "In front of the palace in Stockholm. Didn't he, Kevin?"

"Isn't it wild he won fifteen thousand dollars on *Wheel of Fortune*?" Kevin mused.

"'Member when he threw up on the ferry?" Junior said. "And his big, strong seamen?"

I let out a ha-ha despite myself. "Okay, but Tom has problems."

"Big problems," Junior agreed.

"And all the talk about his *farfar's farfar*?" Kevin said to Becki. Becki laughed. I laughed. Again. Despite myself. Again. Kevin continued, "And how the whole time we were in Stockholm he was whistling?"

"Tom's . . . special." Becki sighed. And the way she said "special," it wasn't good, but it wasn't bad either. Which I guess is what Karen Hamburger means when she says real smarts is just letting opposite truths work together in your brain, much like patting your head and rubbing your belly simultaneously.

CHAPTER EIGHT

HERREGUD!

"I have to tell you something," I said to Declan on the phone the following night.

"I have to tell you something too," he said, sounding hesitant.

I'd spent the entire day in my room at the Rival, the same Stockholm hotel as last time, leaving the king-sized bed only to go to the bathroom or the minibar. Tocke had given us another three-day leave after shooting two episodes back-to-back, and I'd vowed to use these days to get my head on straight, sleep well, eat right, make amends. I'd start a meditation practice, gratitude journal, steam myself clean in the sauna. I'd start just as soon as I finished the minibar.

I broke off another chunk from a tombstone-sized bar of Marabou chocolate and shoved it in my mouth. "You firs'."

"Okay," he said. I heard the turning of pages, the clicking of his mouse. "Actually, no—will you?"

I shoved another piece of chocolate in my mouth. *Courage, Paulie!* "Okay, but befo' I say anythih' I wan' you to know how sorh'y I am. You know thi' i' very unlike me. Or, I mean, mo'shly unlike me—"

"Okay," he said again, sounding even more nervous. "What is it?"

I'd rehearsed a lot of different versions of my confession in front of the bathroom mirror, explaining to an imaginary Declan why and how I'd ended up having feelings for Lars, which had culminated in a sexually charged yet chaste pas de deux at an illegally accessed hotel pool inside the Arctic Circle. The problem was that I felt Declan needed context, and where, exactly, was I supposed to start? With the history of Kiruna? The sinkhole and its filling? The psychological effects of the midnight sun? Reality television? International travel? Tom spiraling? Brock leaving? The male gaze? Stockholm syndrome? Attachment theory? Or should I go back even further, *Tristram Shandy*-style, to the first time I cried as an infant and my mother walked away instead of nursing me?

"I—" I said. My mouth was dry. I took a swig of pomegranate bubbly water. It was too bubbly. Also too pomegranatey. I coughed. "I—" A surge of panic filled my chest. I opened my mouth. "Have you ever shot a gun before?"

I scrunched up my face and covered it with both hands, letting the receiver dangle. "What?" I heard Declan say. "A gun? No. Why?"

"Well, I have," I said, horrified and relieved by my evasion. I broke off another piece of chocolate and put the receiver back to my ear. "A twelve-gauge. And it went straight into a tree and I didn't like it but I didn't hate it, and I had so much adrenaline after that Carolina made me run circles around her house with her vizslas before I went inside—"

"Who's Carolina?" Declan was saying. "Don't you need a license for that?"

"I guess we were licensed by proxy?" I said. I wasn't sure how a person could mangle a confession of emotional infidelity into a discussion of Swedish gun licensure, but here we were. "Becki taught me how to shoot, she's a good teacher, owns a bunch of them I guess—and it's not like they made me do it or . . ." I paused. "Come to think of it, I guess there was some degree of obligation—"

"I don't like it at all," he said darkly. Then: "Becki? The bully?"

"I may have to walk that back." I curled the receiver wire around my fingers. "Due to developments in—"

"Of course they brought up guns," Declan was saying. "The show's a parody at this point. What's next, a football game? Beer bongs? Or maybe you'll form a mob and storm a government building?"

"No, no, it's a Swedish thing, hunting up north," I explained. "With Carolina. She's famous for hunting. We learned where our food comes from and slept at her house, and I ate moose—so good—oh, and Becki's had an abortion, she's actually very pro-choice—she and I have similar, you know, daddy issues—"

"Who owns guns anyway?" Declan interrupted. And then: "*Abortion?*"

"But Declan." I fished a few Haribo gummies off the top of the night-stand. "Don't you ever feel bad that we don't kill our food ourselves? That we buy meat all chopped up from the supermarket with no idea what kind of life the animal led or how it died?"

"No," he said. "It's impossible to live an ethical life under the conditions of late capitalism."

"Well, I do," I said, thinking of Carolina's moose stew. "What about the Dalai Lama?"

"I doubt Becki's using her guns to make beef chili. The Dalai Lama eats meat."

"How do you know?" I said. "And she *could*. You shoot people all the time in your video games. What about Greta Thunberg?"

"They're not guns, they're bellowblast spikethrowers." Declan paused. "Greta's a child."

"She's a very responsible gun owner," I said, my voice rising slightly. "Becki, I mean, not Greta Thunberg. I don't know if she owns guns or not. She might be too young."

"Of course Greta doesn't own a gun," Declan said with a scoff.

"Becki runs a class at her local range on female self-defense. And how do you know she doesn't have a gun? She might."

"Because I know," Declan said with that same confidence I'd heard in Brock's voice, the kind I could never find within myself.

"You're always so sure about everything," I said. I was getting warm. I sat up off the pillows, leaned forward, loosened the belt of the hotel robe. "What about those of us who aren't sure of anything? Don't we deserve a chance to, um, think about things? Shoot a gun to make sure we don't like it? Just because I'm confused all the time doesn't mean I don't have, you know . . ." I was flailing. "Thoughts about . . . policy . . ."

"Paulie," Declan said. He said it gently, the way you might coax a dog at the Humane Society. "Paulie, are you losing your mind?"

The answer was yes. "No," I said indignantly. "Actually, I am finding it. Here in Sweden. My mind is very good in the social-welfare environment. Very strong and . . . healthy . . . and capable of making good decisions . . . and reversing course if certain decisions are maybe not so good . . ."

"Jemma said you left her a really weird voicemail when you were in Lapland. And you never called me back from the hotel."

"Oh, well, that was the bear's fault," I said.

"The bear," Declan repeated. "The bear's fault."

"There was this brown bear in Kiruna, and I looked at him, or it was more of a mind-meld situation—" This had come out a lot better in my bathroom rehearsals. "Anyway, he had a lot of integrity. Or she. They. I'm learning a lot—"

"From the bear?"

"From everybody!" I practically shouted. "This is a mind-altering experience! And I'm sorry if . . ."

"If what?" he said after a pause.

I knew what I was sorry for. And I was really sorry. I just didn't have the courage to say it.

"If *you* don't *get* it," I finished.

"Nice," he said. And he did not sound nice. "Really nice."

"You can't just write Becki off like that. You don't know her like I do."

"True. I only know what you tell me."

"Okay," I said, getting heated again. "But I never told you she was a—"

"You called her a domestic terrorist."

With a pink face I said, "Okay, but I didn't mean it like that."

"And you're right, I don't get it," Declan said, growing rather heated himself. "That's what I was going to tell you. I don't get how someone as smart as you could get sucked into all this bullshit."

"It's not bullshit."

"You actually believe the stories these producers are telling you.

But you're not who you are because of the narratives they're spinning—you're not even Swedish—"

"Yes, I am!" I cried.

"I'm telling you," he said, and in his voice was a new kind of urgency. "That Holocaust study everyone was talking about a few years ago—with the inherited trauma? Turns out it's junk science, they only studied a few descendants."

"Oh, big whoop," I said. "The real problem here is that you've never been on board with the show, and now you're trying to ruin it for me."

"Paulie, I'm serious," Declan said, and the words came out impassioned, blunt and sure: "They're manipulating you. Nothing you're learning has any basis in fact. You really want to live in a world where you're doomed to high blood pressure because your grandpa had PTSD? Nobody knows for sure what gets passed down in generations. No one's ever known. All we do is tell stories, and you're not even deciding for yourself what stories you want to keep—you're just letting them shove them down your throat, one after another. The DNA sites they're probably using for research? They're junk, too, and racist. You know that if you have African ancestry, all they'll point you to is 'Africa'?"

"*That's* what you've been waiting to tell me all week?" I said, feeling my jaw clench. "We've barely talked and you want to give me a term paper?"

"I'm trying to help you," Declan said, exasperated. "Get through this on your own terms. You can say no to them. You don't have to shoot a gun or talk about your trauma or be grateful. They're the ones who should be grateful. You're too open—they don't deserve this much of you—"

"I am on my terms!" My voice rose shrilly. "They're just not your terms! I'm sorry I can't sit at home with you all the time making judgments in front of a screen. Something extraordinary is happening to me here! I can feel it! And I'm grateful I get to feel it! Why do you always have to stick a pin—"

"Because what you're calling extraordinary, I'm calling extreme to the point of being unhealthy," he said. "And I'm worried, and I don't like it. I want to be in real life. With you. Actual reality. Not some three-episode arc a producer—"

"Well, I don't like reality," I said, surprising myself as the words came out. "I like it here. At least here people change. We're not just stuck in the same old—I see new things and hear new points of view—and people actually listen to each other—and it's like—" I sucked in a breath. "Of course I'm made out of who and what came before me. What else would I be made of?"

"What you do now," Declan said simply. "What you did yesterday. What you plan to do tomorrow."

I was so hurt by this. Why was I hurt? Because it was true, maybe, or because it shone a harsh light on my behavior, or maybe, just maybe, deep down, I wanted Declan to cut the analysis and reassure me that, despite our mounting distance, we would be all right. I wanted his affection, not his concern and ideas, which for him were, in fact, tokens of affection, laid at my feet as evidence of care and effort.

But who was I to demand this? To coerce Declan into giving me exactly what I wanted? I, the liar? The scoundrel?

"Fine," I said in lieu of anything meaningful. "Agree to disagree."

"Fine," he said, apparently in the same frame of mind.

How human beings are able to communicate anything at all with this crummy language is a mystery to me.

AFTER WE HUNG up, I plopped down on the bed with a pen and a pad of hotel paper. I needed to think, to process, to clear my head, to heal. *Dear Diary*, I wrote, and paused to lick the top of the ballpoint, the way writers did in the movies. I hadn't kept a diary since the fourth grade, and its sole concern was Ben Meltzer, what with his bowl cut and diamond ear stud. After staring into space, I scribbled, *It's been two and a half weeks.* Another pause. *And so much has happened.* I paused. I tapped the pen on my chin. I took a drink of water from the bedside table and adjusted the pillows behind me. How did Deborah do this? Writers in the movies made it look so easy, but most of the actual writers I'd heard of had become drunks and/or insane. Hmmm. Perhaps it was best not to risk—

Bam, Bam, Bam. A fist on the door. I threw the pen and paper on the floor and rushed to open it so fast you might have thought there was a gigolo on the other side. Junior was standing there wearing sunglasses and holding a split of minibar champagne. "I got Lars's number from Inga." He waggled his eyebrows. "You wanna go out with him and Magnus tonight?"

I hadn't told Junior about what had happened in Kiruna, and I didn't think I could stand to. "Oh—" I gripped the doorframe. "Probably not. Declan and I got in a fight, and I'm super tired, I don't think I'm up for it—plus I don't think Lars is, um, my biggest fan—"

"What are you talking about? He asked if you were coming."

I felt my heart leap from my stomach to my throat. "He did?"

"Come onnnnnnn," Junior said, swanning past me through the open door. He was wearing the metallic blazer he'd found at a thrift store the last time we were in Stockholm. Humming, he pulled a CD off the built-in rack and slipped it into the player. Lykke Li—I'd forgotten she was Swedish. Junior was popping the champagne and dancing around the room, singing about getting blown to pieces. And then: "What else are you gonna do, huh? Sit around and mope?"

I perched on the edge of a Scandinavian-design chair. "For your information, I was writing in my diary."

Junior poured us both coffee mugs of champagne. "Paulie, you don't keep a diary."

"How do you know?!"

He looked me up and down. "Okay, fine," I conceded. "But I *could.*"

The combination of dream pop, champagne, and Junior's staunch refusal to let me wallow in self-pity meant that twenty minutes later we were striding out of the hotel, Junior in his metallic blazer and me in a denim bustier jumpsuit he'd picked out for me during the same shopping trip. "Very ABBA," he'd said with approval when I emerged from the bathroom, self-consciously adjusting my boobs.

"Maybe I should put on something else." I looked down at the bustier, which was not that far off from the bosom-forward looks at Viking Week. "It's a little—"

"Absolutely not," Junior said, and hustled me out the door before I could protest or change.

We walked for ten minutes down Sankt Paulsgatan to a place called the Champagne Bar, which Lars had suggested. On the top floor of a brick building at the edge of a cobblestoned square, with velvet couches, parlor palms, and backlit bar, the place had a roaring twenties gestalt—coupe glasses, plush banquettes. Without phones, we had a hard time finding Lars amidst the packed crowd, but eventually we came upon him and Magnus sitting outside on the rooftop terrace with a bottle of champagne and four glasses. They stood when they saw us. Lars looked different in his "civilian" clothes—a leather jacket and white T-shirt. "Hello," he said to us formally, like a butler at an English manor house.

"Hello." I stuck out my hand. He shook it. We stood there like fools, our hands bobbing up and down. Magnus looked at us quizzically. Junior rolled his eyes, and under his breath I think he said something about straight people, though the music was so loud it was hard to tell. He signaled to the server to bring us two more bottles—thanks to that corporate money of his, I rarely had to buy my own drinks—and it didn't take long for us to drop the awkwardness and formality, thanks to the deformalizing social lubricant known as champagne.

"Thanks for inviting us out!" I shouted in Lars's ear over the thumping sounds of EDM. He had yet to mention anything about Kiruna, and I was pleased he'd seemed to follow my suggestion that we pretend it never happened. "That was nice of you!"

He nodded and smiled, raised his champagne flute. We clinked and drank. Thump, thump went the music. Across the table, Junior and Magnus were engaged in a serious conversation that went something like this:

Junior: "Barbra."

Magnus: "Liza!"

Junior: "Liza?! Are you crazy? You mean Judy."

Magnus: "I take this back. Céline Dion!"

At this, Lars and I looked at each other and laughed. It's fun to conspire with another person, think the same things are funny. It had been months since Declan and I had been on a similar page. I remembered our argument from earlier and blanched internally, then glugged more champagne. "So what do you do when you're not dealing with crazy Americans?"

It was maybe the first question I'd asked Lars, rather than the other way around. He lit up to the extent that a reserved Swede can—maybe twenty watts—and pulled out his phone. On the camera roll was a series of images taken from a public housing complex outside Stockholm. Women in hijabs, men sitting around a table talking, children playing on a dilapidated playground. "A documentary—how do we integrate asylum-seekers?!" he shouted, scrolling through the pictures.

Swedish House Mafia boomed through the speakers, begging children not to worry. Through the din I heard only snatches of Lars's description: "It is a very difficult problem in Sweden! The Swedish Democrats grow every year . . . neo-Nazis . . . language barrier . . . violence in the areas . . . we want them to access jobs and education but . . . 'Swedes for the Swedish' . . . and how do they keep their culture, but not so much that they are isolated . . ."

"Mmmmhmmm!" I nodded, trying to appear interested. Which I was. Yet I was also quite interested in the line of his jaw, the way his thumb flicked across the phone screen just so. Even though I knew I wasn't supposed to be. Especially because I knew I wasn't supposed to be. I wanted to open him up like a hinged door and rummage around until I'd found everything about him, everything that made him, him. I wanted to be an explorer again, tasked with the uncharted, the wondrous, the novel, in lands free of my own dirty footprints and bad habits.

Meanwhile, Lars was saying something about anti-Islamic sentiments in Europe, and then something about Chekhov. The beat dropped with a subwoofing thunk.

"Chekhov! I know him!" I caterwauled. "I've heard *Lolita*'s really good!"

"It is hard to hear you!" he shouted. He motioned to the terrace edge. "Would you like to go talk over there?"

Of course I did. Whether I should have or not was another question. I heard Declan scolding me for being easily manipulated, and out of some mix of spite and desire I stood up and followed Lars to the railing. He kept close to me as we walked. The air seemed to get very quiet then, despite the throngs of people, the clinking of glasses, the Swedish House Mafia. In front of us, the city stood, stately and timeless, lights twinkling and rippling across the canals. It was so beautiful, so startlingly unfamiliar, that it only turbocharged this intoxicating little game I'd started weeks ago called Pretend.

"What would have happened if they stayed?" I heard myself say, letting my hands play the wrought-iron railing like a piano. "My family, I mean. This would all be normal. And my normal wouldn't have to be normal. The strip malls and the highways and the . . ." I let my thoughts drift. "Everyone so scared all the time, thinking they'll run out of money . . ."

"But America is your home," Lars said. He was standing very close behind me. I could feel his leather jacket brush against my bare back, smell his cologne. "You are not homesick?"

"I don't know." I was shaking my head.

"What about your boyfriend?"

"We're not . . . things aren't so great between us right now."

He said nothing.

"I'm sorry I didn't say anything earlier about him. I should have."

I thought we might get into it, then, what had happened at the pool. Recrimination, rebuttal, reversal, refusal. Instead all he said in a husky voice was, "Why are they not so great?"

I turned around to face him. His eyes traveled from my face to my breasts to my hips, then back up again. My body clicked into a heightened gear as I met his gaze. There was, of course, much I could say to Lars to try to explain the impasse at which Declan and I had found ourselves. Different sensibilities, different perspectives, different continents, for heaven's sake. I could complain about his stick-in-the-mud-ness, his cynicism, his criticism, at least partially warranted, of *Sverige och Mig*, which Lars had been loyal to for ten years running. I could protest about not feeling understood or seen. But it turned out I did not want to talk, in the same way I did not want to write in my diary. Language, however crude, has a clarifying effect when used honestly, and at the moment I wanted to stay intoxicated, no matter how badly I'd feel the next day.

Which is why I said nothing, simply turned back around, and brought Lars's arms around me so his hands were resting on my hips. Goose bumps flooded my bare arms. I heard his breath catch. The denim jumpsuit was so tight, I might as well have been naked. I felt his warm breath on my back.

"Just friends," I said lightly, "enjoying a night out together."

Silently, he adjusted his arms around me. I leaned back against him, allowed my body to sing with desire without the caesura of guilt or responsibility, felt the cool night breeze caress my face.

"You smell nice," Lars murmured into my ear as my mind tunneled deeper into the past.

I tumbled through the game of Pretend and turned again to look at him. And beyond him. At the prospect of a new home, of Paradise, of beginning again . . . a new self, a new place, with no mistakes in it. My great-grandmother had started over. Why couldn't I? All she had to pay was everything.

In the near distance, an elevated subway car rattled on toward Gamla Stan. Lars put both his hands on my shoulders, then let them move down my arms. My hair was standing on end; I was shivering, but I was not cold. In the blue light of two a.m., his face was blurred, as if I were looking at him through water. From the heat in his body I felt his desire to overpower me, felt, too, my desire to be overpowered—

For to be overrun by forces was one way to avoid making choices on purpose. Let Lars choose for me, I thought without thinking. Kiss me or don't. Here not there, this man and not that: let history decide, let fate. Let climate change decide, let billionaires, let social media and TV. That way, if things went sideways, I could not be held responsible. If things already were sideways, I was not responsible for that either.

But the moment, pregnant with possibility and portending unknown futures, was cut short, along with the music. A sound system squealed, and then I heard a familiar melody. It was a song from the musical *Pippin*, and I knew there was only one person in the bar ridiculous enough to stop a party in its tracks to sing it. I took Lars by the hand and propelled him back indoors, where we found Junior standing on a velvet banquette as Magnus recorded his performance of "Corner of the Sky" with his phone.

"You Americans!" Magnus said when he saw us. "You are crazy!"

The way Magnus said this, it was not an insult, but an exclamation of fact, like remarking on the size of a cheese plate. Junior had a beautiful voice—he'd studied musical theatre at Northwestern—and a level of showmanship that made the chic, city-slicking Stockholm crowd clap instead of wrinkling their noses. When he was finished, he took a giant bow, then leapt off the banquette and bowed again. Everyone applauded some more, he worked the crowd for a minute or two, and then he sauntered back to us with a canary-eating grin.

"Crazy, crazy," Magnus said, shaking his head. "Why are you all so crazy?"

"Oh, you love it," Junior said. "You're the one who dared me!"

Lars and I looked at each other and laughed. And while I'm not sure if Junior or Magnus noticed, behind this laugh was a whole lot of unfinished business.

THE NEXT TWO days were strange, disjointed, like a dream skipping from one scene to another without transitions. Eating dinner outside in broad daylight at ten p.m. Flipping through paperbacks at a bookstore and not recognizing any words. Ordering kanelbullar and stumbling over the pronunciation, even though my grandma had taught me from an early age. Wandering through a solo show at Moderna Museet, oil portraits composed of imaginary people. Getting chased by geese through Skeppsholmen. Getting lost in the tiny gardens of Långholmen, on the grounds of a former prison. I know I talked to Declan again, and to Jemma, but I can't remember a single word either of them said, save this from Declan: "Paulie, I have never heard you sound so tired."

At the dawn of the fourth day, after a continental breakfast of such marvelous breadth that I ate pancakes, croissants, chia pudding, *and* eggs Benedict, Inga picked up Kevin, Becki, and me—Junior was whisked off for his own "special day"—and drove us several hours until we arrived at the shores of a beautiful blue lake. Atop a crisp, green lawn, multiple two-story red buildings were strewn about like Monopoly hotels. Blond, barefoot children ran about, shouting happily; blond, barefoot teens made bead necklaces at a picnic table. On the periphery, two camera crews were shooting B-roll: wildflowers waving in the breeze, kids paddling canoes, and a suffering Christ figure on a wooden cross staked into the grass.

This was Christ Church, Inga informed us from the van's front seat, a Pentecostal Bible camp where we would be spending the next two days. She'd been cleared by Tocke to explain that the next episode would focus on the history of Christianity in Sweden.

"But my dad always said Sweden's the most secular country in the world," Becki said from the passenger seat.

"Yes, this is the point," Inga said. She was wearing a lavender power suit. "You are learning about Swedish culture, but this is also Sweden—a part most Swedes do not see." She sipped her iced coffee through a straw. "I almost feel bad, leaving you." She put the cup back in the holder and cleared her throat. "But this is my job, yes? And this is your job? I will pick you up tomorrow night, okay?"

We heaved our suitcases onto the gravel drive and watched Inga depart. My stomach was knotting up, the way it always did when I got within a country mile of a church. I hadn't gone since my mom got too drunk to force me. "Take me with you," I said wistfully to the back of the van and the dust it kicked up. Meanwhile, an eerily wholesome man in a denim shirt and Birkenstocks was walking toward us, with Lars, Jonas, and Magnus in tow. Lars smiled at me. I tucked my hair behind my ears and smiled back.

"Americans, you are welcome!" the man said in English, opening his arms like Jesus in *The Last Supper*. This was Karl Karlsson (you can't make this stuff up), camp pastor and television evangelist. His thin fingers, thin blond mustache, and small eyes had a rodentine quality; a meek woman scurried behind him with a baby in her arms. "We have a very special program planned for you today. You are just in time for the war!"

Before anyone could clarify what "war" entailed, I was yanked away by a mob of giggling tweens, who moved with such efficiency I barely clocked they were painting my face yellow and tying my hair into pigtails with yellow ribbon. "*Gul! Gul! Gul!*" they chanted, their youthful breath smelling of licorice.

"Ghoul?" I asked as someone wiggled my arms into a yellow wind-breaker. "Like a ghost?"

"No!" said a darling blond. "Like yellow for Team Yellow!" How did these children speak such excellent English?

When I was yellow as a corncob from tip to toe, the giggling tweens led me to a scraggly field on the other side of the camp, where a brusque, athletic woman wearing a referee shirt was blowing a whistle and screaming instructions in Swedish. Here, we members of Team Yellow began running three-legged races, racing eggs on spoons, relaying with balloons, passing Hula-Hoops, spinning around on baseball bats, and digging a hole in the ground so big—this is not an exaggeration—we could have buried a horse.

This last game, seeing as it was not a game, but a punishment once reserved for prisoners of war, confounded me. I asked our team captain, Oliver, to explain. Oliver, who was aged eleven, plump, and buck-toothed, ran a tight ship and spoke impeccable English. He rolled his eyes. "Paulie, whichever team digth the biggeth hole winth!"

"Okay, well, what's the prize?" I was in the hole, digging, as I said this, up to my ears in dirt.

"Free ice cream," piped up another teammate, a spritely girl named Olivia.

"How 'bout I just buy you ice cream?" I heaved a mound of dirt out of the hole.

Oliver threw up his hands. "Thath not the point!"

Was there a point? I wasn't seeing the relevance to Christianity here, unless it was about obedience to mysterious overlords. Or maybe the ice cream was supposed to represent heaven and our futile toil the strug-gles of Job? Hours seemed to pass in that hole. Just before I was going to throw down the shovel and ask God why he had forsaken us, Karl Karlsson blew his whistle. The blue team, which counted Kevin among its members, had apparently used one of the kids' phones to hire a back-hoe from a nearby farm-equipment outfit. Their hole was six times the size of ours. Game over.

As Karl Karlsson passed out individually wrapped ice creams, Kevin held up a hand, saying loudly for the camera's benefit that he didn't eat processed sugar. Several kids looked fearfully down at their cones. He remained high on his own supply even hours later, after Lars had called for a filming break. It was early evening by then, with a still-high sun, and the sky and lake were the same rich shade of blue as we dragged our suitcases toward the sleeping bunks. Twentysomething counselors were manning enormous grills while teens brought out plates and cups from the mess hall.

"You cheated," I said to Kevin, unable to help myself from the sour cherry of self-righteousness.

"It's not cheating," he snapped. "When did Karl say anything about not calling for help?"

"You broke the norms, then," I snapped back. "Karl shouldn't have to *say* anything about not ordering a backhoe like an Uber."

"You're just mad you didn't think of it," he said smugly, and sped past me toward the male bunks.

Karl's meek wife, whose name I still didn't know, joined Becki and me on the gravel path. "Good evening," she said, her eyes lowered and her posture as bent as a hanger. "I show you to room." She led us to a windowless, cobwebby log cabin, whose sole light source was the slits in the splintered walls. "This is—you sleep here—" she said, and then covered her face with her hands. "I so sorry—my English—"

"Your English is wonderf—" I said, but then forgot to finish the sentence. From the smell, it seemed that someone had recently died in this shack. Or was murdered? Horrified, I ran back outside, just in time to see Junior and Kevin get ushered by rodentine Karl Karlsson into a cheery, two-story cottage, complete with checked curtains and excellent lake views.

"You are welcome to stay forever!" Karl Karlsson was saying to them, tapping the pads of his fingers together in a sinister fashion. "Many find God in this place!"

I ran back into the shack. "Wait till you get a load of this," I said to Becki, who was plopped on the dirt floor, eating a bag of potato chips. Karl Karlsson's meek wife had already scuttled away.

"So?" Becki said once I'd pushed her outside and showed her the men's cabin. She fished around the bottom of the chip bag and licked a few crumbs off her fingers.

I put my hands on my hips. "Well—don't you think that's unfair?"

She shrugged. "Since when's life fair?"

"Um, well, legally, it's supposed to be fair," I said. "Haven't you heard of Title IX?"

"You know I'm not a feminist." She crinkled her empty chip bag. "I don't care, I can sleep anywhere. You know, Paulie, not everything has to be a big deal."

I bristled. "Name *one* thing I've made a big deal about since we started filming."

She snorted and counted on her chip-powdered fingers. "When you tried to get us to strike on the first day, when you started a fight with the host on Gotland because girls weren't allowed to be Vikings—"

"That wasn't a fight, that was a discussion—"

"When you told Kevin he couldn't say the word r—"

Speaking of the devil, an idiom never more apt, Kevin emerged just then from his cheery cottage wearing a white ribbed tank and tight jeans. He sauntered toward us with his hands in his pockets, and from a distance I felt I could see him clearly, which Karen Hamburger says applies to most things in life. He was shorter than average; his ears were too big for his head. At this vantage his confidence seemed shallow, over-reliant on self-improvement and big muscles. He tossed one of his corny salesman smiles at us as he approached. "Nice place you got here."

"Want to switch?" I said, not kidding.

He laughed. "We're good."

"Guess chivalry really is dead."

Kevin smiled again. "That's for chicks I wanna bang, not you freaks."

Becki had the gall to laugh at this.

"*Chicks?*" I said, blood boiling as Kevin peered inside the shack.

"That's a lot of cobwebs." He waved a hand. "Smells like shit."

"Go to hell," I said.

Kevin nodded toward the shack. "Nah, you've got it covered."

I couldn't help myself. "You're a horrible person."

"And you're a spoiled brat."

That set my kettle screaming. In Pippi's world, bad guys—robbers, circus ringmasters, pedantic biddies, greedy millionaires—could always be brought around—or at least neutralized. Robbers softened by a bit of *fika*, biddies drowned out by children's cheering, millionaires lifted up off Pippi's property and plopped back in the front seat of their expensive cars. But in our world, the real world, the world of adults, counteracting malice was not so easy. Perhaps because, for adults, malice was not only an external threat: its potential lurked inside us, like the Epstein-Barr virus, which Else confidently asserted without a medical license was the root cause of all disease. Thus I continued in this vein and not another: "Were you born this way, Kev? Were you not hugged enough as a child? Or were you bullied for being smaller than the other boys on the playground? Help me understand why you're such a—"

"No, Paulie, help me understand."

"Understand *what*?"

Kevin glanced at Becki, who was watching all this with a nonplussed expression. "Why you're so goddamned sensitive."

"Sensitive!" I cried. "As if I'm the only one here who's sensitive! Ever wonder why *men* are never called sensitive? You never called *Tom*—"

"Why's it so important to you, what words we use?" Kevin said. "I'm tired of having to be so careful—"

I interrupted. "Right, right, I know your fascist podcasting bros think they're too cool for—"

"It's like, no shit your dad's a minister, all you wanna do is tell other people how to live—"

"Kevin, chill, don't talk about her dad," Becki was saying. But it was too late: his words had already smacked the big red button on my heart that read Do Not Touch. I could think of no worse insult than being compared to my father, unless, of course, it was being compared to my mother. I bellowed something about how he didn't even know me, and how my father should not be characterized as a minister but a disgraced former minister who happened to be dead, thank you very much, and then Kevin shot back that I was only proving his point, and then I stormed off. Luckily or un-, it was hard to say, I ran straight into Lars, who was tasked with rounding us up for the evening worship service. We hadn't had a chance to talk all day. Sunlight burst through the thunderclouds in my chest.

"Hey," he said, smiling.

"Hey." I couldn't help but smile back.

"How was your day?"

I told Lars about what Kevin said. He rolled his eyes. "*Han har inte alla hästar hemma.*"

"*Han* what?"

"I will tell you later," he said as he ushered me into the barn. "We go out on the lake, after we finish filming for the day."

Inside, Junior was already sitting in the front row, looking pained. Camera crews were set up, and at least a hundred kids were plunked on wooden stadium-style bleachers behind him, wiggling and clamoring toward the cameras. He patted my arm. "I should've known they were going to do religion, what with the two of us. You gonna be okay?"

I took his hand and squeezed it. "Me? Oh yeah. This is the least of my problems." I told him about my argument with Kevin. "Anyway, we can just pretend to listen. Or we don't even have to pretend. What about you? How are you? How was your special day?"

"It was good," Junior said distractedly. "But hey, if I have to get outta here fast, will you come with me?"

"Of course," I said, thinking of what I knew about Junior's backstory: that he'd known he was gay since he was a kid; that the traditional LDS teachings about homosexuality meant not only that he'd be kicked out of the church but go to hell if he came out; that for years he'd chosen his church community over the stirrings of his own heart; that at eighteen, he'd gone on mission to France, fallen in love with a man, and then fallen straight into a spiritual crisis. I didn't know what had given him the courage to leave—when you left the Mormon church in Utah, you really left everything, including your own family a lot of the time—but I knew the material was sacred ground. "Whatever you need."

We kept our hands interlaced as Becki plopped down next to me, and Kevin beside her. I envied their blasé attitudes toward the forthcoming service, as evidenced by their yawns. They could have been in a shopping mall or the DMV, whereas my cortisol levels, though not as high as Junior's, had my knees jiggling rapidly. Karl's meek wife scuttled over to give us each earpieces and explained in halting English that a teen counselor would be translating Karl's sermon for us. "*Tack*," we said dutifully, which meant "thank you," but was also a thing I would have gladly stabbed myself with if it meant getting out of that barn.

Once we got our earpieces in, the service started with a bang—literally. A six-member praise band thumped up onto the wooden stage with the squeal of an amp, blink of a strobe, and puff of a smoke machine. A multicolored digital disco ball began to swirl above us. "*Burbera shooperna keeerna floopsherna!*" a blond woman in skinny jeans called into a professional-looking mic. "*Ett, två—ett, två, tre, fyra—*"

The children behind us screamed so loudly that the barn walls rattled. The band launched into a Christian rock song in English: a word salad of "love" and "sin" and "Father" and "Savior." The singers closed their eyes and lifted their hands to the rafters. Some of the children kept screaming. Others started to cry. Junior and I looked at each other. Alarm passed over his features. "Oh God," he said. "This is worse than I thought."

I wasn't sure whether he meant the screaming or the singing, but I had a similar feeling of foreboding. I thought of the screaming girls waiting for The Beatles to land in New York. I thought of the Germans singing as Der Führer paraded through Berlin. The song ended, and rodentine Karl Karlsson leapt onto the stage with a showman's grace. "*Välkommen!*" he said to us, his arms spread like Jesus. I turned up the volume on my earpiece, and a young, melodious female voice filled up my ear canal:

"Okay, now he is welcoming everybody to the service . . . some announcements . . . congrats to the blue team, who gets victory in Viking Wars . . . talking about tomorrow's schedule . . . sign up for kitchen duty and tomorrow's canoe racing . . . and now he is asking everyone to open their Bible . . ."

I turned the volume down on my earpiece so I could better ponder groupthink and my personal history with religion. After eleven years of attending church twice a week—Wednesdays and Sundays—I knew plenty about the Bible, had read most of it, knew the lovely stories, the ugly stories, the scary and just plain wacko stories. I'd even turned myself on accidentally at age ten while paging through Song of Solomon. But we never talked about the sexy stuff in the Bible, only moral tales of flipping tables and killing giants. Why was that?

I turned the volume back up. Karl Karlsson was still sermonizing. ". . . man must not lie with man . . . Leviticus . . . for homosexuality goes against the . . . sacred role of man and woman . . ."

I took the earpiece out of my ear and turned around instinctively. What I saw broke my heart. These children, naïve as all children should be, absorbing the lessons from their beloved leader without a doubt to its veracity. Plump team captain Oliver, who I was fairly certain was gay, sitting in the back row, his round face shining at Karl with love and hope and trust. I remembered looking at my father that way as he preached on Sundays, so very long ago, before the light in him became overwhelmed by shadow.

I tried to shake off the memory, come back to the barn, as unpleasant as it was. Next to me, Junior was shaking his head as well, his mouth slightly open as if recovering from a blow to the cheek. But despite my best efforts and earlier assurances to Junior, the cortisol that had been jiggling my knees began morphing into flashes of sensation, rioting through my brain, uninvited, like the praise band's strobe lights: the sight of Len kneeling behind the desk in my dad's office at church when I bounded in one day without knocking; the sound of Dad's voice at bedtime, cajoling me into keeping his "special friendship" with Len a "special secret" for him and me; the smell of Chicken Tonight as our parents informed Else and me, two weeks before Dad absconded for New Mexico, that gay people shouldn't be allowed to marry. Grown-ups were so good at saying one thing but doing another. Scarily good. Most of the time they didn't even notice the contradiction.

A wave of nausea passed over me, starting in my lower guts. I thought I might pass out. I thought I might run up the bleachers, gather team captain Oliver into my arms. Instead I just ran out of the barn. I heard my earpiece clatter behind me as it hit the ground, remembering how Mom had started running obsessively after Dad left, losing twenty pounds but never losing her religion, in fact doubling down in those first years, passing out petitions to outlaw liquor-store sales on Sundays when she wasn't nursing a hangover. It broke my brain as a kid, the way people's insides rarely matched their outsides, the way the world pressed on me, flattening my psyche like a hot iron, willing me to accept this fact without complaint.

"What is going through your mind right now?"

I turned around and saw Jonas behind me, filming, with Lars and Magnus at his side. Junior was jogging up behind them. "Please stop," I told them. "I'm not—I can't—"

"Give us a minute." Junior put his arm around my shoulders and held up his palm to Lars. He walked me a few feet away and lowered his voice. "They did this to Tom, too, remember? You're not in danger—it's just a stunt. Like in season seven, when they had two vets, they took them to a military hospital—"

"I can't—I can't—" I couldn't catch my breath; old fear and confusion swarmed like bees. Junior pulled me in tight and told me to breathe with him, so our chests and stomachs were rising and falling in rhythm. It's hard enough, living through some things once. That some idiot producer might go out of their way to create a scenario where you'd have to live through it again—

When we'd managed to get my heart rate back to something resembling normal, I noticed that Jonas was circling around us, filming the whole thing. Lars was standing behind him. I put a hand up to my face. "Come on, Paulie," he coaxed. "We have to see this."

I shook my head, stuck my hand out farther. To Junior: "If you knew they would do something like this, why did you ever—"

"Paulie, almost everyone I talked to who did the show said it was worth it." Junior looked at me with compassion. "It's like life. You make compromises. You try to work within a system. It's not perfect, but it's better than—"

Lars came over to Junior and me, but I turned my body away. He motioned for Jonas to turn the camera off. "Paulie," he said. I ignored him. "Paulie, this is our job—"

"But it's my life." I heard my voice break. "I'm not a personality, I'm a person—"

"Is everything all right?" Rodentine Karl Karlsson was jogging up to us, his tiny mustache puckered with concern.

I wanted to say no. I wanted to lay out, in no uncertain terms, the concerns I had with his little camp and the absolute power he wielded over everybody—but in a frank, playful, yet irrefutable way, like Pippi. Unfortunately my brain remained in a somewhat primitive state, so all I told Karl was this: "I hate you. I really, really, hate you."

It felt good to say, bad-good, like when I'd told Mom she was pathetic after she'd come home from treatment. We'd met for coffee; I was still living with Jemma's family, and I'd gotten a dark thrill from seeing her eyes well up with surprise and hurt. "You're not the victim here," I'd burst out after an hour of listening to her explicate her suffering, not yet understanding that most grown-ups are hurting, all the time, and there was no point in turning pain into a track meet. I'd stood up so fast I'd knocked my chair over. "I am! I am! I am!"

I went off on Karl a lot more after that. I remember calling him a Philistine and telling him I was going to call the cops on him and that his mustache made him look like a rat, and if he really were all about what Jesus would do, maybe he would give his wife a break once in a while so she could wash her hair and buy herself a new dress instead of waiting on him hand and foot. No, mine was not a graceful rebuke to authoritarian powers; it had about as much Pippi as a pincushion. But someone had to be punished for my pain, and it was sure as hell not going to be me.

In fact, I think I was still bellowing ad hominem attacks about Karl's facial hair when Junior and Lars dragged me away from him and toward the lake, whose rippling pinks, purples, and blues mirrored the cloudless sky. At some point Junior must have retreated, for when I looked up, it was just Lars standing beside me. Through the fog of anger I remembered what I'd proclaimed to Brock about Tom after the mine incident: that it was never acceptable for someone to lose their temper so violently.

"Oh dear," I said, and hiccupped.

Lars walked me out to the end of the dock, where lake water lapped against the wood like the sound of a dog drinking. We sat down, took off our shoes, and put our feet in the water. It was bracingly cold. The dock rocked us side to side; the slosh of water had a somnolent effect. Behind us, I heard children's laughter on the lawn; the service must have finished. My whole body was suddenly exhausted from the day: the giant hole we'd dug in the ground, in my heart. I leaned back on my hands. Lars removed his hands from his knees and braced his palms on the dock behind him. His pinky finger brushed mine, purposely or not. I felt the hair on my arms stand up. "Do you want to talk about it?"

No. Yes. No. "You're not going to like what I have to say."

He raised his eyebrows. "Try and we will see."

So I told him that Declan was right, that filming *Sverige och Mig* was extreme and unhealthy, and cribbed all his arguments from his media and cultural studies degree and his research into genealogy: the peddling of trauma as entertainment, the manufacturing of drama for ratings, the concoction of meaning out of junk science and amateur research. When I was done, Lars frowned and shook his head. "But these other reality shows—they do not care about the people the way we care about you." He cleared his throat and quickly amended, "All of us who work on *Sverige och Mig*, we love the Americans. We love seeing the changes, what this show does to you. This is why we come back year after year."

"You come back 'cause it's good money."

Lars gave me a look. "Come on, Paulie. It is public television."

"You come on. That was an ambush. You at least could've given me a heads-up—"

"But I do not think you are mad only about this." He was shaking his head. "There is something else—"

As he said this, two off-duty counselors bumped into the dock with their rowboat. They said something in Swedish to Lars, who said something back. He looped a rope around the dock pole and helped them climb out, then motioned to me to climb in.

"No way," I said. "One rowboat this trip is enough for me, thanks."

Lars again nodded toward the boat. He smiled a little when, finally, I groaned and capitulated, then held my hand as I clambered onto the seat not attached to the oars. He stepped in gracefully, untied the rope, and grasped the handles of both oars. His arms looked magnificent in his black T-shirt. Neither of us said anything until we were far out on the lake, the sun well behind the pine trees, turning the neon colors of the sky to pastel. When Lars stopped rowing, he rested the oars on his lap. "I am sorry I did not warn you."

I made a sound of acknowledgment and looked out on the water.

"I care about you."

I looked at him. He had an expression of utter seriousness. "Well I— I care about you too."

A dragonfly swooped down and landed between us. Or no, it was two dragonflies, one right on top of another, with slim, iridescent blue bodies. Then came another. And another. And another. And another. And Lars and I were pointing at them, and marveling at their wings, and with so much presence in the present, the past faded back into the past.

But alas, it left a sticky residue, the way the past always does: when I looked at Lars again, I felt myself wanting to cling to him like flypaper. Self-obliteration does not solve the unsolvable problem of what happened long ago, but it sure can put it off for a while. Which is why, despite every bit of good sense I'd managed to accumulate over thirty-five years, I got to my knees, crawled across the bottom of the boat, took his face in my hands, and kissed him.

Lars's mouth felt familiar, easy, as if we'd practiced this in another life a thousand times before. I ran my fingers through his hair; he caressed his hands over my waist, hips, lower back. I made a sound, overcome with a desire to devour him—or was it to be devoured? His tongue plunged into mine; his hands traveled to my thighs. The boat pitched and rocked, and I gripped him for dear life.

"Paulie—" He broke away, breathless. "We cannot do this."

"Yes, we can," I said between kisses to his neck.

He took me by the shoulders and pulled me up. "No. Not like this. Not when there is someone back home."

"It doesn't matter," I insisted. Because at the moment, it didn't seem to matter. Because like at the Champagne Bar, we were playing Pretend. Because at the moment nothing but Pretend mattered. Nothing mattered except my overpowering desire to no longer be myself. I went to kiss him again, but he kept me at arm's length. "I cannot do this. Not after my—"

I think he went on to explain himself further, but I could no longer hear him, deafened by my own humiliation. I looked around blindly, trying to hatch an escape plan. "I will take us back," Lars was saying in a reasonable voice, except I was beyond reason. "No, no," I heard myself say. "No, no, no." And I stood up, looked down at the midnight water, and jumped in.

I SLEPT AS poorly as you might expect that night when I finally made it back to camp. My ingenious escape hadn't been so genius after all: Lars insisted on accompanying me back to the dock, rowing beside me as I huffed and puffed through the water, freezing cold and disgraced. Once I'd heaved myself up onto the shore, I grabbed my shoes and fled to the murder hovel, where Becki was snoring. I woke up with the sniffles the next morning and used them as an excuse to get out of more Pentecostal programming—Bible study, creationism chat, iconography arts and crafts. I joined the others at lunch, careful to avoid Karl Karlsson, and sat on the sidelines in the sunshine while the others played Capture the Flag. Junior checked in on me from time to time, but I waved him off, saying I'd blown off all the steam I'd needed to and was simply tired from the exertion. Thank God Lars and his crew were nowhere to be found.

"Did you survive?" Inga asked all of us when she pulled up in the van at six that evening.

"Paulie didn't," Kevin said, laughing as he climbed into the back-back seats. "She went apeshit on the minister last night."

"Shut up, Kevin," Becki and Junior said simultaneously.

Inga drove us to a country hotel some forty-five minutes away. I slept for fourteen hours, hoping to erase my memories from church camp along with my shame. It didn't work, but at least my sniffles were gone by the time I joined the others in the Sprinter van. We drove for another forty-five minutes before arriving at an open field with a crew, a crane, and the makings of some kind of absurd obstacle course not unlike the first competition. This time the weather was cool and overcast, with no signs of rain; pockets of blue peeked through the gray in a way Karl Karlsson would have found significant. As I clambered out of the van, I saw Lars looking in my direction, but he quickly turned away. As did I.

I noticed Kevin was limping as he made his way toward the coffee. Junior told me that he and Becki had gone out last night and partied at a local bar, and he'd fallen into the bushes on his way home.

"What's the matter, Kev?" I called. "Too sensitive to Bud Light?"

He stuck his middle finger in the air without turning around.

"Let us pray," I said to Junior, and lowered my gaze. "Heavenly Father, please send that idiot back to hell today, otherwise known as Florida in the summer."

"Walking shots, *allihopa*!" chipper pregnant producer Anna called, clapping her hands beside the crane. "*God morgon!* Time for walking shots!"

The competition before us had a name: *Vad Skulla Jesus Göra?* ("What Would Jesus Do?") Its purpose was to put us through the paces of Jesus Christ's life from birth to death. What this meant, in practice, is that first we would pack a manger full of straw; then assemble a three-legged IKEA stool made of raw pine; then flip a table filled with heavy accounting textbooks; then "raise the dead"—that is, find a hidden button on a wooden casket to make a mannequin pop to a seated position—then wash our own feet in a basin; and then drag a life-sized crucifix across the field until we crossed yellow police tape labeled Golgotha. Here, on the other side of the yellow line, we would recite three of the seven phrases Jesus said on the cross, words we would find at the beginning of the course taped to the manger. Obviously, the fastest Jesus would win, the slowest flown back to America with a proverbial boulder over their tomb.

"Questions?" Anna asked.

I shot my hand in the air. "Can I go first?"

I don't know if it was residual anger, hurt, humiliation, or the innate wildness of the preacher's daughter, but I shot through that course like a New Testament demon, screaming "I thirst why have you forsaken me father forgive them for they know not what they dooooooo!!!" at the finish line before spiking an invisible ball into Golgotha's end zone. I raised both my arms into the sky, index fingers up, and strutted around like a Super Bowl MVP until Tocke yelled at me to get off the course. "I'll get off when I'm ready to get off!" I yelled back, and then immediately got off.

Becki was lumbering through the challenge at that point, looking like Lazarus pre-raising because of her hangover. Then Junior zipped through, then Kevin. I didn't watch much; I was too busy trying to make sure, subliminally that is, that Lars knew I was a woman of high morals and poise for whom the other night meant nothing, was just a bout of temporary insanity that was actually his fault due to manufactured duress. When everyone had finished, we gathered around the casket, and as the cameras rolled, affable host Erik Lundgren announced with long pauses and elaborate fanfare that Junior would be going home.

"WHAT?" I caterwauled. Junior looked like he'd been punched.

"It was very close," Erik Lundgren explained. "Pauline, you are the winner."

"WHAT?" Now it was Kevin's turn to be shocked.

"It's okay, I was expecting it," Junior was babbling, though I could tell he was trying not to cry. "I couldn't find the button on the casket and the soap for my feet kept slipping out of my hands—"

"Becki," Erik Lundgren said, "you came in second. Kevin, it was very close, but you are staying."

Kevin took off his regulation polo and threw it on the ground.

"Say your goodbyes to Junior!" Tocke yelled from somewhere in the scrum of crew. "This is for real, you guys!"

"You're not leaving!" I said, turning to Junior and bursting into tears. "I can't do this without you!"

He gave me a hug and said into my ear: "You've got this. Just keep your head on straight. Remember, there's nothing they can bring out in you that wasn't already there, nothing they can show you that you don't know deep down already—"

But before he could finish, Becki came at Junior like a missile. "JuJu, I'll miss you so much!" She gave him her signature death-squeeze. "I have to come see your burlesque in Nebraska!"

"It's—not—burlesque"—he gasped—"it's—cabaret—"

"Please," I said to Tocke, once he'd called a wrap on the episode. I could see Junior across the field, talking with chipper producer Anna. He seemed to be laughing, at least. I wanted to cry. "Please let me say goodbye to him one last time."

"No," he said, scrolling through his phone, as matter-of-fact as if I'd asked if it were raining.

"Why, though?"

"Because I say so."

But I'd had enough of male authority. I was sick to death of it, as sick as a leper colony. "You love having this much power, don't you? Making us your pawns in some sick game? Do you know how much this is costing us? Our mental health? Our relationships? And for what?"

Tocke looked up, eyes narrowing with anger. "And you think this is not costing me?!"

"Not nearly enough!" I cried. I cupped my hands around my mouth. "JUNIOR! HEY—JUNIOR!" I called.

Junior turned and waved. He sang something to me, something about rivers and eagles. I remembered this. And I knew just what came next. "*My corner!*" I sang back to him as I jogged closer. "*Of the sk—*" And was sadly cut short by Tocke screaming in my ear and dragging me back across the field.

CHAPTER NINE

FÖRLORAREN
STÅR LITEN

The next morning at ten, in a foul temper, I went down to meet Becki in the hotel lobby. We'd made plans while driving back to Stockholm the night before to visit the ABBA Museum, for Tocke had given us two more days off, and Becki'd said she had to go as a delegate of the official ABBA fan club. Yet when I tromped over to the front desk from the free breakfast, having emotionally eaten a half dozen Swedish pancakes, the only person I saw was Kevin, wearing the tiny California shirt from H&M he'd bought earlier on our trip. "Becki told me I could come," he said defensively before I could say anything. "You can't stop me."

"*Psh*, I'm not going to stop you, Kevin," I said. "I'm going to pretend you don't exist."

So I stared at the ceiling, counting light fixtures, while, across the lobby, Kevin huffed his way through his Wim Hof breathing. *HEE HOOOOOO HEE HOOOOO.* Five minutes later, I had spots in my eyes, Kevin sounded like an asthmatic donkey, and Becki was charging out of the elevators, wearing a T-shirt that read Dancing Queen in neon letters.

"Cut the crap, you two," she said to us, tightening the fanny pack around her waist.

I held up my palms. "I wasn't doing anything!"

Becki rolled her eyes. "It might be our last two days in Stockholm—can't we just try to have a nice time?"

"Fine." I also rolled my eyes.

"Whatever." Kevin rolled his eyes too.

With Becki serving as buffer, the three of us walked through the Stockholm drizzle to the Slussen subway station, then hopped on the aboveground tram that went along the canal and down Djurgårds-vägen, or "Animal Garden Way." We passed the Nordic Museum; the Vasa Museum, an homage, according to Deborah's guidebook, to an epic seventeenth-century naval fail; the Viking Museum; and Skansen, Stockholm's zoo.

"Hurry up!" Becki said, hopping off the tram and jogging across the street to the sleek, square ABBA Museum with its floor-to-ceiling windows. On the patio, you could take pictures with life-sized, faceless wooden cutouts of Björn, Benny, Frida, and Agnetha. I'd brought my Polaroid, and before we went in, I made Becki stick her face in the hole atop Frida's body. *Snap.* "Kevin, come on!" Becki hollered, motioning to the Björn-sized hole next to her.

"No, thanks." Kevin was hot on the heels of a clump of blond, twenty-something Australians. "Hey, how y'all doin'," I heard him say. "I'm here filming a TV show."

"Gross," I said to Becki as we passed them on our way to the ticket window. Kevin was talking about how much money he made selling solar panels.

"Like watching your little brother masturbate," she agreed. To the ticket-seller: "Two, please."

"Oh," I said, reaching for my purse. "I can—"

"My treat," she said, waving my hand away.

Except then her credit card was declined. The second one she offered was declined too. "It must be the system," Becki kept repeating as the back of her neck grew pinker. Finally, feeling funny on her behalf, I shoved my own card at the ticket-seller and it went through just fine.

"You didn't have to do that," she said shortly as we headed through the rainbow-colored gift shop. "It would've worked eventually."

"Maybe they put a hold on since it's an unfamiliar charge?" I ducked around a corner.

"Yeah, maybe," Becki said, showing our tickets to the guard. "Not a big deal." But her neck and cheeks were still pink.

I decided to leave the matter, along with our bags, downstairs in the museum lockers. After a trip to the cotton-candy-pink bathroom, we rounded a black hallway into the campy, retro universe of Sweden in the '70s, complete with bell-bottoms and Volkswagen buses, immersed first in ABBA's formative years, then the romance of Agnetha and Björn, then the romance of Benny and Frida, and then, complete with lots of television footage, the story of how this posse of friends/lovers turned their Eurovision-winning performance of "Waterloo" into years of super-stardom. In the next section we attempted to engineer a new version of "Money, Money, Money" on a digital soundboard, auditioned for ABBA with karaoke tracks in tiny sound booths, toured the band's recording studio, and "traveled" to the island of Viggsö in Stockholm's archipelago, where Benny and Björn composed much of ABBA's music. We meandered past makeup mirrors, sheet music, awards, platform boots, spandex, spangles, and state-of-the-art wax figures. The lighting was theatrical and the atmosphere festive, with ABBA music tunneling constantly through speakers. Within a half hour, I was high on disco, having forgotten all about Lars and Junior and Kevin. Disco was life! Disco was joy! Disco scoffed at despair, guilt, and sulking! I belted out "Mamma Mia!" with a Russian oligarch, sang "Take a Chance on Me" with two Brazilians, and crooned "Voulez Vous" with a gang of late-middle-aged French snobs. Earworms make for such funny companions: you never knew what you might grow to love via some combination of proximity and helplessness.

And it was with a similar kind of love that, in the last room of the museum, I watched Becki climb onto a sizeable black stage to become, as the sign suggested, ABBA's Fifth Member. She fiddled with a monitor, took her hair out of her ponytail, and straightened her T-shirt with en-dearing self-consciousness. And as the first bars of "Dancing Queen" slid

across the impressive sound system, Becki started strutting around with
her hands on her hips and was suddenly joined—surprise!—by life-sized,
lifelike holograms of Benny, Björn, Frida, and Agnetha.

She screamed when she saw them, though she knew they were coming,
and I laughed at her delight. The tension in Becki's forehead, jaw, and neck
dissolved, and for just a moment I saw the girl she had been long ago: loud,
bossy, sensitive, fearless. She threw both arms into the air, singing into the
microphone about having the time of her life. I sang along with her and,
at the relevant moment, pointed at the stage and shouted: "BECKI'S
THE DANCING QUEEN!"

"Okay, your turn," Becki said breathlessly, running over to me with a
slap to my upper arm when the song was done.

"But I don't know that much ABBA," I said as she propelled me toward
the stage.

"The lyrics are right there." She pointed to the monitor hung alongside the stage lights. "Can I pick yours? Lemme pick yours. Please?"

Before I had answered, the piano started plunking, the backups started
aaaaaahing. Words appeared on the monitor. I started singing. Apparently
I wasn't into talking? About stuff we had been through? I stopped singing.
"Becki, I don't know this one."

"Sure you do," she said. "Just wait till the chorus."

The lyrics were coming fast now on the monitor. I put the mic back to
my mouth. "See?" Becki called. "You're doing great! Just close your eyes
and pretend you're on Eurovision."

So I did, and sang about playing all my cards. Hmmm, oddly topical.
I remembered the taste of Lars's mouth. I remembered the sound of
Declan's voice, the fights we'd kept having. I remembered shouting at
rodentine Karl Karlsson and shaming Tom for doing the same thing in
the mine. I remembered all my shame, my regrets, my hurts and anger.
I closed my eyes as the chorus arrived, because, it turned out, I did know
it. "*The winner takes it all!* " I put a hand over my heart and launched
into the chorus; a great rush of feeling swelled along with the music's
crescendo. "*The loser's standing small!*" Yes, yes, that was it, exactly. I had
to tell someone about Lars—I had to tell Becki. I was standing small if
I didn't, I thought I might burst if I didn't get it out—

"I have something to say," I told Becki, relaxing the mic as the song marched into the second verse. Agnetha and Frida were holding hands on one side of me while, on the other side, Hologram-Björn strummed away on his guitar. "But don't judge me."

Becki was clapping along but stopped. "What?"

"Lars and I—" I said, and propelled by some great force, the force of disco: "We made out the other night. At Jesus camp. It's a whole thing—it almost happened a bunch of times—"

She leaned back on her heels as if I'd smacked her. "*Lars* Lars?"

"Yes, Lars Lars," I said. "But he stopped it, 'cause—" The chorus was coming up. I put the mic back to my mouth.

"Damn. He's hot," Becki said. "Was it hot?"

"Yes." I flushed. Hologram-Björn wandered closer, strumming his guitar. "No. I mean, I dunno, he ended it, 'cause of Declan—" I put the mic back to my mouth and sang. The beat picked up. Rather than explain—not that I could justify any of it, it was unjustifiable—I started step-and-touching with Hologram– Frida and Agnetha. I lost myself in the music for a while, or rather, I escaped into it. The relief I felt at unburdening myself was as physical and palpable as a bowel movement. When the song finished, I was panting, feeling about ten pounds lighter, and Kevin was standing at the front of the stage next to Becki with a smirk on his face. He fished a pill out of the prescription bottle he was always carrying. Wait—Kevin?

"How long have you been there?" I demanded, crouching down on the stage.

Kevin was chewing gum. He snapped it. "Long enough."

Becki said, "Came in during your second dance break."

"What happened to the Australians?"

He cracked his gum again and smiled meanly. "We're meeting up later. You gonna meet up with Lars later too?"

"Shut up, Kevin," Becki said.

"It's against the code of conduct, you know," Kevin said. "I bet Lars told you about the Jesus contest and that's the only reason you won yesterday. What do you think Tocke'll say when I tell him? You think he'll send you straight home or just rig the competition so you lose automatically?"

And then—then!—Kevin had the nerve to laugh. Nothing infuriates me more than mocking laughter. I saw red, or thought I did, or was that the theatrical lighting? The rage that had been coiled in my torso since our first fight at Viking camp unfurled itself across my body. I felt my muscles tense as I launched off the stage without a whiff of forethought, tackling a surprised Kevin and scrambling for the pill bottle that flew out of his hand and went skittering across the floor. I grabbed it and read the label before he crawled over and snatched it from me. "Steroids!" I crowed. "Really, Kevin, have you been 'roiding this whole time? You think Tocke's going to like that any more than—"

"They're for my back!" he roared. "It's a weight-lifting injury!"

"Stop it! You guys! You're gonna get us kicked out!" Becki was saying as an eight-year-old assumed the stage and started belting out "Gimme! Gimme! Gimme!" Her mom, who was recording the performance, glowered at us and whispered something to the guy next to her. He nodded and headed toward the gift shop.

"So you say," I scoffed. "Even if they are, all I need to do is say the word 'steroid' and Tocke's gonna hit the ceiling. You know he is."

Kevin opened his mouth, closed it, opened it again, closed it. Then he pointed at me. "I hate you."

"I hate *you*!"

"That's enough—" Becki said, but before she could finish, she was interrupted by the sound of a telephone ringing, an old-fashioned *brrrrring*. The museum had been crammed with tourists when we arrived, but it was almost empty now, the sound echoing through the halls like a dream. "Hold on, I know what that is—" she said, and took off running back through the museum. Kevin and I glanced at each other despite ourselves and took off after her. Becki skidded to a halt in front of a small podium I had previously missed, upon which sat a red rotary phone. A sign read: If the Phone Rings, Pick It Up. It's ABBA Calling. The phone was still ringing. Becki's face was very pink. "I'm scared," she said, out of breath. "I don't know what to say."

"Answer it!" Kevin and I shouted. We glanced at each other again.

Becki snatched the receiver. "Hello? Yes? Yes, I'm here." Pause. "Uh-huh. America. Becki."

Kevin and I fell into a stunned silence as Becki listened. She listened for a good while. "Got it," Becki said. "I won't. 'K thanks, bye." She hung up and looked at us.

"Well?" I demanded.

Becki looked shocked. "That was Benny."

"Benny?" I said. "*Benny* Benny?"

Becki nodded her head, dazed. "*Benny* Benny."

Kevin said, "Probably AI."

"Shut up, Kevin," Becki and I said simultaneously.

"What'd he say?" I asked her.

"He said—" Becki paused. "He said the three of us have a story, and we need each other, and we're in this together like prizefighters or something."

"What the hell is that?" I said. "A Zen koan?"

"'I Still Have Faith in You.'"

"Becki." I touched my palm to my chest. "Thank you."

"Paulie, it's one of their songs."

"Oh. Right."

"So it's a recording," Kevin said.

"It wasn't! He told me his name, I told him mine, and he said it back."

"AI can do that," Kevin said.

"Shut up, Kevin," Becki and I said again simultaneously. Then Becki said, "He called for a reason. Do you think he has cameras hooked up? Did he see you guys fighting?"

"You think Benny wastes his time looking at tourists on CCTV?" Kevin said.

Becki ignored him. "There's a message here, there's got to be."

"Maybe he says the same thing to everybody," I offered.

"No, no, there's got to be," Becki repeated, just as a security officer rolled up and asked us to leave the premises.

"Sir, I apologize," I said to the guard as we fetched our bags from the coatroom.

"So do I," Kevin added, not to be outdone. "A lot, actually."

Meanwhile, Becki kept muttering the lyrics to the song over and over to herself as the guard escorted us to the door and made sure we headed for the tram stop. To the drizzly sky she said, "But what the hell is it?"

WHEN I TALKED to Declan that night, I kept the conversation solely on him, telling him I was tired of arguing, he'd heard more than enough about my travels, and I was eager for updates from home. So he gave me news from the neighborhood (the city had come by and pruned a bunch of trees on the boulevard, to the point of mangling), told me about coding something new in Python, uploading a free troubleshooting tutorial online for new programmers, and his obnoxious new CEO, whose favorite word was "meritocracy" but whose arrival had caused a bunch of women to quit. I focused intently on his words, almost like a meditation, and in doing so found it possible to slam shut all sorts of doors that opened into upsetting questions of deceit and infidelity and regret and shame and the possible repercussions from Tocke coming if Kevin opened his big fat mouth. This must have been how my father had survived all those years in his own house of cards: cordoning one section off with spiked nails, to be entered only under the cover of night, and when no one was looking. In fact, if I concentrated enough on being a good partner to Declan, it was almost as if that cordoned-off area wasn't there. Almost.

I spent the next day browsing the English-language bookstore in Stockholm and devouring a leather-bound copy of *Pride and Prejudice* over a steady diet of coffee and open-faced sandwiches at an outdoor café. The day after that, we started filming again, but this time we didn't have to pack our bags: Inga announced we'd be filming the episode in Stockholm. Becki went off early for her "special day"—her relatives were from Trosa, about an hour south on the coast—and Inga drove Kevin and me to what looked to be a recording studio in Östermalm. Thank God it was only a twenty-minute ride, including traffic, otherwise I'm not sure I could have survived Kevin alone.

At the studio, or in front of it, as the warm sunshine hit our backs, I spotted Lars and Jonas milling about as Magnus put a mic on me. Great, just great. I kept to the perimeter of the group, noting that Lars had his eyes trained on the pavement while Tocke explained to us that due to the massive global success of Swedish pop artists like ABBA, Robyn, Ace of Base, the Cardigans, Avicii, and dozens of others—gob-smacking, considering Sweden only had ten million people—Kevin and I would be spending the entire day writing and recording our own pop song about our time in Sweden with Swedish pop sensation Tove Orönso. There was a lightly political element to this segment, Tocke said: right-wing government leaders were considering cutting funding by half to Sweden's culture schools, or *kulturskolan*, which offered free music classes to Swedish kids. But a lot of people, Tocke continued, credited Sweden's disproportionate success on the global charts to the country's long-standing support of children learning music, believing it just as important as math and science, which was maybe why around twenty percent of Swedish adults still sang in organized choirs.

"*Hej*," Tove said, emerging from the studio as Jonas pivoted the camera. She was in her late twenties and wearing baggy pants, puffy sneakers, and a bespangled bra under a gold lamé jacket. I was immediately starstruck. Tove was famous for her explicitly feminist and sexual lyrics; she had an entire EP called *Lady Boner*. She was also extremely hot, or at least I seemed to get very hot as she smiled a superstar smile at us. "Welcome to Sweden." And to me: "Wow! You are very tall!"

"Thank you?" I said as Kevin said, "*Hej*." I could almost see his tongue falling out of his mouth and rolling toward her like a carpet. "'Sup. Dig your music."

As if he knew any of her songs! "I actually love your music," I said to Tove, accidentally-on-purpose jostling Kevin out of the way. "When 'Coolest Girl' came out, it was all my best friend, Jemma, and I listened to for weeks—I'm a huge fan." Tove took this in graciously. I said to Kevin, less graciously: "So what's your favorite song?"

"Oh—" he said, blinking. "Um—"

"Most people say 'My Worst Habit,'" Tove said encouragingly.

He snapped his fingers. "Exactly."

After more introductions, this time to the studio manager and engineers, Tocke set the three of us up in a small soundproof studio. Jonas was also there with the camera, but the room was small enough that Lars and Magnus stayed in the hallway, thank goodness. I sat on a small nubbly orange couch with my back to the door as Tove picked up an acoustic guitar, and Kevin, to my surprise, picked up an electric bass. "Had a band in high school," he told Tove. "Called L 4 1. The numbers, not the letters." Then he starting playing, not *for* her, exactly, but *at* her, that way some guys do, until all that's left of you is a frozen smile while your insides metaphorically trash a hotel room.

But Tove, instead of getting trapped by a wall of sound, waved Kevin off. He stopped playing immediately. "Do you play any instruments?" she asked me.

"A lot," I said, thinking back to my grandma's house, the piano and dulcimer and zither. "But badly."

"Can you sing?"

"Um." I flashed back to the ABBA Museum. "Does karaoke count?"

Regardless of my hesitation, Tove gave me a tambourine and a kick drum and told me to show her what I could do. I guess I could do enough, because from there we started riffing, then putting our riffs together. Over the next few hours, the feeling in the studio became not unlike my long-lost days in the darkroom: process took over personality, and finer points of consciousness relaxed. For example, I did not want to throttle Kevin every time he swallowed. Somewhere in the late morning, Inga brought us *fika*; next thing I knew, I blinked and it was lunch. Neither Tove, Kevin, nor I wanted to quit, so while the crew went for pizza, we worked on lyrics. Tove's sounded something like this:

In the land of the midnight sun, where the stars align
I found a love so wild it makes my heart ignite

Whereas Kevin's went something like this:

Hey, hey, hey Sweden, you know you're more than okay
Girls just as hot and easy as in the U.S. of A.

"I do not like that," Tove said, wrinkling her nose. She appeared not to know or care about the other golden rule: that you never tell a man that he's done a bad job. Even with Kevin, my sworn enemy, I had an impulse to tell him he had a beautiful singing voice instead of explaining flat-out that his lyrics sucked. His singing seemed to soften all his hard edges. He nodded at Tove's criticism, took it in without defensiveness or complaint, and tried again, noodling about birch trees and swimming naked in the Baltic. I grabbed my Polaroid off the couch and took a picture. *Snap.*

Tove nodded in approval at Kevin's efforts. "That is much better. Because we want Sweden to be the object of desire, not just Swedish girls." She laughed. "Though we are very nice. You have a good voice."

I nodded, too, albeit begrudgingly. "I agree."

Kevin smiled at us, then, but not his usual lizard smile. "I never thought so. My mom hated it when I sang."

I felt a ping in my chest. Empathy has a way of sneaking up on a person, especially when music's involved. "Why?"

"She was hungover a lot," he said with false casualness. "Said the sound hurt her head."

"Oh," I said. Then: "Relatable."

"Yeah," he said.

"Yeahhhhh," I said.

Then he shrugged. Then I shrugged. Then we picked our instruments back up.

The song didn't really come together until about midnight, maybe later. We didn't mind, not even Tove. Inga kept bringing coffees, and Magnus handed out packets of *snus*. He told Kevin and me to keep it in only for a minute so we didn't puke. (And we didn't!) It was after two a.m. when we got back to the hotel, and Tocke thankfully permitted us a lie-in. I woke up around ten and wandered over to Becki's hotel room to see how her special day had gone. She opened the door just after I knocked, and the state of her shocked me: puffy-faced, wild-eyed, and splotchy, with yesterday's makeup smeared under her eyes. Two empty bottles of wine were sitting on the TV stand, and the room smelled terrible, a mix of artificial vanilla and feet.

Before I could even ask, Becki told me her day had been awful. "Horrible," she said. "I've been looking forward to it for months, I thought I'd learn all these things and"—she made a gesture that looked like an explosion with her hands—"everything in my life would make sense. Like it did with you. But it didn't. And they kept trying to get me to cry and talk about my dad—you know I don't do feelings, Paulie . . ."

She teared up and turned her face away. "And that made me mad and then they got mad 'cause I wouldn't cry, and then we walked around the town and saw the place where my great-grandma hanged herself after people found out she'd been having an affair with the shopkeeper's wife, and I had to lay a freaking wreath on the tree where she did it—"

She kept talking for a while, but it was hard to follow what she was saying. "I thought it was gonna be different than that," she said finally. "I thought it was gonna be happy. Why'd they have to go and—I didn't want to know all that—"

I didn't know what to say, though I knew exactly what she meant. I'd spent most of my life wishing I hadn't known what I did about my dad and Len, wishing I hadn't been the one to find Mom unconscious on the bedroom floor. It seemed to me when I was younger, and even now, that if ignorance wasn't bliss, it certainly was freedom: freedom from hard things.

How I wished to sit Becki down on the bed and tell her this, but also that I had to believe, seeing as there was no way for a person to unknow what they know, or undo what's been done, that another form of freedom beckoned beyond the first. I didn't know what it was yet, and maybe I never would, but when I closed my eyes and tried to picture it, what I saw were rows of faces, like a living Guess Who? board, throwing their hair back and laughing, or wiping tears from their eyes, or baring their teeth, or gazing forward with expressions of grave solemnity, and while they had different shapes and colors and textures, the thing all these faces had in common was that their eyes were clear, their jaws relaxed, and no shadows passed across them.

"Paulie?" Becki was saying. "Paulie? Hello? I said did you get breakfast?"

"Oh." I opened my eyes. "Right. Um, no, not yet. But first let's—"

But instead of saying any of that, since none of the words would come out right anyway, I picked up the wine bottles, put them in the trash, opened the drapes, cracked the windows, and made the bed while Becki splashed her face with water and lined her underarms with deodorant. As we waited by the elevator, she said, apropos of nothing, while jabbing the Down button over and over: "You know, just because depression runs in your family doesn't mean you'll automatically be depressed."

"It's true," I agreed as we stepped in the elevator, thinking of what Declan had said about epigenetics. "But if it does happen, it doesn't mean you're bad or anything."

The elevator shuddered downward. We waited in silence. "I hooked up with a girl once," Becki said. She looked at me like it was a test. "Twice."

"Hey, that's great," I said. "I haven't, but all my friends have. Why not?" She narrowed her eyes. "It doesn't mean anything, though."

"No, not at all." I paused. "No big deal. But if it did, no big deal either."

She sucked in a breath, then exhaled so completely it was like the air in the elevator doubled. When the doors opened, she stepped in front of them, and I noticed that her shoulders were no longer up by her ears. "God, I'm starving," she said, a little too loudly. She turned to look at me, and I saw the vulnerability in her eyes. "You hungry, Paulie?"

"Oh God, always," I said.

She said, "Man, me too."

WE SPENT THAT afternoon filming at the Spotify headquarters in central Stockholm, learning about the company's unlikely rise to global dominance and talking to engineers about the finer points of the site's mechanics. For an episode ostensibly centered on music, we heard very little about the fine arts over those several hours, and more about how the founders had outsmarted old-school executives, bested Silicon Valley, done away with something called "lag," and created the best algorithm in the world. Had it not been for the occasional reference to Swedish artists, we might have been talking about any number of internet services, including pornography. "You must trim the fat!" our guide kept saying. "No fat allowed!"

From there we grabbed a quick dinner of kebab pizza, a Swedish specialty, before heading to a famous rock venue called Debaser, nestled on the canal in Hornstull. Tocke, who hadn't come with us to the Spotify offices, was waiting for us by the coat check with matching T-shirts and baseball caps that said Rap Sverige. "Put these on," he instructed us as more Swedes—mostly young, white, suburban guys—streamed into the venue. The rappers that night, a duo of two short white men with tattoos, gold chains, and guaranteed state pensions, spat verses about—well, I'm

not sure, since they were in Swedish. Every once in a while they'd shout
English words—"Word!" "Baller!" "Party!"—as they ran and jumped like
little boys when they wanted to make a point.

Meanwhile, Becki was drinking a lot of beer throughout the concert.
We all were, including Kevin, who generally avoided it due to strict carb
regimentation, but Becki could drink us under the table. Tocke had
instructed Inga to cap us at two pints each, but by this point in filming,
the crew was just as tired as we were, as insubordinate too. "This shih's
weird," Becki slurred near the end of the set. She pointed to the stage.
"Theh're like babies. Baby rappersh—" The thought made her laugh.
"Baby rappersh! Straigh' outta Compton, NOT—hahahahaha—"

I saw Lars elbow Jonas, who swung the camera in Becki's direction.
She was pushing her way toward the front of the crowd, which was
remarkably easy compared to an American concert. I followed Becki,
and Lars and Jonas followed me. Partly I was worried about her, partly
I was horrified to see what she might do.

"Booooooo!" she was yelling. "Boooooooo!" It was hard to hear her
over the music, but not impossible.

"Fucking Americans," I heard a guy behind me say as I passed.

Like an elephant through brush, Becki kept trampling until she reached
the bottom of the stage. "Boooooo!" she was still yelling. "Booooooo!"
Except the rappers must have thought she was saying "You! You!" because
they were looking at her, and at Jonas's camera looking at her, and smiling.

"*Hej*," one of them said into his mic at a song break, pointing at Becki.
"Would you like to come on the stage?"

At once, Becki's face transformed into an expression of great en-
thusiasm. "Wooooooo!" she hollered, throwing her hands in the air.
"Wooooooooooo!"

The rappers gestured toward the steps that led to the stage, which were
manned by two burly security officers. To my surprise, as Becki staggered
toward them, I was hit with an acute and poisonous envy. Despite my
growing affection for Becki, this envy wriggled like a worm in the fat,
red apple of my heart, leaving a thick trail of slimy thoughts: how unfair
it was that loud people with zero self-awareness and poor manners often
got exactly what they wanted in this world, whereas, O woe, my good

manners (relatively), self-awareness (sometimes), and modesty (low self-esteem) had gotten me exactly nothing. The worm tunneled from Becki's antics to the politicians and celebrities of our day; to the entitled children I tutored; to the most successful artists in my graduate program; and all the way back to the third grade, when Marilyn Hoffer stole all my friends with the successful propaganda campaign "Paulie Is Poopy."

It was not, I told myself, that I wanted to climb up onto that stupid stage myself; it was more that I didn't want Becki to go up there, nor to want to go up there. Because of the principle, I told myself. Because of the politics. Not, I told myself, because this secret part of me envied her shamelessness, her ability to know and pursue her desires so straightforwardly. And thus the worm made its way through my heart, gobbling up its soft and juicy parts, until it seemed perfectly reasonable—or, more than that, honorable—to hang back and say nothing as I watched Becki head straight for an anaconda-sized extension cord on the floor, catch her big toe on its edge, and then, as if in slow motion, go facedown with a *splat* onto the set of stairs.

The music didn't pause, but everyone around her did. We gasped. She put a hand up. "I'm fine! I'm fine!" Then she turned her head. It was covered in blood. I put a hand over my mouth. The rappers paused, stared, then got back to rapping. Someone poked me in the arm. I turned. It was Lars. "Why didn't you help her?" he said as one of the tiny men shouted, "*Skål!*"

I stiffened. "How could I? There was no way to get there in—"

"You let her fall." Then he pushed through the crowd to get to Becki. Someone from the venue came over with a first aid kit; a security guard cleared some room. I went over and hovered, chewing a hangnail and racking myself with guilt. After some initial probing, it became clear that nothing was broken, just scraped. Becki good-naturedly submitted to rubbing alcohol and a few Band-Aids. "This is nothing," she kept saying. "You should've seen me after blink-182."

When Jonas led Becki over to the bar to get some ice water, I took my chance with Lars. "No, I didn't!" I said, drawing him over to a dark corner so that no one would overhear. "It was an accident!"

His face remained a stone. "One that you could have prevented."

"If that's true, then you could've too!"

"I was behind you. I would not have gotten there in time."

"It happened too fast, I didn't have—" I could feel myself getting hot. "You know what? Leave me alone. I'm not talking to you."

I turned to go, but he grabbed my arm. "You are just mad because of what happened. At the lake."

"Why would I be mad when nothing happened?"

"Because I made us stop."

"*You* made us stop? I'm the one that jumped out of the boat!"

"Paulie."

"I haven't thought about it since. Don't tell me you have, that's pathetic—"

"You are not telling the truth."

"How would you know if I wasn't? You don't know me! I haven't been myself in weeks! I'm nothing but a rat in this stupid maze—"

"Because all I have done for a month is watch you! You think I don't notice? You think you can pretend this is nothing when I see in your eyes—?"

"Who's pretending? You're the one who's pretending—"

And then, as though everything we'd said was but an idle prelude, I was kissing him, and he me. He backed me up against the black wall of the venue and pressed against me. I pressed back. It seemed we might break right through the plaster: he interlaced his fingers in mine and pinned them beside my head. I plunged my tongue into his mouth. I hated him. I wanted him. This was wrong. This was everything. He moved like an animal—powerful, primal, assured. I tugged at his lips with my teeth. Our mouths were so tightly pressed it seemed a hole was opening up in the middle of that wet, pink darkness, dropping us—

I don't know what we would have done, how far down we would have traveled, had one of the rappers not sounded an airhorn. The lights went on, the concert was over. "*Shmerbeel hjurna flicpa* AFTER-PARTY!" the rapper shouted, or something like that. Lars and I stepped apart. I looked at him, a stranger. He looked at me, a stranger. None of this made any sense.

"*Hej, hej,*" Magnus said, coming over. "There you are." He looked at us. "Why are you so red in your faces?"

"Oh, um," I said, angling my body away from Lars. "I guess I just really liked the music, ha ha. Anyway, I guess I should check on Becki. Wouldn't want her to get confused or . . . lost or . . ." I was nodding like a bobblehead. "Okay, well, bye."

Then I turned and fled. So fast, in fact, that I didn't notice the anaconda-sized extension cord on the floor, either, and soon went flying across the fast-emptying room like an acrobat without a net.

AND SO IT was that on the following morning, Becki and I both arrived with black eyes and bandaged faces to the Skansen zoo for competition day. Becki thought it was a hilarious coincidence, I thought it a fitting karmic punishment, and Tocke thought it ridiculous, positively criminal, that we both managed to get so scraped up before a filming day. "I am telling you!" he roared in the midst of his twenty-minute tirade as he paced in front of a miniature thatched barn. "On no other show do I have this many problems. You are teenagers! You cry and scream, you listen to no one, you waste time and go out of your way to cause trouble, and why?"

I lifted a tentative finger. "Tocke, I'm not trying to make excuses here, but the amount of pressure you've put us under—"

"Pressure!" he shouted. "You want to talk to me about pressure? When it is me that the network comes to every day? This is not about pressure—it is that you must always have your way! The world must always revolve around the Americans, isn't that right—"

I lifted my finger again, but Becki swatted my hand down. "Just let him finish," she murmured as Tocke started ranting about American hegemony, linguistic arrogance, emotional infantilism, and our inability to adapt to the customs of the country. "I am so sorry not even our toilet paper is good enough for you," he said mockingly. "Not soft enough for your soft little asses."

I'd heard quite a few tirades from Tocke by this stage of our journey, but this one put me over the edge. I'd arrived that morning feeling contrite about last night on many levels, planning on putting my best foot forward and my bad foot far back, but by the time he had finished, my hands were balled into fists. Tocke made Becki and me apologize and shake his hand and promise to get in line for the last two weeks of filming. But as I took his big, meaty paw, I looked into his eyes and in my head popped the words, *Don't tread on me*, a phrase I hadn't thought about since ninth-grade history.

Skansen was a charming zoo, old-fashioned and quaint, not unlike Marie Antoinette's hobby farm at Versailles. Ducks and geese waddled all over the place, unsupervised, and across a gravel path, two cows were masticating. Yet the competition that day, according to affable host Erik Lundgren, had nothing to do with the animals. Instead our challenge, both mental and physical in nature, was to memorize a list of twenty Swedish pop songs, along with the artist name and date of release, and then run across a field to a large wooden board and arrange wooden tiles, each one printed with a song title, artist, or date, in correct and chronological order. If we forgot something, we could run back to check, but it would cost us time and energy. "The loser, as always, will be faced with a return trip to America," said Erik Lundgren affably. "On your marks, get set—"

Before he said *går*, we were already going, the three of us, jostling to get to the three tables where the song lists waited. Whether it was because of Tocke's rant, our cumulative fatigue, or the pressure of the semifinal, the air around us had a negative charge. I shielded my body from Becki and Kevin so they couldn't discern my memorization process; when I saw Becki drop a piece of paper, I didn't pick it up. After a few minutes, Kevin took off across the field, and as I saw him run, I was overcome with that same red feeling—was that what people meant by killer instinct?—that had caused me to tackle him at the ABBA Museum. Though I had not finished memorizing, I ran after him, determined to best him at whatever cost. "Robyn, Tove Lo, the Shout Out Louds, The Cardigans, Ace of Base, Peter Björn and John," I said breathlessly, trying to keep it all in my head, once I'd sprinted up to the boards. "Benjamin Ingrosso, 1970, 1996, 2008—"

"Shut up, Paulie," Kevin said, covering his ears with his hands and straddling the wooden tiles on the ground.

"ABBA, The Hives, Avicii, 1950, 2018, 1979—"

"I said, shut up!" He jogged over to my board, picked up the basket that held my wooden tiles, and threw it across the field. It went surprisingly far.

"Leave her alone, Kevin!" Tocke shouted from across the field.

Kevin turned. "She's trying to confuse me!"

I shouted, "He's sabotaging me!"

Kevin shouted, "Only 'cause she's sabotaging me!"

"Stop!" Tocke shouted. "That is it! Stop the time!"

He stormed over just as Becki ran up, silently mouthing a list of song titles. *Hate to say I Told You Dancing on My Don't You Worry Child Sommaren*—"What do you think you are doing?!" Tocke demanded of Kevin and me. "Don't you understand this is a family program?! That little children watch it every year with their *mormors* and *farfars*?!"

"It's Paulie!" Kevin burst. "She's trying to kick me off the show!" He looked around wildly and pointed at Lars. "But you should kick *her* off the show! She's broken the code of conduct! They're hooking up!"

I felt a dark hush descend upon my body. I looked at Lars. He looked away from me. The darkness thickened around me, curdling into panic, until—

"Well, did you know *he's* taking steroids?" I jammed my thumb toward Kevin. "Been taking them this whole time? How else do you think he's been moving so fast?"

"THEY'RE FOR MY BACK!" Kevin bellowed.

In contrast to our screams, Tocke was ominously silent, flicking his blue eyes back and forth between Kevin and me. Flick, flick. Flick, flick. Like a dog at a tennis court.

"That is it," he said after what seemed like an unbearably long pause. "I can take this no longer."

Kevin and I both took a step back, chastened by the finality in his voice. "You." He pointed at me. "You." He pointed at Kevin. "And you." He pointed at Becki. "I am done with you. No"—he corrected himself— "I am done with Americans. Done with your egos and your explosions. Ten seasons and I am finished."

"*Our* egos and explosions?" I exploded.

"*Me?*" Becki said, affronted. "What did I do?"

"I don't have ego and explosions." Kevin looked taken aback.

"You don't?" Tocke guffawed. "Have you seen anyone in Sweden shouting while you have been here? Or shoving? Or complaining? Or crying? Or laughing so hard at their own jokes? And you," Tocke said, turning to Becki. "You think the rules do not apply to you, don't you? Because you are from Texas? Well, you are wrong. We know all about your secret phone."

My mind flashed to that long-ago night in the Hotel Rival lobby, after everyone had gone shopping, when I saw Becki hiding a plastic bag under her butt. Tocke continued, "After you spent the first week asking everyone to borrow theirs? Then you stop and two days later you are suddenly friending everyone in production on social media? You think you are too smart for us? Or we are too nice? The nice, polite Swedes will never notice? That because we are not bullies we will not fight back?"

"I needed to transfer money," Becki said weakly as she turned several shades of pink. "I'm having some trouble with—"

"And did you know," Tocke said, gesturing to the three of us, "that none of you were even going home today? That you ruined this shoot and each other for nothing? No," he answered himself. "Of course you did not know. You know nothing but act like you know everything. This is the American way, no? Well, it is not the Swedish way." He turned and announced to the crew, "We are done here. Lars, I must now talk to you."

The crew looked at one another in confusion. "Done?" I said. "You mean, done-done?"

"I don't know what I mean," he said hoarsely. "But I do not wish to see you. Please leave."

"But Tocke—" producer Anna said, no longer chipper. She put a hand on his forearm and continued in Swedish. She gestured toward the set. He shook his head, said something back, gestured to us, crossed his arms, and nodded. "You can go," Anna said to us finally as Tocke strode off, gesturing for Lars to come with him. She handed Becki and me our purses, which Inga had fetched from the van.

"But where?" Becki said. "Until when? We don't have phones—" She flushed again. "Or, they don't have phones—"

"We will call you at some point. At the hotel." Then Anna dismissed us with a flick of her wrist.

Alone on the field, Becki, Kevin, and I stared at one another like kids who had just gotten suspended and were waiting for our parents to pick us up.

Becki was the first to speak. "Well, whatever, Tocke." She scuffed her shoe in the dirt.

"I don't even care about the show," Kevin said.

"Me neither," I said. "It's toxic. Toxic and dumb. Declan says production uses the same techniques as the CIA." I tapped my forehead with my index finger. "Mind control."

"Man, I believe that," Becki said.

"Know who's got more ego and explosions than all of us combined? *He* does," Kevin said.

"Right?!" I said. "If they fire us—no, you know what? I won't let them fire us. Before they try anything, I'll quit."

"Me too," Kevin said, surprising me with his agreement.

"Me three," Becki said. We were walking away from the field now, away from the others, though none of us knew where we were going. She continued, "Like he has any right to go off like that! All you've done for weeks is push and push and push till we freak out and give you the reaction you wanted. Well, Tocke, guess what? If you're gonna keep pressing our buttons, you best believe they're gonna pop off even when you don't want 'em to."

Kevin whistled in agreement. "Amen," I said.

"Talk about being a teenager," Becki said. "He's the biggest teenager."

"He eats too much sugar, you can tell," Kevin said, and I couldn't help but laugh.

We kept trudging along. My shoes were getting wet from the dew in the grass. "He wants it to be a family show, why doesn't he start by treating us like family?" I said. "'Member what I said, Becki? If the point of the show is to meet our Swedish families, why the hell do we have to do all this? It's torture. It's *literal torture*."

We all looked back at the field, the wooden boards, the tiles, the dozens of people milling around, the cameras, the geese, the cows, the hullabaloo.

"And it's stupid," I added.

"Stupid," Kevin said.

"So stupid," Becki said.

But I noticed we all kept looking back.

✤

CHAPTER TEN

ETT MELLANSPEL

What makes a family, anyhow? After I separated from Becki and Kevin, telling them I wanted to walk back to the hotel instead of heading to the subway, I dodged bicycles and passed pedestrians along a canal and considered the question. There seemed to be no easy answer, if answers even existed. Tocke kept harping that *Sverige och Mig* was a family show, one that Swedes of all generations gathered to watch every Sunday, but what did that even mean? That there was no violence? No cruelty or mayhem? Even though violence and cruelty and mayhem, at least in my family, were as routine as a Thanksgiving turkey?

For years I'd been worn out by people waving the family flag like Tocke did when he wanted to make us feel bad. It boiled down to power, as most things did. So much was excused or protected or justified for the sake of an abstract, if not imaginary, family. Focus on the Family, ha! People had children because that's what people did. Having children was hard and tiring, and because it was hard and tiring, and because people were guaranteed to mess it up due to, among other things, being tired, they told each other constantly what a good and noble thing it was to do.

And then, goodness and nobility assured, they did all sorts of things, bad and good, that forever went unexamined, because to examine a family the way one examined, say, Congress, would rip society's fabric to an unmendable degree. And if this lack of examination happened to annoy a person, or strike a person as fatuous or hypocritical—

"You'll see, it changes you," a wealthy mom had explained, patting my arm at one of Jemma's sponsored parties. Jemma had told me this woman had recently fired her nanny, who was working below minimum wage, for watching too much TV. "It's the best thing I've ever done, really. You think you'll start trying soon, Molly?" Before I could answer, she tinkled a laugh and squeezed my forearm with her bejeweled hand. "If you have any questions, don't hesitate to reach out!"

"Has it changed her?" I asked Jemma after we'd escaped to the buffet. I hadn't had a chance to mention my name was not Molly.

Jemma popped a cucumber sandwich in her mouth and cocked an eyebrow. "I mean, yeah," she said, chewing, "jus' not the way she thinks."

Jemma, dear Jemma. What about the fact that Jemma was a Hungarian Jew, no blood relation, yet we routinely finished each other's sentences? Or that my mother, sister, and father were the people in the world most foreign to me, though we shared skeins of DNA? Or that my grand-mother, a hero in my mind, had to die before my dad would come out of the closet? Or that my fourth-great-grandma, whom I'd encountered thanks to *Sverige och Mig*, was both a role model and a figment of my imagination? Or that Karen Hamburger, who I saw biweekly in a beige office for fifty minutes, was the best parent I'd ever had?

And Declan—even recalling his name brought an ache to my chest. I knew every inch of Declan's body, had a hard time falling asleep without the weight of it next to mine, yet even when we were not half a world away, arguing on the telephone, he often made as much sense to me as the code he spent too much time writing. Did that count as family? Would it count more if we were married? If I knew his parents better? If we ignored the fact of each other's strangeness and focused instead on holiday rituals and date nights? And why did all these people inside my screens back home, or smiling happily in their Christmas mailers, or even here on the canal in Stockholm, pushing strollers or holding hands, seem unbothered by these questions? How did they think about family without this ache in their chest? Or if they did ache, as I did, why and how did they hide it?

But others must ache. In fact, I'd borne witness to such aching for weeks: Deborah, who'd been adopted by a family that omitted her from their tree; Kevin, whose family had buried—had been forced to bury—essential truths about their Sámi heritage; Tom, whose father's death continued to undo him; Becki, whose family patterns, once discovered, had taken the wind right out of her. Families were horrible! Genealogy was horrible! Think of the despicable regimes, from the Nazis to the Brahmins to the Boers to American slaveholders, that had declared that a person's personhood was defined by and limited to patrimony. Think of the despicable families that hid evil behind the fortress of blood ties. And yet we—I—continued to bang my head against the wall of heredity, or was it a prison, praying a hidden door might swing open to—what?

A young guy dressed in crisp business wear passed me, then, listening to big headphones, and I heard the faint strains of David Bowie's "Life on Mars?" Declan loved Bowie to the same degree he hated genealogy. We'd watched a Bowie documentary over the winter, and I'd been shocked to discover that he'd grown up in a very conventional, middle-class family in South London, about as far away from Mars as you could get. After the movie, Declan had asked me why I was so surprised. "I guess I never thought of him as coming from anywhere," I'd told him, realizing my answer only by saying it aloud. "He seemed to just fall from the sky."

The same was true for Nan Goldin, Diane Arbus, all the women artists I loved and most admired. They lived on the vanguard, unimpressed by nostalgia and institutions of any kind. Yet I found myself arguing with myself as I crossed a bridge over the canal, wandered past the Slussen subway station, and took a left to meander back along the water on the opposite side. Self-invention had its own problems. It was all right and good to discard old ideas, but what about discarding people? What about the lonely people in Los Angeles, with their stage names and their empty mailboxes? The fraying of social ties? The epidemic of isolation inspiring countless internet think pieces? I was so lost in thought I practically ran into Fotografiska's brick exterior before realizing where I was. I'd been avoiding the photography museum for nearly a month, even after Tom had sung its praises, and yet I'd somehow made my way straight to it when I wasn't paying attention. Tourists chattering in multiple languages—French, German, Japanese, Dutch—streamed past me toward the entrance. I felt my chest tighten, the same feeling I used to get before critiques in art school. Perhaps an inherited feeling, perhaps the same feeling my great-grandmother had when arriving at Ellis Island, perhaps a plain-old human feeling, longing and loss mixed up in a stew.

Whatever its origins, I let the feeling lead me inside Fotografiska, past the airy gift shop, to the ticket desk, and through a revolving turnstile that led to the exhibits. The museum was busy but not crowded, and I soon found myself alone in the first room of the ground-floor show. The headline exhibit was called *Migrations*. On the black walls, under stark spotlights, hung blown-up images of Swedish emigrants, all taken at the Gothenburg harbor in the late nineteenth century. No one in the pictures smiled. Even the children's faces looked weathered. Their bodies looked bigger than their thin necks suggested; they were likely wearing all the clothes they owned.

I sat down on the hard wooden bench and looked at these strangers. Really looked. Didn't just run my eyes over the images, hoping for instant gratification. These were not beautiful pictures; these were not beautiful people. You could not call the compositions artful, nor the subjects particularly revealing. And yet the sum, somehow, transcended the parts. The longer I sat, the more it seemed I could feel the anticipation humming in their bodies, the fear hiding beneath grim resolve. One of the children, a boy, gripped a small wooden toy with one hand. This one detail seemed to open up the whole world inside the frame: ordinary and extraordinary, same as mine; filled with desire and lack, same as mine; expectation and disappointment, same as mine.

The same thing happened in the next room, which was busy with photographs of Swedish immigrants in America from the same era. What I noticed first was that the necks were even thinner, the faces even more weathered. Rough-hewn cabins, hand-felled trees, and community-built churches loomed in the background, along with thick, old-growth forests. One wall was devoted to Swede Hollow, a ghetto in St. Paul, Minnesota, where, according to a wall panel, Swedish immigrants had lived in squalid conditions while installing the city's first plumbing system. The Swedes were replaced by Italians in the early twentieth century, then by Poles, until the neighborhood was razed by the city, having been deemed both an eyesore and a public health hazard.

I expected the next room to be similar in both subject and era, but what I saw instead, stepping into the darkness, were contemporary portraits of asylum-seekers taken by an Afro-Swedish photographer. *Välkommen?* read the first wall panel. The migrants were living in small towns and large cities, based on the backgrounds. Some wore headscarves, some didn't. Some looked at ease, others didn't. A watchfulness pervaded the space behind their eyes; their necks were also thin, their cheeks also lined, their clothes secondhand and oversized. The next wall panel informed me that Sweden had opened its doors to refugees in the previous decade, but then slammed them shut after nearly two hundred thousand migrants entered en masse. According to the panel, "Europe's greatest example of tolerance morphed into suspicion within eighteen months." Just as Lars had said during our discussion of his documentary at the Champagne Bar. My heart rat-a-tatted at the thought of him, though whether out of regret or longing it was hard to say.

The exhibit's next and final room was filled with portraits, not of people but of birds, taken by the same Afro-Swedish photographer. Specifically, species of birds that were dying out, losing centuries of hard-wired migratory patterning due to light pollution. When they began to fly in autumn, they became disoriented and ended up freezing to death in places too cold for them to survive. One of the images showed a blackpoll warbler, dun-colored and plump, perched on a thin branch, its orange claws hooked just above a clump of leaves.

Before I knew it, I had plopped down on the bench in the middle of the room and was weeping bitter tears, not bothering to rub my face when other tourists wandered through. My high school photography teacher used to say that, like chiaroscuro, an artist cannot capture real beauty without also capturing real ugliness. "People think they want sunsets and smiles and beaches," she'd say, writing with such force on the blackboard that the chalk squealed. "You must remind them that what they really want is the truth."

Still sniffling, I stood up and went through the exhibit all over again, letting the chiaroscuro crash through my body. Human beings wreaked a lot of havoc on the world, and I was no exception. I gazed at the sandpipers, the wild geese, the pregnant Syrian, the hollow-eyed Irani, the exhausted immigrants, the hopeful emigrants, until at some point, somewhere in those dark rooms, the contradictory forces of beauty and ugliness turned into physical energy in my body. It itched to move, to make, to wreak its own kind of havoc, not of destruction but creation. And because it couldn't bear to stay in the hushed walls of the museum, I left without seeing any of the other exhibits, the energy driving my feet out the door.

Outside, the air was breezy and cool, and the sun played peekaboo with gray cashmere clouds. I took my Polaroid out of my backpack and saw that I had three pictures left on the cartridge. The energy propelled me over to a wood-and-iron bench overlooking the canal. An older woman with a shock of short red hair sat on it, her hands resting atop her cane, her cane resting on the earth between her feet. She wore thick black glasses, an oversized lavender blazer, and wide black pants. "Hello, *hej*," the energy said before my mind could catch up. "May I take your picture?"

She looked at me. She seemed neither shocked nor particularly interested. "Why?" she said in English. Her voice was gravelly, her accent thick.

I startled, answered honestly: "I don't know."

"Are you a photographer?"

I shifted my weight. "No. Yes. I don't know."

"It seems you do not know very much."

A snort of a laugh escaped my nose. A smile threatened the corners of her lips. She said, "I do not like to have my picture taken."

"Why not?"

She adjusted her hands on her cane. "I never look like myself."

"I can help." The energy pushed the words out before I had the chance to balk at their audacity. "May I?" I motioned to the space on the bench next to her. She nodded. I sat and set my camera down beside me. "Where are you from?" I asked.

Thus began an hour-long conversation whose subject matter ranged from her childhood in Karlstad to her work as the only female architect at one of Stockholm's most prestigious firms to sex to travel to relationships to old age. "It scares me," she said later in the conversation, referring to death. "To grow old, it is like the frog in water growing hotter and hotter. I do not always notice how much of myself I am losing."

This rang true to me, even though I had never heard anyone speak in this way. I stayed quiet, hoping she would say more. Eventually she concluded, "It is terrifying." And then she burst out a deep, throaty laugh. Which made me laugh. So we laughed together for a brief and glorious time as the clouds chased the sun across the sky.

"I know this sounds strange," I said after the energy had settled. "But I wonder if you would let me take your picture now."

And perhaps because I'd spent some time with her, or because we'd laughed together, she did. She even took off her glasses and set them gently in her lap. After a moment, I heard her breath deepen, saw her face relax, saw a softness come around her eyes. I picked up my Polaroid silently, looked through the viewfinder. "Open your eyes," I said from behind the camera. She did. *Click*.

We sat in silence as we waited for the print to develop. The breeze from the water sounded like a seashell in my ears. After ten minutes, I turned it over on the bench. There she was. Not all of her, but maybe as much as my old Polaroid could get.

"Yes," she said, nodding with approval. She picked it up and gazed at herself. "I am beautiful, no?"

I laughed. "Oh yes."

She pulled it toward her chest. "I keep this?"

A split-second of grasping, then I felt my hand unclench. "Of course," I told her. "It belongs to you."

She thanked me as she stood up slowly, straightened her clothes, and gestured with her cane toward the subway station. "I mean to ask you before I leave," she said, turning around after a few feet. "Why are you in Sweden?"

The answer seemed like it belonged to a different world. "I'm filming a TV show."

She looked at me thoughtfully, then pointed at me with her cane. "*Crying Americans*."

My eyebrows rose. "*Sverige och Mig*. How did you know?"

She shook her head and said in a forthright way, "Well, you are American, and when you first talk to me, you are crying."

"Was I?" I touched my cheeks.

"I like this show. It is a nice show. The family reunion is very moving." She turned around again. "I will cheer for you."

"Here," I said, hurrying to her side. "I'll walk you to the train."

We started thumping along the canal, me with my camera, her with her cane.

"You Americans," she said, placing her cane deliberately in front of her. "We like how you show your emotions. This helps us. My friend's husband cries once a year, on the final episode."

"That's a nice way to think about it," I said. "The producer says we're like spoiled children."

"That is true," she said with that same forthrightness. "But what most Swedes will not say is we wish to be open like you. But we are too ashamed."

We had reached the subway station then. "Thank you," I said. "*Tack så jättemycket*."

"*Tack så jättemycket*," she said, correcting my pronunciation. "I hope you keep photographing. You seem to enjoy it, yes? I am still drafting every day, even at my age. It is a pleasant way to spend the morning."

"A pleasant way to spend the morning," I echoed.

As she made her deliberate way inside the subway station, I realized I had never gotten her name. Then she was gone. I turned and walked back across the bridge where I'd come from that morning, feeling a peace I hadn't felt since my early days with a camera, when I'd take it with me to parks and parties and the late-night diner where Jemma's and my friends would play dumb games like how much milk could you drink without puking. It gave me something to do, something that felt important, and I didn't care that no one found it important but my friends and me. Only later had the pictures become currency to trade, subject to market forces and thus vulnerable to capricious elements like tastes and trends, supply and demand, things that had nothing to do with their making.

I stopped at the center of the bridge leading to Gamla Stan, my heart thudding. Two teenagers were standing next to me, making out, the boy's hands cupping the girl's rear, the girl draped over the boy like a fainting couch. The sight was garish and outré, especially compared to the austerity of the old-fashioned architecture surrounding them. It was stupendous. "Excuse me, *ursäkta*," I said. They turned to me, their eyes half-lidded, dreamlike. "Can I take your picture?"

They stared at me. "*Foto*." I held up my camera. "Hard copy. You keep it."

"I guess?" the girl said in perfect English as the guy adjusted his erection.

In a flash, they had posed in a way I'd seen before, a copy of a copy of a copy of something someone saw on the internet. The girl pursed her lips. The boy put on a tough face. Both of them made the peace sign. "Not like that," I said. "Like you were before. Like I'm not here."

They looked at me like I was insane. But I had their hormones on my side, plus the element of stealth. I walked to the other side of the bridge. After twenty minutes or so they were going at it again like they'd been before, and I crept over. *Click*. I handed them the film. They stared at it the entire time it developed, as if they'd never seen a Polaroid before. Perhaps they hadn't. "Huh," the girl said finally. The boy said something to her in Swedish. She laughed.

I kept walking without a destination in mind, carried on by the urge to create. I had one picture left in the camera, and I sensed the subject would reveal itself to me without having to search. I wandered all the way through Gamla Stan and across the bridge to Kungsträdgården, where old men were playing chess. Over and up through Norrmalm, with its bustling hotels, restaurants, and shops, and the famed Centralbadet spa. Past one leafy park, then another, then another, until I found myself tripping on a sidewalk across from the park at Odengatan. When I regained my balance, a gold plaque on a stately gray stone building facade practically stared me in the face:

ASTRID LINDGRENS HEM
DALAGATAN 46

Her house? Astrid Lindgren's house? A runner was exiting the building entrance, tucking headphones into his ears. He turned left and started to jog. On instinct, I grabbed the heavy door just before it closed and ducked inside. The air in the vestibule was cool, the light dim. Large pastoral oil paintings hung above the wainscoting, and a tacked-up piece of paper listed the residents and apartment numbers. Astrid Lindgren, 1tr, Gatuhus, it read in Times New Roman, plain and unadorned.

As if possessed, I stepped farther inside, passing the old-fashioned gated elevator and making my way up the curving stone steps. Astrid Lindgren's apartment was one floor above street level, and next to the door was a little library made from a wooden milk crate, filled with her books. I sat down, removed an old paperback of *Pippi Långstrumpf*, and started leafing through the pages. Though it was in Swedish, I knew the stories well enough to recognize them in any language. Pippi goes to school, Pippi goes to the circus, Pippi goes to *fika*. Curled up on the floor, leaning against Astrid's door, my joy at seeing this funny little girl live and do as she pleased was undiminished from childhood. She never let anyone get the best of her: not policemen, not burglars, not judgmental neighbors. Even when she disagreed, or misunderstood, or refused their terms, she happily gave them her rare gold coins and served up strong black coffee. And while I had failed, again and again on this trip, to live up to Pippi's unconditional friendliness, rereading these stories felt like singing along in the shower to one's favorite song: the point, maybe, was not to sound like the music but to catch the tail of the feeling that created it. And maybe marvel at the fact that a regular person, a person just like you, had briefly transcended the slop of daily life and reached out and touched the truth.

There was a red bookmark inside the back flap of the paperback, decorated with a drawing of Pippi. Down its length it said something in Swedish that I could not decipher. I was just about to stand up and make my way outside to find someone to translate for me when the door I'd been leaning against opened, and I fell backward into Astrid Lindgren's vestibule, the back of my skull landing with a thud on the parquet floor.

"Owww," I said when my eyes opened, feeling for the back of my head.

A very old woman with short gray hair, a thousand wrinkles, and gentle blue eyes was peering down at me like a bird. She said something in Swedish as I scrambled to my feet. "I'm sorry," I said, "I don't speak—"

"Who are you?" The question seemed driven by curiosity rather than suspicion. I took a few steps out of the apartment, and she moved the door close around her frame. I could still see a raincoat hanging in the hallway and a duck-handled umbrella in a stand.

"Oh—um—" I held up the copy of *Pippi Långstrumpf*. "My name is Paulie—Pauline Johannson. These books are—sorry, the door downstairs was open—"

A white lie, which seemed to amuse the woman. Yet all she said was "There are no tours." She motioned behind her to the apartment. "There are at other times of the year, but the building is getting new plumbing." I noticed, then, the old woman was wearing wooden clogs. A sliver of striped sock was visible beneath her sensible slacks.

"That's okay," I said, backing away, the paperback still in my hand. "I shouldn't be here—I'm so sorry for intruding—here, I'll put this back—"

I knelt down to place *Pippi Långstrumpf* back in the milk crate, but the old woman waved her hand. "Keep it," she said, a smile passing across her face. "I have plenty more."

"Thank you." I clutched it to my chest. "Truly. I'll treasure it."

"Goodbye, then." She started to close the door, but—

"Wait!" I said, putting an arm out to stop her. I pulled the bookmark from the paperback. "Before I go, could you please tell me what this means?"

The old woman leaned forward, squinting at the small type. Then she laughed a little. "Of course," she said, as if remembering something. Then she looked me dead in the eyes. "'When you are very strong, you must also be very kind.'"

I THUDDED DOWN the stairs, out of the building, across the street to enter the park off Dalagatan. It was late afternoon, and the green was filled with families and old couples. Gripping my paperback like a precious stone, I managed to snag an empty bench near an impromptu soccer scrimmage. I flipped through the pages, looking for an author photo, but there was none. I was almost positive Astrid Lindgren was dead, for the government surely didn't put plaques on living authors' apartment buildings. But then who was that woman? And why didn't she seem at all shocked to see me at her door?

"Paulie? Is that you?"

I looked up from my book and did a double take. Standing in front of me was Lars. Two young girls, clad in shin guards, were peering out behind him. "You have children?" I blurted.

He smiled, nodded, said something to them in Swedish. "This is Ingrid," Lars said, gesturing to one of his daughters. "And this is Birgit." They waved shyly. I waved back. They looked a great deal like their father: tall, slender, serious faces, light-brown hair. He told them, "Paulie is one of the Americans on *Sverige och Mig*." And then to me: "They are in English school, but they are scared to practice."

"You didn't tell me you had kids," I said, not accusingly but not-not.

"You didn't ask."

"What are you doing here?"

"I live here." He pointed to Astrid Lindgren's apartment building.

"You live in Astrid Lindgren's house?"

Lars laughed. "Not her house, but her building, yes."

"I didn't see your name on the—" I said, and then realized that despite all our—I didn't know what to call them, fraught exchanges?—I never did catch his last name. Ingrid and Birgit were staring at me in that guileless way children have. "It's okay, you can practice your English with me," I told them. Then I said all the Swedish words I knew, five in total, and my pronunciation made them laugh.

"How do you like it here in Sweden?" Ingrid, the older one, said.

"I like it very much," I said, and for the first time since arriving I felt my heart clench with longing. "But I miss home too."

Birgit nodded. She pointed at my Polaroid, whose box chain strap was still looped around my shoulder. "What is that?"

I explained it was a camera, but the old-fashioned kind, and as I did I understood exactly what to do with my final piece of film. "May I take your picture with it?"

Birgit looked at her father, who nodded. "All of you," I said, standing up from the bench. I arranged them where I'd been sitting: Lars in the middle, a daughter on each side. I sat on the ground and chatted with the girls for a while, in the hopes of putting them at ease. I had a bag of strawberry licorice in my purse from 7–Eleven, and with Lars's permission I offered it as tribute. "So, um, is everything okay with you and Tocke?" I asked Lars at one point while the girls started bickering in Swedish.

He shrugged. "You know Tocke, he loses his temper over everything, especially when things don't go as he plans. I do not take it seriously any longer."

"Oh. Well, that's good."

Unspoken words and unfinished business hovered in the air, heavy and viscous like glue. Lars turned his head and said something to Ingrid in Swedish. She retorted, and Birgit joined in, seemingly on her sister's side. It was a familiar, familial scene, the intimacy among them revealed through small gestures: the tugging at a sleeve, the exasperated sigh, the eye roll, the razor-thin vocal line between irritation and endearment. Quickly, before they could remember I was there, I raised the viewfinder to my eyes and took the picture. *Snap.* They looked at me in surprise. "It's perfect," I assured them, and gave the film to Birgit to shake.

When it finished developing, the photo revealed exactly what I had seen: a family. An unmistakable unit, as recognizable as a tree. Lars was mid-sentence, Birgit was scowling, Ingrid had her palms open in response to her father. I looked at it closely. Yes, this was a family. And it was not my family. Whatever Lars had been to me, it was not and would never be this.

The girls thought it was hilarious. They were laughing and talking to each other in Swedish.

"My gift to you," I said to Lars. Our eyes met. "An apology."

He gave me that half-smile of his. "No need for an apology."

"Then a thank-you."

"No need to thank me either."

Tears sprang behind my eyes. "Then a goodbye."

He nodded soberly. I stood up and held out my hand to Birgit. "It was awfully nice to meet you." Then to Ingrid. "And you." Then to Lars. "And you."

Yes, we'd see each other the next day—that is, if both of us weren't fired—but it would be different. And that difference would make us a little sad, but a little relieved too. "I will never forget," he said.

"Nor I," I said.

He passed me the photograph. "Please keep it. *En minne.*"

"What does that mean?"

He smiled. Not a half-smile, all the way. It was beautiful, partly because I knew I would never see it again. "A memory."

IT WAS AFTER nine when I knocked on Becki's hotel door holding a Swedish *Prinsesstårta*, a princess cake, that I'd snagged from a bakery on my long walk home. She opened the door wearing matching pajamas, her blond hair in pigtails, her black eye fading. It was such a far cry from the tough, abrasive Becki I'd met in Copenhagen that I felt my mouth stretch into a smile before either of us had said anything.

"What's this for?" she said, standing aside so that I could enter.

"It's an apology cake," I said, and told her about how I could have prevented her from going spread-eagle on the concert stairs. "I was—" I started to say, and halted. "You're so confident," I said finally. "Here I am, going on and on about, you know, women's issues, but I still fall into this trap where I think there's not enough—"

"I get jealous of you, too, you know," she said, shrugging.

"You do?"

"Even though I hate how much you talk about emotions, I wish I could do that sometimes."

"You do, though," I said. "You have."

Instead of acknowledging this, Becki went over to the minibar area to pull out a couple plastic forks. "I take them from restaurants," she explained, holding up the forks. "You never know when you're going to need them."

It was such a domestic, almost motherly, thing to do. In that moment, I swear I saw Becki anew, saw something in her that was easy to miss, something she may have, in fact, actively tried to prevent me from seeing, and the fact that she tried so hard to hide it only made it more precious. She handed me a fork and opened the plastic lid on the princess cake. It was covered with green marzipan and, according to the baker, filled with sponge cake, jam, and whipped cream. An elegant pink rose sat in the center, which the baker said traditionally went to the person being celebrated. I nudged Becki to take it. "So, yeah, about feelings," Becki said as she dug her fork into the flower. "The reason I bought the phone and didn't tell anybody about it was because—"

She chewed, swallowed. She took a sip of wine from an open bottle on the TV stand, then passed it to me. "Because—"

The story came out haltingly and not in the right order, the way difficult events do when they haven't had time or space to cohere. Eventually I came to understand that Becki had spent a lot of money on her dad's cancer treatment over the past several years, money she'd ordinarily have been funneling into her landscaping business to keep it afloat. She'd stopped taking a salary, too, relying on her lash-extension side hustle to make up the difference, but she kept coming up short, both in the business accounts and in her personal ones. For months she'd essentially been playing a shell game, moving money around as soon as it came time to pay the minimum balance on maxed-out credit cards and overdue bills.

"Why didn't you tell me?" I said with my mouth full of cake. "Or tell Tocke?"

"Because it's embarrassing." She took a huge forkful of cake and stuffed it in her mouth. "I'm supposed to be—I've always taken care of myself. And now ..."

"You'll be all right," I jumped in. "You have so many people who love you and wanna help. I'll help." I puffed my cheeks, thinking. "We could start a GoFundMe! When the show airs! You'll get tons of donations. Or we could—"

"We . . ." Becki was saying, almost to herself, when the phone rang. We looked at each other. I nodded toward the receiver. She got up, dusted the crumbs off her pajama top, and went over to the nightstand. "Hello? Oh, hi. No, she's here with me. Okay, sure."

She turned. "It's Tocke. He wants me to put him on speaker."

"Oh God," I said as my heart rocketed into my stomach. I mouthed to Becki, *Are we about to get fired?*

She mouthed back, *Maybe?*

"Hello?" a tinny Tocke was saying. "Can you hear me?"

"We can hear you!" I said.

"Listen, guys, about this morning," Tocke said. I braced myself. I ate a bite of cake. I prepared myself for yet another treatise on American self-indulgence. I ate more cake. Finally, my cheeks bursting with marzipan, I heard him sigh. "I am sorry."

"Sorry?" Becki and I both said with our mouths full. We looked at each other, incredulous.

"The thing is, I really am under a lot of pressure," Tocke said in a rush. "The ratings for *Sverige och Mig* are not as good as they used to be. The network is threatening to cancel the show if they do not improve and replace it with"—he said something in Swedish—"it is a home-makeover show where the children do the demolition. This worries me a lot. I cannot sleep. My doctor says I must stop working so I do not have heart attack." Here, I could have sworn I heard his voice crack. "But *Sverige och Mig* is like my child. I would do anything for her."

"Oh no," I said, and in my heart I felt genuine sympathy.

"I know my, how do you say, my temper . . ." Tocke the Viking sounded almost frail.

"No, I'm sorry, Tocke," Becki said, jumping in while I stared at the phone. "I shouldn't have gotten that burner, it was stupid. It's just that I'm this close to having to declare bankruptcy and I was too proud to tell anyone, so I was just moving money around, trying to make it work—"

"And I'm sorry too." I stood up, my cheeks flushed with sugar or courage or both. "About Lars. I know the code of conduct says no hanky-panky. For what it's worth it was only hanky, not panky"—oh dear God—"and I swear I didn't get a single piece of intelligence as a result—"

There was a knock at the door. "One sec, someone's here," Becki said into the phone. A moment later, she returned with Kevin. "Hey Tocke," he said to the receiver. I gave Kevin a small wave.

"I was just telling the others that I am sorry for this morning," Tocke said from the phone.

"And I'm sorry too," I said to Kevin.

"And me too," Becki said to the phone.

Kevin looked at the princess cake, then at Becki, then at the phone, then at me. I could tell he was calculating the advantages of exploiting our vulnerability versus sharing his own. Kevin loved having the upper hand, whether in conversations, solar-panel sales, or body-fat percentages. But this time he surprised me. "You know what?" he said, taking my fork out of my hand and digging into the cake.

"That's not keto—" I started to say.

"I'm sorry too." Kevin took a huge bite and said with his mouth full, "I can be a real douche canoe." He swallowed. "Those steroids really are for my back, though."

"They are," I said to the phone. "I shouldn't have said otherwise, that was stupid."

Kevin dug out another forkful. "And Paulie and Lars only hooked up once."

"Well, twice, but I guess it depends on your definition . . ." I said, trailing off.

"And I only used my banking apps," Becki said, then paused. "Okay, and Facebook. And I guess I listened to music once in a while, but that was just to help me sleep."

"Have you ever heard of the Swedish term *lagom*?" Tocke said.

We shook our heads until Becki realized he couldn't see us. "No," she said into the phone.

"*Lagom* is a very important part of Swedish culture. It means not too much, not too little. This ritual comes from the Vikings. When you passed around a bottle of mead on the ship, you were supposed to be *lagom*. Enjoy, but save some for your neighbors.

"After ten seasons, I do not think Americans are so good at *lagom*. 'Too much' is your medium and you scream and cry at 'too little.' This makes me crazy, but it is also good TV. And it is"—he took a deep breath—"*you* are what make this show special."

"But Tocke, I want to be more *lagom*," I said, startled by my own urgency. "I don't want to let Becki trip or tackle Kevin at the ABBA Museum or tell Brock I'm gonna kill Tom or fall in love with Lars after five minutes when I don't even know the guy. I don't want to give up photography just because I'll never be famous and I don't want to give up on my relationship just because Declan's no longer a fantasy—"

Becki interrupted: "And I don't want to be tough all the time, I want to have feelings too—"

"And I don't want to be keto anymore," Kevin said. He ripped off a huge chunk of cake with his fingers and stuffed it into his mouth. "And I want to keep singing."

I took a step toward the door. "I'm sorry, I have to go."

"Go where?" Becki said.

"I'll be back in a few." I leaned over to the phone. "Just to be clear, Tocke—are we fired?"

"No," he said. "Everything is *lagom*."

I SPRINTED BACK to my room, then over to the telephone, where I dialed Declan's number. I didn't even wait for him to say hello. "I figured it out," I said breathlessly. "*Lagom*."

"Paulie—I'm—la-what?"

I briefly explained what Tocke said. "Like, with you and me," I huffed. Hmm, maybe I should start doing cardio with Kevin. "We make each other *lagom*. I get you out of your head, you get me into mine. You slow me down, I speed you up. We don't need to see eye to eye on everything"—I smacked my palm on the bed—"we just need to find the middle way!"

"Yes," Declan said amiably. "Paulie, I hear you. But I'm also on the other line with my CTO."

I looked at the clock. Right smack dab in the middle of Declan's working hours. "Right-o," I said. "Of course. Not very *lagom* of me, ha ha. But I had to tell you."

"I'm glad you did." And he sounded glad, truly glad. Then: "I really have to get back to this call."

"Oh! Of course. Okay, bye."

I replaced the receiver, replaced the film in my Polaroid camera, and ran back to Becki's room, which she'd left propped open for me. She was playing ABBA from the room's impressive speaker system, and both she and Kevin were dancing. Half the cake was gone, and the wine was gone too. Their cheeks were pink from sugar. Kevin had taken off his shirt, and Becki was using her hairbrush as a microphone. "*People need love!*" they sang.

These crazy people, these Americans. "*People need love!*" They were not who I ever planned to love, not even who I wanted to love, what with their weird habits, crackpot politics, and various unpleasantness. But they were also—I put my hand on my chest, as if to make sure—they were who I loved. And I think they loved me back—tolerated me, humored me, forgave me for my own tall stack of weird habits and unpleasantness. And standing there in the doorway, I thought that if anyone got to see them as I did, with their innumerable layers and impossible contradictions, they couldn't help but love them too.

CHAPTER ELEVEN

✦

MÅTTET PÅ EN KVINNA

Becki, Kevin, and I were laughing the next morning at breakfast over thick layers of Swedish pancakes, strawberry jam, and whipped cream, remembering a moment from the night before when Kevin had put on Becki's sunglasses and lip-synced to Elvis Presley's "Jailhouse Rock."

Don't be fooled—it wasn't that Kevin and I had become best friends overnight. More that we had decided to give up on being enemies. The transition reminded me of the fights Else and I'd had as girls over God-knows-what—Else's bossiness, my stealing Else's toys—fights that ended with screaming declarations of hatred and ill will. For an hour we would stay locked in bitter and mutual resentment. Sometimes two. And then one of us, inevitably, faithfully, would pad over to the other and make a very specific sound into her ear, a hopeful chirping. And in that sound lay dozens of layers of meaning: *I'm sorry* and *This is boring* and *Do you want to play some more* and *I'm not mad* and *Are you mad* and *Don't be mad* and *I can wait if you're still mad* and *But please don't make me wait forever*. One of the great tragedies of my adult life was that Else and I had at some point lost the ability to move fluidly between love and anger, delight and betrayal, hope and disappointment. Yet something about the night before had jostled Kevin and me out of a similar trench warfare and into a no-man's-land free of grudge. I didn't know how long we'd be able to stay there, but the fresh air felt pretty good.

"Your hips!" Becki practically screamed, falling into her orange juice at the thought of it, when Inga appeared in front of us in the hotel restaurant, dressed in oversized pants and a crop top and jingling the van keys. "You are in a good mood for three people almost fired yesterday," she said, raising an unplucked brow. "Why is this?"

"We had fun last night," Kevin said. He was hoovering a pancake, a food so far from keto he might as well've been sliding around Candy Land.

Inga looked at us, moving her gaze from one to the next. "Fun," she repeated. "You had fun. You have not taken drugs or stolen money?"

I blinked. "No."

Inga narrowed her eyes. "Did Magnus take you on the *Patricia* last night?"

The *Patricia*, I remembered Magnus telling me back at the Champagne Bar, was a former yacht turned multistory nightclub permanently parked on one of Stockholm's canals. "No *Patricia* either," I said to Inga, pushing my chair back. Becki and Kevin pushed theirs back, too, and grabbed their suitcases, which had surrounded our table like a fortress wall. Kevin handed me my bags without my asking. I said, "Thanks, Kev."

He said, "No prob, Paul."

Inga's face looked skeptical. Then she jingled her keys, sighed, and motioned to the door. "You Americans, you are so crazy."

We had to go back to Skansen for about an hour that morning and don our competition polos, so Tocke could film our ersatz reactions to affable host Erik Lundgren's announcement that none of us would be going home. Tocke said he planned to cut that in with the truncated footage they already had from the competition, and they'd finish the episode with a "music video," aka clips from previous episodes, set to the song Kevin and I had penned with Tove Orönso. Which was all to say that, by some miracle, if we played our cards right, no viewer would ever know we'd all gone a little nuts on one another and been nearly fired on a grassy field across from a petting zoo.

After we'd finished reacting and syncing, we climbed back in the van, and Inga drove us a couple hours to a pretty little city called Norrköping, southwest of Stockholm, where we arrived in time for lunch. The town, according to Deborah's atlas, had been an industrial center in the nineteenth century, then kind of died out in the twentieth, and now was apparently trudging back to life thanks to a fledgling tourism industry and a remodeled downtown that hugged the Motala River.

We were there, Inga told us over a light lunch of various spreads on toast, to learn about the Swedish education system: one of the best, Inga said, in the world. Though school was about to let out for summer, we'd been invited to volunteer at an English-intensive middle school in the waning days of the term. Kevin, Becki, and I were thereafter outfitted with microphones and greeted at the front door of an old-fashioned building by the principal, a well-dressed older woman by the name of Lise. Lise led us inside to a cafeteria/auditorium, where a large crowd of teens sat on small chairs. They looked, more or less, like American middle schoolers: hair of various length and color, clothing either enormous or minuscule in size. Though a majority of the students were blond and blue-eyed, there were a small number of non-white students, and I couldn't help but recall the rise and fall of Sweden's open-arms immigration policy. Lise strode up onto the stage. "Here are the Americans I was telling you about," Lise told the students in English. "Please welcome them and the crew from *Sverige och Mig*." The teens clapped wanly, as only teens can.

"Somnolent" is the word that best describes the remainder of the assembly, what with the thick warmth of adolescent bodies, the creaks of an old building, the drone of a kind authority figure speaking in a foreign tongue. I must have passed out in my little chair, for the next thing I remember was Becki thunking me on the arm. "C'mon, they're taking us to a sex-ed class, can you believe it?"

I followed Kevin and Becki obediently out of the auditorium and into a classroom, where Lars, Jonas, and Magnus had already set up.

They nodded and waved as the middle schoolers filed in. We nodded and waved back. The sex-ed teachers—two men, both in their forties, both handsome enough to make me blush at the thought of them saying "penis"—were telling their students to sit. We sat. Later, Magnus told me that the teachers had been instructed to act like we weren't there, which explained the fact that I had no more squeezed my rear end into a teen-sized chair when one of the hot teachers pulled up a PowerPoint on his laptop. The other pulled down a projector screen from the board, and before I could make up a safe word, the word "porn" popped up in the title slide, which was illustrated with a painting of Rubenesque naked women.

I think I said, "Oh God." There was a twelve-year-old boy sitting on one side of me—Becki was on the other—who looked like he belonged in a Swedish boys' choir: rosy cheeks, blond hair, blue eyes. "Do not worry," he told me with the utmost seriousness. "I will translate for you."

"Oh," I said. "That's very nice, but you don't have—"

He motioned to the screen. "This means, 'Things You Will Not See in Porn.'"

"Oh," I said again, wondering if it was medically possible to die from discomfort.

"You are from *Sverige och Mig*?" the boy beside him asked.

"Yes," I said, relieved to change the subject. "Do you like the show?"

"Only old people watch it," he informed me, and to my surprise I found that my feelings were hurt.

"What about families? They say it is a family show," I said. And then: "It's won an Emmy."

The two of them looked at me dispassionately but said nothing. Before we could get to the bottom of who did or did not watch *Sverige och Mig*, the two handsome teachers started their presentation. Though I was able to more or less guess at the content of the lecture, thanks to graphic hand-drawn illustrations, my new little friend, along with his friend, insisted on translating.

"This means, no smells—no, not smells, odors—"

"This is—they do not have the sounds of sex, from the bodies rubbing to the . . . ah . . . vagina sounds—"

"This says that it is okay if there is—not water—*jaha*, liquids from the bodies—"

I would have thought the boys were trolling me, had they not seemed so earnest about helping. I coped by keeping my eyes a solid foot above the projector and recalling my own sex-ed teacher, Mr. Butz, pronounced "Boots," whose primary teaching appointment was shop class. I'd never forgotten the day he guided my hands on the band saw to make a wooden boat in the morning and then, in the afternoon, used those same hands to dismantle a bust-sized model of a vagina. The plastic clitoris had fallen out and rolled across the floor, and we'd spent most of the period trying to fish it out from under the radiator instead of learning what it was for.

The PowerPoint ended with an efficient run-through of sexual positions one also wouldn't find in porn, ostensibly because they deprioritized the male gaze. Kevin, Becki, and I could only stagger to our feet when the bell rang. When the students had finished filing out, Lars called the three of us over and asked us to do a quick sync about the difference between Swedish and American sex-ed programs. Becki went first. "I went to school in Texas," she told the camera. "So, yeah, all we learned about sex was not to have it. And if you did have it, you better pray to God to forgive you for being a slut."

What about gay sex, Lars asked. Becki startled a second before letting out a *pfff*. "It was the late '90s, no one was gay in Texas."

Kevin went next and told a complicated story about a girl in his class he'd had a crush on who had somehow ended up mishandling a condom so that it ricocheted across the classroom, slingshot-style, and hit him in the eye. "After that they called me Dick Eye," he said, and I could still see his abashment.

Then it was my turn. "Wow," Magnus said, looking back and forth between Lars and me. "This is pretty big moment! Two lovers talking about sexual education, very exciting. I am steamy just thinking about it ha ha! Do you want us to leave so you can—"

"NO," Lars and I both said. Then we both laughed, because what else was there to do, and everyone else laughed, too, and in this way we lubricated the moment past its initial awkwardness. I told the story of Mr. Butz, and also described the pamphlet about periods I was supposed to read for sex-ed homework but instead kept hidden in my backpack, fearful that my mother would find it, for Mom didn't believe in sex and periods the way some people in Florida don't believe in climate change. (Just because a person is personally affected by something doesn't mean they have to accept it exists!) I found myself explaining that it'd taken me two years to figure out how to insert a tampon, which was funny in hindsight, but also sadder, because I'd remembered Jemma's mom had taken her out for a whole special day to celebrate her "flowering" and she'd come back with her first manicure.

"And what do you think about this Swedish system?" Lars asked. "We are very open about sex, as you see."

"Well, gosh, I think that the Swedish attitude toward sex is just great," I said brightly, because I always had to include the subject of the question in my answers. And then, to my surprise, I burst into tears.

WE SPENT THE night at a hotel and all the next day back at school, learning about Swedish immigration. There were a number of former refugees in the school, Lise the principal said, though not nearly as many as in the big cities. Apparently, the children in town had adapted far better than the adults. Lise had a friend who was married to a Chilean, and he wanted to move to Stockholm as soon as they could afford it. "Small towns, they are the same everywhere I think," Lise explained.

"It's not just small towns," Becki said, and told us her Dallas-born father would have disowned her if she ever dated a Black kid. She laughed uncomfortably. "Good thing he's dead, 'cause my boyfriend's Puerto Rican."

I didn't want Becki to feel like we were hanging her out to dry, so I added, "My dad used to make racist jokes, but when I told him not to, he said I needed to lighten up."

"Hey, Paulie, don't look so sad," Kevin said. He put a hand on my fore-arm. "My dad still makes racist jokes."

Though this was awful, not funny, Kevin's earnestness cut the tension, and we laughed. After school, we got two hours of respite back at the hotel before Tocke gathered us at a riverside park for what the crew kept calling the Last Supper. With the help of a portable propane grill and a picnic basket filled with cooked sausages, pickled herring, smoked salmon, fresh bread, a variety of local cheeses, and white wine, Becki, Kevin, and I clinked glasses, ate to bursting, and fought off mosquitoes while being walked through a reflective conversation by Tocke, whose prompts went something like this:

- Talk about how far you have come since you first arrived in Sweden. Talk about all your emotions. If you cry, that is okay.
- Talk about your friends who have already left the show and how you miss them. Also what they might say to you if they were here. If you cry, that is great!
- Talk about what you love about Sweden. Don't worry about going on for too long, because we can always cut it down. Consider crying as you say this.
- What are some of the big differences between Sweden and the U.S.? Talk about how it will be hard to go home because Sweden has changed you. You should be crying by now.
- Talk about how America is not as civilized as Sweden. Remember that Sweden barely has a military and how much America spends on theirs when they could be spending it on health care like we do. Again, don't worry about going on for too long. If you are not crying you are doing something wrong.
- What do you wish you could tell your Swedish families, who are all waiting to meet you and hoping you will win the family reunion? It should be hard to talk now, what with all the crying.
- Talk about how you all are such good friends. Talk about how it will be hard to do tomorrow's competition because one of you who has gotten so close to winning will now be sent home, and they are also your good friend. If you need to take a break because you are crying so hard, that is perfect!

And so forth. Yet somehow, unlike in the first weeks of filming, our semi-scripted conversation managed to transcend the artifice of its scaffolding, and affection swelled in me over that dinner hour. For leading as they were, Tocke's questions gave way to something real inside us, something deep and true. We did miss our old friends who had already left! We did love Sweden! We were good friends! It would be sad for one of us to go home the next day! As I watched Kevin eating bread and Becki visibly moderating her wine intake, I was struck by the sense of knowing them, and they me, in an intimate way, a way that relatively few people had ever known us. Maybe this was what arranged marriage was like, or any marriage. Maybe shared history was what people meant by family.

The nights were getting shorter and shorter by then, even south of Stockholm. Midsommar was just a few days away, and the air was filled with anticipation. On the walk back to the hotel I saw a stand filled with small red strawberries, as plump and juicy as kisses. The store displays were filled with mannequins wearing eyelet dresses and flower crowns. I slept poorly that night, full of anticipation myself, and woke up with my period. And I mean a real period, none of that warm-up business. I stuffed in a tampon, thinking of my mother despite myself, and asked Inga to pick up ibuprofen after she drove Becki, Kevin, and me back to school.

After greetings from Lise, we were led into a large classroom filled with crew members and affable host Erik Lundgren. The room was set with three desks at the front of the class, with the whiteboard behind them. On each desk was a small dry-erase board and a black marker.

"*Hej, hej!*" Erik said to us as Magnus handed us mics. "Are you ready for your pop quiz?"

"Pop quiz?" I said, but before anyone could clarify, Tocke ushered us into the desks. I was in the center, Becki was on my right side, and Kevin my left. We were informed by Erik, with the cameras already rolling, that in honor of our school episode, the competition that day would be a test, *Jeopardy!*-style, about everything we had learned thus far on our grand Swedish tour. The person with the fewest number of correct answers would be sent on the next flight home. "I hope you have been studying!" Erik said, and winked at us.

"Studying?" I said to Becki while the crew paused to set up the dolly.

"Studying?" Kevin said to me.

Becki looked at us like the exasperated leader of a group project. "You haven't been studying?"

Kevin and I looked at each other. ". . . No?" I said.

"What's wrong with you?" Becki said. "Didn't you watch the old seasons? They all have a quiz at the end."

"Why would I watch old seasons of a show that I'm literally going to be on?" Kevin said. "That's so boring."

I pointed at him. "Thank you!"

"Let's start easy, *allihopa*," Erik Lundgren said affably. "How many provinces are there in Sweden? Please write down your answer on your whiteboard and wait until I tell you to reveal them."

I picked up my marker as a cold sweat started in my armpits. Provinces in Sweden? When had we learned this? After a moment's reflection I remembered Lapland, and Norrland, and I figured Gotland might be another one, maybe Stockholm too. After that things got a little fuzzy, so I just tacked on a number that seemed reasonable and scribbled the total down.

"Please show us your boards," Erik said. I glanced at Kevin, who had written "3." I had written "12" in what I hoped was confident penmanship.

"Twenty-five," Erik said. "Becki, you are correct. Please erase your answers and prepare for the next question."

"Twenty-five!" I said. "That's way too many!"

"Thank you for your feedback," Erik said, somewhat less affably. "Next question: what year did Spotify 'go public,' as you say in the States?"

Beside me, Becki practically jumped onto her whiteboard. My mouth hung open. It was as if they had expected us to actually pay attention on those infernally long informational tours, and not just daydream idly!

"Correct," Erik said to Becki. "Pauline, you are ten years off. Kevin, I'm sorry, the internet had not been invented at that time. Next question: how many tons of ore does the Kiruna mine export each year?"

Becki knew that one, the next one, and the one after that. "Oh, Paulie," I heard Magnus say to Jonas from halfway across the room. By the time I guessed, incorrectly, the year that Sweden had last revised their constitutional monarchy (1975, not 1612), the score was 11–0–0, and I desperately needed to change my tampon. I raised my hand. "Can I go to the bathroom?"

"No," Tocke said.

What was I, a kindergartener? "I really have to go, though."

"We do not want you cheating while you're in there." Tocke raised one brow.

"I'm not going to cheat! How would I cheat?"

"You might ask someone for help."

"How could I, when I don't even know the questions? When have I ever cheated?" At this my eyes landed upon Lars. I felt my face turn pink.

"Jesus, Tocke she has to change her tampon," Becki announced to the room. "Even in Texas guys know that if a girl suddenly has to use the bathroom you don't try and stop them."

"Guys too," Kevin piped up. "I've got IBS."

Across the room Magnus beamed. "And me too!"

After an inordinately long discussion about when a person had the right to physically stop a fellow adult from using the bathroom (during a hostage situation, during a home invasion, at a wedding if you were the one getting married), Tocke finally agreed to let me go, but only if Inga accompanied me. "This is humiliating," I grumped in the child-sized stall, fishing around for the tampon string that always seemed to go missing at the most inopportune moments. "Oh wait—I found it!"

"Nineteen sixty-five," said a growly voice outside the stall.

"What? Inga, is that you?" I ripped open a Tampax.

"Remember the year 1965."

"Inga, why are you using that weird voice?"

"Paulie, I am trying to help you," she said in her normal tone, sounding exasperated. I flung open the stall door as she said, "Just go with it, okay?"

I started washing my hands, pumping the dispenser for extra soap. "Tocke would kill you if he knew you were doing this."

"I know, I know," Inga said. She fluffed her hair in the mirror. "But between you and me, I cannot let Kevin win."

I burst out laughing, despite myself. "What? Why? Kevin's really grown on me."

"And on me too," Inga said. "Like a wart that needs to be burned away."

She said this so seriously that I burst out laughing again. She continued: "Kevin doesn't need to win. But you and Becki . . ." She paused. "You are a little bit more pathetic, you see?"

I stiffened. "Okaayyyy"—I dried my hands—"you know I have an MFA, right?"

"He has his vitamins and his money, and he is so confident. You and Becki, you are like ducks swimming in circles, using energy without knowing where you are going. You are always . . . how do I say . . . running into the rocks and the trees. You understand?"

"Well—" I said. The skin on my chest prickled as the truth sank in.

"We girls have to stick together," Inga said, pursing her glossed lips in the mirror before linking her arm in mine. As she kicked open the door to the bathroom with her foot, she said loudly, "And this is why I must also tell you about the best Swedish vibrator. Remind me and I will show you. It will make you happier than any man."

Back in the classroom, affable host Erik Lundgren announced that because Becki was so far ahead, she would be excused from the rest of the competition, which would become a sudden-death match between Kevin and me. "The first one to get the right answer will be safe," Erik said. He looked hard at Kevin and me. "Please try to be quick so I can get back to my wife and son in time for dinner." Then his demeanor changed, became slightly more camera ready: "The first question in sudden death is: what year did Ingmar Bergman move to the island of Fårö?"

Nineteen sixty-five. It had to be. I looked at Kevin. Kevin was staring at his shoes. I wrote down the number in giant print and coughed slightly. Kevin looked over, and just as he did, I angled my whiteboard toward him and jiggled my foot, which I hoped he read as "pay attention." Why did I do this? I cannot say, except that I could no longer imagine doing the opposite. Yes, Kevin was a boor, but he was *my* boor. And I wasn't going to hang him out to dry if I could help it.

"Both of you are correct," Erik said when we revealed our answers.

From the back, Inga widened her eyes at me. I widened them back. If I was going to beat Kevin, I tried to say with my eyeballs, I was going to beat him fair and square.

Which was noble in theory, but what happened in practice was that Kevin and I had to sit up there and sweat for two more hours as we both bombed question after question. Eventually Tocke called a break because they'd run out of trivia and had to make up a bunch more. "Thanks for that back there," Kevin said, thumping his desk toward mine while Tocke huddled with the other producers. "How'd you know that?"

"Oh, a little bird told me," I said airily. "Anyway, you would've done the same for me."

It's an old saying, one I'm not sure exists in other languages, that functions either as a fact or as a wish. In truth I had no idea if Kevin would have done the same if the roles had been reversed, but I wanted him to be that person, and so I reflected that person back to him, partly by being that person for him.

Still, despite the positive fellow feeling growing between us, our so-called sudden-death round was more like an extended torture session. It wasn't until after three in the afternoon that, at last, I put the competition to bed. "What is the name," Erik Lundgren asked, "of Astrid Lindgren's most famous literary creation?"

With a bolt of euphoria, I scribbled Pippi's name on my whiteboard, in Swedish and English, and drew a little picture of a girl with pigtails. We revealed our answers. Erik said, "Paulie, you are correct. Kevin, I believe Curious George is American."

I leapt up as if I'd won an Olympic medal rather than limped to second place in a multi-hour contest that was supposed to take thirty minutes. Becki, who had been watching in the back, ran over to hug me. Then the two of us ran over to hug Kevin. Kevin was crying, though he would tell you he wasn't. He squeezed us both so hard that I could feel his heart, the way you can feel when an avocado's ripe. Firm yet soft. "You did good, Paulie," he said.

"You did good." I pulled back so I could look at him. My face was wet. So was his.

He was smiling. It had taken me weeks to see that smile, the real one. Like a little kid's. "I'm proud of you."

"I'm proud of you."

"I'm not proud of either of you," Becki declared. "That was humiliating."

"It really was ha ha!" I heard Magnus call before Tocke shushed him. They were filming all of this.

"We have to say goodbye now," I said to Kevin, though I was talking to myself.

"I'm gonna miss you guys," he said.

I said, "We're gonna miss you too."

And while I fear I shall put too fine a point on what comes next, and thereby render it moot, the moment I kissed Kevin on the cheek in farewell I knew that it was possible to love anyone, anyone in the whole world. Many hours trapped in a Sprinter van + foreign country + social isolation + no phones + a series of bizarre locations and subcultures + reality television was but one set of circumstances to inspire such love, but I was sure there were more, there were many. This love was neither conditional nor rational, it was not predicated on similarities or agreement or culture or language; it was just a big, fat, sloppy love, like a golden retriever's. When Kevin and I pulled back and looked each other in the eye, I had this sense that he was a person I could call at any time, in any crisis, and he would run to my side; and what's more I'd run to his too.

"See you chicks later," Kevin said, and I didn't even mind the slang.

"He's a real sonofabitch," Becki said with a sigh, rubbing her face with her palms after Inga had led Kevin out of the room and toward whatever taxi would take him to the airport.

I wiped my eyes with my shirtsleeves. "He really is."

"Congratulations, Paulie," Lars said, coming up to Becki and me with Magnus. "I mean, you did bad, but you did good."

"Thanks." I sniffed.

"Really bad," Magnus said before giving me a hug. "Awful. Silly little Paulie."

"I'm six feet tall!" I blubbered into his shoulder.

"*Little Paulie, little Paulie*," Becki sang, poking me in the ribs until I giggled like the Pillsbury Doughboy, and she laughed, and Magnus laughed, and Lars laughed, and I laughed some more, and then I cried, because there were so many wonderful people in the world, so many kind and wonderful people. Who knew how many kind and wonderful people were at this very moment wandering around just waiting to be revealed? Oh, sure, beneath the surface of this world is a deep old sorrow that'll break your heart, but beneath that, what if there's love, too, ready to geyser up to the sky like Old Faithful—an abundant, inexhaustible force just waiting to be uncratered?

CHAPTER TWELVE

✥

HUVUDET SOM BÄR KRONAN

Because Midsommar was just three days away, we had to jump right into filming the season finale. After our farewell with Kevin, Inga drove Becki and me the two hours back to Stockholm and gave us strict instructions from Tocke to rest. "It is going to be a very long, very hard day tomorrow," she said before she booted us out of the van in front of the hotel. "I do not envy you a little bit."

Becki and I looked at each other, a mutual exchange of surprise and unease. "What does that mean?" she said after Inga had peeled off, ostensibly to sink herself into a sensory-deprivation tank.

"I don't know," I said, but already my mind was tumbling around possible reasons for the foreboding: fires, beds of nails, eating bugs, sharks—were there sharks in Sweden? "You've seen other seasons—do they make you do terrible things to win?"

"Not terrible," Becki said, but her voice was far from convincing.

We ordered room service together and watched *Bad Mommies* on the English-language channel before turning in early, both vowing, as we had back in Norrland, to help each other as much as we could. The next morning, bright and early, before the Baltic waves could get too big, Tocke took us on a small boat out to Vaxholm, the closest island to Stockholm in the region's massive archipelago. Becki threw up on the hour-long ride, either from seasickness or nerves, while I managed to stave off both by reading about the island in Deborah's atlas. Apparently an old king had built a fortress there in the sixteenth century to protect Stockholm from the Danes and the Russians and other Eastern invaders. Then it had become a prison, and now it was a prison-themed bed-and-breakfast at which people with lots of freedom and money could pretend to have no freedom and no money. How strange!

It was a popular tourist destination—the whole island of Vaxholm, not just the bed-and-breakfast—with a famous ice-cream shop. Hmmm. If the competition involved eating ice cream, I felt confident in my abilities. In fact, I'd once won a Monster Sundae contest at a local diner, polishing off a mixing bowl of banana split without throwing up. I still had the T-shirt, too bad I hadn't brought—

"Paulie?" Inga was saying. "Paulie, we must get off the boat now."

"Oh." I looked up and blinked, torn from my recollection of standing on the diner booth and holding the mixing bowl high in the air, like a gladiator. "Right. Coming."

We disembarked at Vaxholm's charming little harbor. It was a brilliant day, the sky a crisp blue, the sun warming the skin under my lightweight sweater. Magnus gave us our mics, and Jonas filmed Becki and me walking along the harbor and had us stop right in front of the famous ice-cream shop about which I'd just read. Kismet! It was painted in pastels and looked as menacing as cotton candy. If this was any indication of the timbre of the day, perhaps Inga had been wrong, the competition wouldn't be so bad—

We paused our walking shots so Jonas could go inside and prep. Another camera was set up in front of the building. I turned to Becki. "So the trick is to open your throat."

She was fussing with her foam mic bit, which had gotten twisted in her necklace. "What?"

I knocked my head toward the shop. "When you have to eat a lot at once, the trick is to open your throat. And keep your mouth wet. Take sips of water."

"They're not going to make us do an eating contest, they've never done that," Becki said, just as affable host Erik Lundgren emerged from the ice-cream shop with a jolly-sounding "*Hej, hej!*" as Jonas followed with the camera. Erik explained that our final competition would be a timed, three-part challenge in three different parts of the island, all celebrating different Midsommar traditions. Whoever was ahead following the first part would get a head start in the second, and so forth. "Only one of you will meet your family after today," Erik explained in his serious, yet still affable, way as Jonas roamed around him. "Only one of you will get what you have spent these past weeks and your blood, sweat, and tears— especially tears, yes?—trying to achieve. The stakes are high. Are you ready?"

Becki grabbed my hand. "Yes."

As Jonas continued to circle us like—well, like a shark—Erik explained the first part of the competition: on his signal, we would run into the ice-cream shop's kitchen and each make thirty homemade waffle cones under the watchful eye of Brunhilda Hildagård, the store's elderly matriarch. Erik said Swedes loved ice-cream cones, especially around Midsommar, but they were also quite particular about what constituted a good one. Therefore, if our waffle cones fell apart or were too mushy, they would not count toward the total.

"Are you ready?" said Erik Lundgren. "*Ett, två, tre—*"

And then we were off, sprinting inside the shop doors, skidding past the customer counter, and heading to the back, where Brunhilda and another camera crew were waiting for us in the kitchen. On the countertop sat two waffle irons, two bowls of batter, and a bunch of stainless-steel racks. "You've got to burn your fingers," Becki whisper-panted as she slopped some batter in the iron. "I worked at Cold Stone in high school. The cone won't stick together unless it's really hot."

"And use less batter than you think you need," I panted back. "Other-wise it'll spill out the sides and you might run out."

It was hot in the kitchen—too hot, considering it was an ice-cream shop—and it wasn't long before Becki and I had both peeled off our

sweaters and rolled our jeans up over our ankles. Becki was right—you
did have to burn your fingertips. After I'd done about ten cones, I could
barely feel them. She was much better than me at the rolling, but I had
a small edge in the baking, and by the time we'd both made thirty cones
that were up to Brunhilda's surprisingly exacting standards, we were only
fifteen seconds apart, with Becki holding a slight lead. "Jesus," she said
after the segment producer had called cut and we burst back out, panting,
into the brilliant sunshine. "I thought I was gonna have a heart attack."

"Same." I heard my stomach gurgle. "What a sad way to die."

"*Crying Americans!*" a tourist said cheerfully, pointing at us as she
passed by with a friend. "I love this show!"

I smiled and waved like a normal person, even though I could hear my
heart *rump-a-pumping* in my ears. "They'll never know how stressed we
got," Becki said, watching them pass with her hands on her hips, her eyes
squinting at the sun. Her voice had a mix of wistfulness and resentment.
"It'll all look so fun and easy."

Inga told Becki and me to take a *fika* break while the crew set up the
next location. "Have a coffee, why don't you," Tocke said, and motioned
to the catering guy holding a giant carafe and paper cups. Swedes were
always telling us to have coffee. Coffee in the morning, afternoon, night.
In Norrköping, I'd seen an old lady order a cup at the hotel restaurant at
ten p.m. without blinking. This was after I'd had to explain to the server
what I meant by "decaffeinated" after she'd said such a thing didn't exist.

"It is worse in the winter," Inga had said when I'd asked her about
her nation's prodigious habit later. "It is so dark you drink it just to stay
awake."

"Like you drink how much?" I'd said.

Inga had counted in her head. "I would say seven cups per day."

Becki said, eyeing the coffee: "Is it a trick? He wants us to get hyper or
something?"

If it was a trick, it worked. We waited around for a while and had
time to drink several punishingly strong cups before Inga finally led
us down a gravel lane, through a stone-wall entrance, and onto a lush
lawn on which a white tent had been erected in front of a large brick
manor house. After we'd put on crisp white aprons with the *Sverige och*

Mig logo, affable host Erik Lundgren announced that the second part of the competition would be a pickled-herring-eating contest. "Sill is one of our favorite Midsommar traditions," he said grandly to us and the camera. "But for some reason it has not gained the same popularity in other countries." He laughed, and we laughed, for the sake of the viewers, though I could already feel bile roiling in my belly along with the coffee. "The sill from the Baltic is very lean. Here in Sweden we use very strong vinegar. There is much flavor, ho-ho-ho! Your goal is to eat a jar of sill in as little time as possible. Becki, because you have the lead, you will start fifteen seconds before Pauline. On your marks, get set—"

"Water!" I cried as she took off. "Don't forget the water!" She gave me a thumbs-up behind her back.

When it was my turn, I looked up to the sky and asked Grandma to wish me luck before I started running. We'd had herring every year at her house at Christmas, and I'd hated it the way only kids can, with noisy and operatic fervor. When my parents forced me to clean my plate, I'd cut the herring into tiny pieces, swallow it with milk like Tylenol, and find sport in trying to make the most disgusting sounds and faces for Grandma's amusement. "The horror!" I would cry, clutching my throat. "Oh, the horror!"

In the tent, Becki was staring down her open jar, which was maybe three times the size of a can of tuna. It smelled of vinegar and sea and stinky fish and stinky spices. She fished out a piece of fillet and dropped it into her mouth, swallowed, grabbed her water glass, drank. "The water helps."

"It'll go down easy," I said reassuringly. Then I opened my own jar and was assaulted by odor. Why people in one of the richest countries in the world chose to eat such things was a great and powerful mystery. I gagged. "Oh sweet Jesus."

I was hoping for commiseration from Becki, but she was in a rhythm now, the way I imagined she was when laying sod in people's yards: workmanlike, efficient. Me, I dumped all the pieces of fillet on the provided cutting board and started breaking them into pieces the way I had as a kid. *You can endure anything for five minutes*, I told myself, like an incantation. (Strangely, the image that came to mind as I chanted was of American troops clambering up Omaha Beach.) Though my small-piece approach was slower than Becki's, I had to take less time between swallows, whereas she, every few fillets, had to put her head between her legs and fan off her mouth from the vinegar. I finished fifteen seconds before her, which meant that by the end of round two, our times were exactly even. "This is the closest finale we have ever had," Erik Lundgren said to the camera. "Who will be the tenth-season winner of *Sverige och Mig*?"

"Good question," Becki said before leaning over and puking into a bucket. The smell of her puke plus the herring did a number on me, and within a few seconds I was doing the same.

"Does this disqualify us?" I panted, wiping my mouth with the back of my palm when Inga came over with a towel. "Do we have to start over?"

"God no," she said, tossing a towel at Becki. "We are surprised you do not throw up earlier."

Our nausea did not abate when we were packed into a small, polished wood motorboat and sped across to the islet that housed the Vaxholm fortress-turned-hotel. I could see why the Swedish king had built it: huge and imposing with a hard brick exterior, it certainly would have put me off as a potential invader. Becki and I both puked again, this time into the Baltic, and when chipper producer Anna offered us gummy candies, I puked into the small cellophane bag. My clothes had the rancid odor of thrown-up coffee.

"This is *not* a family show," I kept saying between vinegary belches. But no one was listening. It was like a wedding that way, filming a reality-show finale: each person floating in a private bubble of stress and excitement. Once we docked, Becki and I were shepherded inside the fortress and through the museum and dungeon, past the old torture instruments used at the prison, and into a cheery commercial kitchen belonging to the bed-and-breakfast. Affable host Erik Lundgren had come across in an earlier boat. He was waiting for us in front of a butcher-block countertop covered in tea towels. "And now, the third and final contest in this finale," he said to us grandly. "The very best part of Sweden's Midsommar tradition. You will each make a Midsommar cake"—he pulled the tea towels off the table, revealing tidy stacks of ingredients—"with only a very basic recipe. The person who finishes the fastest without their cake collapsing into pudding will win this season of *Sverige och Mig.*"

I breathed a sigh of relief. A cake! I could bake a cake, no problem. Next to me, I heard Becki suck in her breath. Becki didn't bake. She'd told Kevin and me that the closest she'd ever gotten to home cooking was adding a fried egg to her DoorDashed Chipotle.

"But there is one twist," Erik added. "In honor of our tenth anniversary." From behind his back, he pulled out a bottle of aquavit. "You drink to your season before we begin."

"Oh no," I said, just as Becki whispered, "Oh, thank God."

We clinked tiny glasses with Erik. *Skål!* Tocke halted filming to move the cameras, and in the pause I felt my head start to swim. My stomach was acidic and empty, and the single shot of aquavit hit my bloodstream like a Viking siege. I gripped the butcher-block countertop. "Paulie?" Becki asked, as if through a tunnel. "Paulie, are you all right?"

I was going to say yes, but when I opened my mouth, all that came out was a rank, vinegary belch, loud as cannon fire. Becki snapped to attention like a military colonel. "Crackers, someone get her crackers," she announced to the room. "Ginger ale, 7-Up, or Sprite—anything like that. Okay, fine, sparkling water will have to do—"

She made me hop up and sit on the counter while someone handed me a piece of knäckebröd and a plastic bottle of water. "Breathe," she commanded, and thumped on my back. "You'll be fine. I've seen worse than this. Hell, I've been worse than this. Did I tell you about the time at a Blake Shelton concert when I—"

"Not now," I stammered weakly. I was gnawing on the crisp bread, which tasted like rye cardboard, but in a comforting way. Tocke came over to inspect me, but Becki shooed him away. I heard her tell him that we needed ten minutes and then I'd be "good as gravy."

This seemed impossible, given how acute nausea seems to signal, at least to me, that the end is nigh, but Becki was right. After a little while, the mix of liquids, carbs, and sugars plonked into my system managed to stave off the worst effects of coffee, sill, and aquavit. "Thank you," I said to Becki as I clambered off the counter. "I know you didn't have to—"

"Oh, shut up, Paulie, not everything has to be such a thing," Becki said. But she was smiling a little, and she reached out her hands, and before I knew it we were dancing together, in a silly way, the way we'd done with Kevin back in the hotel room.

When we stopped, the crew burst into applause. "We should have filmed that," Tocke said when everyone'd calmed down and we'd taken joking bows. To Becki and me, in a tone of voice that was less a question and more of an order: "Can you do it again?"

Because Tocke was the boss, we did do it again. Except it wasn't as good, the way artificial versions of real things, like spontaneity and Christmas trees, are never as good, despite what producers and advertisers and influencers try to tell you. "You are not so good on command," Tocke said, throwing up his hands, to which Becki clapped back, "No, we just don't like taking commands from *you*."

Affable host Erik Lundgren looked back and forth between Tocke and Becki. "Okay, so, um, back to the competition," he said after a pause. "Your times are exactly even. So. Ah. On your marks, get set—"

The recipe for the Midsommar cake, which was really just a strawberry sponge cake with vanilla cream, wasn't a recipe at all. Here it is in its entirety:

1. Make sponge cake
2. Make vanilla cream
3. Cut strawberries
4. Assemble cake with layers of sponge, cream, and berries

But I had baked sponge cakes with my grandmother since the moment I could stand on a chair beside her in her fragrant kitchen. The real instructions were imprinted on my being: whisk the sugar and eggs in a double boiler while heating water in the saucepan, sift and fold in flour to the warm egg mixture, then butter. I pulled the ingredients to the front of my workstation and started cracking eggs. The sound of the shell breaking, and the hiss of sugar being poured into the bowl, evoked sense memory: calm entered my body like cool water into a glass. I was four years old again, and I was warm and safe, and if I didn't know how to do something, Grandma would show me without yelling or scolding, and I could lick all the spoons at the end of the day.

I turned on the electric mixer and saw Becki from the corner of my eye. She was standing, terrified, before her ingredients, moving them around in a random fashion like one might go about solving a jigsaw. We'd been instructed not to look at each other's workstations, but I knew that if I did nothing, this was the end of the line for Becki, even if she tried to follow my lead from across the room. So I would win. I would get my family reunion. Though it would not be entirely fair or entirely square, given the fact that Becki had paused the entire production to wipe me off the floor after that shot of aquavit, it would be fairish and squarish, given that I could have done that for myself. Right? And it was the humane thing for her to do, right? And probably someone from the crew would have noticed eventually that I wasn't quite myself, even if she hadn't. Right?

The mind, when nudged, can rationalize anything. The body, on the other hand—

Another sense memory emerged, breaking through the surface of my consciousness while the mixer whirred and whirred. I was sitting in Grandma's lap while the cake was in the oven. We were reading *Pippi Longstocking*, the chapter where Pippi goes to the circus. She pays too much for her tickets, gives the extra money to the ticket lady, startles an equestrian by hopping onto her horse in the middle of the ring. The ringmaster asks if anyone is brave enough to wrestle the strongest man in the world: if they do, they might win a hundred dollars. So Pippi, who is the strongest girl in the world, raises her hand, and before anyone can stop her, she goes right up to that giant man, lifts him up over her head, and carries him around the ring.

And boy, oh boy, is that strong man mad. And the ringmaster is mad, and the equestrian is mad, because funny-looking girls with no parents are supposed to be pathetic and lonesome, not talented and strong and funny, and they all think Pippi has ruined the circus. But actually the audience loves her, and they insist the ringmaster give her one hundred dollars, but Pippi only likes gold pieces so she hands the money back. The ringmaster then tries to have Pippi removed from the circus, but she is so strong and sturdy that no security guard can pick her up, so in the end they let her be, just like the policemen and the burglars and the mean ladies in town who say Pippi has bad manners let her be. Because that's what strength eventually gets you: freedom. And when you are very strong, you must also be very—

I blinked my eyes rapidly over the mixer. I could not lift Tocke over my head. I could not climb to the tops of birch trees. I could not give away my chest of gold pieces. But Pippi was in me, somewhere. I knew she was. If I could only figure out what she might—

"Combine the eggs and sugar in a bowl!" I called to Becki, startling myself with the sound of my voice. "Then put the bowl inside a saucepan with water in it and turn on the burner!"

"Cut!" Tocke said. "Cut, cut, cut!" He strode over to me, his long dark hair streaming behind him. "Pauline, what are you doing?"

I ignored him and started measuring the flour. To Becki: "Get the water hot but not boiling! You should still be able to touch it with your finger!"

"Becki! No! Paulie, stop!" He said this in a voice that was supposed to be soothing but came off as menacing. "This is not how the competition works," he said. "You are friends? Fine. This is nice. But there can only be one winner of *Sverige och Mig*."

The way he said this, you would have thought he was repeating some indisputable fact: the world is round, an object in motion tends to stay in motion, humankind can only bear so much reality. But the fact that *Sverige och Mig* could have only one winner wasn't an indisputable fact: it was an arbitrary rule that Tocke himself had made up ten years before. People were always doing this, trying to bring you to heel over this dogma or that. "Says who?" I said. "It's a free country."

"That is how the show works," he said, trying to stay calm but sputtering a little. "One winner. You cannot just come in here and change all the rules because you decide you do not like—"

"Okay," I said to Becki, angling my body away from him. "Now turn the mixer on high and whip the eggs and sugar while they're getting warm in the saucepan—but don't let any water get in the bowl. I'll wait for you—then when you're done we'll add the flour and butter."

Tocke was starting to look like a cartoon now, getting all red in the face, huffing and puffing like the circus ringmaster. "Stop it."

I smiled my very politest smile at Tocke, the one I used to reserve for church on Sundays. *If you are very strong, you must also be very kind.* "But I can't stop! If I stop now the eggs'll lose their air and we'll have to start over. You want to finish filming today, don't you?"

Becki was hunched over the burner, whirring away with the mixer, Igor to my Dr. Frankenstein. "Think of what a wonderful surprise it will be," I said to Tocke. "Two winners! That's way better than that show you're worried about, the one where little kids demolish houses. Hell, maybe this'll get you another Emmy." I patted his arm. "You'd like that, wouldn't you?"

Tocke's face changed as I said this. The purple-red aspect evolved into something cooler, bluer, and more calculating. His breath slowed. I patted his arm again. "No one will see it coming. You will do something new and they'll call you a visionary. They'll say it is exactly the kind of thing we need in these troubled times. Some other producer will think of it eventually—wouldn't you rather be first?"

The aspect of Tocke's face changed again, became lighter. "You think it will work?" he asked, and his voice was filled with wonder. Tocke had been in charge of people for so long that a hard crust had grown on top of his skin, like the chicken pox I'd had when I was a kid. Sometimes the hard crust did all the talking for Tocke. Most of the time. *Your armor isn't what's beautiful,* my high school photography teacher had told me during our self-portrait unit. If it was true for me, it was true for everybody. If it was true for everybody, it was true for me. Either everyone's beautiful or no one is. Either everyone's a person or no one is.

"'K, I'm ready for the flour!" Becki called from the other side of the kitchen. Tocke looked at me. I nodded at him. He nodded back, almost imperceptibly, then turned to the crew and gave instructions rapidly in Swedish. They were moving the cameras closer to Becki and me, moving our workstations closer together. "Now talk to us about how the Valkyries inspired you," Tocke was saying, stepping back into director mode. "Talk about how you and Becki are your own little Swedish female army."

"Oh, I wasn't thinking of the Valkyries," I said, dumping flour into my bowl. "I was thinking of Pippi Longstocking."

At that, to my great and everlasting surprise, Tocke started crying. His eyes became very blue, and his face very pink. I thought maybe he was thinking of his childhood, or his grandmother, or his own children or his country, or the human capacity, unique to our species, to change our minds in every sense. And maybe he was, I'll never know, the way we can never really know other people. Still, as Tocke wiped his tears with one meaty paw, what he said was, "Fucking hell, this is so great, we are definitely going to win that Emmy."

LATER, BECKI AND I pulled out our Midsommar cakes from the oven at the exact same time, assembled them at the exact same rate, and when we, together, presented our cakes to affable host Erik Lundgren, he, too, started to cry. I don't know why, but seeing all these Swedish men get teary over TV endings and cake cracked me up. I started laughing, and then Becki did, too, and then Tocke got mad and said we were ruining the moment. I thought of my grandma laughing over Pippi, and I, too, burst into tears. This made Becki laugh even more, and then she was crying, too, and I mean really crying—big, juicy, shuddering sobs, tears she seemed to have held in for a good long time—and my God, it was magnificent.

What I'm trying to say is that the finale was a mess, but a genuine mess, certainly one we put our all into. This became even more clear when Becki and I took turns calling our families back home to tell them the big news. Tocke gave us his phone, and I dialed Declan's number while Jonas stuck his camera in my face. "Paulie?" he said over speakerphone.

"It's me. I have something to—"

"They kicked you off, didn't they," he said darkly. "Those bastards."

Tocke, who was standing right above me, shifted his weight. "Um," I said. "Actually, I—"

"Okay if I call you back?" Declan said. "I have to present in five—I'm on a Zoom—in the meantime tell those fuckers they can go—"

Jonas exchanged a glance with Magnus. Tocke crossed his arms over his chest. Lars, who had been nearby, came over and leaned toward the speakers with interest.

"Declan," I said, trying to be calm. "Declan, you're on speakerphone right now. The producer is right here, and I'm being filmed, and I'm supposed to tell you that I won this season of *Sverige och Mig*—well, Becki and I both—"

"Oh," he said. A beat. "Oh shit." A beat. "Did you say speaker?"

"Yeah," I said. "But hey, isn't that great?"

"That's—wow—I mean, that's not what I expected you to—" Declan corrected himself. "I'm happy for you! But the thing is, Paulie, I'm on this Zoom—"

"We're gonna have to do this again," I heard Tocke murmur to Lars.

"Because he's a person," I told Tocke. "Not a character."

"A what?" Declan said. "Is someone else talking?"

I raised my voice. "I'm just telling everyone that you're a person! Not a character on a show! So you can't be expected to react—"

"I'm doing a bad job, aren't I?" Declan said. His voice sounded worried. "Let me try again after this call. I didn't know you were filming—"

"Oh please, how could you?" I said. "There's no script for any of this!"

Becki's call went similarly—her sister told her she was on the toilet and it was going to be a little while, and they could talk while she was on the toilet, but actually her sister preferred to play a game on her phone while she was pooping if that was okay with Becki. She screamed when Becki told her about the cameras and speakerphone. Poor gal! Whatever expectation Tocke had set up for us—that we'd have some magical, teary victory call like the ones you see on TV—went straight down the (literal) toilet after that. But maybe that was for the best, because life was so much better than TV, no matter what anyone said.

The next day was Midsommar Eve, which meant the crew would spend it with their families. Meanwhile, Inga was on the phone with Becki's and my Swedish relatives, arranging for transportation and hotels for our family reunions, which would take place two days after Midsommar. I thought Becki and I would just hang out at the hotel in

Stockholm for the holiday, but to my surprise, Tocke invited us to his family's *stuga*. "There is a small guesthouse where you can stay," he said. "You will see Sweden at its very best."

"That's so generous of you," I said, thinking of all the horrible things I had thought and, occasionally, said about him. When would I ever learn that there was no point in drawing conclusions about anyone? "Thank you," I said.

"Just, please, no more *sill*," Becki added.

We took the motorboat back to Vaxholm from the fortress's islet, then a bigger ferry from Vaxholm back to Stockholm. The crew was buying us drinks, buying themselves drinks—the air was jubilant, with that last-day-of-school energy brought on in part by the holiday and also by the end of the season. Only a small crew would stay on to film our family reunions, including Lars and Jonas and Magnus, and I was glad for this. I loved all three of them, a summer-camp love, a different category from "real" love but meaningful in its own way. Perhaps the trick was to name what kind of love it was before it rolled you over like a wave. Perhaps the trick was to surf it, not seize it, let it come and go in its own way.

The waves beneath the ferry were thunking up against the metal sides as I stood and looked out at the water and considered the nature of love and man. It seemed like I was really getting somewhere, but then Becki and Magnus ran out carrying an extra beer and Magnus thunked me on the head with the bottle. "Paulie, what you doing out here, trying to solve math problem? Do not be so serious—it is party time, okay?"

"Okay, okay, okay," I said, taking the beer from him while Becki whacked me on the side. "I know what we're gonna do when we land," she said. She opened her mouth to tell me, but burped instead, right in my face. What a smell: herring, aquavit, coffee, cake, beer. In a comic stage whisper she slurred: "We're gonna'ge' tatTOOS!"

"Tattoos?" I said. I looked down at my tattooless body. "I don't know about—"

"Shhhhh." She put her finger to my mouth. "Shhhhh. Jus' trus' me. It's gonna'be beau'iful—"

Which is how, one hour later, I found myself standing beside Becki in a tattoo parlor in Gamla Stan, flipping through a binder of designs.

I had missed other tattoo phases I'd seen my friends go through: after breakups, big trips, or what Jemma's assistant called her "Saturn Return." My mom had thought them unseemly, and what she had said about my sister's ankle tattoo (a butterfly) had always stuck in my head: "It'll look even trashier when she's older." But I was a little drunk, and a little giddy, and more than a little raw after the events of the day-week-month, so when Becki pointed triumphantly at a tiny image of a Midsommar cake and cried, "*Tack så mycket!*" I found myself nodding and pointing simultaneously, and adding: "*Ja, tack!*"

We stumbled out an hour later with bandages over our forearms, under which shone our matching cakes. "Wanna see our tattoos?" we asked passersby. "Wanna see?" No one did. Oh well. The thing is, these tattoos didn't need to be seen to be important. They didn't need to be admired to matter. They just needed to be there, to remind us of—of—of—

CHAPTER THIRTEEN

❖

DET HAR ÄR MIN FAMILJ!

What can I say about Swedish Midsommar that hasn't already been said by the memoirs and travel guides and coffee table books and movies? Not much, which is why I've saved myself the trouble and composed a simple list of pros and cons about the nation's most celebrated holiday:

Cons: spotty weather, chance of hangover, hand-weaving flower crowns much harder than anticipated.

Pros: lakes, birdsong, endless daylight, breakfast cake, milky coffee, flower-drenched country lanes, crowded hayrides, dandelion fluff, flower crowns made by professionals (preferably teenage girls), white dresses, country village maypoles (*Midsommarstångar*), country village accordionists, traditional folk costumes, traditional songs, traditional *fika*, non-traditional ice-cream novelty items, strangers apologizing for the weather, strangers asserting proudly that they have visited New York, strangers asking if you know their cousin in North Dakota, strangers worrying that you are not having a nice enough time, more strangers apologizing for the weather, late-afternoon swimming, late-afternoon aquavit, boiled potatoes and sour cream served alfresco, smoked salmon, grilled lamb, Midsommar cake, evening boat rides, a complete lack of fireworks, a complete lack of national anthems, a complete lack of oversized vehicles including and especially those with truck nuts, and, conversely and importantly, a complete abundance of wild strawberries. In Swedish these strawberries, which you can find in woods and thickets and on the side of the lane, are called *smultron*, different from *jordgubbar*, which are the strawberries you buy in the stores. And if you, for example, find a secret hollow on the lane containing a bunch of *smultron*, a place where you maybe eat so many you find yourself lying down on the cool grass and daydreaming contentedly for an afternoon, you might call this secret hollow your *smultronställe*, or "wild strawberry place." But the thing about a *smultronställe* is that while it can be an actual, special place to find wild strawberries, it might also be a special somewhere or someone that gives you what approximates to a "wild-strawberries feeling." This may not make much sense, seeing as it's a word and thereby a feeling that doesn't exist in English, but that's to our detriment. For that wild-strawberries feeling is the quiet cousin of ecstasy, and couldn't we all use a bit more of both ecstasy and quiet?

"THANK YOU," I said to Tocke as we stood in the driveway the morning after the celebration, waiting for the cab to come and collect us. And though it hardly got to the heart of it, I added: "We had a wonderful time."

"*Varsågod*," he said, which means "you're welcome" and "please" and "here you go," but in this case I thought it might mean the latter, as in, *Here you go, this is my country, it doesn't get better than this.*

The cab pulled up then, and Becki and I tucked our luggage in the back and climbed in after saying our last goodbyes. When we arrived back at the Hotel Rival, We got rooms next to each other on the hotel's second floor, and spent the afternoon and evening picking out clothes for our reunions, washing our hair, and pretending we were not as terrified as we were. Or was it excitement? Keyed up, perhaps, is the right way to put it: my body was an accordion and someone was pumping the bellows and playing all the keys simultaneously. Becki kept opening the mini-fridge in her room, then closing it. She had said she didn't want to drink before the big day, but I could tell she was regretting her avowal. "Hell," she said after she had gazed at the beers a third time. "I feel like I'm getting married or something."

"I know what you mean," I said. I was sitting on her bed, scrunching the waves in my damp hair, feeling the knots in my stomach flip.

"I guess it's been so built up . . ." she said, somewhat unconvincingly.

"I hope they're nice," I said. "I hope they like me." *I hope they love me*, I didn't say. *I hope I belong.*

"Of course they'll like you," she said brusquely. "Don't be stupid."

I shook my head. "You don't know my family."

Though Becki and I had found a surprising number of overlaps in our psychological Venn diagrams, she remained a person who had absorbed the myth of the happy family so intensely that, even as events in her life had challenged or outright contradicted the myth, her belief remained steadfast. Unlike mine. Yet as I sat there ruminating over my tortured relationship with my family of origin, Becki seemed to read the hurt and cynicism steaming across my cloudy face, for she conceded a bar of Marabou chocolate and a Coca-Cola from the mini-fridge and tossed them on the bed next to me before she sat down.

"Goddammit, Paulie, your problem is that you can't let go of family being some awful thing." She unwrapped the chocolate foil. "So you had a bad roll of the dice coming out of the chute. Baddish—not like you were beaten or anything. You didn't starve. You got to go to college. But now you're so convinced that's all there is that when you see people being happy—just, like, normal, regular people—Paulie, don't look at me like that when I say 'normal,' you know what I mean—you think it's a big lie, or that something horrible's about to happen." She took a big bite of chocolate. "Well, maybe it's not a lie. Maybe it's just a different experience. You've only had the one. For someone who thinks she's soooooo open-minded . . ." She paused to chew her chocolate. "It's like, shouldn't you try to get some more evidence before giving up on the whole thing?"

Was the secret to being a grown-up that simple? Becki opened the Coke can with one hand, and it fizzed over the top. She offered it to me, but I shook my head. "Caffeine doesn't affect me," she said, taking a big swig. "Alcohol neither. Guess I'm not as sensitive as you, ha ha, Paulie."

Not true: I had seen her be profoundly affected by both. "Guess not."

She finished the soda, put the can down, thumped on her chest, and let out an airy belch. "You think I'm right, don't you? That's why you're not saying anything." She looked pleased with herself. "It's like, for someone smart you're pretty dumb, but for someone dumb I'm pretty smart."

"I never called you dumb," I said. "Who called you dumb? That's crazy."

Her face clouded over. "Oh, people," she said vaguely, waving her manicured fingers around, and for a split-second I saw her step outside herself and straight into another life, armed with an MBA and a power suit, terrifying a corporate board with her frank pragmatism. It excited me, though I knew it would likely never happen, for that kind of class-hopping and reinvention was the exception back home, not the rule. It had taken us just two hundred years to invent our own rigid hierarchies, based mostly on money, to the point that Becki would see such upward mobility not as progress but as a betrayal. Which perhaps it was. But it also seemed like Becki's life was slightly too small for her, like pants you can button but can't easily move around in, and I believed that everyone deserved a life of well-fitting pants, both real and metaphorical. And if this was just another belief based in American delusion, well, it was not one I was willing to cede just yet.

"Let's go to bed," Becki said, just as I said, "I just want you to have pants that fit, okay?"

She looked at me like I was having an allergic reaction. "I'm not wearing pants, we decided on that blue dress, remember? Honestly, Paulie, I don't know what's going on in your head half the time."

"That makes two of us," I said, and saluted her like a departing general.

I WOKE UP before six with that accordion feeling again and could not fall back asleep. I did some stretches, went down to breakfast, took a long bath, reread *Pippi Longstocking*, did my hair and makeup, put on my nice, flowered dress and leather strap sandals, and was just about to crawl out of my skin when Becki knocked on my door wearing her bathrobe. "Jesus, I can practically hear your panic through the walls." She held up her burner. "Here. I downloaded Scrabble for you."

I took the phone. "How'd you know I love Scrabble?"

She rolled her eyes and told me she had to get ready. I played sixteen games of Scrabble, and then I called Jemma on the burner.

"Paulie, is that you?" she answered sleepily. "What time is it?"

"Ummm—" I glanced at the alarm clock. "Too early. Sorry, I forgot about the time change—"

"Are you okay? Did something happen?"

"Something did happen." My lower jaw started to tremble. "I'm about to meet my family."

Her whoop was so loud I wouldn't have been surprised if Becki heard it through the walls. "I knew it. I *knew* it! I'm so proud of you!"

"But Jemma—" My mouth was having a hard time moving. "What if—what if—"

But I couldn't quite put the words on what I was afraid of. The words just drifted, weightless, through canyons of pain and grief that had been carved out ages ago by the tumultuous waters of nature and nurture.

"Paulie," Jemma said, her voice immediately clearing of sleep. I could hear her rustling up to a seated position in her bed. "Paulie, I'm going to tell you something and I need you to listen to me. Okay?"

I nodded silently. My jaw was still trembling away.

"There is no possible way—and I mean it, no possible way—that they can hurt you. Okay? At least not the way you think they might."

I nodded silently, again.

"But if they did—and again, I guarantee you they won't—I will be on the first flight to Stockholm to take you home. Right?" More nodding. "Because we're not kids anymore, right? And you're not trapped, and you're not alone—not that you ever were."

I nodded and nodded and nodded as her warm, familiar voice airlifted me out of those bottomless canyons. The lap of my dress was wet. "I love you," I said, my voice wobbling.

"I love you too." I could tell she was also crying. "Jesus, this is what happens when you win? Thank God you didn't lose."

This made us both laugh. We talked of lighter things for a while as I readjusted to solid ground. "Go back to bed," I finally said. "Dream of the thousand souvenirs I have for you."

"If one of them's not a Swedish elkhound, I'm never talking to you again."

We hung up. I took off my dress, dried it with a blow-dryer, and reapplied my makeup.

At five minutes to one, Becki knocked on my door and we took the stairs to the lobby together. "Christ, my hands are sweaty," she said.

"*Hej, hej!*" Magnus blasted through the doors, holding up his boom mic. "Are we ready for the big day?" Anders, another sound guy, came through on his heels to collect Becki.

Becki and I stood up from the lobby bench, smoothed the fronts of our dresses, and looked at each other. "I'm scared," I said.

"Me too," Becki said. "But we have to do it anyway."

"But why?"

A pause. She seemed to seriously consider the question. "'Cause we're the strongest girls in the world, that's why." Then she pecked me on the cheek and left.

I spent the next two hours with Lars, Magnus, and Jonas as they put me through my paces for what was presumably the last time in my not-yet-existent television career. Walking shots, more walking shots, shots of me looking out over the canals, shots of me gazing at a tree that looked (kind of) like the tree at my family's farm, and interview questions designed to solicit sentimental reactions that, as usual, worked like a skeleton key in the lock of my heart. Was I happy to be here. Was I glad to be the cowinner of *Sverige och Mig*. Was I sad that the rest of my family was not here to celebrate with me. Was I sad that the rest of my family, in general, was incapable of celebrating with me, due to unbroachable differences in our sensibilities. (I'm paraphrasing here, Lars's English wasn't quite that good.) What would my grandma say if she were here. What do I wish I could have told my grandma, could she listen. What would my father think. My sister. My great-grandmother, who emigrated all those years ago and nearly died to give me a better life. My cast members, who were all home in America wishing they were me.

"And your boyfriend?" Lars said, studiously looking me in the eye from behind the camera.

"Yes, my boyfriend, Declan, I wish he were here too," I said, and burst into a fresh round of tears.

I knew, even then, that I was not being very articulate, and I apologized to Lars as Jonas packed up the camera. He waved his hand at me, not unaffectionately. "Nobody will be listening to what you are saying anyway. They only want to see the emotion on your face." He saw that I was trembling a little, and he put his arm around me. The charge between us had not entirely gone away, and likely never would, but it was different now, earthbound, well out of the realm of fantasy. "I know you do not want to hear this right now, but all of these emotions will make very good TV."

And for the first time, through the fog of my own mania, I glimpsed that the intensity of my feelings on the show were in no way contagious but in fact were mine alone, as impossible for Lars or Declan or anyone else to comprehend as it was for me to understand Swedish.

"I'm an idiot," I said to Lars, putting my arm around him too. "I'm so sorry for what I—you must think—I think this whole thing's made me a little crazy."

Lars's face was amused but kind. He squeezed my ribs. "You only notice this now?" Magnus said, looking up from the sound mixer around his neck. "Ha ha, Paulie!"

"Every year, they always are," said Jonas, who again had worked on the show since its inception. He hefted his camera on his shoulder. "If it makes you feel better, you are less crazy than most."

"Put that on my tombstone," I said as we started walking the few short blocks to the place where my family was waiting for me. Jonas ran out in front of us and started walking backward for one last series of walking shots. "Oh, and before I forget," I said to Lars, and briefly explained my pilgrimage to Astrid Lindgren's apartment. "Do you have any idea who that old woman in the building was? I'm guessing a docent? I want to send a thank-you."

Lars looked at me, puzzled. "That apartment has been empty for months. No tours. Something about the plumbing—I have seen workers going in and out, but that is it."

I got the strangest chill up the back of my spine. "But that doesn't—"

I started to say as we turned left on a street corner and passed a tall row of hedges on my left side. I was so taken aback by Lars I'd nearly forgotten what we were doing.

"Forget all that," Lars said. "Your family, they are on the other side of these trees. They are waiting for you."

"Oh jeez Louise," I said, already starting to cry. "Put that on my tombstone instead, why don't you?" And with a deep breath, I turned to meet the rest of my life.

I CANNOT TELL you the exact story of those next six hours, because I have no story. What remains of that precious afternoon are fragments, images, smells, candles dripping down to the tablecloth as the hours slipped by. Karen Hamburger says that the part of the brain that stores anguish has no access to language, but sometimes I wonder if the opposite is also true—that our happiest experiences exist outside the realm of language, our inner analysts napping beneath the desk, allowing our sensing selves to run free, hair streaming out behind us, being without thinking, which, at least for me, is the truest definition of happiness.

Still, it seems miserly, given as we've reached the climax of my great Swedish adventure, to not at least try to cull the fragments from my family reunion. Such as: rounding the corner of the hedges and discovering fifty people, all resembling me, from young children to the very elderly, waving Swedish flags and cheering. Clinking glasses of champagne handed to us by production. Shaking hands with the older generation, hugging the very young. Clapping my hands—I remember I could not stop clapping, for reasons I could not decipher. Playing tag with the children in the grass. Asking people, over and over, "And how are we related?" These were all the descendants of my great-grandmother Esther's sister, who had had four children, some of whom had never met each other before. Someone said we were related to King Gustav, generations back. "In Sweden, everyone's related to some king or another," someone else said wryly. "I am afraid everyone ends up marrying their cousin."

There were cameras in our faces, all the time, but I had grown so accustomed to them at that point that I hardly noticed. My relatives did, however, fiddling with their microphones, blanching when Tocke barked out an order, looking perturbed when they were cut off mid-sentence in order to film something again. "I wish they would leave us alone," my cousin Alma said, giving Tocke a dirty look. She told me she had given Tocke hell on the phone when she realized that, back in late May, she and her family had been traveling through Helsingborg at the same time we were arriving in Sweden. "He refused to let us meet. I asked why not. He said it would ruin the reunion, and I told him he was a horrible man." She laughed gaily. "I don't think I will apologize. I was worried about you! Every few days we would hear an update from someone named Inga about whether you were still in the competition or not. It made me sick! I thought, how could it not make you sick too? Eat something now, you're much too thin. Here, I'll get you some pasta."

We were sitting, at that point, around two large rectangular tables in-side a studio that had been repurposed to look like a restaurant. Catering had ordered Italian food, and I could see that everyone was struggling to eat their spaghetti in a manner dignified for national television. The strangest part of sitting there, beyond all the obvious strangeness—the cameras and the rehearsals and the microphones and the retakes—was how familiar these strangers seemed. Not just their faces, which resembled mine in large and small ways, with their blue eyes and high foreheads and long faces. Their wry humor, their self-effacement, their intelligence and skepticism of the powers that be—I had a sense of not déjà vu, or already seen, but déjà felt. I took to their company as if I'd been among them my whole life, but whether that was because some genetic signal had been flipped or production had groomed me for such a reaction was impossible to say.

Others seemed to feel it too. "This is much easier than I thought," a cousin named Elisabeth said. She was a stylish older woman dressed impeccably, right down to the pearl brooch on her lapel. "I must tell you, I had some fear about today. What we hear about Americans in the news . . ." She trailed off, then patted my wrist. "But you are lovely."

"We aren't all like that, I promise," I assured Elisabeth. "Not even most of us. Forty percent, maximum."

From behind the camera, Magnus broke the fourth wall. "You are lucky," he said. "Sometimes the Swedes at these reunions are real . . . how can I say? They talk like potatoes. Very plain. And the Americans, well—Paulie knows, Americans are crazy! But you all, you seem to—you seem to fit with each other, no?"

Elisabeth and I looked at each other and smiled. "I would agree," Alma said from my other side. Alma and Elisabeth in particular gave me an uncanny sense of familiarity, though perhaps that's just because they were the ones I was seated beside. Alma had the same eyes as me, chin-length light-brown hair, and was one of the founders of an innovative publishing house in Stockholm. We fell easily into conversation and became so engrossed that I had nearly forgotten that the purpose, and the financial imperative, of all this fuss was to sing and dance for Tocke's and millions of unnamed viewers' amusement.

"Paulie!" Tocke barked. "Focus! Talk about how you are feeling!"

So we had to have more contrived conversations—the similarities and differences between America and Sweden, the similarities and differences in our personalities, the similarities and differences in our families, and so on—and funny questions put forth by the children. It took some time before we could once again just be people. It took, to be precise, the cameras moving away to do B-roll of flowers and candlelight. Before Jonas went outside to film a wide shot, I asked him to fetch my backpack, which was sitting in a corner.

"May I take a picture of you?" I asked Alma, pulling out my Polaroid.

"Of course. Are you a photographer?" she said, starting to take her lipstick out of her purse.

"Oh, don't worry about that," I said, putting out my hand to stop her from applying the lipstick. "And yes—no—I don't know. I was, a photographer I mean. I've taken a lot on this trip. It's made it fun again—I'd stopped having fun a long time ago." *Snap.* I caught Alma just as she was looking up from her handbag, a sort of deer-in-the-headlights quality to her eyes.

"You have them with you?" Alma said, motioning to the camera. "May I see?"

I rummaged through my backpack. "I have a few." I handed them over to her. It was a real mishmash—Kevin sleeping in the Sprinter, the Vikings in Gotland, Becki outside the ABBA Museum. Alma flipped through them without saying anything. "You know," she said after a moment. "I have a friend who has a small gallery in Gamla Stan. I could introduce you."

"Oh," I said, startled. "No, that's okay, these are just for—"

"With the tie-in to the show, I am sure she would be interested," Alma continued. "What I like about these is how, how do you say, casual they are. You seem to have caught people in a private moment. Like we are seeing something we almost shouldn't see."

"Literally in some cases," I said, thinking of Kevin snoring. "But you don't have to, it's—"

"Yes, but I want to," she said. She cocked her head, gave me a good, long look, then broke into a smile. "This is what family is for, yes? We are family now." She waved a hand around. "And we are Swedish. Nothing is just for show."

"Oh—um—yes, wow, I guess that is what family's for," I said, though actually I'd had no idea, because, as Becki had pointed out, I'd drawn a lot of conclusions about family without gathering much evidence. At the same moment, Elisabeth, who had disappeared, came back into the room holding a princess cake. The children started clapping, and the rest of us joined in. Elisabeth set the cake down in front of me. "The rose in the center? This is for you," she said. "Welcome to our family."

"This is the happiest day of my life," I wept, and sank the cake knife right through it.

"Oh, do not say that," Elisabeth said, settling back into her chair. "The pasta is not even very good!"

I would have laughed, but I was trying not to get my tears on the cake as I cut it into pieces and started passing it down the table. Everyone was laughing and talking, and the children were playing, and glasses were clinking and forks scraping, and the light was golden from early evening coming through the windows and the dripping candles, and there was so much love in the room, so much love, that I knew that it had to be a collective effort. I could see it on my family's faces, in their eyes and mouths and voices and hands, and it was the first time I had ever felt such a thing, ever, certainly the first time in the context of traditional family, not that anything about this moment could really be called traditional, and I finally understood what the fuss was about. It had never made sense to me before, why people would sacrifice everything for a group of other people. But it was for this feeling, this one precisely. And yes, if this love could bring out the worst in people—tribalism, greed, insularity—then perhaps—joy, kindness, humor—it could also bring out the best.

Snap went my Polaroid. *Snap, snap.* I'd try to remember that. *Snap.* I'd treasure it for the rest of my life.

"Paulie, stop it!" Tocke roared. "We need you outside!"

Sighing, I trooped out the doors of the studio and into the grass, where my relatives were amassing into rows like an old-fashioned class picture. "Go stand in the middle," Tocke said to me. "In the back. And on the count of three, you are going to say 'This is my family!' and the rest of you are going to cheer and wave your Swedish flags." He said something rapidly in Swedish to the others.

"What? No!" I said, stuffing myself into the back row. "That's so corny!"

"Corny?" Jonas said from behind the camera. "*Corny?* Five weeks of corny and you worry about it now?"

"It is not corny, it is good television," Tocke barked. "Okay, is everyone ready? Children, stop moving around. You, there, I need you to—"

"Thank you everyone," I found myself saying as Tocke continued on with his last-minute adjustments. "Thank you. Thank you so much."

"Look happy," Tocke said. "Look like it's the best day of your life."

"It *is* the best day of my life," I said.

"Mine too!" said one of the children. They had a juice mustache on their upper lip.

"And mine," Alma said, and squeezed my hand.

"Right, okay, sure, whatever. One," Tocke said. "Two, three—"

We cheered so loud that cars on the street stopped and started honking. We cheered so much I thought my voice would break along with my heart. Somehow it didn't. We made good television. And in the aftermath of this triumphant set piece, as the crew started packing and my cousins started making noise about heading to their cars, I found myself answering Alma confidently when she asked when I'd be returning to Sweden: "Very soon, yes, yes, very soon."

"You sound so sure," she said, laughing.

"I've never been surer of anything in my life," I said.

"I knew I liked you," she said thoughtfully.

I said, weeping, "I love you too."

CHAPTER FOURTEEN

✴

BUMPY LANDINGS

"Guess this is it," I said to Becki at the airport in Reykjavík, Iceland, fourteen hours later.

She hefted her backpack on her shoulder. "Guess so."

When we had arrived back at the hotel the previous night, Inga had unceremoniously dropped a plane ticket in each of our laps and given us instructions to be waiting outside at seven a.m. for the airport taxi. "Tocke says to remind you that if you try to stay in Sweden after tomorrow, or come back before the show airs in January, you will have to pay 100,000 kronor fine. Okay, time to go, it was nice to meet you!" She had given me a hug so light it was like getting brushed by tissue paper. "Bye-bye!"

Becki and I had been on the same flight to Reykjavík, and on the way we'd regaled each other with tales of our reunions, having been too exhausted the night before. She had found the experience more stressful than I had, perhaps because over a hundred relatives had shown up to shake her hand. She had been right after all: the day really had been like a wedding, with only a few seconds to talk to each guest. "Except I didn't know who any of them were!" she'd complained. "Tocke beat us over the head: family, family, family, don't you want to meet your family. But then when it is time to meet the family he doesn't make it good! It's all, get the footage and get out. It's bullshit." She'd taken a slug of Bloody Mary. "I thought it was gonna be like a real reunion. That it wouldn't just look happy, it'd *be* happy."

"It's a TV show, not a charity," I'd reminded her. "That's what Junior always said."

Becki's flight to Dallas was now boarding, and she looked glum. She gazed toward the long line of people jockeying in the queue. We had heard our fellow Americans in the airport before we saw them, shouting through the corridors about snacks and bathrooms. At the first sign of my fellow countrymen, my heart seemed to shrink a few sizes. They were so large and unwieldy, in all senses: chewing with their mouths open, dressed in pajamas, staring at their phones while charging down the corridor, forcing others to scuttle out of the way. One guy with a Big Ten college sweatshirt was double-fisting beers at a café while noisily blowing his nose. A group of twentysomething girls were screaming and taking selfies. "Oh my God, do not post that!" one of them said while pursing her lips and staring at herself. "Oh my God, Tessa, do NOT!"

Becki, apparently still thinking about her reunion, said, "I guess I had this idea in my mind of what it would be like, and it was nothing like that."

I watched the guy with the beers get up and abandon his table, leaving a snow pile of dirty tissues. "It never is, is it?"

Becki blinked. "So whaddya think's gonna happen when you see Declan?"

I felt my chest constrict. "I have no idea." How I wished I'd read *The Odyssey* and not just the CliffsNotes! Odysseus had probably known just what to do after hooking up with Circe. He probably brought back Penelope an elegant laurel wreath or a pile of gold, not the novelty apron I'd found for Declan that read I ♥ Swedish Girls and the apology I'd rehearsed a thousand times already. "I hope I can make him understand it didn't mean anything—or, it meant something, just not what he thinks—" I covered my face with my hands and groaned. "How do you explain temporary insanity?"

Becki let out a small burp. "Just don't overthink it."

I removed my hands from my face. "I'm not overthinking. I'm thinking."

Becki thumped me on the back. "You're being r—d."

"You can't say that anymore."

"I can say whatever I want, I'm going back to Texas."

"It's not funny," I said, in a tone rather self-righteous for the circumstances.

"Well, whatever, I'm leaving," Becki said. "So you'll never have to listen to me again."

Her face was defiant as she said this, but I knew her better now, enough to know that her defiance was a smoke screen. There was a gentle person way down in there. Way, way down. Way, way, way—

"Listen, I'll come visit you," I said. "I've never been to Texas—except Austin—"

"Austin isn't Texas," she said flatly.

"Well, then you'll show me Texas."

"I doubt your friends in Minneapolis would like that."

"Would you shut up?" I said. "They'll get a kick out of you, I'm serious, anytime—"

As I said this, Becki adjusted her backpack, and I spotted a button on the strap that I'd somehow never noticed. Stand for the Flag, Kneel for the Cross. I don't know what was so funny—that Becki, the most profane and least Christlike person I'd ever met, was hawking this particular maxim; that she seemed unbothered by her contradictions; or that I, too, was unbothered by her contradictions, and in fact enjoyed them, thereby revealing my own contradictions, which I felt loose enough to forgive.

"What's so funny?" Becki said. I pointed to the pin. A smile twitched on Becki's lips. But she frowned. "It's not funny."

But she couldn't help it. In the face of my laughter, which was out of love, not contempt, she started laughing too. Really laughing. The more she tried to resist, the more demanding her laughter became. Tears collected in the corners of my eyes, and in hers. And in a moment of divine grace, or human inspiration, in the midst of this fit, Becki slipped away from me and into the line of passengers, and disappeared down a Jetway before either of us could say goodbye.

TEN HOURS LATER, I was standing outside the baggage claim in Minneapolis, my heart thudding, waiting for Declan to pick me up after a seven-hour flight and a grueling interrogation by the U.S. Immigration and Customs officer:

OFFICIAL BEHIND BULLETPROOF GLASS: You were doing what?

ME: A reality show. In Sweden. But I wasn't paid, it was just a per diem—

OFFICIAL: Did they pay you in goods, then?

ME: Oh, no, nothing like that—I just have a few wooden horses, souvenirs, you know, and some clothes—

OFFICIAL: Lemme get this straight: you were gone for five weeks and you got paid nothing but wooden horses?

ME: Like I said, I got a per diem—plus, you know, there's the free hotels and the—

OFFICIAL: I've never heard of anything like this. (*calls OFFICIAL 2 over, explains*) But, see, she don't have a work visa.

ME: Because technically I wasn't working.

OFFICIAL 2: What were you doing, then?

ME: It was a kind of—journey of self-discovery—

OFFICIAL 2: But was it paid or unpaid self-discovery?

ME: I guess I don't know how you guys count a per diem—

OFFICIAL: I'd give my left nut for five weeks of—what'd you call it?—self-discovery. With a per diem! (*pronounced purr deem*)

OFFICIAL 2: What kinda job you got where you can go off and do that?

ME: Oh, I'm a college admissions—

OFFICIAL: Bet she gets all the holidays off too.

OFFICIAL 2: We're gonna need to see your suitcase.

ME: Okay, um, you really don't want to do that—

OFFICIAL 2: Why not?! You trying to hide something from us?!

ME: No! It's just that I haven't done laundry in three weeks—

A car horn honked, and I looked up. There was Declan in the driver's seat of his reliable Japanese import. He'd shaved and gotten a haircut, and was wearing a clean, albeit wrinkled, button-down shirt. He got out of the car and came to give me a hug, and I was startled by his smell, which was probably how he always smelled, except it smelled different to me now, foreign. He hadn't brushed his teeth. "Hi," he finally said, releasing me and picking up my suitcases. "You ready to go home?"

"I—I—yes," I said, and without saying anything else, slid into the passenger seat.

The fifteen-minute drive back home felt elongated, unfamiliar. The roads were so wide, the cars so big, the billboards so shouty with their admonishments to ask Gary and buy ugly houses and turn dinner into a winner with gas station pizza. I blinked slowly and turned my head from side to side, feeling like Rip van Winkle. Everything was different, or I was different. Minneapolis was ugly, or maybe it was just plain. I'd been spoiled by the beauty in Stockholm, both natural and man-made, and there was a distinctive thud of disappointment in arriving back to a second-tier city with so few tourists that, if you happen to encounter one, your first question is "Why are you here?" And why was I here? Why was anyone? My ancestors had risked life and limb and sanity to get to Minnesota, and *this* was the New Scandinavia? A brown, capitalist marsh? Declan had the windows down, and the air was so humid it felt like you had to drink it. An unlovely corner of the world, flat as a cookie sheet. Cheap rent and lots of trees, but—

Declan reached across the parking brake and took my hand, and I felt my body settle, the thoughts dissipate. "So how was it?" he said. We were pulling off the highway and passing the unhoused people who had, over the past several years, taken to living and/or begging on the exit ramps. I startled, thinking for some reason that he meant kissing Lars, made eye contact with a man holding a cardboard sign that read Sober Dad, Widowed. Anything Helps. "Um, how was what?"

"The reunion? Or are you too tired—"

"Oh. Right." That had been exactly twenty-four hours ago. How strange to live in a world that moves so fast. My mind felt soft and curdled, a pan of scrambled eggs. "It was, um, wonderful. Or—it was amazing. It was—it was one of the best days of my life—"

He pulled up in front of our duplex. How about that: he'd managed to keep my geraniums alive. He grabbed my suitcases from the back, and I realized I had butterflies as we went up the front walk. Butterflies with Declan! Declan, the man I slept beside and burped beside and chided about the water glasses he left on every surface of our house. I'd thought that phase was long over, ended as soon as we started sharing a bathroom.

Inside, the house was spotlessly clean, or as clean as someone relatively unused to the physical plane can make it. There were peonies on the dining-room table, fresh bread, and several gift-wrapped packages at my seat. "You shouldn't have done all this," I said, looking around, when what we both knew I meant was *I love that you did all this*. "I'm the one who should be giving you presents. And I have them"—I gestured toward my beat-up suitcases—"somewhere in there . . ."

"Let's wait on that," he said. "I'll have dinner ready in a few minutes. Sit down and relax."

I followed him into the kitchen. "I've been sitting for fifteen hours. Let me help."

Declan's culinary skills must have improved rapidly while I was away, for he told me we'd be having salade Niçoise. Did I mind spinning the lettuce and trimming the green beans? I did not. While he halved new potatoes and whisked a vinaigrette, we talked on the surface of things— how the travel went, the logistics of the reunion, developments at Declan's work—while the animals inside us slowly crept out and sniffed the air. He opened a bottle of Sancerre he'd purchased and been chilling, my favorite, even though he preferred red. I praised the potatoes, which he'd boiled in sea-salty water, and expressed admiration that he'd overcome his fear of artichokes. The early evening summer sunlight streamed through the windows, giving a golden cast to Declan's skin and hair; the wine slid down my throat like nectar. How do you find someone again after being far away? How do you keep finding them? We should have signals for this, symbols, like Batman or Zorro. *I am here. Come and find me.*

By the time we sat down at the table, we were holding hands.

"I missed you so much," I said. "Let's never do that again." I noticed only after I said it the implied *us*, when what I'd meant was me.

"I missed you too," he said. "That was a long time."

So he'd felt the distance too. Of course he had. It'd been there for a while, even before I announced my trip to New York. Declan was eating fast, as he always did, and had forgotten to put the cloth napkin he had included in the table settings on his lap. I reached out with my fingers and touched the laugh lines around his eyes. How on earth had I mistaken the chemistry I had with Lars for love? *For someone smart, you're pretty dumb, Paulie,* Becki had said. And she was right.

"All your mail's on your desk," Declan was saying as he speared some green beans. "And you probably saw already, but I organized the emails that came in in a new folder called Sweden. All the junk I just deleted."

"Thank you," I said. "I know I asked a lot of you—too much, given the circumstances—"

"About that." Declan put his fork down and reached for his wine. "I was doing some more research—"

I felt a pin approach the area around my heart, primed for deflation, but then Declan continued down a surprising avenue. With a potato in his mouth, he said, "Interestingly, a lot of it ended up tying back to queer studies, starting with these support networks that emerged during the AIDS crisis after the government failed to step in." He proceeded to give a detailed history of legal rights, or lack thereof, for gay families in the 1980s, including the realms of health care, marriage, and adoption, and went on to explain how community-run AIDS clinics, phone trees, and hospice centers managed to create a powerful web of noninstitutionalized care.

"The point is," he continued, "when traditional institutions fail—in your case, your nuclear family—it's possible for nontraditional yet equally effective support systems to emerge to take the institution's place. Maybe even more effective, like the flower growing through the sidewalk." He took a sip of wine. "My mistake was that I didn't see *Sverige och Mig* as your effort to seek out this kind of nontraditional support system. I believed it was just a lark, which it may have been

initially, but it clearly became something else." He picked up his fork
again, put a giant forkful of salad into his mouth. Chewing, he said,
"'Chosen family' is the common term for this in the LGBTQ community, but in your case I think 'found family' is better. Because you're
always searching for something. You're always discovering new people to
love." He swallowed. "Anyway, sorry it took me so long to understand
this. Do you want some more bread?"

I had tears in my eyes, which I only knew because Declan was swimming in front of me, his clear hazel eyes looking at me, the way you
look at a person when you have their number but plan on putting that
knowledge to only good use. What a person he was. What a person!
I felt ill with deception. He didn't deserve what I had done. He was
too good for that. For me. But then again, perhaps he didn't need to
know . . .

This last thought, as it uncoiled from the back of my brain, appeared
to have been lurking for a long time. It was ancient, powerful, with the
force of human history behind it. It was the same thought my father had
had, I was sure of it, when he made the choice to lie to everyone he knew
about his sexuality. The same thought my mother had when she hid her
drinking. The same thought as Becki's family, burying her ancestor's
suicide. As Kevin's family, hiding their Sámi identity. As Deborah's
family, hiding her adoption. If I had learned anything in Sweden, besides how little I knew about everything, it was that secrets destroyed
families, even if it didn't seem like it at first, even if it took a long, long
time. And if that was true, perhaps the converse might also be true: that
honesty could save families. Even if it didn't seem like it at first. Even if
it took a long, long time.

It was the last thing I wanted to do, and the one thing I needed to do.
If I wanted my family to be different, that difference would have to start
with me. I put my fork down and took a sip of water. "There's something
I have to tell you."

In a halting voice, with none of the rhetorical flourishes I'd thought
up on the plane, I told Declan about Lars's and my intimacies, large and
small, which culminated that night at Jesus camp and decrescendoed with

a grimy embrace in the corner of a Swedish rap concert. What struck me more than anything while confessing all this was how dumb it sounded. Divorced of intensity, and examined in the cold light of day, it was not a story of sex and desire but a story of stress and fear and embarrassment and a longing to escape one's circumstances no matter the cost. Not unlike the episode from junior high when Robbie Irwin invited me to the spring dance but spent the whole night trading Pogs with his friends, which meant I spent the whole night grinding on Evan Holowinski in retaliation. What a piece of work is man, honestly. What a piece of work is me!

But Karen Hamburger liked to say, whenever I got too down about human nature, that while *Homo sapiens* had indeed turned out Hitler, it had also popped out Shakespeare. "Variation is the keystone of our species," she always said. In other words, there were infinite ways to live, more than there were toppings on a pizza, some closer to Hitler, some closer to Shakespeare, and a whole lot of tomato sauce between.

"I just want you to understand—not as an excuse—that we were so isolated," I said, fumbling my way through the gray. "Bewitched, even. And you weren't under the spell but on the other side of the world, and no matter what I did I couldn't seem to get out of the trance and back to you—"

"I knew it," Declan said. "I knew it." Though he'd remained eerily still as I spoke, he now pushed his chair back from the table and stood up. His lower jaw was trembling. "I knew even before you went that something like this was going to happen."

"But how did you know?" I said, picking up my fork. "When I didn't know! When I could never have—"

"Because I know you!" he cried. "Because I notice everything about you! Even when you think I'm not, I'm paying attention." He picked up his napkin, twisted it between his hands, then let it fall to the floor. "You get swept up in things, that's what you do. And you get so swept up riding whatever wave you're on that you—that you forget there are people on the shore, waiting for you."

And before I could respond to him, not that I'd thought of anything to say, he walked straight out the front door. I heard the screen door close with a bang before I jumped up and ran after him. "Don't follow me!" he shouted without turning around, and put an arm up in the air in warning.

I didn't follow Declan, but I did watch him. Slightly bowlegged, a slightly shuffling walk. Declan was right: he knew me, but I knew him too. Knew his worry and his thoroughness and the way he yelled at machines when they weren't working, just like his mother. Knew exactly how he cleared the sauce from a plate with his index finger and exactly how much he hated group sing-alongs (a lot). Knew the way he clutched his fists to his bare chest while he slept and the coolness of the skin on his upper arms in the mornings.

And I was standing there, in the depths of despair, wondering why so often knowing someone, and loving them, also meant hurting them badly, when Jemma pulled up in her electric car and stepped out onto the sidewalk with a bottle of French champagne. Declan must have told her to come over—I was so tired I'd forgotten to text.

"What's wrong?" she said when she saw my face.

"Declan left," I said. "I told him I hooked up with someone else."

Jemma sucked in a breath. The humidity was doing wonders for her hair. "Is he mad?"

"Of course he's mad!" I cried. "He's furious! We're probably going to break up and it's all my fault—also, you look amazing, I missed you so much—"

"Come on," Jemma said. She propelled me indoors and sat me down on the couch and returned with two champagne flutes. When she popped the cork and handed me a fizzing glass, I said, waving her off, "I'm not really in the mood to celebrate."

"Not in the mood to celebrate?" Jemma pushed the glass into my hand. "You won a Swedish reality-TV show and you're not in the mood to celebrate? You haven't seen your best friend in five weeks and you're not in the mood to celebrate?" She leaned forward to clink her glass with mine. "Well, too bad, Paulie, 'cause we're celebrating."

"Did you not hear what I said?" I took a sip of champagne, despite myself. It was delicious. "I did something awful. Truly awful. Declan's never gonna forgive me."

Jemma drank her champagne. "So did you sleep with him or what?"

"The guy? No. He's a segment producer, though, and we spent a lot of time, like, you know, being"—I lowered my voice—"emotionally intimate—"

"And you told Declan this, what, five minutes after you got home? Are you crazy?"

I thought for a second. "Yes."

"So you got dickmatized," Jemma said matter-of-factly. "It happens."

"I think it was more of a general hypnosis—"

"Like a cat in heat. Hormones, man." Jemma sighed heavily. "Remember when I was dating that John guy and he broke up with me over the phone and then I called him back and I said . . ." She covered her face with one hand while the other balanced her champagne flute. "I can't even say it, it's too embarrassing—"

I was laughing, despite myself. "You told him that day or night, he could call you and you'd—"

"STOP!" Jemma was waving her hand. "You have to stop. I'll die. I'll literally perish."

"Why aren't you yelling at me?" I asked. "Why aren't you telling me I'm an awful person?"

"Because blame and shame make the world insane," she recited, something her mom had taught us when we were little kids. "You want some more champagne?"

"But this is different," I said. "I betrayed Declan. *Betrayed.* While he was here taking care of everything while I was away." I was making myself very warm. I stood up and started pacing around the living room. "It's genetic, isn't it? I'm doomed, Jemma, I knew it. I've always known. If I don't end up in the loony bin like my mom, I'll end up"—pant, pant, pace, pace—"leading some kind of double life, sneaking around like my dad and—how can Declan ever trust me again? How can I ever look him in the eye? How can we keep building a life together if—" I went on like this for a while. Jemma crossed and uncrossed her legs. Once in a while she poured herself more champagne.

"Are you done?" she said when I came up for a breath.

I wiped my forehead with the back of my hand. It was damp. "For the moment."

She leaned forward on the couch. "Do you really need to turn another good moment into a bad one? Are you dying to condemn yourself?"

"I'm not dying to, I have to—"

"Because if you do, it's fine." Jemma put down her glass. "But I'm not going to sit here and listen to you tell the same old story about what a failure you are and how you'll never get out from under your family and you're bound to end up like your parents blah blah blah blah blah." She stood up. "I've heard it too many times—I don't need to hear it again. So just call me when you're ready to do something."

She made for the door. "Jesus Christ, Jemma!" I put my champagne flute down on the coffee table. Jemma turned around. "You're not going to let me spiral for even a little bit?"

"Not even a little bit," she said calmly, and made her way back to the couch. "Now, where's your phone? Let's call him."

THAT WAS SUNDAY night. On Tuesday morning, I went back to Premiere Prep. Declan had taken to sleeping on the couch, though I tried to insist that should have been my job. He'd barely spoken to me on Monday, was either out of the house or barricaded in his office. "Give him time," Jemma had said, but what on earth could time do? Pain didn't pass with time—it simply changed, became a part of you. Look at me with my parents, and them with their parents, and back and back and back—

It was in this macabre frame of mind that I stepped into the Premiere Prep offices. Before I could even get my bearings, my boss, Garance, pulled me into her office. As always, it smelled not good, exactly, but expensive, like a Nordstrom bathroom. We both sat down. Garance asked, "And how was your vacation? Did you remember to mention Premiere Prep every day?"

"Oh! Um, about that—" I said.

"I wanted to catch you up on the new strategy we're onboarding," she interrupted. She proceeded to rattle off a number of recent trends in college admissions, including a keen interest in hardship and the overcoming thereof. "We're not having them write about volunteer work anymore," she continued, "or even anxiety or ADHD. Our clients have trauma. Do you know how much pressure they're under, coming from so much privilege?"

I thought of Tristan, almost a high school senior now, struggling with his ancestral call to dentistry. "I mean, I don't know about trauma, but sure, they're pretty stressed—"

"How are they supposed to own their privilege when their parents refuse to?" Garance said, clicking her painted nails on her desk. Her voice grew passionate. "How can they confront their own racism when racism is baked into the structures paving their way to guaranteed success? Trolls calling them nepo babies, I find they're paralyzed by privilege—oh, that's good"—she uncapped a fountain pen and started scribbling on her notepad—"paralyzed by privilege," she murmured. "Something, something, 'the burden of inheritance.'" Garance looked up. "You want a pen?"

I did not. The same feeling of *wrongness* I had encountered while watching Tocke justify his decision to drag Tom underground was re-emerging through my skin, as palpable as heat rash. I'd spent the last five weeks wrestling with the so-called burdens of inheritance, not to mention the last four years in Karen Hamburger's group therapy. And while these burdens were real, and from time to time had me acting out and/or losing my mind, to align myself solely with these burdens as authentication of my identity felt insanely reductionist, the difference between a jingle and a song. Which is what Declan had been trying to get me to understand since January: that I was not just the result of events long in the past, and my life could and should not be distilled into a tidy, one-trick tale that a bunch of producers in Sweden made up for television. In the same way that Deborah was not just a result of adoption, or Tom a result of his father's untimely death, or Honor her professional bona fides, Brock evangelicalism, or Junior Mormonism, or Becki conservatism, or Kevin masculinism. Heaven forbid! We were so much more than the worst things that happened to us, and moreover, the worst things we did.

"I'm sorry," I said. "I don't think I can do this."

Garance looked up. "I know it's a lot to catch up on, but you left right in the middle of this big pivot—left me quite in the lurch, may I say—"

"I mean, I did ask several months in advance, and wrote out plans for all my—" *Paulie, this is no time to split hairs!* I took a breath. "Garance, I'm so grateful for the years I've spent here at Premiere Prep and everything you've taught me"—the customer is always right, name-dropping is never wrong, what you can't win through sycophancy you can often win through passive aggression—"but I think it's time that I headed in another direction."

Garance exhaled. "Well, this is a surprise." After a beat, she added: "And a relief, actually, because in your absence, I'm afraid I learned I didn't need you, strictly from a financial standpoint. Efficiency, you know." I started to cry. Garance patted my knee. "Oh, Paulie, I'm sure you'll land on your feet. Well"—she paused—"maybe not sure-sure, but given your age and race I think it's likely—"

I didn't have the wherewithal to tell Garance that I wasn't crying because I was leaving Premiere Prep. I was crying because, in Declan's absence, I'd learned just how much I needed him, and I feared that he no longer needed me, given all my foibles. "I'll give you a reference, of course," she said, somehow standing me up and getting me out the door, for the next thing I remember is leaning against the elevator. "I use the Harvard letterhead—it's very effective. Anyhow, good luck, Paulie, keep in touch and dream big!"

And with that, I was in the elevator, feeling as if I'd just woken up from a dream, only it hadn't been a dream, it'd been five years of my life. My phone buzzed when I got to the lobby. It was Alma, my Swedish cousin—we'd exchanged numbers on Saturday evening. (Had that only been Saturday?) *Welcome home, Paulie! I hope you are getting some rest. I spoke with my friend who owns the gallery, and she is interested in seeing your photographs. Here is her contact info. She is expecting to hear from you soon. Kram xx Alma.*

I started texting back a thank-you, but before I could finish I ran over and puked in the lobby trash can.

"GUILT, OBVIOUSLY," KIRA clucked. I was back in Karen Hamburger's office the next day, sitting in the cesspool of my life while my fellow group-therapy members waded through looking for buried treasure—or trash, in Kira's case. "Of course she was going to have an affair—no offense, Paulie—did anyone else see it coming or just me?"

"It wasn't an affair," Todd interrupted. "It was a dalliance. Brought on by stress. Like my flirtation with heroin when I got to art school."

I looked at him with horror. "What, you think I *enjoy* when good things happen to me?" he said, then took a giant bite of his sandwich. Chewing with his mouth open, he said, "Sometimes I think I'll never be as happy as when my mom and I'd steal hot pizza from the Little Caesars dumpster."

"Frankly, I'm surprised she didn't turn to something stronger," Sheila said drily. She looked around at the group. "Come on, y'all, at what point do we need to call the behavior from these so-called reality-show producers what it is?" Sheila had been horrified by ninety-five percent of the things I'd said I'd done under Tocke's authoritarian hand, particularly the Jesus stuff.

"Oh, *psh*, the show's not abusive," I said. "Amoral and manipulative, at worst—"

"Immoral!" Sheila cried, fanning herself with her hand. She'd grown up Baptist, but she'd left the church when her pastor said he didn't believe in trans people. This when he'd had one standing right in front of him!

"At best, like a Janus-faced Santa Claus?"

"Stop using big words," Kira complained. "You only do that when you're intellectualizing."

"Weigh it for us, then," Ayisha, the actuary, said. "Was it worth it?"

"Language," Karen Hamburger intervened in a mild tone. Karen didn't believe in using market words like "worth," "cost," "expense," "buy it," and so on, in a therapeutic environment.

"Fine," Ayisha said. She stared up at the sky, thinking, before snapping her eyes back to me. "Do you find you have more regret than satisfaction in the aftermath of this journey?"

I sat back in my chair, my Mediterranean Veggie sandwich from Panera nestled in my lap like a pet. I thought I would need time to think, but then—"No, not at all," I said. "What makes it all worth it is that I found my family—sorry, not 'worth'—"

Then I started crying. Again. Everyone but Todd shifted in their chairs. Sense memories slid through my brain: hurling myself around inside an inflatable chess piece, dancing to ABBA in bars and hotel rooms, visiting Fotografiska, taking pictures, skinny-dipping in Norrland, scream-singing The Beatles in the Sprinter van with everybody, eating wild mushrooms cooked on an open fire, tromping across Stockholm, watching the midnight sun, and—and—"And it was pretty fun."

A pause. "Hmmm," Ayisha said. "Fun?"

Fun's a hard thing to explain, don't you think? Like trying to explain an orgasm. I tried anyway. "It's like, the fun just happened, even though the producers tried to control everything. You can't plan for fun, and you can't spoil it either. It happened with people like Becki and Kevin who at first I hated. But I also love them, because we had a lot of fun. Do you see what I'm getting at?" I found myself getting warm again. "If you can hate someone and love them, and if this gets easier when you have fun—"

"For God's sake, Paulie." Kira was rolling her eyes. "I don't need to go halfway around the world to figure out that you can hate and love the same person. Why do you think I come back here every week?" She had not taken a single bite of her chicken salad sandwich, which went against the rules of group. Then she said, somewhat begrudgingly, "But I'm glad you found your family. They sound nice."

"You want my two cents, Pauline?" Sheila folded up the paper from her sandwich and placed it neatly on an end table. Karen Hamburger gave her a look. "I mean—you want my input?"

I nodded. "The reason you had fun is that you were making choices." Sheila said the last two words deliberately. "You've spent a lot of time waiting around for things to happen to you. A gallery or a grant to say yes. Your mother to apologize. Your father to come back from the dead and explain himself. Your sister to snap out of cuckoo land. The right career to fall into your lap. You and Declan to decide—or not—about getting married. But making choices, it's finally gonna turn you into an *ac-tive par-tic-i-pant* in your life. Am I right?" She crossed one leg over the other, interlaced her fingers on top of her knee, and smiled with satisfaction. "May I just say, it's been a long time coming."

"I just quit my job, Sheila!" I said, though not unappreciatively. "Give me a break!" Then: "When I'm done licking my wounds, remind me to thank you."

Sheila nodded, pleased that I had accepted her read. "Oh please, you'll be fine," Kira said waspishly. "You're always fine."

"How am I gonna be fine?" I said. "I'm not even remotely fine. I'm jobless, my boyfriend, possibly ex-boyfriend, wants nothing to do with me, I've got terrible jet lag, and I—"

"Because you have this way of landing on your feet no matter what happens to you." Kira put her untouched sandwich down on the end table and cleared her throat. "I'm jealous of that, all right?"

"That's brave of you to say, Kira," Karen Hamburger said after a pause. "Paulie, would you like to respond?"

I cleared my throat too. "You're brave, too, Kira. I know how hard these last couple years have been for you."

"Thanks," she said gruffly. "And thanks for the cookies after Mom died. I don't think I said that back then." She put her sandwich back in her lap. Her voice went back to normal. "The thing is, you guys—sorry, Sheila, y'all—I think I've gotten addicted to—" She named a popular fitness app. "And I can't fall asleep until I do at least one class a day. I try to do five. Like one of every category. It's not all exercise—there's, like, breathing and stretching and stuff. I mean, I know it's healthy for me. But is that healthy?"

The rest of us shifted in our chairs, having known the answer from the second Kira opened her mouth. Why was such clarity self-evident when it came to other people and never when it came to oneself? "We're not talking about this until you have some sandwich, Kira," Karen Hamburger said gently. Where this woman gets her patience is, like the location of Cleopatra's tomb, one of life's enduring mysteries.

THERE IS NO better comfort in the midst of life's troubles than baking bread. For the rest of that week, as Declan continued to give me the disappearing act, that's what I did, just as my grandma taught me, measuring and mixing and kneading and shaping and baking until I was balancing pyramids of whole-wheat and oatmeal loaves on the limited counter space in our kitchen. Was it dumb to use the oven during a heat wave? Yes. Did I do it anyway? Yes. I biked around my neighborhood with hot bread in my basket, handing loaves out to whoever wanted one and taking pictures of the recipients with my Polaroid, including the widowed man whom I'd seen on the highway exit ramp. At stop signs I texted with Becki, Brock, Kevin, Junior, and Deborah, who were, like me, struggling to settle back into their lives. Kevin had taken to going on long drives. Junior had also quit his job and was considering opening up a cabaret bar. Becki was thinking about breaking up with her boyfriend, and Brock was going out dancing every night after putting his kid to bed. Deborah had started writing a memoir, tentatively titled *Mother/Land*, about her adoption and our trip to Sweden. She was writing five thousand words a day. *I think I'm manic*, she wrote. *Tocke drove us so hard I can't seem to calm down!* They told me to keep baking, to stop worrying, or *over-thinking* as Kevin and Becki called it. *You're tougher than you think*, Becki said. *For fuck's sake your* [sic] *a reality television champion!*

At night, alone in bed, I read and reread *Pippi Longstocking*. Pippi did a fair amount of baking herself: bread, hot buns, ginger cookies, sugar cookies. I scribbled notes to myself, proto-recipes, and compared them to the ones my grandma had passed down. One particularly hot evening, Jemma dragged me out to Queen and bought me a giant vanilla cone. I told her that the official genealogist from *Sverige och Mig*—a distant cousin, believe it or not—had sent over a giant spreadsheet of my relatives in America, numbering well above five hundred. "Eh," Jemma said, licking her cone as we sat at a red wrought-iron table. "Take your time on that."

"You think?"

"I mean—" Jemma licked ice cream off her thumb. "Just because you opened the door a teeny crack on family doesn't mean you need to let everyone in. It's not an all-or-nothing situation."

As if in reply, the phone rang. I put my mother on speaker and set it on the table. "Hi, Mom."

"Hi, honey, are you back from Switzerland already? That was fast."

"It was Sweden, Mom. I was there for five weeks. What's up?"

"You told me Switzerland. Anyway, I'm calling because Gail's daughter's applying for college in the fall, and I told her you'd love to talk with her about the process." Gail, if you'll recall, ran the equine therapy barn at Healing Waters.

"Actually, Mom, I'm not doing that kind of work anymore, I left Premiere Prep—"

"It's immature, Pauline, to not help others when you've benefited from so much help yourself." My mother pronounced it *im-ma-tour*, something she did when she was feeling better. Some people speed right down the track from suicidal despair to moral certitude. "It will take no time at all, and it's about lifting out a hand and—"

Jemma took my hand, squeezed it. She knew what I was feeling, I'd had the same reaction to my mother for thirty years. I could feel it rising again, starting in my chest: fury, sorrow, the *wah-wah-wah* of my baby self. What did this have to do with love? My mother was still talking. "Like when I taught Rose in equine therapy how to brush Chester properly—"

While she continued to talk, as the baby inside me continued to *wah-wah-wah*, something strange happened: I heard the baby inside my mother too. *Wah-wah-wah*, she cried. *Wah-wah-wah*. Beneath the words I heard her longing for someone to listen to her, someone to pick her up, someone to rock her, pay her attention, lavish her with care, which was not a human luxury but a human right. Her mother, my grandmother, had been too busy taking Seconal to parent; God knows her father wasn't up for the job. *Wah-wah-wah!* my baby-mother cried, at the root of her lecturing. *Listen! Tell me I matter!* This poor baby, I thought for the first time. All alone in the world except for Chester. Oh, what a piece of work is man.

I thought of what Sheila had said in group, that making choices could finally transform me into an active participant in my life. I could make a different choice with my mother, something besides recrimination. This required nothing of her, and a lot from me, but who knew, maybe it really could change my life.

Meanwhile, Mom went on talking, and Jemma went on holding my hand, and the reactivity in my chest continued to rise, but beneath it I started summoning the force I felt when I was saying goodbye to Kevin. Love: that vast, impersonal thing. The thing beneath all the other things. Old Faithful. And I pictured Old Faithful, which my grandparents had taken me to when I was eight, steadfastly bursting into the air at Yellowstone twenty times per day, and I tried to imagine that much love just waiting around beneath the surface of our world, waiting to burst through the surface of somebody or something, and I invited it into my body, starting in my feet. *Come on*, I told it. *Come on. Come on. Burst through me.*

It did not come. All that hurt and resentment and anger stayed right where it was as my mother prattled on about Healing Waters. But I kept at it, I kept making the choice, I kept picturing Old Faithful, and for extra strength I started summoning, too, all the love I'd gotten at my family reunion, all the love they'd poured into me, and the love I felt from Jemma's hand in mine, right there, and Declan's food and my grandmother's bread and Becki's hard hugs and Kevin's singing and Deborah's insight and Brock's laughter and Junior's camp and Honor's honor and Tom's haplessness, from the Baltic Sea and the Midsommar pole and the midnight sun, from Karen Hamburger and Todd and Sheila and everyone at group, from my teachers and mentors and neighbors and friends, from—oh! oh!—the sun with its brightness and the water with its coolness and the earth with its nourishment and the animals with their truthfulness and the plants with their carbon dioxidinal generosity—

And there it was. Oh thank the gods, there it was. Came erupting through my heart and my mouth and my ears and my eyes, to the point it seemed unfathomable that I could ever again be held captive by matters so mean and small. Love coursed through my veins and loosened out my fascia and unkinked my muscles and ungripped my joints and, like a lighthouse, swung its golden light through the dark corners of me. It did not demand these dark corners depart but presented, in a gentle yet indisputable way, proof of their impermanence. Like Pythagoras's theorem, a proof that had the power to reshape the world as I knew it. Which is perhaps why, by the time this love had finished its eruption, the baby in me, the one that had been crying, was nestled up quiet in my chest.

Meanwhile, my mother was explaining how she'd been wronged by someone named Susan, who, she explained, "had no interest in what I had to share about astrology."

"Mom?" I said a moment later. "I'd be happy to. With Gail's daughter."

"What? Oh good, Paulie, I knew you'd come—"

"But Mom?"

"What?"

"I have to go now. I love you. I'm glad you're doing well. It makes me happy, hearing you like this."

"But Paulie, I haven't even told you about Chester's—"

"I love you, Mom, but I really have to go."

After a few more attempts, I finally got off the phone. "Jemma, something just happened to me."

"Did you get your period? I have a tampon—" She started rummaging in her bag.

"No, I mean something—it's like I don't—" I tried to figure out what I meant. Eventually I said, "I don't have to hate her."

Jemma patted the top of my head. "No, you don't. But I might?"

This made me laugh. I put my phone back in my pocket. "But the thing is, if I'm not hating her, what on earth am I supposed to do with her?"

"I've got a few ideas." Jemma crunched her cone. We sat in silence for a while in the gloaming. Then she said, "So did you figure it out? In Sweden?"

I took my last bite of cone. Chewing, I said, "Figure what out?"

"How you managed to fall so far from the tree?"

"Oh, *psh*, not so far, if you consider how big the tree is." I crushed my napkin in my fist. "You climb far enough up the tree, you pretty much find everybody."

Instead of answering, Jemma gave me the rest of her ice-cream cone, not because she didn't love it, but because she did.

DECLAN WASN'T HOME when I arrived. His absence was deafening: no clicking away on the keyboard in his office, no turning the pages in a Serious Magazine, no methodically moving pots around in the kitchen. Alone, I popped myself popcorn for dinner and flopped down on the couch to watch a famous Swedish film Alma had recommended. It was about a nineteenth-century family that decides to make the perilous journey to the New World, and fifteen minutes in, I understood why Alma had told me to watch it. There were obvious parallels with my own family: dead children, poverty, starvation, the dream of Shangri-La by way of Minnesota. Their journey across the Atlantic is horrifying: more starvation, more dead children, darkness, dankness, rats. In America, they're reviled, hoodwinked, confused, cast off to the wilderness. The mother grows depressed, blaming the father for their poverty and isolation, missing her family in Sweden, ruing the day her husband came to believe that simply by changing continents they could change their lot in life. The Native people, whose land they stole, are initially ignored, then feared, then praised as noble savages. Eventually the mother dies. An apple tree the family brought from Sweden survives, which is supposed to be hopeful. The father has cleared the land, which is supposed to be progress. The kids go to school, which is supposed to be good.

The film was long, and by the time it was over, the house was pitch-black. I sat in the dark, thinking to myself: Where is the happy ending? No wonder America was crazy. A bunch of traumatized crackpots running around in the woods—what else was going to happen? I got up from the couch, went into the kitchen to wash my popcorn bowl, and in a fit of pique I pulled down the baking ingredients from the cupboard. I needed somewhere to put my disappointment, or no, not just my disappointment, this excess of feeling in my body that so wished the world was better than it was. Rye bread, another of my grandma's recipes, the kind the mother had made in the movie before she died.

It was midnight when Declan came home, and the bread was on its second rise.

"Where were you?" I asked lightly, trying not to sound accusatory.

"Just walking," he said. He looked at the countertop, where the dough was proofing. "More bread?"

"I got inspired by this movie—you know what, it doesn't matter."

Declan took a glass from the cupboard and filled it at the sink. When he walked past me toward the living room, a new strand of gray in his hair caught the light. "Wait—" I said, catching him by the hand. "There's something I have to tell you."

"Something else?" he said, not turning around. "I think I'd rather not."

I knew I deserved that, but still. I closed my eyes and plunged ahead. "I just want to tell you that to me—you're the apple tree. You're the *smultronställe*."

"The what?" When I opened my eyes, Declan was looking at me with a face both cold and puzzled.

"It's from this movie—never mind, I won't summarize it," I amended, "but it's about how most people in this world have a bad time of it and either lose hope and die, or just work till their backs break and *then* they die. But these people in the movie lugged an apple tree across the world to have something near them that felt like home and gave them hope even when everything around them looked hopeless. Like you do for me."

Before I knew it, I was getting down on one knee in front of Declan. "You're not just home for me, you're hope for me. You're so decent and patient, even when you have no reason to be so. You don't rush to judgment and you're slow to take sides. You make me think that if human nature is so variable, but it can turn out someone like you, then maybe we're not doomed after all. Maybe love really is the thing beneath all other things. Like Old Faithful." I was wiping my eyes. "Because I would endure any amount of eruptions for the chance to share my life with you. Will you marry me?"

I didn't know I'd asked the question until it was hanging there in the silence, the air thick and heavy as if ghosts were gathering inside it, ghosts like my grandmother and great-grandmother and Astrid Lindgren and, yes, there she was, Pippi Longstocking. I could almost see them, smiling down at me, clasping their hands in pleasure. *Just try*, they murmured. *Just try, just try, just try*. And I knew what they meant without them having to say any more. That despite and because of everything that happened to us, everything that came before, we had to try. We had to try to do better. We could not choose much about this world, but we could choose, every day, who we wished to become by the things we chose to do.

"Marry me," I said again, and my voice cracked. "Just try."

He pulled me up to my feet, and just like that, his arms were around me. "All right, Paulie," he said huskily into my hair. "All right."

BIG IN SWEDEN

We were married a year later, Declan and I, the Saturday after Mid-sommar, in the gardens of the Swedish consulate and cultural center in Minneapolis that had, in the wake of *Sverige och Mig*'s ratings-busting season finale, generously offered to host us for free. Jemma officiated in a stunning black tuxedo. I wore a white eyelet off-the-shoulder dress and a crown of flowers in my hair that one of Alma's children wove, and Declan wore his best suit, which was also his only suit, and heroically kept his tie on for forty-five minutes before declaiming it was too itchy.

Everyone was there, or at least, everyone who mattered, including a number of people who surprised me. My sister, Else, left a silent retreat early so she could attend, yet she maintained her vow of silence through-out the festivities, which meant we could only communicate through gesture, which actually improved our relationship by leaps and bounds. Though it pained her, my mother briefly left Chester at Healing Waters to fulfill her role as mother of the bride, which she took to with aplomb, or at least enough not to ruin anything, which was the primary worry for Jemma and me. Jemma and her mom, who called herself my bonus mom, took turns babysitting my mother, but after a while Mom didn't need it, so happy was she to sit at her honored table and regale anyone who wanted to listen with stories of horses and healing, and it turned out there were a fair number of girls ages eight to twelve and women forty-five to seventy who were interested in that very thing. One of them was Deborah, who had composed an original poem to read during the ceremony, and by the end of the night my mother and Deborah were clasping hands as bosom friends, not something I ever expected to see and more proof that people, even mothers, can always surprise you.

Deborah wasn't the only one from *Sverige och Mig* who was kind enough to not only attend but participate in the nuptials. After Junior sang "Till There Was You" from *The Music Man*, accompanied by his boyfriend on piano, there wasn't a dry eye in the house. He'd made good on his wish to quit corporate life and open a cabaret bar, and the bar (called Elphie's, in honor of the Wicked Witch and Wizard of Omaha Warren Buffett) had just received a rave review in *Nebraska Life* magazine. Becki, who came to the wedding solo, told me later that the performance was the kick in the pants she needed to switch the settings on her dating apps from "looking for men" to "looking for women and men." She looked fabulous, and the GoFundMe I helped her set up in the wake of the show's success had managed to pay off all her debts and even give her a small raise at her landscaping business. Becki did all the flowers for us, including the centerpieces, and refused to accept a single cent. They were gorgeous and natural and wild: blue borage and foxglove and daisies and honeysuckle and coneflowers and prairie grasses. "You bought my ticket to the ABBA Museum," she'd say, waving her hand when I protested. "Now we're square."

Kevin, too, astounded me with his generosity. Buoyed by the surprise success on the Swedish charts of the song we'd written with Tove Orönso, Kevin started a wedding band, fronted by him, and funded by the massive profits of his solar-panel salesmanship, and he flew all the members out to play at our reception. Their repertoire leaned heavily on ABBA, but Kevin had recently started taking *joik* lessons, traditional Sámi singing, over Zoom with a Sámi elder, and I could already hear the influence in his riffs during the intros and outros. He brought me up onstage at one point to sing the song we'd cowritten, and as I looked over at him during the refrain, we smiled at each other, and he put his arm around me, and I around him, and it seemed impossible—unfathomable, really—that I had once tackled this man at the ABBA Museum and had to be escorted out by security.

"Wait, what?" Brock said when we told him the story of karaoke gone wrong after Kevin's band went on break. I thought Brock might be hurt that Kevin's band was playing the reception instead of his, but he didn't seem to mind at all. "Dude, I get it, our stuff's a little cutting-edge for a wedding crowd," he drawled. He played DJ during the breaks with turntables he'd lugged on the plane from Colorado, and ducked out from behind the booth at one point to dance with his daughter. The dance floor was full, but Honor, who had flown in from D.C., never made it on, for she spent the entire reception engrossed in conversation with the executive director of the Swedish cultural center, discussing how the organization might best support present-day immigrants arriving in Minnesota from all over the world, not only Sweden, with particular regard to affordable housing.

Tom was sitting at Honor's table, and he appeared to be listening intently to this conversation. His wedding gift, which had arrived the week before, was a framed photograph he'd taken of Becki and me laughing together, from the afternoon we'd spent with widow Gullvi in Kiruna. I went to thank him when I first got a chance, and also to apologize. "I'm sorry I went off on you like that after Brock got booted," I said. "What happened to you in the mine—it happened to me later in filming. I get now why you were so upset, and I wish I could have had more empathy."

He nodded. "Thank you," he said. He apologized, too, for his numerous outbursts, said he'd been sober for four months and counting, and that he and his wife had started couples therapy. He coughed a laugh and took a sip of sparkling water. "Didn't think I'd ever be doing shit like that, but then we did a lot of shit we never thought we'd do, didn't we?"

"Ain't that the truth," I said, shaking my head. "Things no one else would believe."

"Say, you and your husband ever want to come to Milwaukee, you're welcome anytime. Only six hours from here, that. We got an art museum and everything."

"Yeah?"

"Yeah."

"Well, maybe we will," I said, baffled by his invitation, and baffled more that I was accepting it, and not only out of politesse.

And speaking of welcome, we welcomed a whole phalanx of Swedes to the festivities: Alma and her family, Elisabeth and her family, Jonas, Magnus, and Lars—yes, Lars! He brought his new girlfriend, who looked to be twenty-five, and made fast friends with my art-school pals by discussing experimental documentary films. Magnus became an instant favorite among the Americans for his humor and goofy accent, while Jonas sneakily violated our "no cameras" rule by snapping candids with his phone. Which I didn't mind, in the end, for the scenes he captured were glorious: Elisabeth dancing with Brock, Becki taking shots with Junior and his boyfriend, Deborah and my mother laughing, Else and me making funny faces. The "no cameras" thing was Declan's idea, and in hindsight it was brilliant, even if I balked at first, seeing as it went against every grain of American cultural life as well as my own interests and experience. But some moments, Declan argued, need to be lived without being documented and proven, were private rather than public affairs, and while the line between public and private may be constantly eroding everywhere else, it could stay foundational in our family. It was the way he said "our family" that made me shiver and ultimately agree. A solid thing, but also inviting. Like . . . like . . . cheese.

Which had made it relatively easy to refuse when Tocke called one day in April, asking if I had any interest in filming our wedding for a *Sverige och Mig* reunion special. The season had aired on Swedish public television throughout January and February, and had proven to be a ratings bonanza. I'd quite enjoyed my fifteen minutes, probably because the bulk of it took place four thousand miles and an ocean away, and primarily consisted of heartwarming messages from strangers who believed we were cousins, and teenagers who had also struggled with broken families and mental illness. After hopping on a few local radio and talk shows, and giving interviews to a handful of Swedish podcast hosts, my brief and modest moment in the spotlight faded, leaving me more relieved than anything else, and also cured of any desire to live out that newfangled American dream of becoming rich and famous by turning one's life into a digital performance. Though I'd barely grazed the dream with my fingertips, that alone had sent me bonkers, and it turned out I preferred sanity to pretty much anything else, including the crown of public affection.

"Thank God," Declan had said while I was working these conclusions out before bed one night while idly rubbing his chest. I'd propped myself up on my elbow and asked him if now was a good time to buy some backyard chickens to become internet henfluencers, and he'd thrown a pillow at me, and I'd started giggling, and then he'd started to—oh, it was a wonderful night.

Anyway, Tocke took my refusal to let him film our wedding better than I expected. He even had the production company send a giant crate of Swedish *godis*, or candy, to serve at the reception. Which we did, along with the giant Midsommar cake I baked myself, which by some miracle did not melt or topple before we served it. As Declan and I shared the first slice, I looked down at my tiny cake tattoo and smiled, and when I looked up, Becki was smiling at me, too, and she pointed to hers, and to mine, and even though she was halfway across the garden I could feel her right there next to me.

After dancing the night away, sleeping for maybe three hours, and hosting a Swedish pancake breakfast at our house for out-of-town guests, Declan and I boarded a plane and flew to Sweden for our honeymoon. Alma had generously offered the use of her family's *stuga* north of Stockholm for a week, and we spent seven glorious days sleeping, swimming, reading, dozing in the sunshine, and eating *smultron* we'd foraged on the side of the road. By the end of the week I'd recovered enough to actually enjoy the opening of my very first solo photography show, entitled *Crying Americans*, in Gamla Stan the following Friday. Thanks to the lingering goodwill from the *Sverige och Mig* finale and decent press coverage, the small space was packed, and we sold out within a couple hours, much to my surprise and the gallerist's delight. Jemma, who had flown out to support me, cried the whole night, so much so that a number of Swedes came up to me and asked if she was part of the show, a kind of performance art. I assured them she was not. "It's so you," Jemma kept saying as she looked around. "You figured it out, Paulie, oh, you finally figured it out."

Declan, Jemma, and I left Stockholm the following morning, after giving assurances to the gallerist that yes, indeed, if and when I was ready for another show I would let her know immediately. I wanted to show them Svea's farm in Västra Götaland, and we also had somewhere important to be: more relatives of mine were hosting another family reunion for those who had missed the televised one, and others who had reconnected with the clan as a result of the show after time and distance caused them to drift. I introduced Declan as my husband—what a strange and lovely word, coming out of my mouth!—and Jemma as my sister, and we spent the day meeting everyone and eating smoked salmon and hard rolls, and the night learning Swedish drinking songs and getting sloshed on *snaps*. The reunion happened to take place on the Fourth of July, obviously not a holiday celebrated in Sweden, yet my relatives surprised us with a brief yet fizz-banging fireworks show of which they were so proud we could not help but stand up and cheer. "AMERICA!" we hollered, clinking our forks against our *snaps* glasses, somewhere between ironically and not. "AMERICA!!!!!"

"WE HAD FUN, didn't we?" Jemma said, sliding out another piece of pizza from the box.

It was two months later, Labor Day evening, and the three of us were reminiscing about the trip while sitting on the wood floor of the soon-to-be-open Smultronställe Café, which was taking over the storefront across the street from our house, the one Declan and I had been mulling and arguing and fretting over for ages. Thanks to Jemma's angel investment, the brisk sales from the gallery show, and the small sum my father had willed to me when he died, it had been much less scary than I expected to take the plunge into small-business ownership. Garance, my ex-boss, had, in a leap of good faith, insisted on mentoring me on financials, Karen Hamburger and company had been walking with me through my fear, Declan had built the website, and my grandma had given me her recipes, which had also been her grandma's recipes, that I would now be able to share with the entire neighborhood. Pippi Longstocking's recipes, too, or what I imagined they would be: sugar cookies and rhubarb crumble and buns and hard rolls inspired by her books. We were importing Swedish coffee and serving it black and strong unless asked otherwise, and had chosen what Jemma had taken to calling a "Pippi cottage aesthetic": poplar wainscoting, sturdy crockery, sheer curtains, mismatched silverware, hodgepodge tables, hand-hewn chairs, and lots of natural light. The whitewashed walls were as yet bare, for I dreamed of filling them with Polaroids of customers and community members, either framed in simple birch or hung with clothespins and fishing wire. So that maybe people could feel at home when they walked in. So that maybe it could live up to its name, become a real *smultronställe*. Not that *smultronställe* is a feeling you can force, though, is it? After all, what makes a *smultronställe* a *smultronställe* is there's no forcing of any kind.

Declan handed me a beer and nudged me to take some more salad. He'd been like this ever since work on the bakery had gotten really hectic: dropping off snacks, reminding me to drink water, making dinner with lots of vegetables so I didn't get scurvy from a flour-and-sugar diet. The past week, I'd been on a hiring kick and had just brought on Tristan, dentistry-hating high school graduate, for his gap year, and a couple of distant cousins I'd found who were eager for work and able to make the commute from the countryside. "Fun's one of Paulie's strengths," he said to Jemma.

"And a weakness," I conceded, shoving a forkful of Caesar salad in my mouth.

"And a weakness," he agreed.

It was getting dark outside. It was getting dark earlier and earlier, the first sign of autumn amidst still-balmy summer afternoons. I lit the candelabra on the other side of the pizza box, a small ceramic gem I'd found at a charity shop in Midköping with Jemma. Then I picked up my beer. "Should we make a toast?"

Jemma raised her bottle before asking, "To what, though?"

I looked at her, then I looked over at Declan. Saw their eyes shining with candlelight in this sweet little place we had built together. This sweet little place that, if we were lucky, would open its doors and become a sweet little place for everybody. Love: the thing beneath all the other things. Old Faithful. I did not have to will it this time. It poured out the top of my head, my eyes, my mouth, my heart, my hands.

"To family," I said. And I meant it in both the small way and the largest and most capacious way, the way that left out nobody and nothing.

"To family," they repeated. We clinked. And in that moment, a warm breeze swept through the large open windows like a burst of laughter and snuffed out the candlelight.

ACKNOWLEDGMENTS

This book burst out of me like a star being born, and I had incredible support throughout the white-hot and exuberant process. My agent, Michelle Brower, who is wise about all things, told me to put another manuscript aside to write it, and it was the best piece of advice she's ever given. Thank you, Michelle, for your counsel and friendship. I also need to thank Emma Törzs for the crackpot idea to apply to a Swedish reality show in the first place, and for the kind of "Yes, and" energy that leads to careening around Sweden in a free Volvo. Thanks also to consummate little sister Jesse Törzs, for always laughing in the backseat.

I sat at the feet of wonderful teachers while working on this project, all of whom gave so much of themselves. Thank you to Charles Baxter, for imbuing me with the belief that books matter. Thank you to Christopher Bayes at The Pandemonium Studio, for showing me how to let the little one drive. Thank you to Jan Jirak and Nicole Grunzke for teaching me to be strong and kind. *Tack så jättemycket* to my Swedish teacher, Liz Stopka. Thanks to Robert McKee for your master class in story, and special thanks to Meg Ryan for your extraordinary mentorship, and for teaching me to "just try."

Thank you to my editor, Kate Nintzel, for acquiring this book when it was not much more than a twinkle in my imagination, and thanks to Molly Gendell for pinch-hitting when a certain small creature forced us to move up our timeline. Both of you made this book so much better with your perceptiveness and generosity. The same can be said of Natalie Edwards, who helped me course-correct dozens of times in early drafts. Thanks also to Lara Avery for reading the first pages and knowing what jokes to keep. Thank you, Erin White, for your crucial late-stage read, and thank you to Sugi Ganeshananthan and Curtis Sittenfeld for the sparkling conversation. Thanks to Katherine Heiny for reading your fan mail in 2019, and to Julie Schumacher for permanently putting to bed the question, "Are women funny?" Matt Burgess: you're my favorite ragamuffin. Oron Stenesh: you're the king of cabaret. No one on this earth gives hugs like Ellie Roscher. Thank you to Kate Galle for so many things, but particularly for making sure I'm never hungry.

This novel bears little resemblance to the real-life reality show that inspired it, but I would be remiss if I didn't thank Christer Åkerlund for inviting me on the trip of a lifetime in 2021. Thank you also to my castmates, Nicole Archer, Sharon Febriz, Bret Goss, Erika Newell, Trevor Ohlsen, Bubba Palmer, Brittany Pearson, Jon Strand, and Melody Sky Weaver. You have nothing in common with Paulie's pals except that, like them, you grew my heart ten sizes and were excellent company in a Sprinter van. Special thanks to Erika for letting me steal her diary and to Nikki for being my resident reality TV expert. Thanks, too, to the entire AFS crew and to Tilda Saulesco for playing mama bird. Thank you to Alexander Laving for all the jokes, good and groan-worthy. A giant hug and thank-you to Ola Fredholm for your friendship, travel advice, and for throwing the party of the century—and sorry again about the mirror!

In the Arctic Circle: thanks to Dan Lundström, for the rich historical tour of Kiruna, and to Nutti Sámi Siida in Jukkasjärvi for introducing me to the reindeer. If you're not headed to the far north anytime soon, but you'd like to learn more about the Sámi and Sápmi, Ann-Helén Laestadius's novel, *Stolen*, and Linnea Axelsson's *Ædnan* are both powerful entry points. I'd also like to thank the American Swedish Institute in Minneapolis for its cultural, linguistic, and culinary programming, and to Bruce Karstadt for bringing me into the fold.

I'm lucky to have incredible representation on both coasts and beyond. Many thanks to Dana Spector and Allison Warren for your advocacy and always being game to talk turkey. Allison Malecha, you're the queen of foreign rights. At Mariner, thanks to marvelous marketing doyenne Liz Psaltis for getting my work into so many readers' hands, and thanks to my publicist, Martin Wilson, for going to bat for me again and again. That you all work so hard on my behalf means more than I can ever say.

Penultimately—I swear, we're rounding the bend toward the finish line here!—I have to thank a motley crew of family and found family for all the affection and encouragement: Nancy Angelo, Isaac Butler, Suzanne Carreker-Voigt, Ginny Green, Janette Greenwood, Liz Greenwood, Anil Hurkadli, Laurent Maertens, Nick Mangigian, Nancy McCauley, Gail Mooney, Jordan Poast, Jackie Polzin, John Sessler, Freddy Törzs, Alex Voigt, and Jeff Voigt. Gratitude to my relatives in Sweden, whose sudden arrival in my life feels like winning the Powerball, but for love. Special shout-out to Gullvi Ohlsson Rigland and the Varberg clan, especially Kiki, Anders, and Britta Källgård. Nina, Anders, Filip, Kasper, and Tova Viberg—I can't believe that so much joy can come out of reality TV, but we are living proof of it. F, K, & T: Gröna Lund!!!!!

Lastly, it wouldn't feel right to pen a whole book about genealogy if I didn't acknowledge my parents, their parents, and so on, who struggled and sacrificed and endured much hardship so that I might spend my working hours playing make believe. My life is a consequence of and conversation with the lives that came before me. And thank you, finally, to Ben and Harriet. You are the real story to which all fiction pales in comparison.